BALTAZAR FRANCO GIARRUSSO

ENCOUNTER

WELCOME TO THE TEAM!

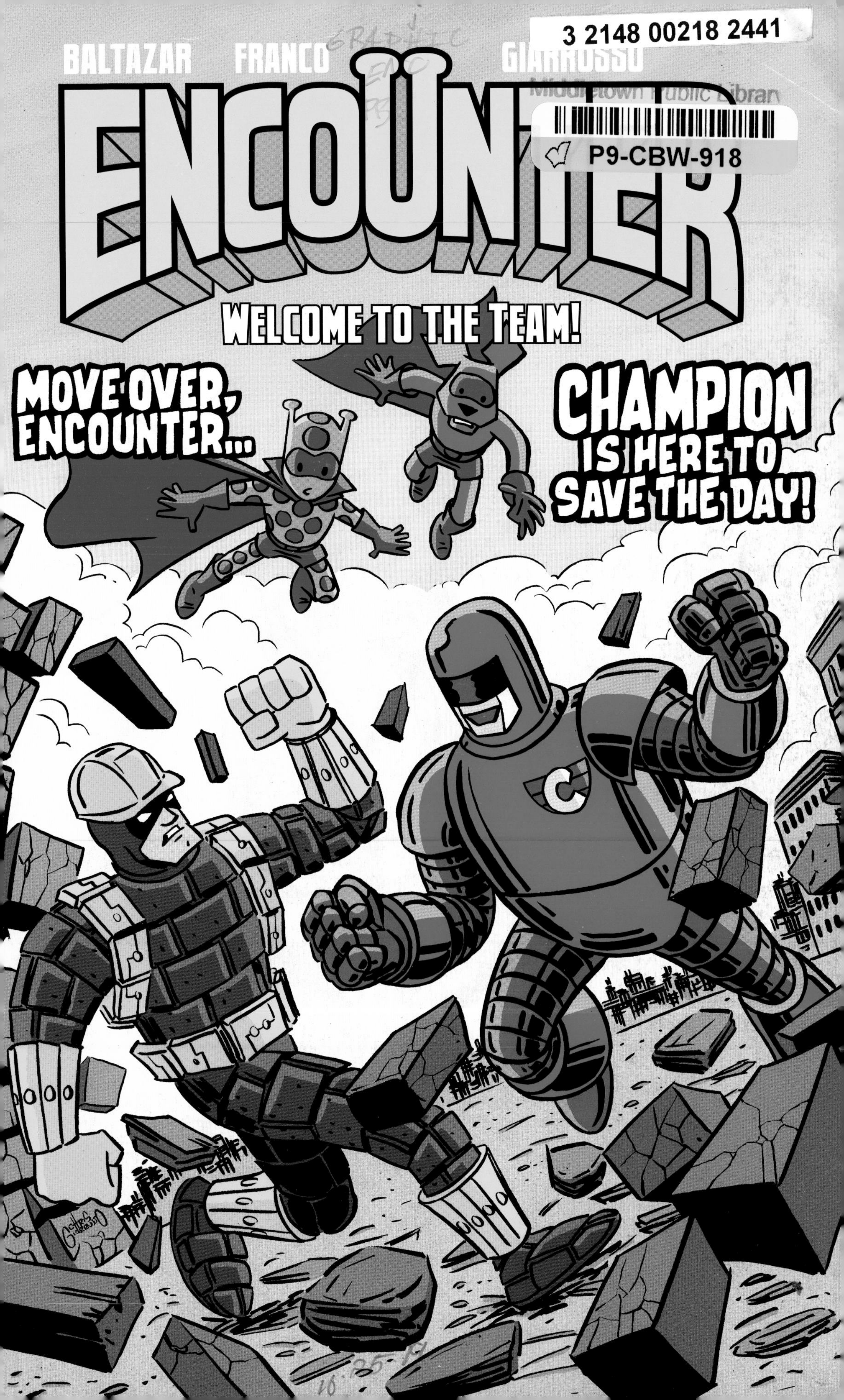
MOVE OVER, ENCOUNTER...
CHAMPION IS HERE TO SAVE THE DAY!
C

ISBN: 978-1-5493-0271-8
Library of Congress Control Number: 2018932769
10 9 8 7 6 5 4 3 2 1

ENCOUNTER™

WELCOME TO THE TEAM!

STORY BY
**ART BALTAZAR,
FRANCO &
CHRIS GIARRUSSO**

ART, LETTERING & COVER BY
CHRIS GIARRUSSO

COLORS BY
STEPHEN MAYER

BACKUP STORY BY
**ART BALTAZAR &
FRANCO**

BACKUP ART, COLORS & LETTERING BY
ART BALTAZAR

EDITOR
HAZEL NEWLEVANT

ASSISTANT EDITOR
AMANDA VERNON

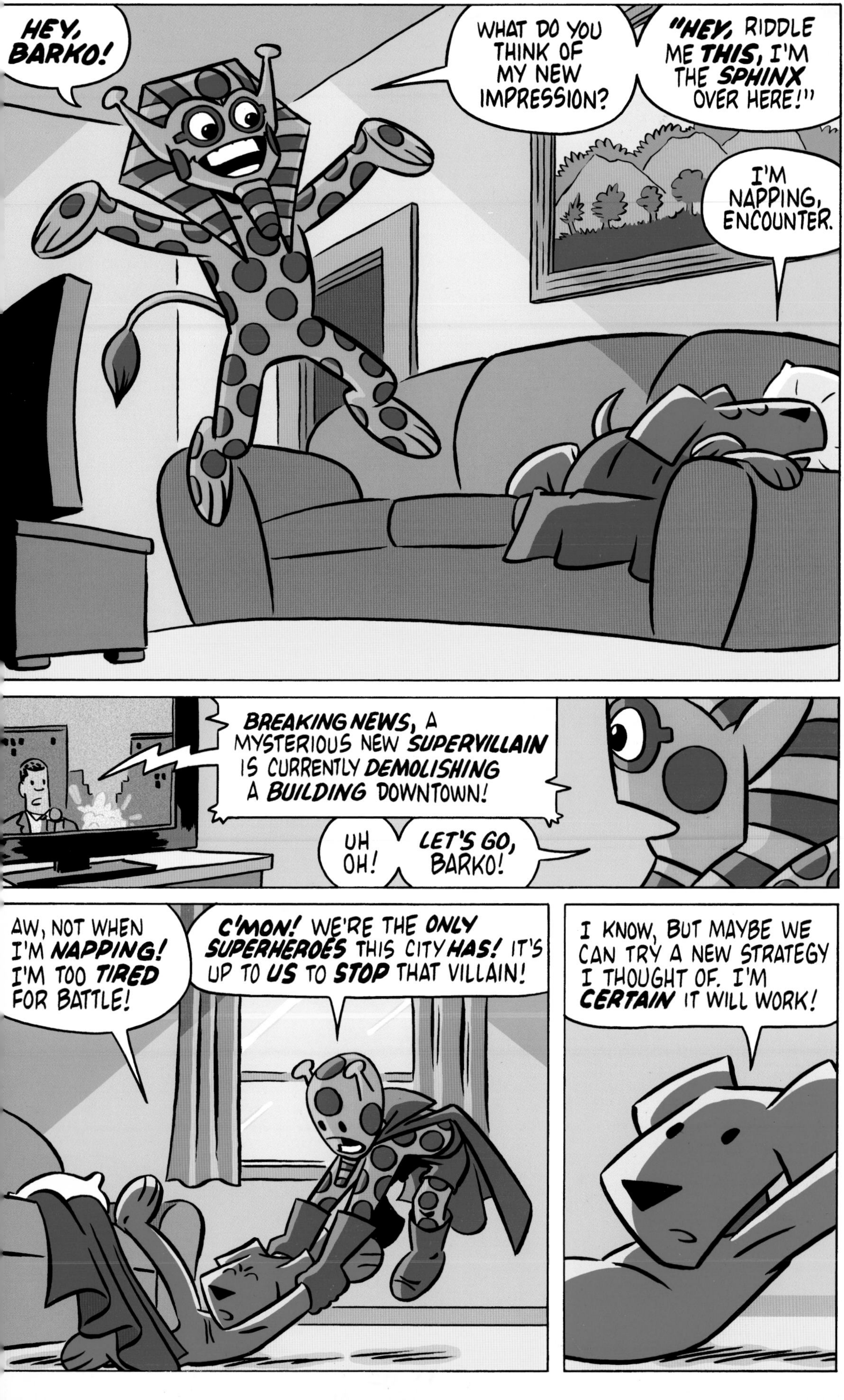
HEY, BARKO!
WHAT DO YOU THINK OF MY NEW IMPRESSION?
"HEY, RIDDLE ME THIS, I'M THE SPHINX OVER HERE!"
I'M NAPPING, ENCOUNTER.
BREAKING NEWS, A MYSTERIOUS NEW SUPERVILLAIN IS CURRENTLY DEMOLISHING A BUILDING DOWNTOWN!
UH OH!
LET'S GO, BARKO!
AW, NOT WHEN I'M NAPPING! I'M TOO TIRED FOR BATTLE!
C'MON! WE'RE THE ONLY SUPERHEROES THIS CITY HAS! IT'S UP TO US TO STOP THAT VILLAIN!
I KNOW, BUT MAYBE WE CAN TRY A NEW STRATEGY I THOUGHT OF. I'M CERTAIN IT WILL WORK!

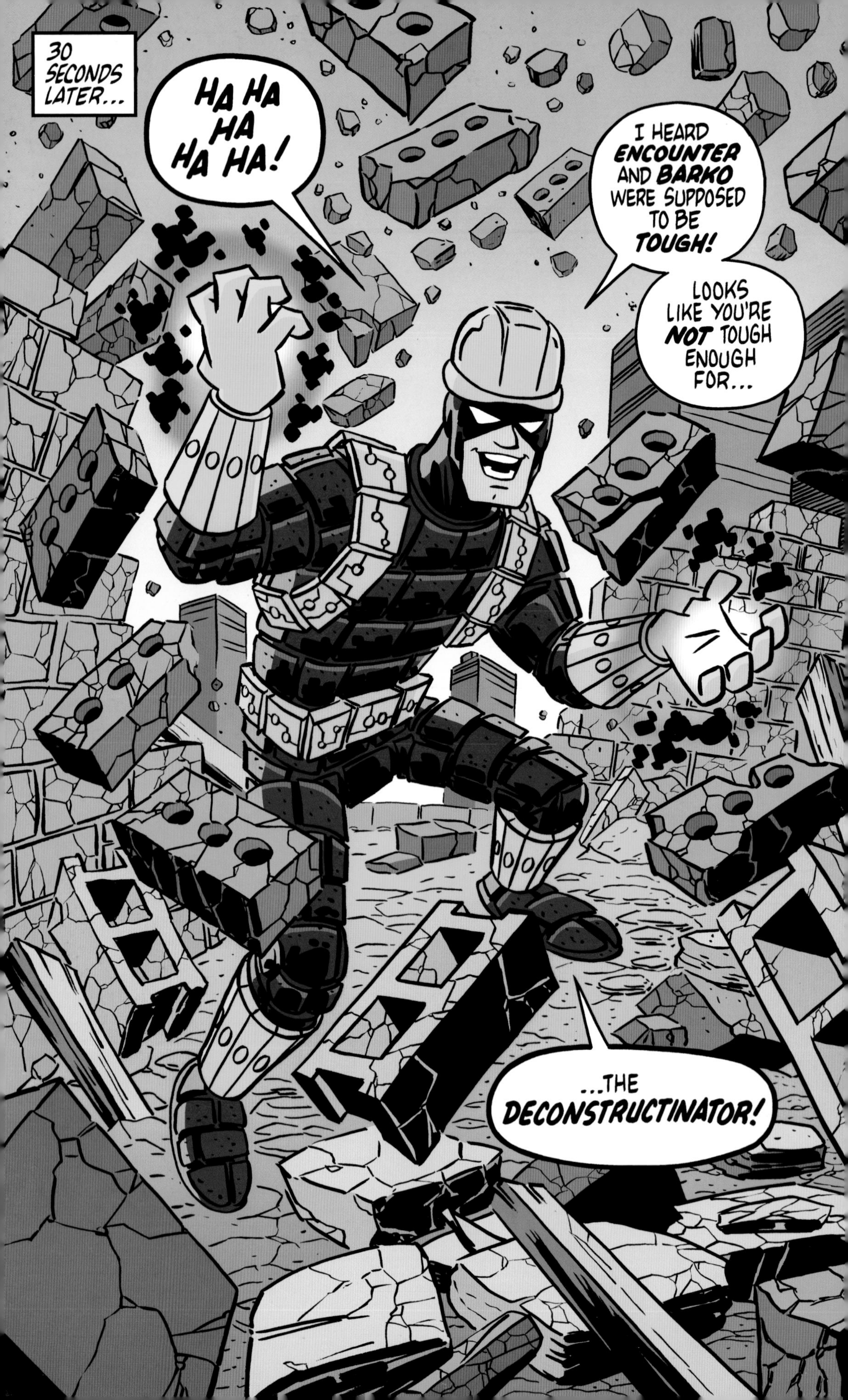
30 SECONDS LATER...
HA HA HA HA HA!
I HEARD ENCOUNTER AND BARKO WERE SUPPOSED TO BE TOUGH!
LOOKS LIKE YOU'RE NOT TOUGH ENOUGH FOR...
...THE DECONSTRUCTINATOR!

I TRAPPED YOU CHUMPS IN **SECONDS!**
GREAT STRATEGY, BARKO.
CAN WE DISCUSS OUR STRATEGY LATER?
THERE WON'T **BE** ANY LATER FOR **YOU** UNLESS YOU GIVE ME THE **PODS!** WHERE **ARE** THEY?
ANOTHER VILLAIN AFTER THE PODS, JUST AS WE SUSPECTED.
WHO SENT YOU?
I'LL BE ASKING THE QUESTIONS! AND IF YOU DON'T ANSWER, I'LL **DECONSTRUCTINATE** YOU RIGHT DOWN TO YOUR **ATOMS!**
I COULD TAKE YOU APART LIKE A **JENGA GAME!**
THAT SOUNDS RATHER **IMPOSSIBLE.**
NOT FOR ME!

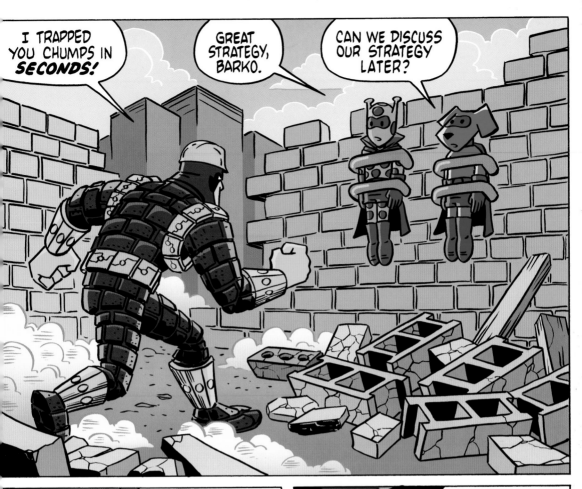

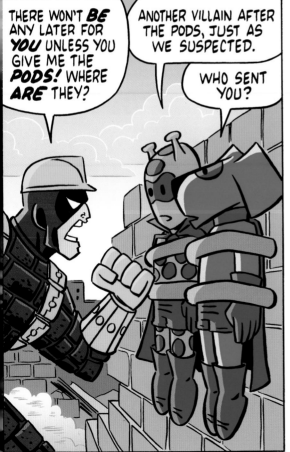

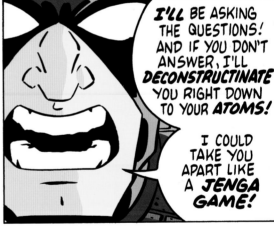

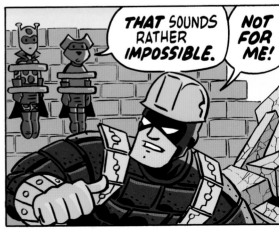

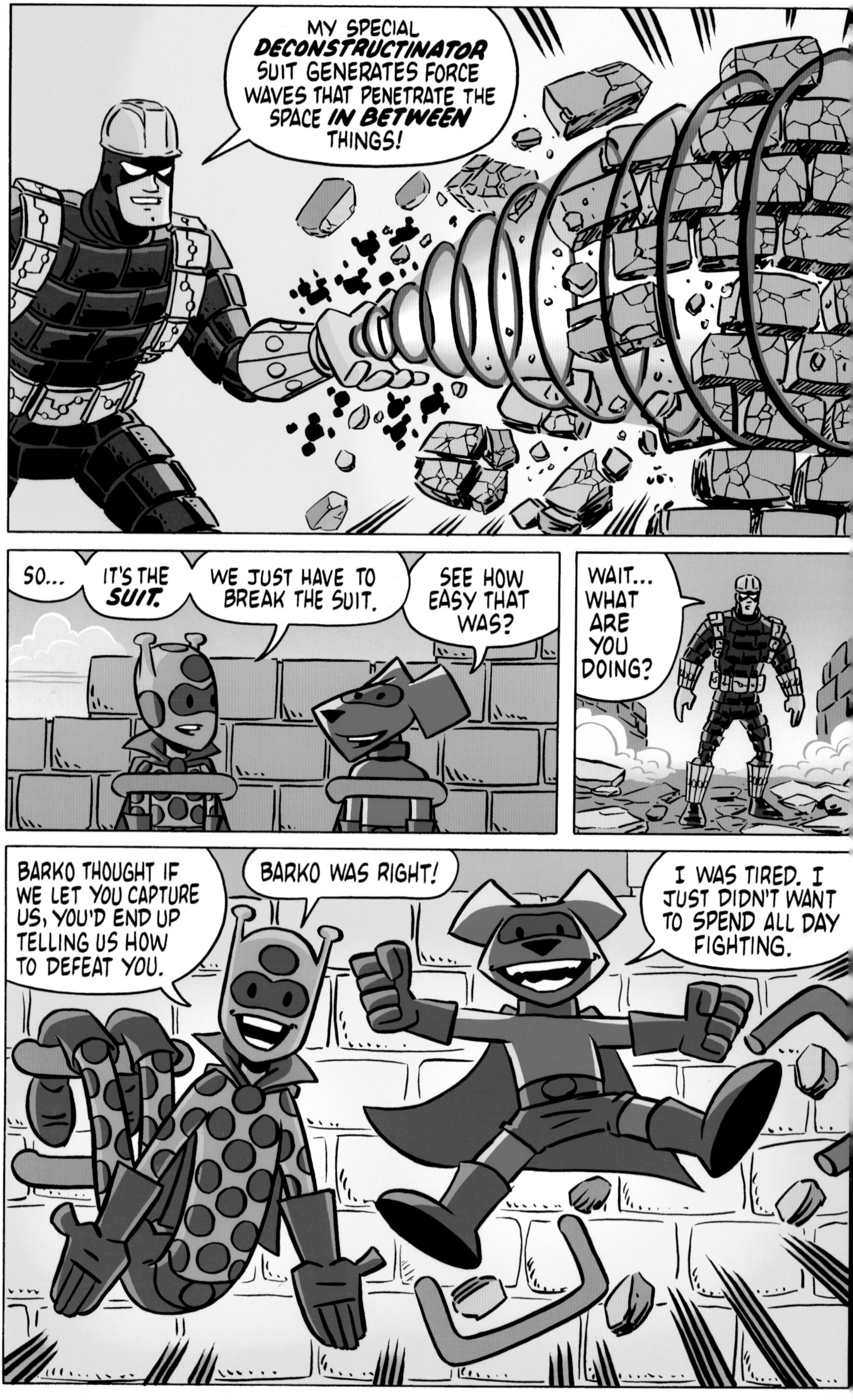
MY SPECIAL DECONSTRUCTINATOR SUIT GENERATES FORCE WAVES THAT PENETRATE THE SPACE IN BETWEEN THINGS!
SO...
IT'S THE SUIT.
WE JUST HAVE TO BREAK THE SUIT.
SEE HOW EASY THAT WAS?
WAIT... WHAT ARE YOU DOING?
BARKO THOUGHT IF WE LET YOU CAPTURE US, YOU'D END UP TELLING US HOW TO DEFEAT YOU.
BARKO WAS RIGHT!
I WAS TIRED. I JUST DIDN'T WANT TO SPEND ALL DAY FIGHTING.

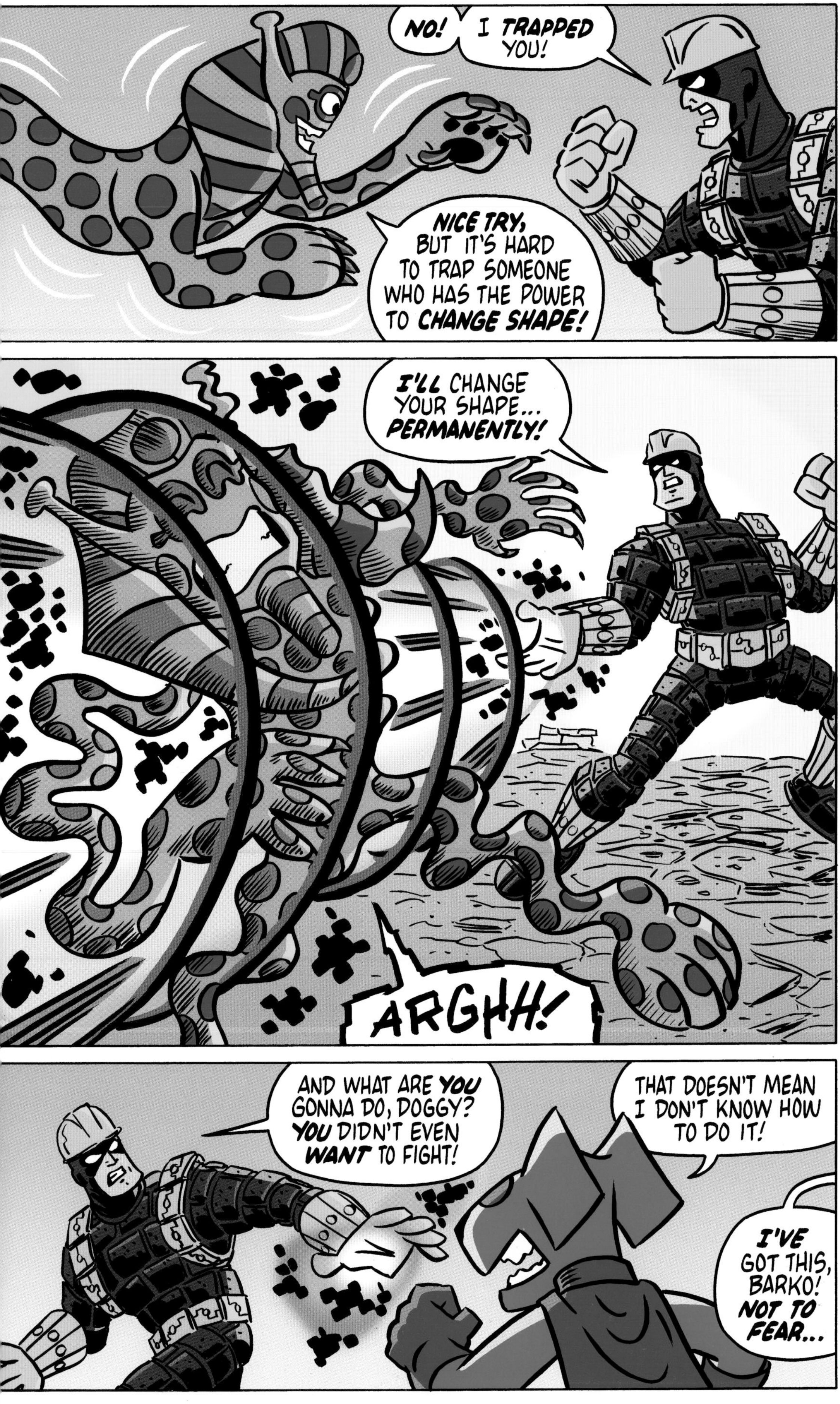
NO!
I TRAPPED YOU!
NICE TRY, BUT IT'S HARD TO TRAP SOMEONE WHO HAS THE POWER TO CHANGE SHAPE!
I'LL CHANGE YOUR SHAPE... PERMANENTLY!
ARGHH!
AND WHAT ARE YOU GONNA DO, DOGGY? YOU DIDN'T EVEN WANT TO FIGHT!
THAT DOESN'T MEAN I DON'T KNOW HOW TO DO IT!
I'VE GOT THIS, BARKO! NOT TO FEAR...

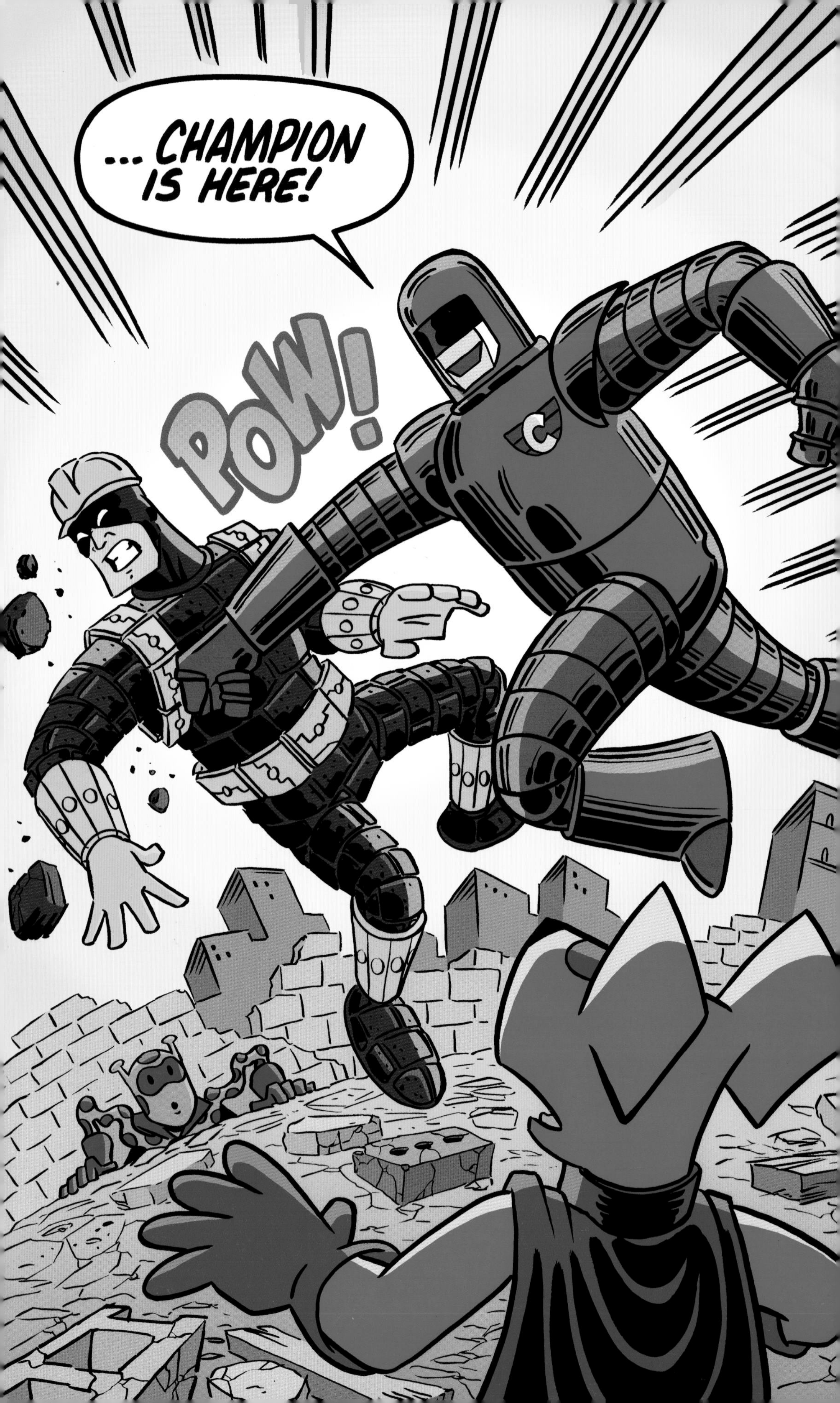

...CHAMPION IS HERE!
POW!
C

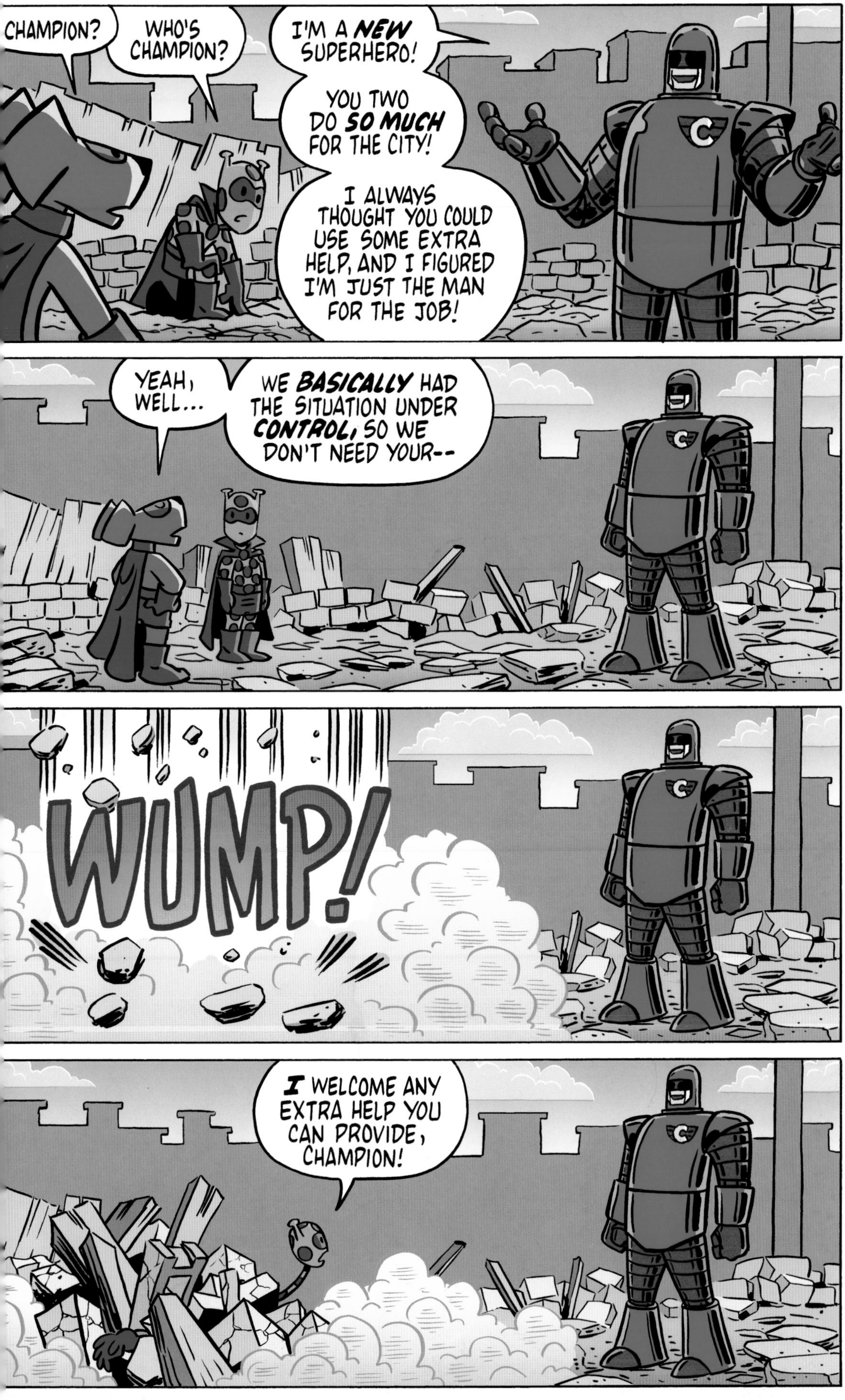
CHAMPION?
WHO'S CHAMPION?
I'M A NEW SUPERHERO!
YOU TWO DO SO MUCH FOR THE CITY!
I ALWAYS THOUGHT YOU COULD USE SOME EXTRA HELP, AND I FIGURED I'M JUST THE MAN FOR THE JOB!
YEAH, WELL...
WE BASICALLY HAD THE SITUATION UNDER CONTROL, SO WE DON'T NEED YOUR--
WUMP!
I WELCOME ANY EXTRA HELP YOU CAN PROVIDE, CHAMPION!

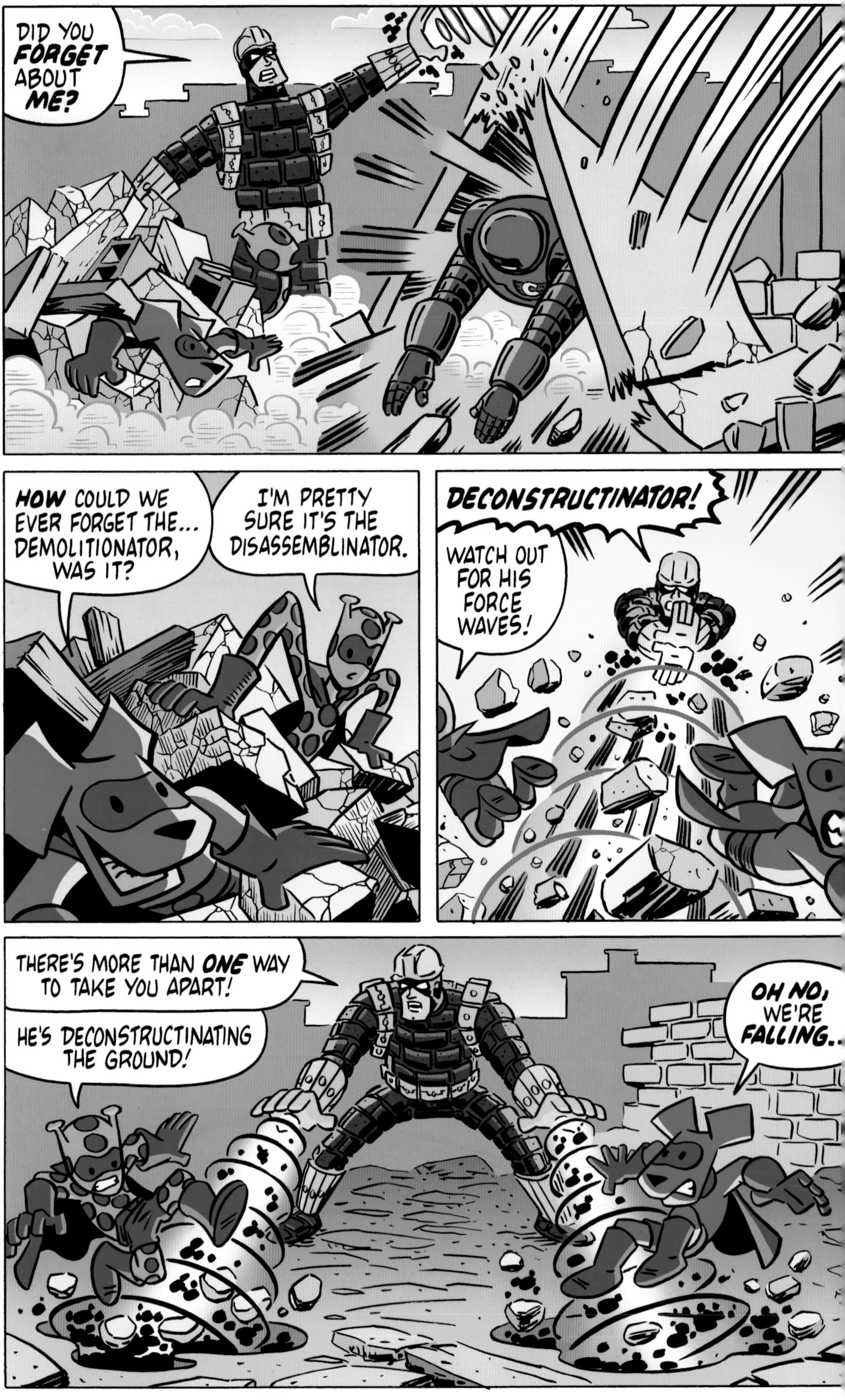
DID YOU FORGET ABOUT ME?
HOW COULD WE EVER FORGET THE... DEMOLITIONATOR, WAS IT?
I'M PRETTY SURE IT'S THE DISASSEMBLINATOR.
DECONSTRUCTINATOR!
WATCH OUT FOR HIS FORCE WAVES!
THERE'S MORE THAN ONE WAY TO TAKE YOU APART!
HE'S DECONSTRUCTINATING THE GROUND!
OH NO, WE'RE FALLING..

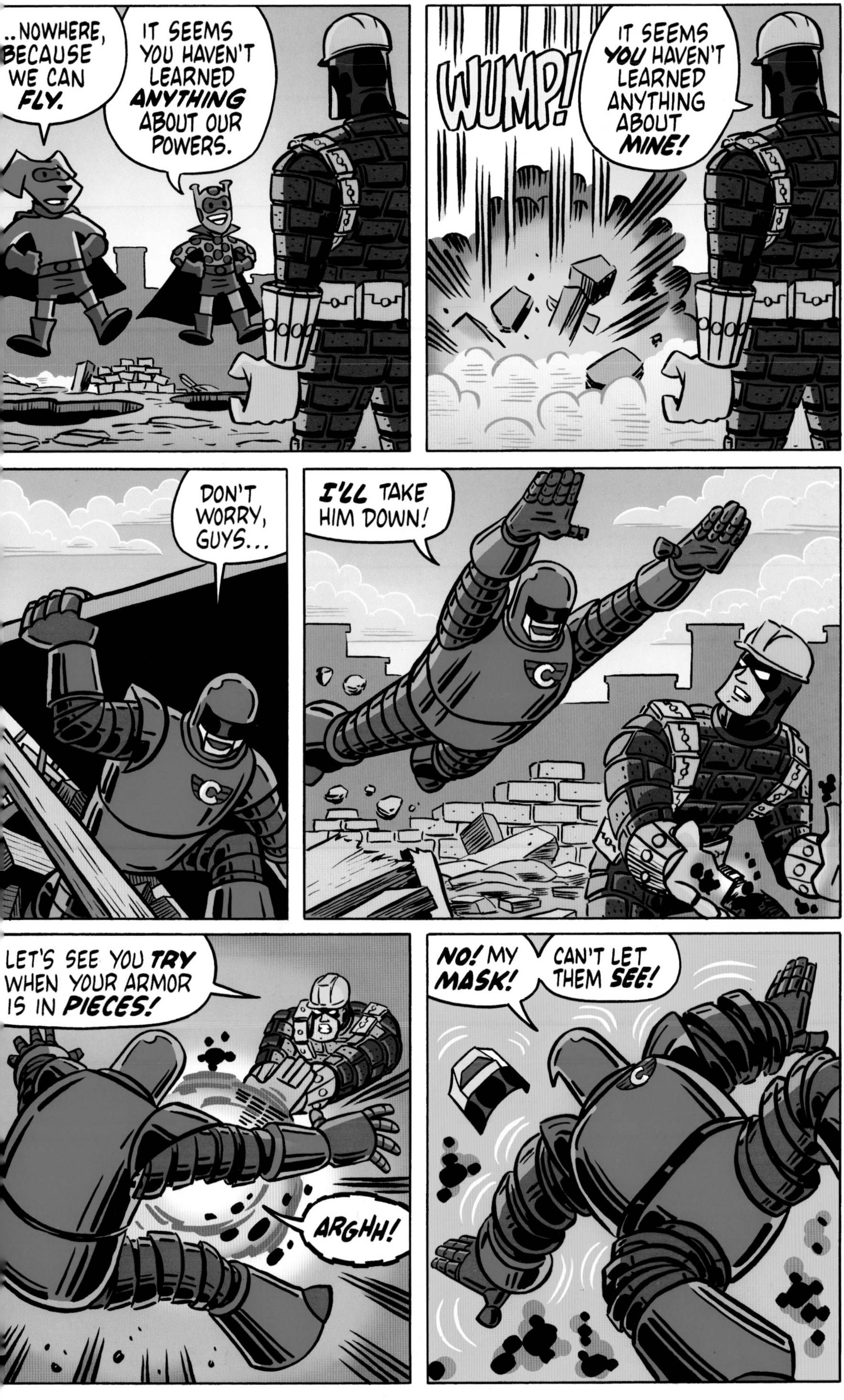
..NOWHERE, BECAUSE WE CAN FLY.
IT SEEMS YOU HAVEN'T LEARNED ANYTHING ABOUT OUR POWERS.
WUMP!
IT SEEMS YOU HAVEN'T LEARNED ANYTHING ABOUT MINE!
DON'T WORRY, GUYS...
I'LL TAKE HIM DOWN!
LET'S SEE YOU TRY WHEN YOUR ARMOR IS IN PIECES!
ARGHH!
NO! MY MASK!
CAN'T LET THEM SEE!

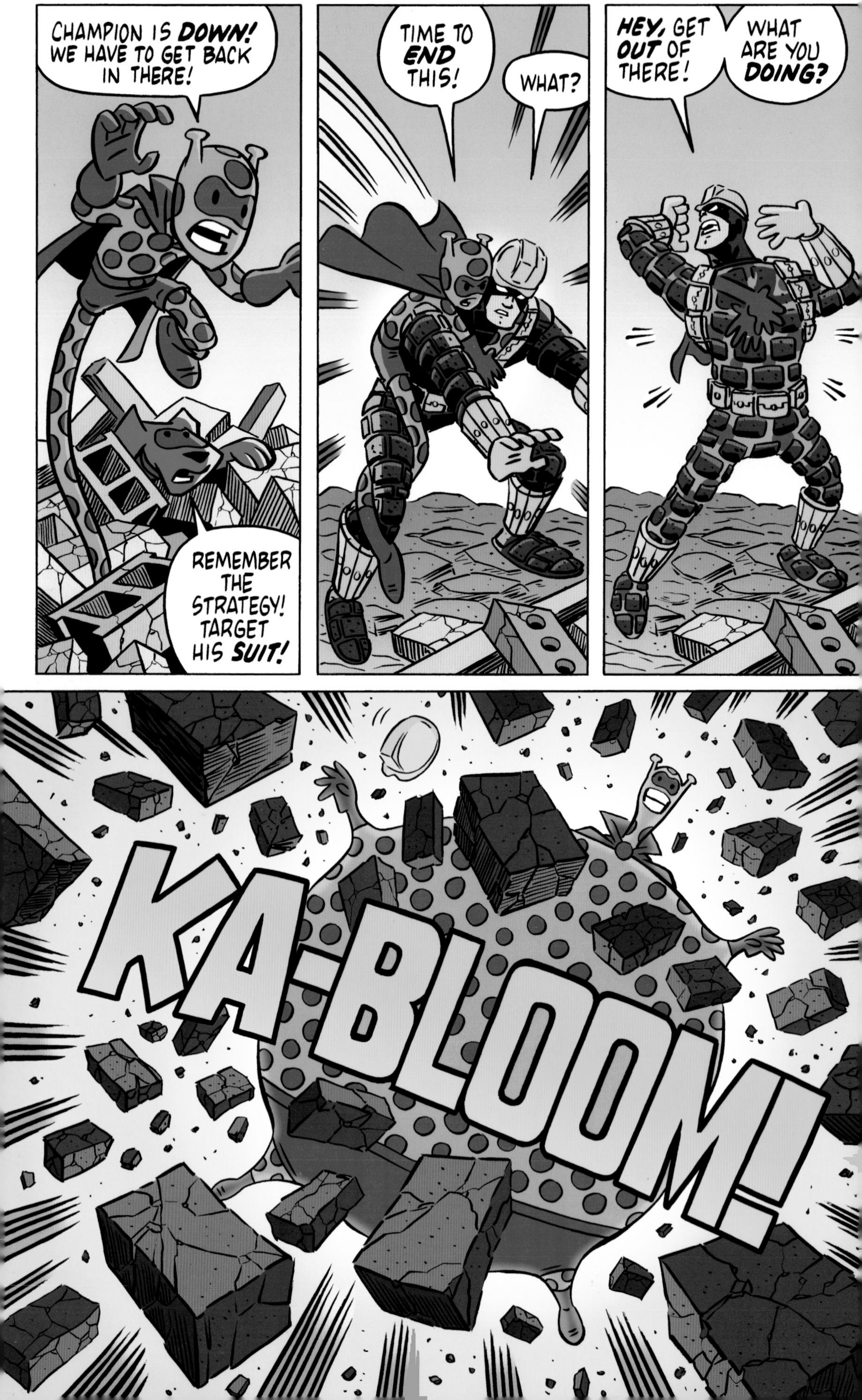
CHAMPION IS DOWN! WE HAVE TO GET BACK IN THERE!
REMEMBER THE STRATEGY! TARGET HIS SUIT!
TIME TO END THIS!
WHAT?
HEY, GET OUT OF THERE!
WHAT ARE YOU DOING?
KA-BLOOM!

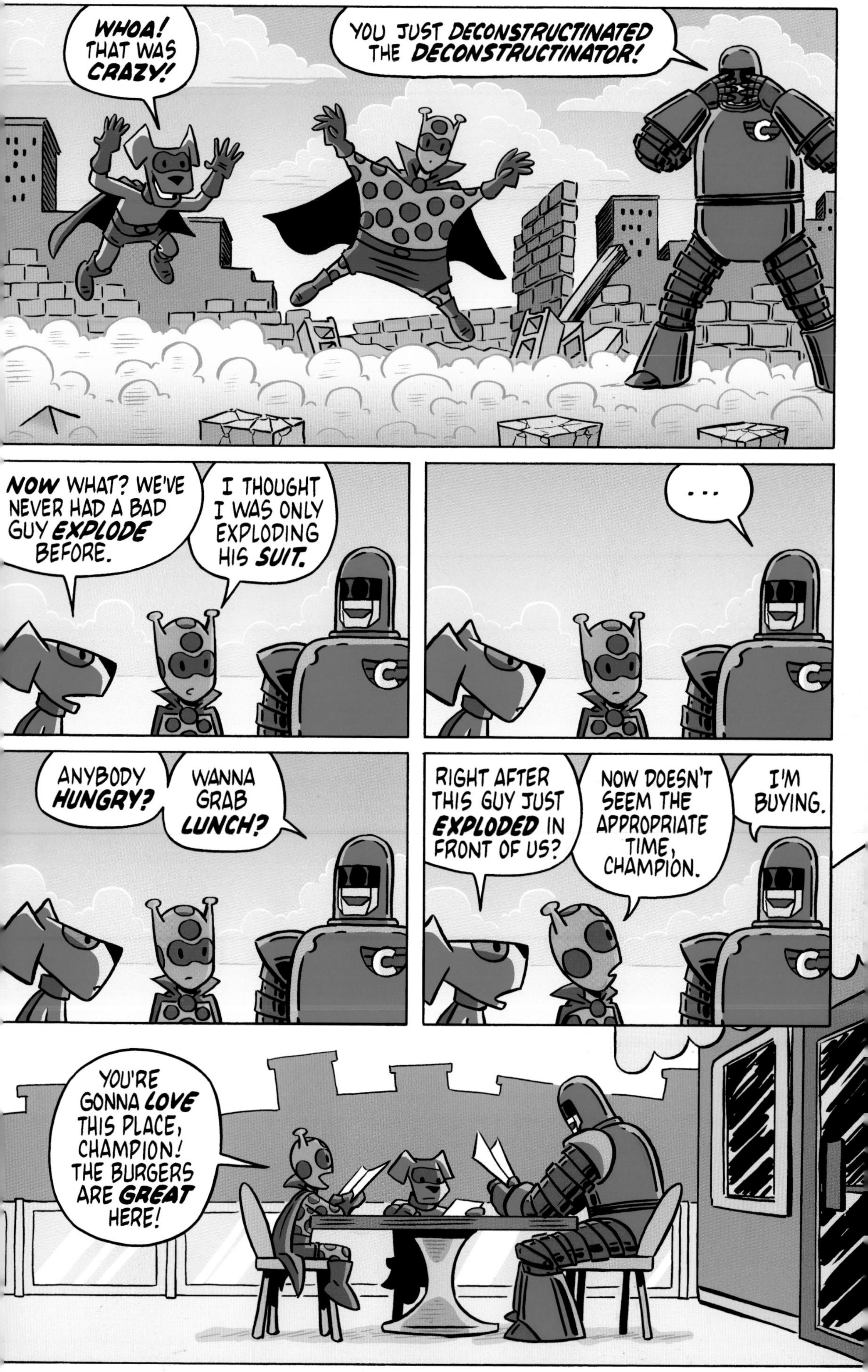
WHOA! THAT WAS CRAZY!
YOU JUST DECONSTRUCTINATED THE DECONSTRUCTINATOR!
NOW WHAT? WE'VE NEVER HAD A BAD GUY EXPLODE BEFORE.
I THOUGHT I WAS ONLY EXPLODING HIS SUIT.
...
ANYBODY HUNGRY?
WANNA GRAB LUNCH?
RIGHT AFTER THIS GUY JUST EXPLODED IN FRONT OF US?
NOW DOESN'T SEEM THE APPROPRIATE TIME, CHAMPION.
I'M BUYING.
YOU'RE GONNA LOVE THIS PLACE, CHAMPION! THE BURGERS ARE GREAT HERE!

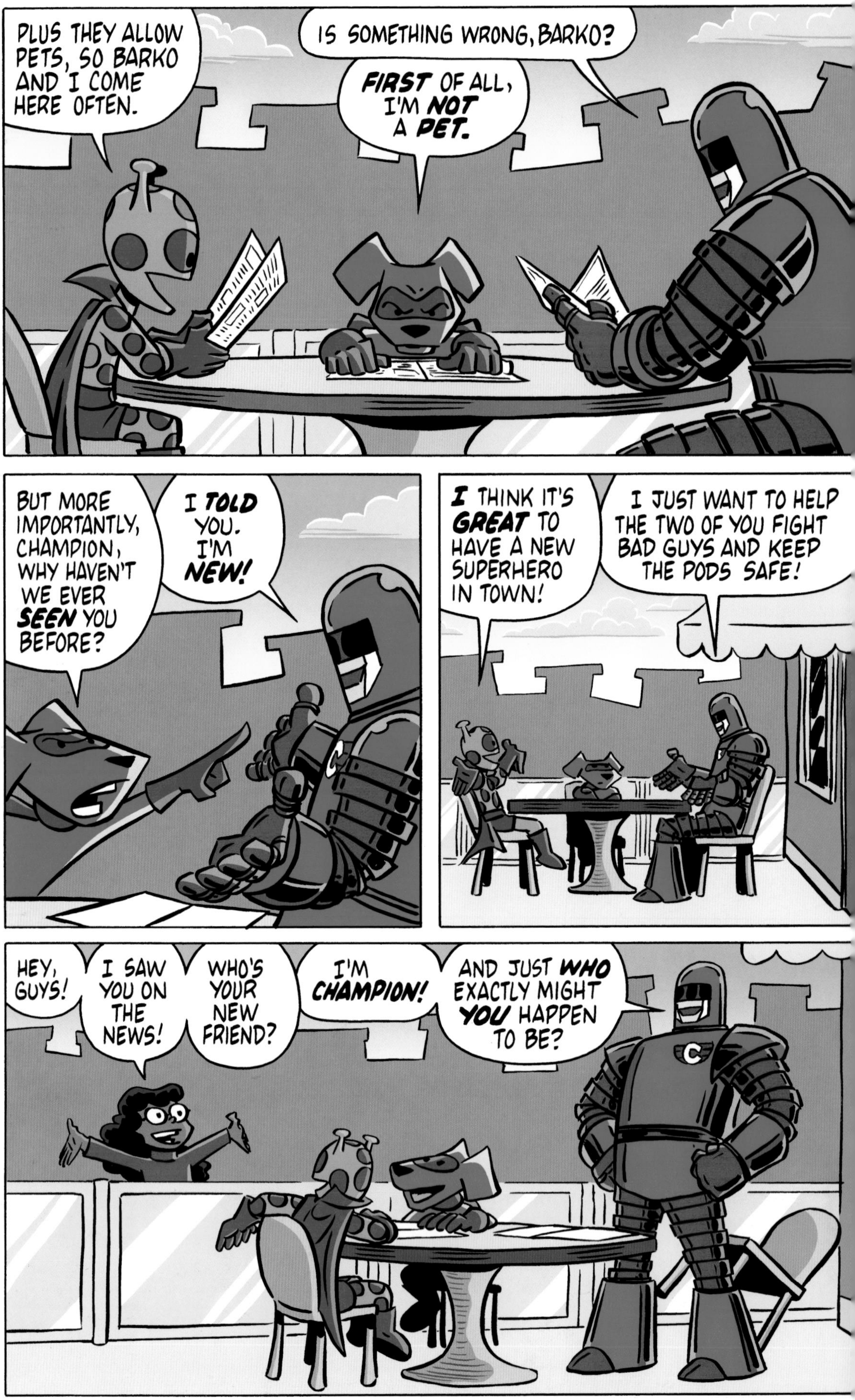
PLUS THEY ALLOW PETS, SO BARKO AND I COME HERE OFTEN.
IS SOMETHING WRONG, BARKO?
FIRST OF ALL, I'M NOT A PET.
BUT MORE IMPORTANTLY, CHAMPION, WHY HAVEN'T WE EVER SEEN YOU BEFORE?
I TOLD YOU. I'M NEW!
I THINK IT'S GREAT TO HAVE A NEW SUPERHERO IN TOWN!
I JUST WANT TO HELP THE TWO OF YOU FIGHT BAD GUYS AND KEEP THE PODS SAFE!
HEY, GUYS!
I SAW YOU ON THE NEWS!
WHO'S YOUR NEW FRIEND?
I'M CHAMPION!
AND JUST WHO EXACTLY MIGHT YOU HAPPEN TO BE?

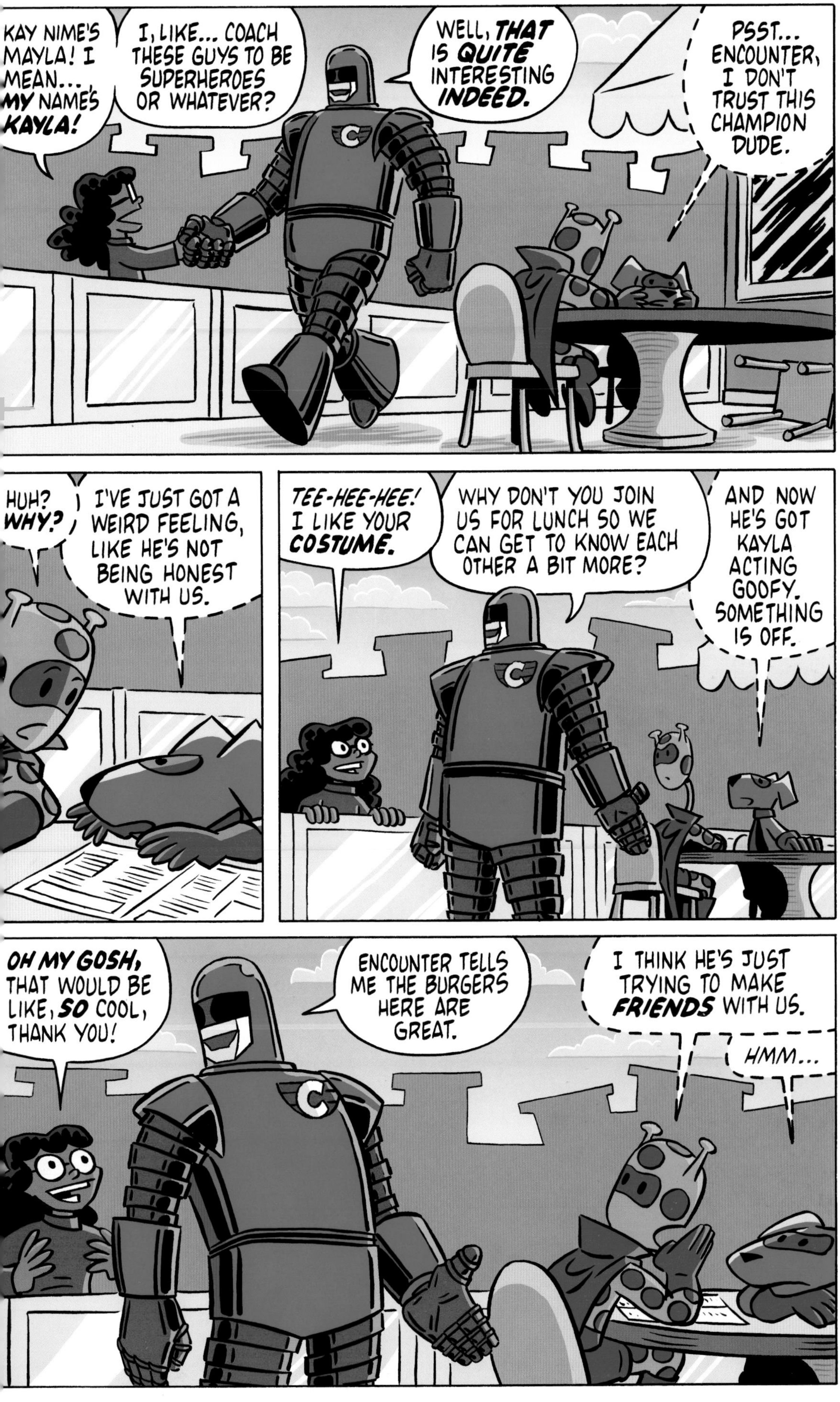
KAY NIME'S MAYLA! I MEAN..., *MY* NAME'S *KAYLA!*
I, LIKE... COACH THESE GUYS TO BE SUPERHEROES OR WHATEVER?
WELL, *THAT* IS *QUITE* INTERESTING *INDEED.*
PSST... ENCOUNTER, I DON'T TRUST THIS CHAMPION DUDE.
HUH? *WHY?*
I'VE JUST GOT A WEIRD FEELING, LIKE HE'S NOT BEING HONEST WITH US.
TEE-HEE-HEE! I LIKE YOUR *COSTUME.*
WHY DON'T YOU JOIN US FOR LUNCH SO WE CAN GET TO KNOW EACH OTHER A BIT MORE?
AND NOW HE'S GOT KAYLA ACTING GOOFY. SOMETHING IS OFF.
OH MY GOSH, THAT WOULD BE LIKE, *SO* COOL, THANK YOU!
ENCOUNTER TELLS ME THE BURGERS HERE ARE GREAT.
I THINK HE'S JUST TRYING TO MAKE *FRIENDS* WITH US.
HMM...

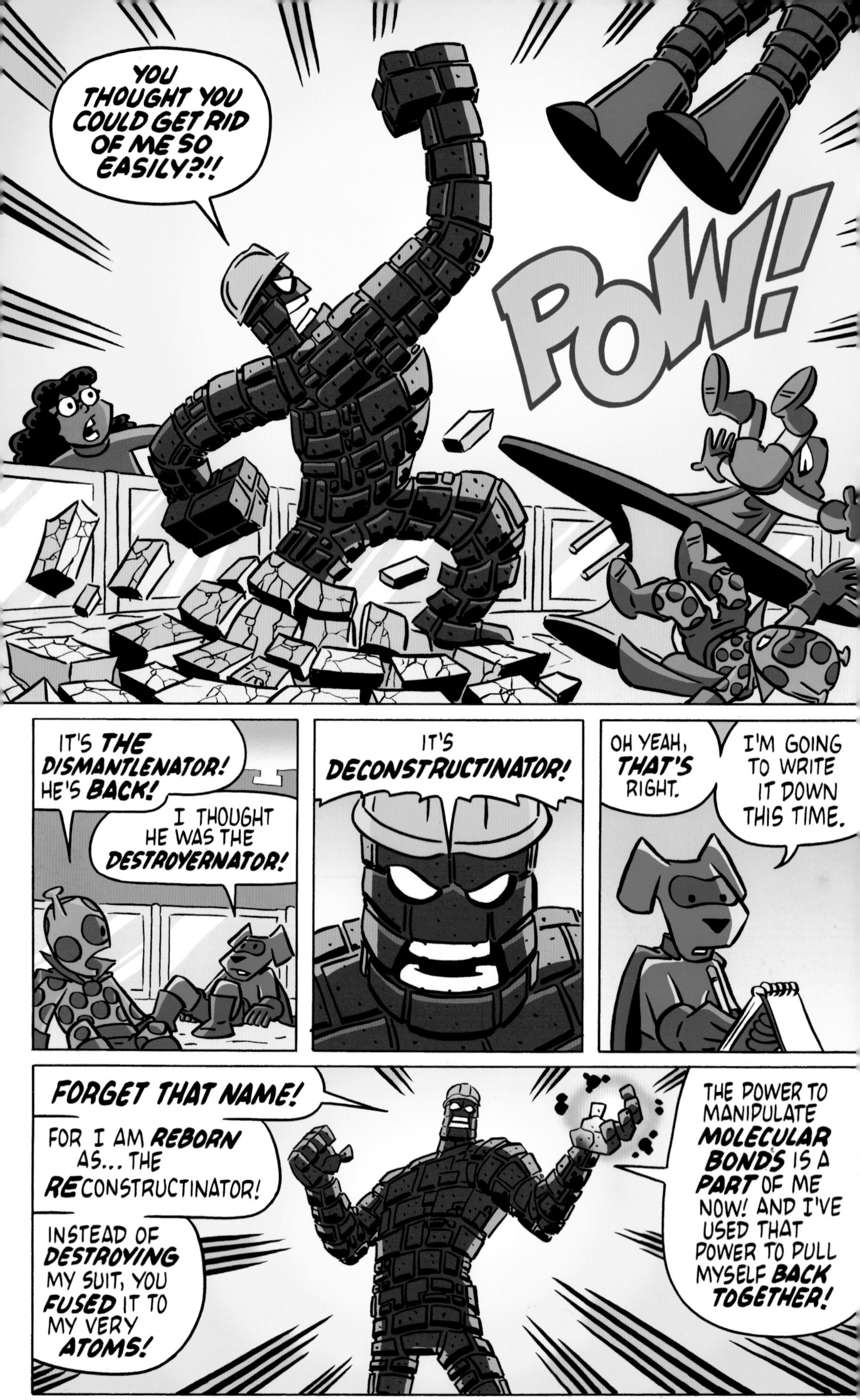
YOU THOUGHT YOU COULD GET RID OF ME SO EASILY?!!
POW!
IT'S THE DISMANTLENATOR! HE'S BACK!
I THOUGHT HE WAS THE DESTROYERNATOR!
IT'S DECONSTRUCTINATOR!
OH YEAH, THAT'S RIGHT.
I'M GOING TO WRITE IT DOWN THIS TIME.
FORGET THAT NAME!
FOR I AM REBORN AS... THE RECONSTRUCTINATOR!
INSTEAD OF DESTROYING MY SUIT, YOU FUSED IT TO MY VERY ATOMS!
THE POWER TO MANIPULATE MOLECULAR BONDS IS A PART OF ME NOW! AND I'VE USED THAT POWER TO PULL MYSELF BACK TOGETHER!

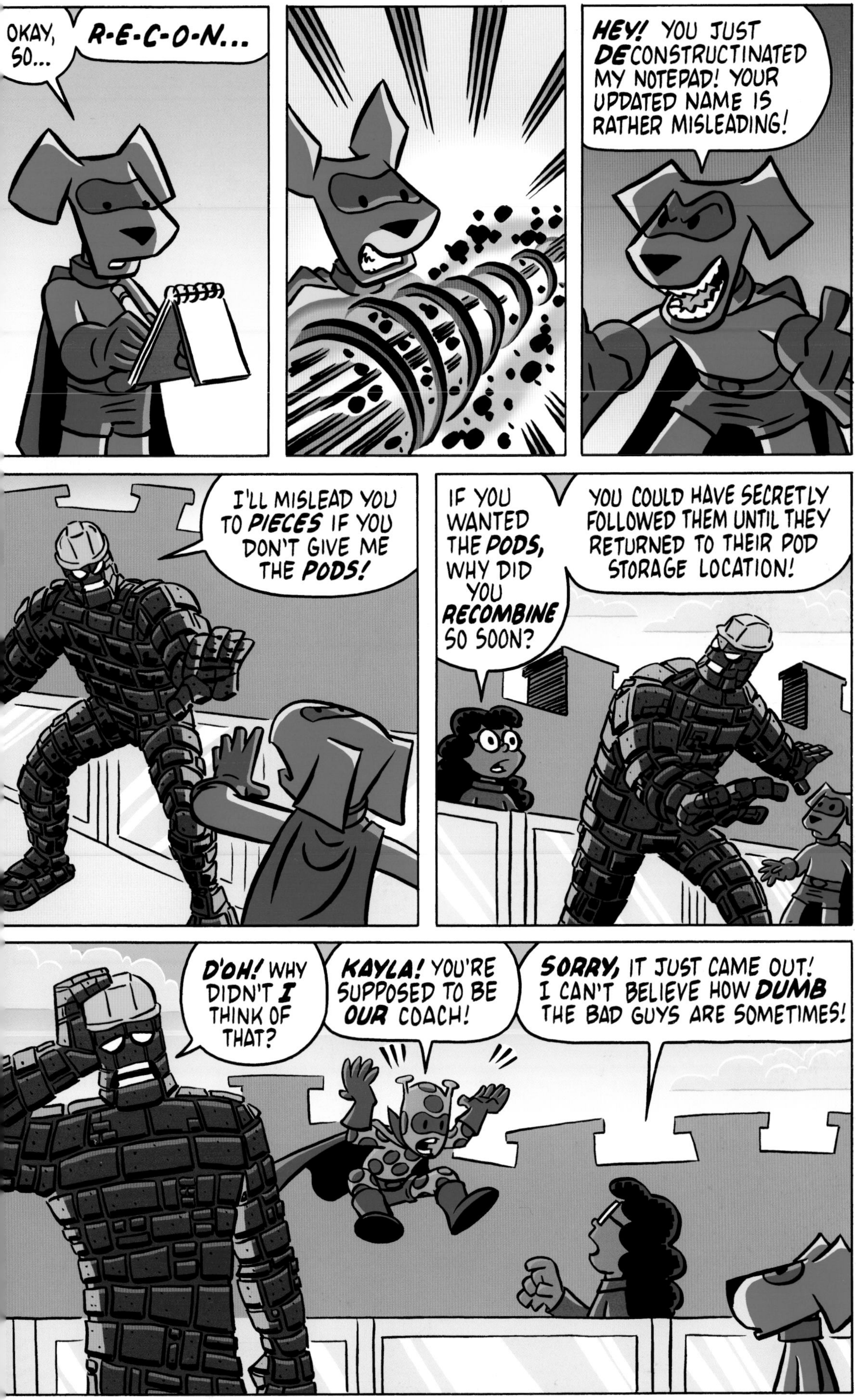
OKAY, SO...
R-E-C-O-N...
HEY! YOU JUST DECONSTRUCTINATED MY NOTEPAD! YOUR UPDATED NAME IS RATHER MISLEADING!
I'LL MISLEAD YOU TO PIECES IF YOU DON'T GIVE ME THE PODS!
IF YOU WANTED THE PODS, WHY DID YOU RECOMBINE SO SOON?
YOU COULD HAVE SECRETLY FOLLOWED THEM UNTIL THEY RETURNED TO THEIR POD STORAGE LOCATION!
D'OH! WHY DIDN'T I THINK OF THAT?
KAYLA! YOU'RE SUPPOSED TO BE OUR COACH!
SORRY, IT JUST CAME OUT! I CAN'T BELIEVE HOW DUMB THE BAD GUYS ARE SOMETIMES!

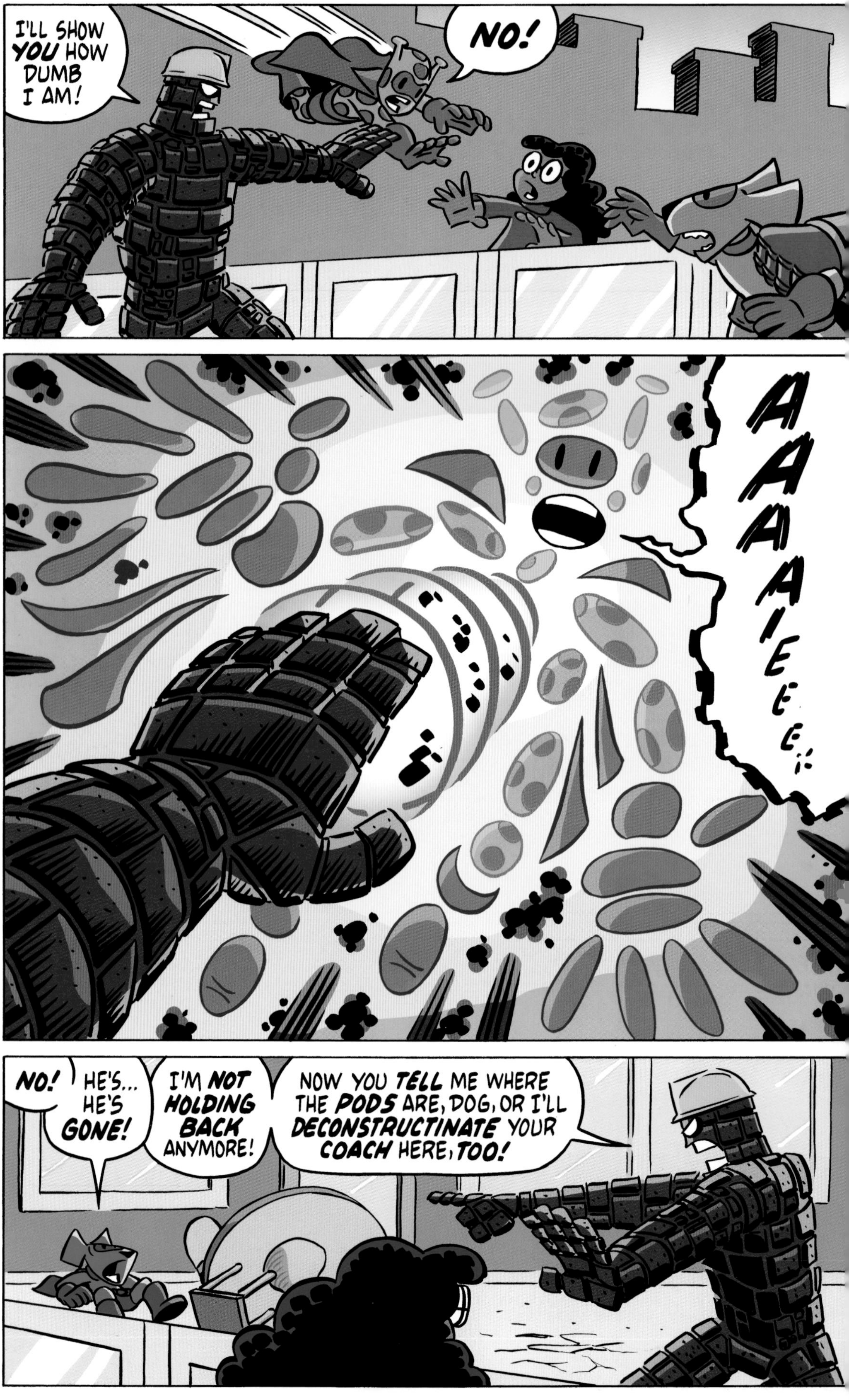

I'LL SHOW YOU HOW DUMB I AM!
NO!
AAAAAIEEEEE!
NO!
HE'S... HE'S GONE!
I'M NOT HOLDING BACK ANYMORE!
NOW YOU TELL ME WHERE THE PODS ARE, DOG, OR I'LL DECONSTRUCTINATE YOUR COACH HERE, TOO!

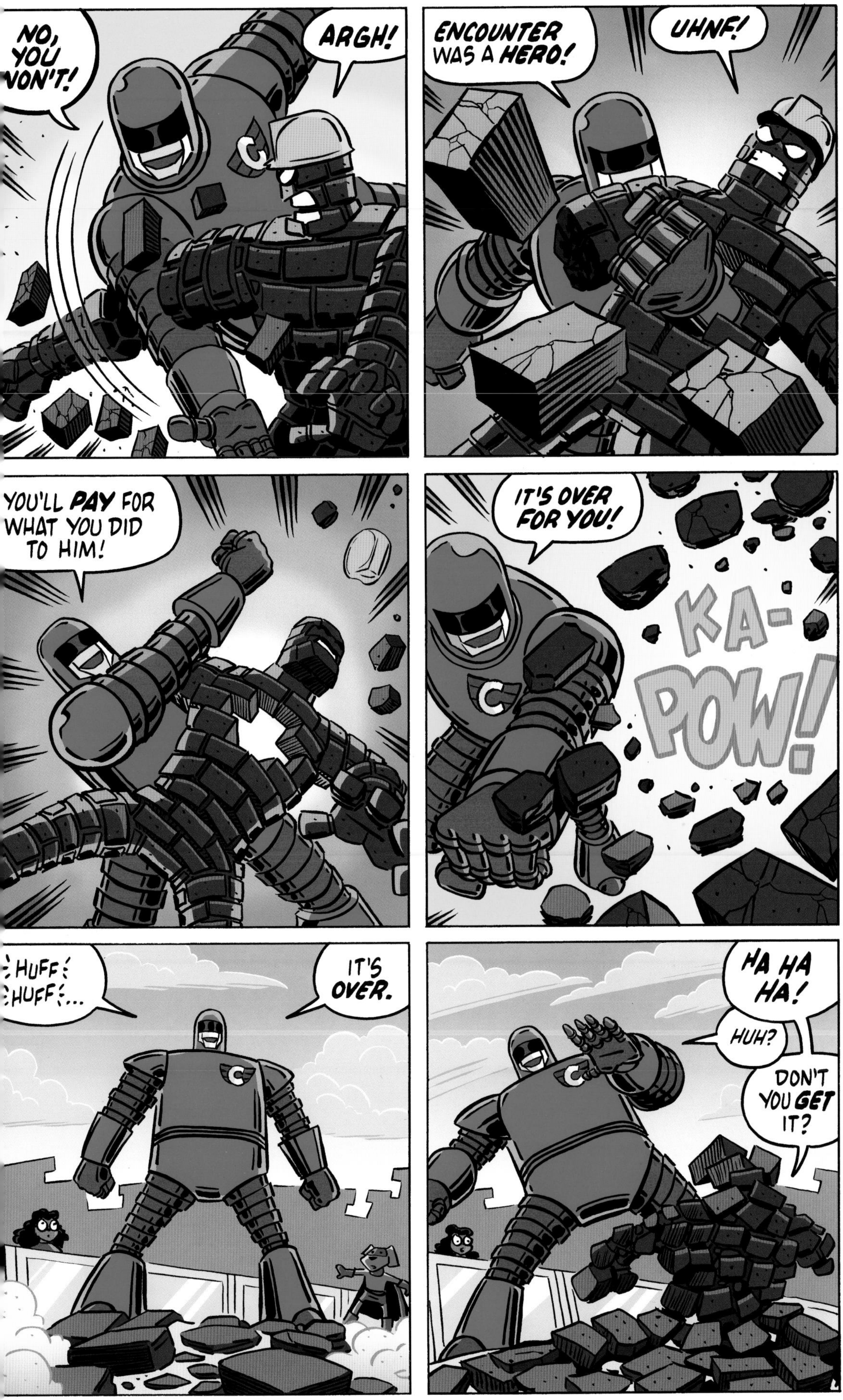

NO, YOU VON'T!
ARGH!
ENCOUNTER WAS A HERO!
UHNF!
YOU'LL PAY FOR WHAT YOU DID TO HIM!
IT'S OVER FOR YOU!
KA-POW!
HUFF HUFF...
IT'S OVER.
HA HA HA!
HUH?
DON'T YOU GET IT?

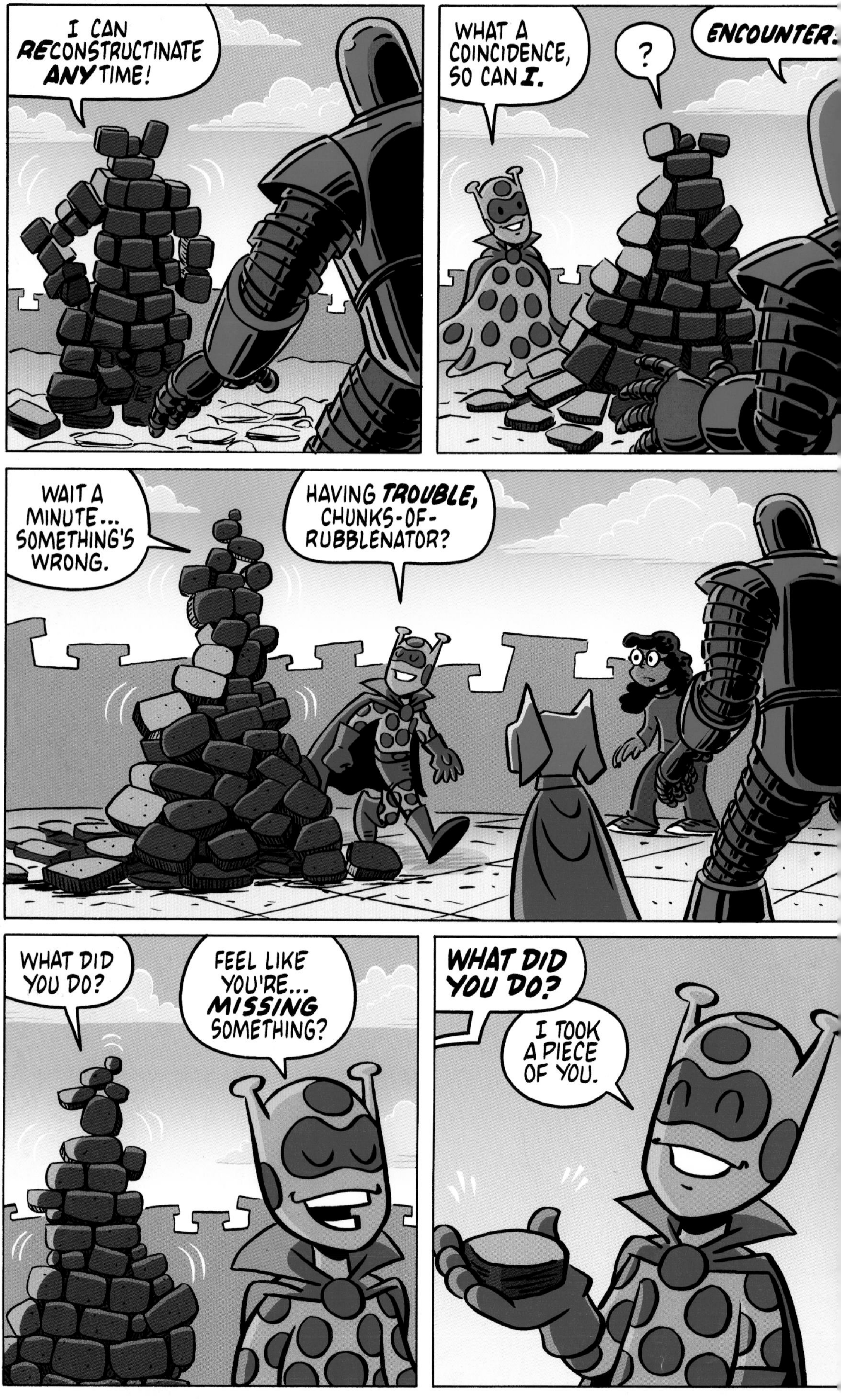

I CAN RECONSTRUCTINATE ANY TIME!
WHAT A COINCIDENCE, SO CAN I.
?
ENCOUNTER.
WAIT A MINUTE... SOMETHING'S WRONG.
HAVING TROUBLE, CHUNKS-OF-RUBBLENATOR?
WHAT DID YOU DO?
FEEL LIKE YOU'RE... MISSING SOMETHING?
WHAT DID YOU DO?
I TOOK A PIECE OF YOU.

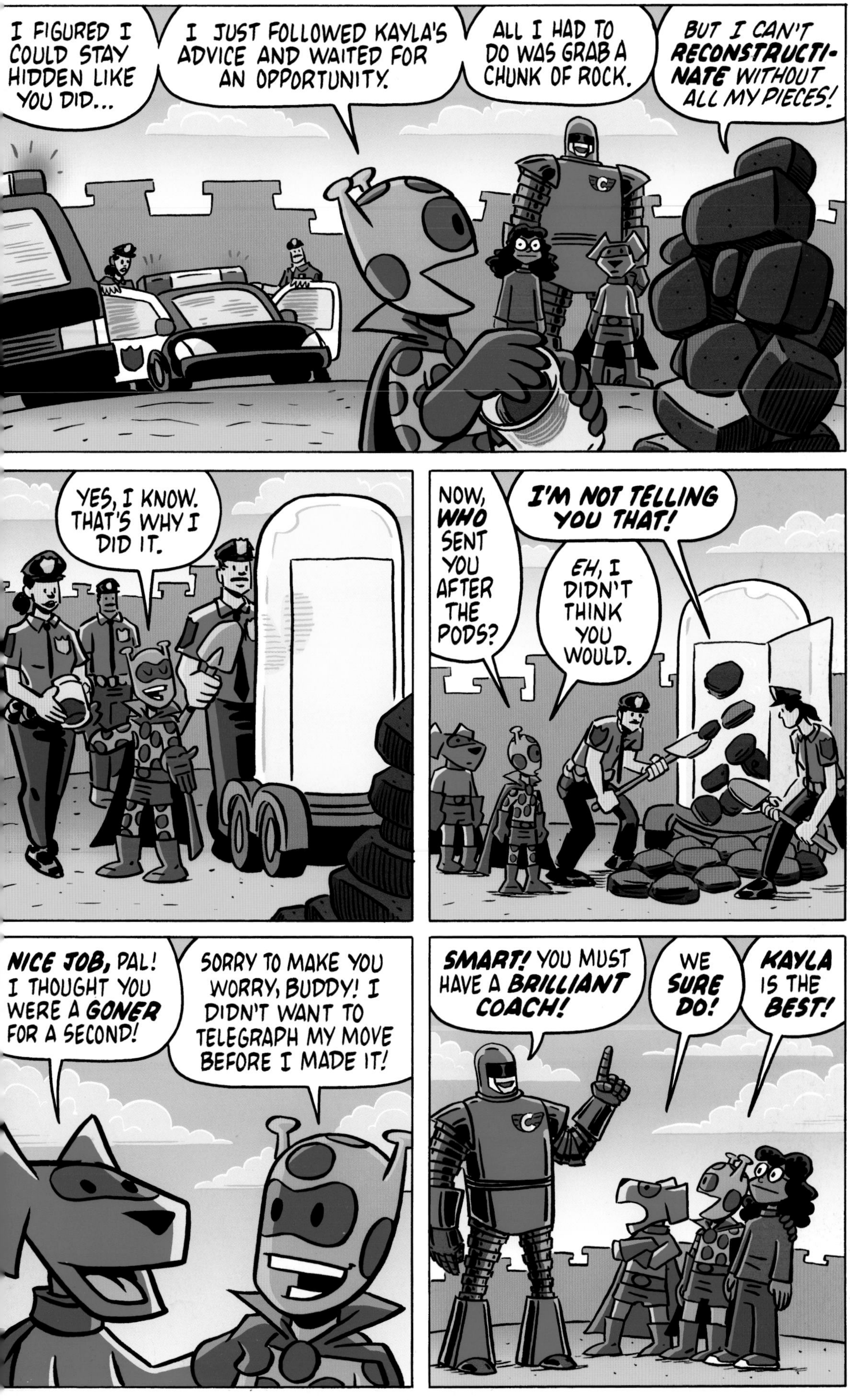
I FIGURED I COULD STAY HIDDEN LIKE YOU DID...
I JUST FOLLOWED KAYLA'S ADVICE AND WAITED FOR AN OPPORTUNITY.
ALL I HAD TO DO WAS GRAB A CHUNK OF ROCK.
BUT I CAN'T **RECONSTRUCTI-NATE** WITHOUT ALL MY PIECES!
YES, I KNOW. THAT'S WHY I DID IT.
NOW, **WHO** SENT YOU AFTER THE PODS?
I'M NOT TELLING YOU THAT!
EH, I DIDN'T THINK YOU WOULD.
NICE JOB, PAL! I THOUGHT YOU WERE A **GONER** FOR A SECOND!
SORRY TO MAKE YOU WORRY, BUDDY! I DIDN'T WANT TO TELEGRAPH MY MOVE BEFORE I MADE IT!
SMART! YOU MUST HAVE A **BRILLIANT COACH!**
WE **SURE DO!**
KAYLA IS THE **BEST!**

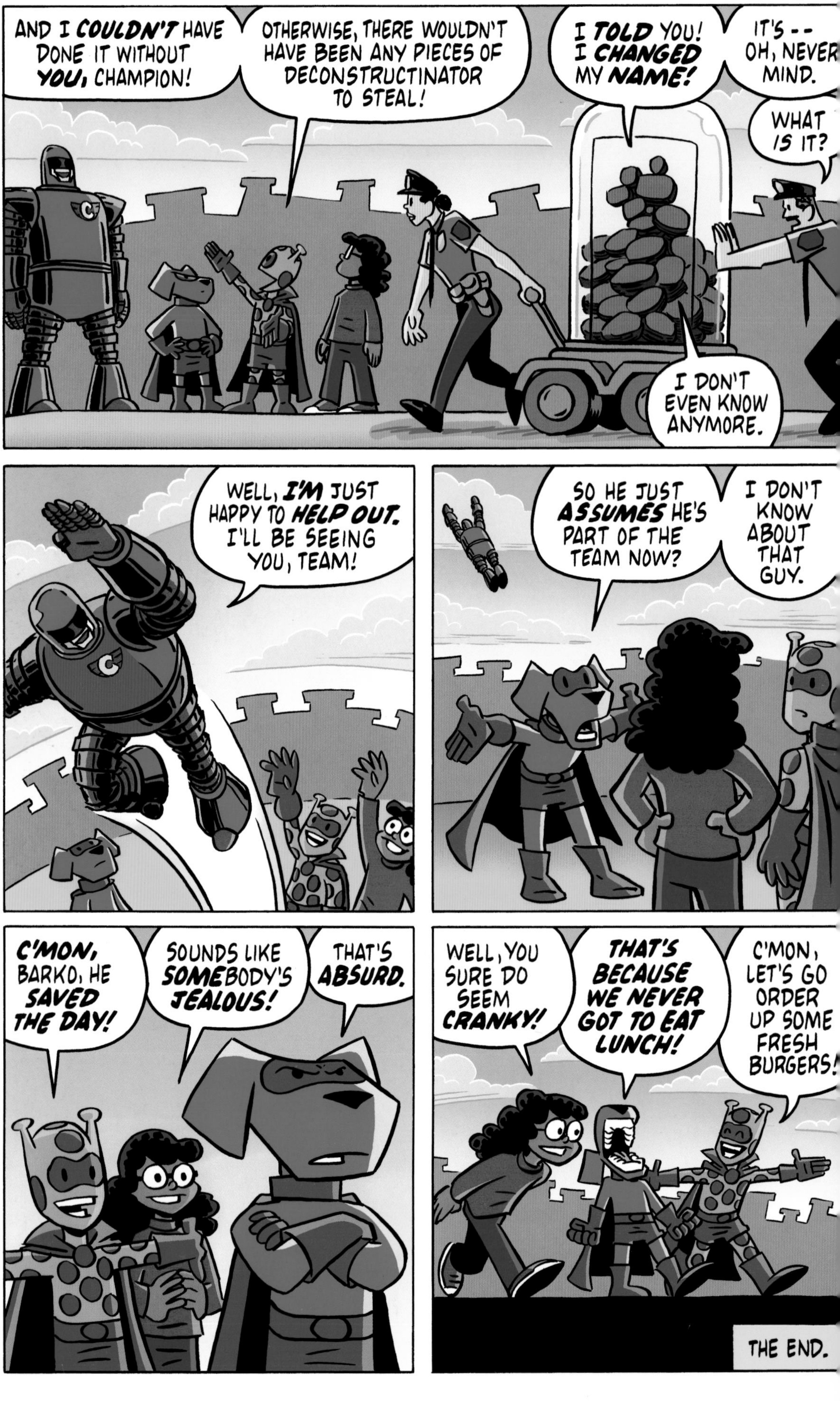
AND I COULDN'T HAVE DONE IT WITHOUT YOU, CHAMPION!
OTHERWISE, THERE WOULDN'T HAVE BEEN ANY PIECES OF DECONSTRUCTINATOR TO STEAL!
I TOLD YOU! I CHANGED MY NAME!
IT'S -- OH, NEVER MIND.
WHAT IS IT?
I DON'T EVEN KNOW ANYMORE.
WELL, I'M JUST HAPPY TO HELP OUT. I'LL BE SEEING YOU, TEAM!
SO HE JUST ASSUMES HE'S PART OF THE TEAM NOW?
I DON'T KNOW ABOUT THAT GUY.
C'MON, BARKO, HE SAVED THE DAY!
SOUNDS LIKE SOMEBODY'S JEALOUS!
THAT'S ABSURD.
WELL, YOU SURE DO SEEM CRANKY!
THAT'S BECAUSE WE NEVER GOT TO EAT LUNCH!
C'MON, LET'S GO ORDER UP SOME FRESH BURGERS!
THE END.

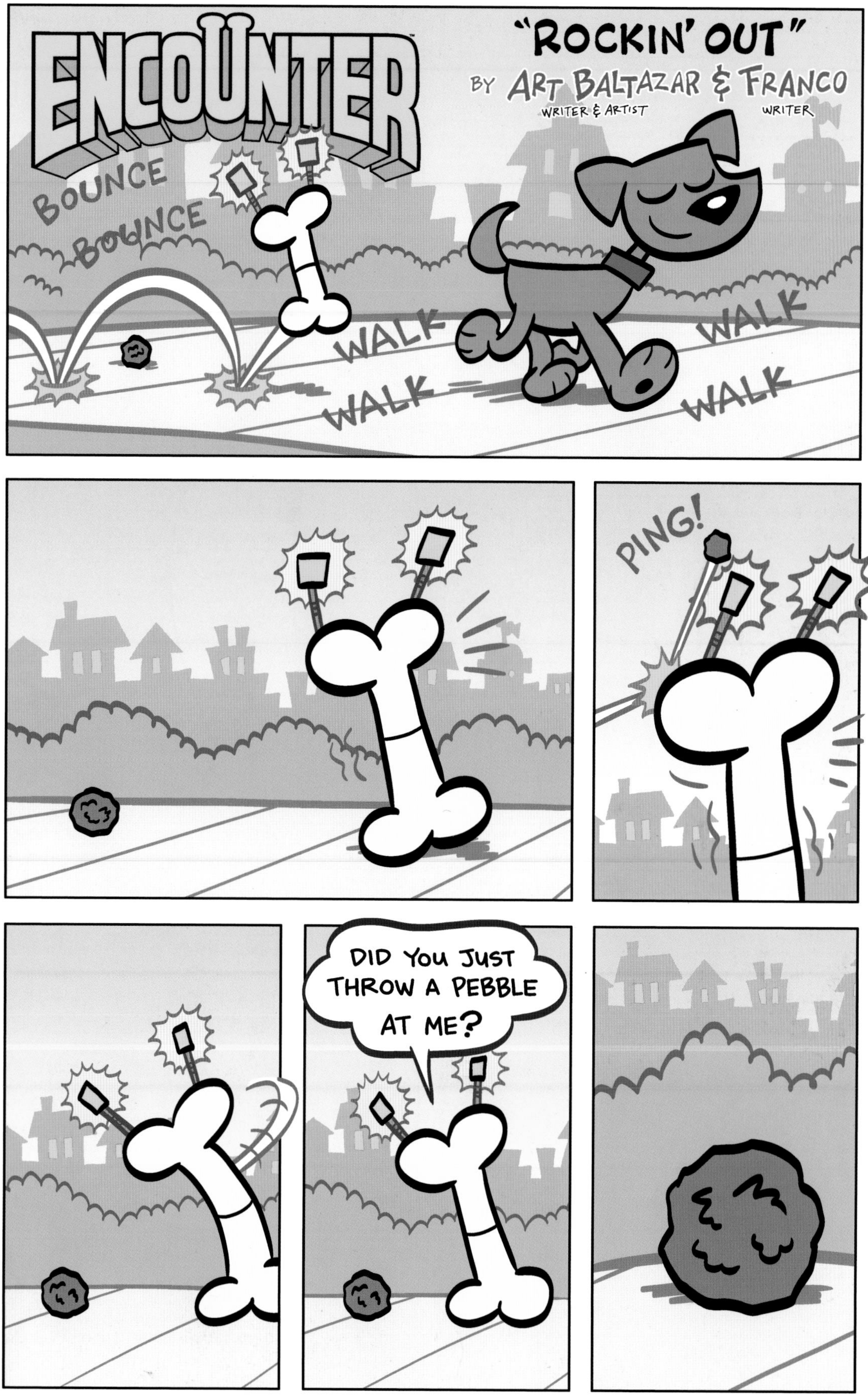
ENCOUNTER
"ROCKIN' OUT"
BY ART BALTAZAR & FRANCO
WRITER & ARTIST
WRITER
BOUNCE
BOUNCE
WALK
WALK
WALK
WALK
PING!
DID YOU JUST THROW A PEBBLE AT ME?

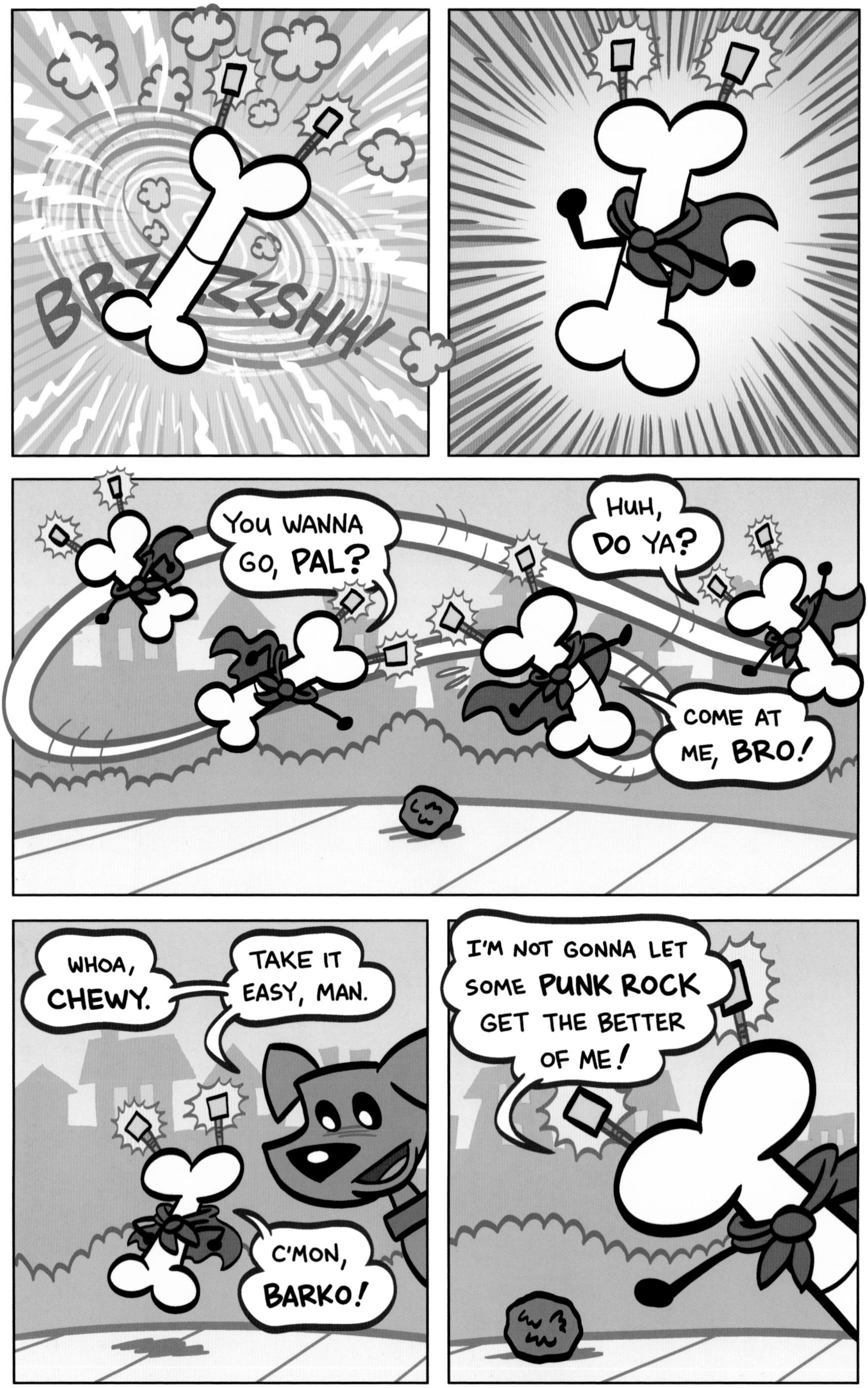
BRZZZSHH!
YOU WANNA GO, PAL?
HUH, DO YA?
COME AT ME, BRO!
WHOA, CHEWY.
TAKE IT EASY, MAN.
C'MON, BARKO!
I'M NOT GONNA LET SOME PUNK ROCK GET THE BETTER OF ME!

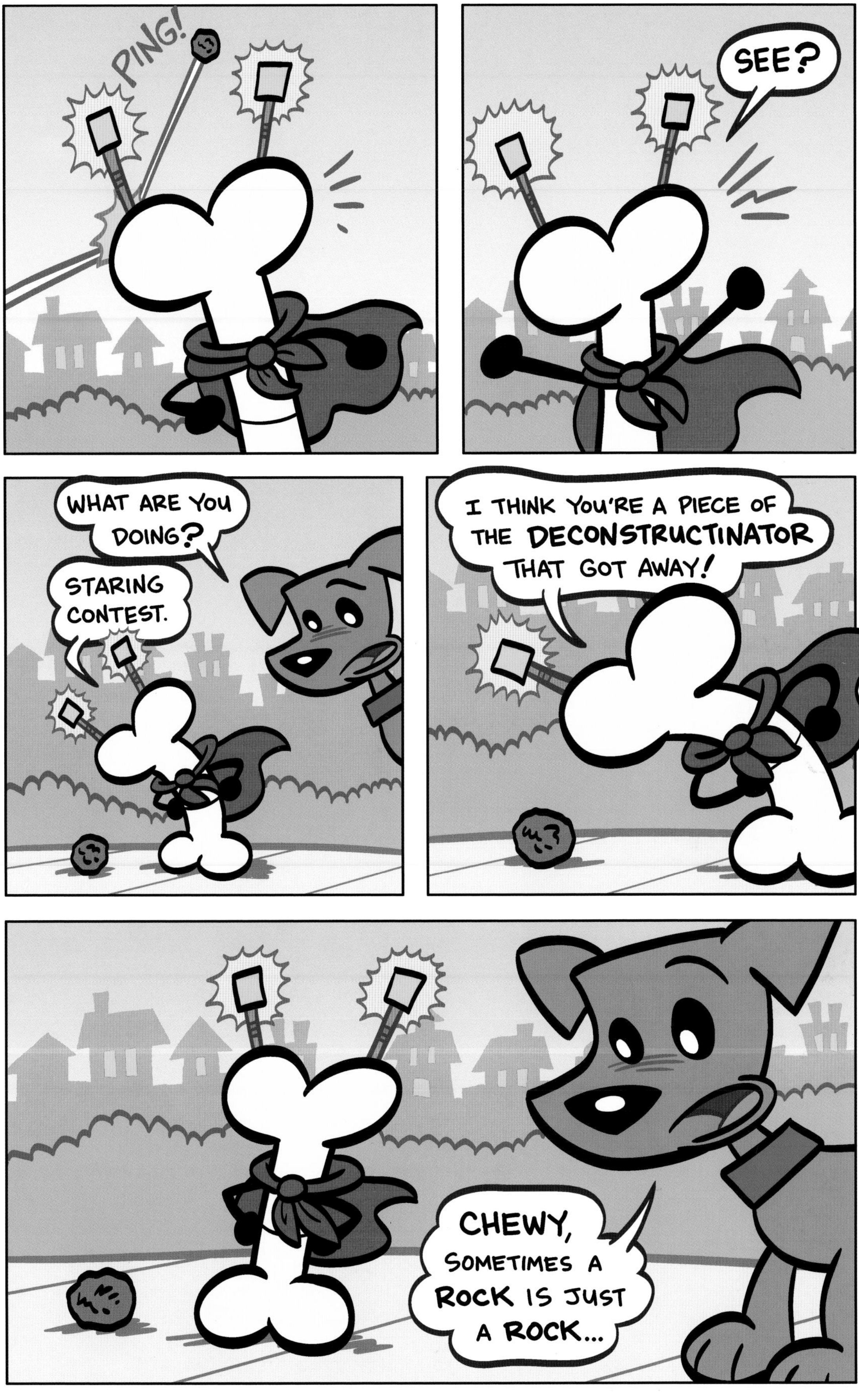
PING!
SEE?
WHAT ARE YOU DOING?
STARING CONTEST.
I THINK YOU'RE A PIECE OF THE DECONSTRUCTINATOR THAT GOT AWAY!
CHEWY, SOMETIMES A ROCK IS JUST A ROCK...

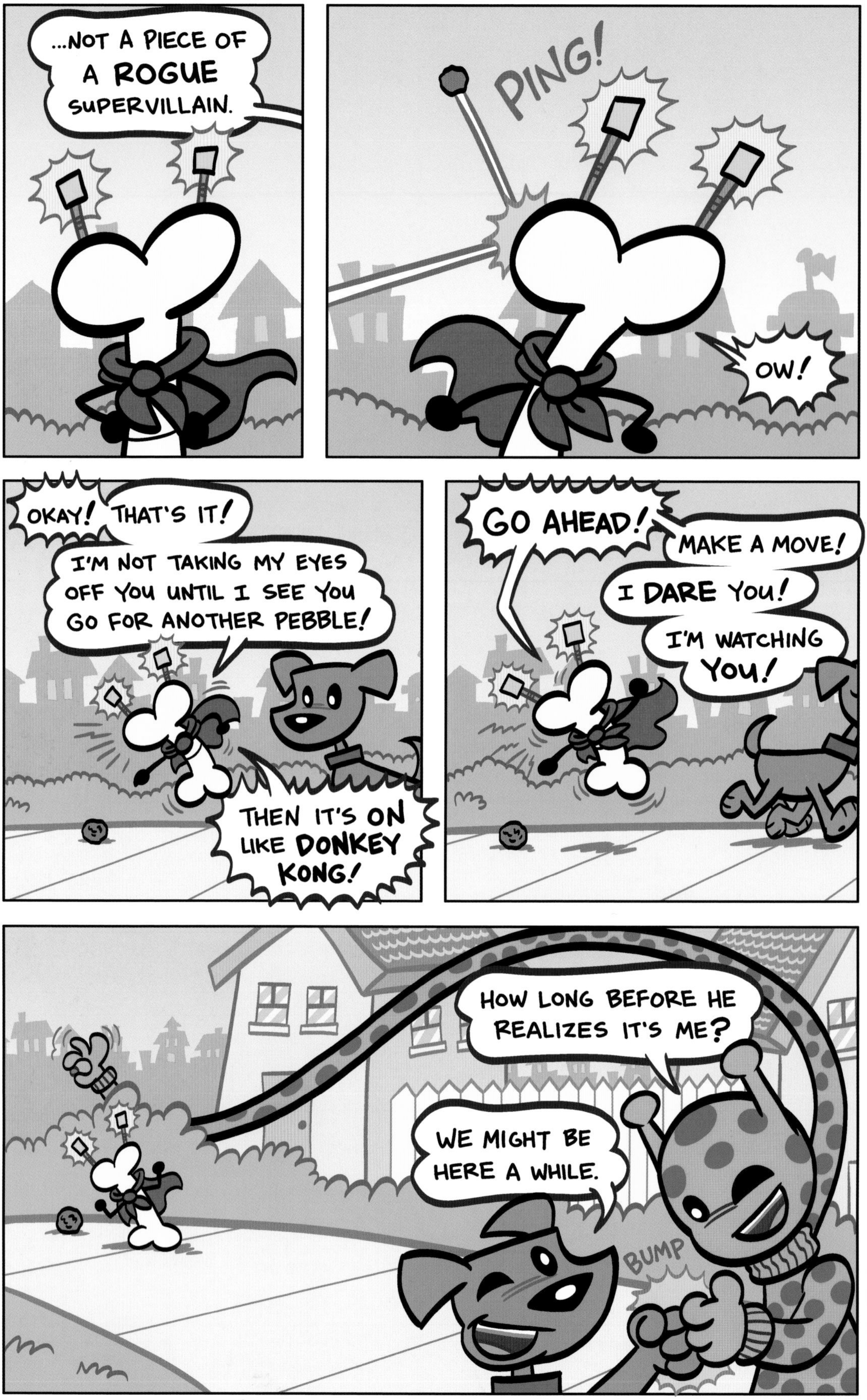
...NOT A PIECE OF A ROGUE SUPERVILLAIN.
PING!
OW!
OKAY!
THAT'S IT!
I'M NOT TAKING MY EYES OFF YOU UNTIL I SEE YOU GO FOR ANOTHER PEBBLE!
THEN IT'S ON LIKE DONKEY KONG!
GO AHEAD!
MAKE A MOVE!
I DARE YOU!
I'M WATCHING YOU!
HOW LONG BEFORE HE REALIZES IT'S ME?
WE MIGHT BE HERE A WHILE.
BUMP

–COME AT ME, BRO.

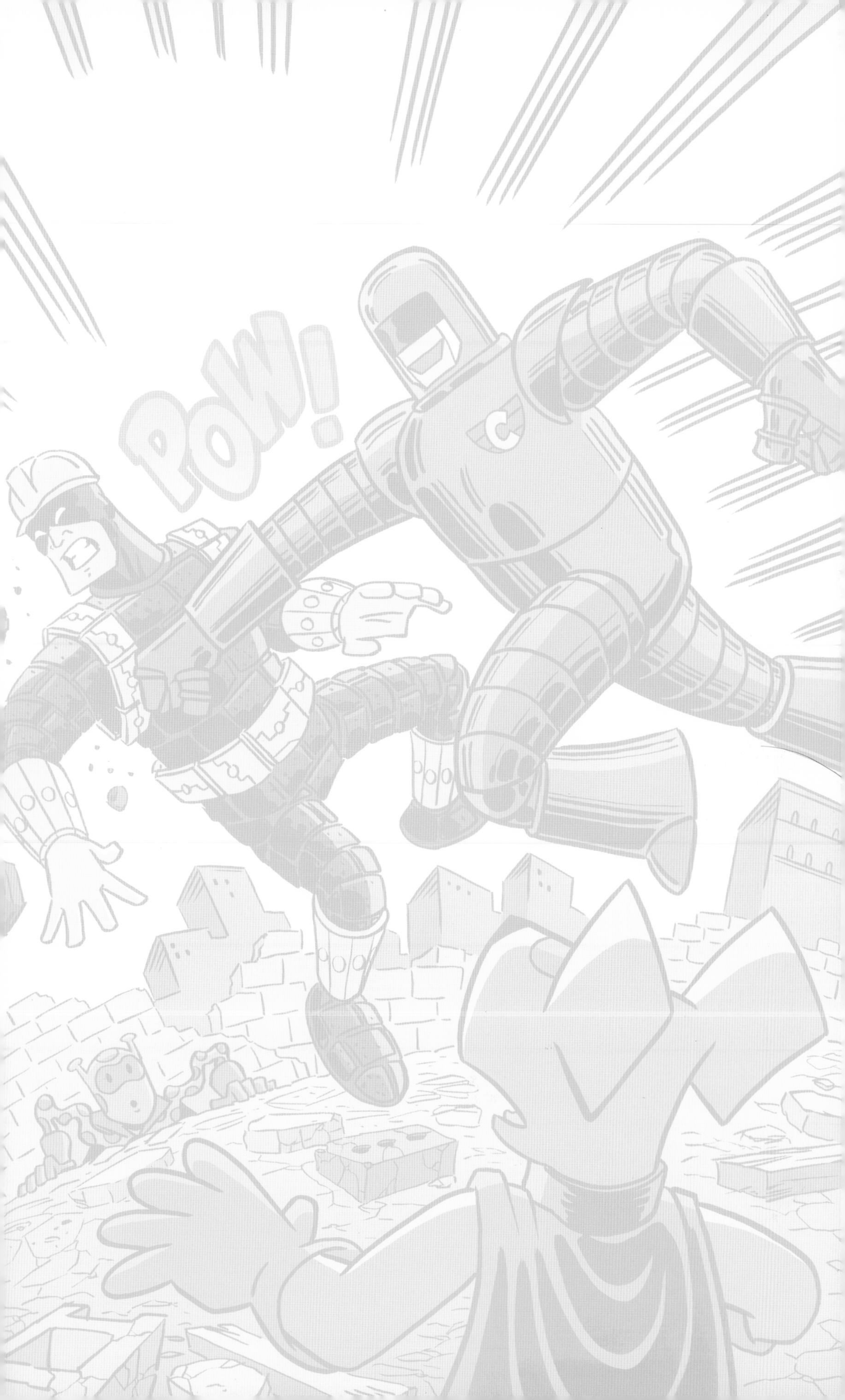
POW!!

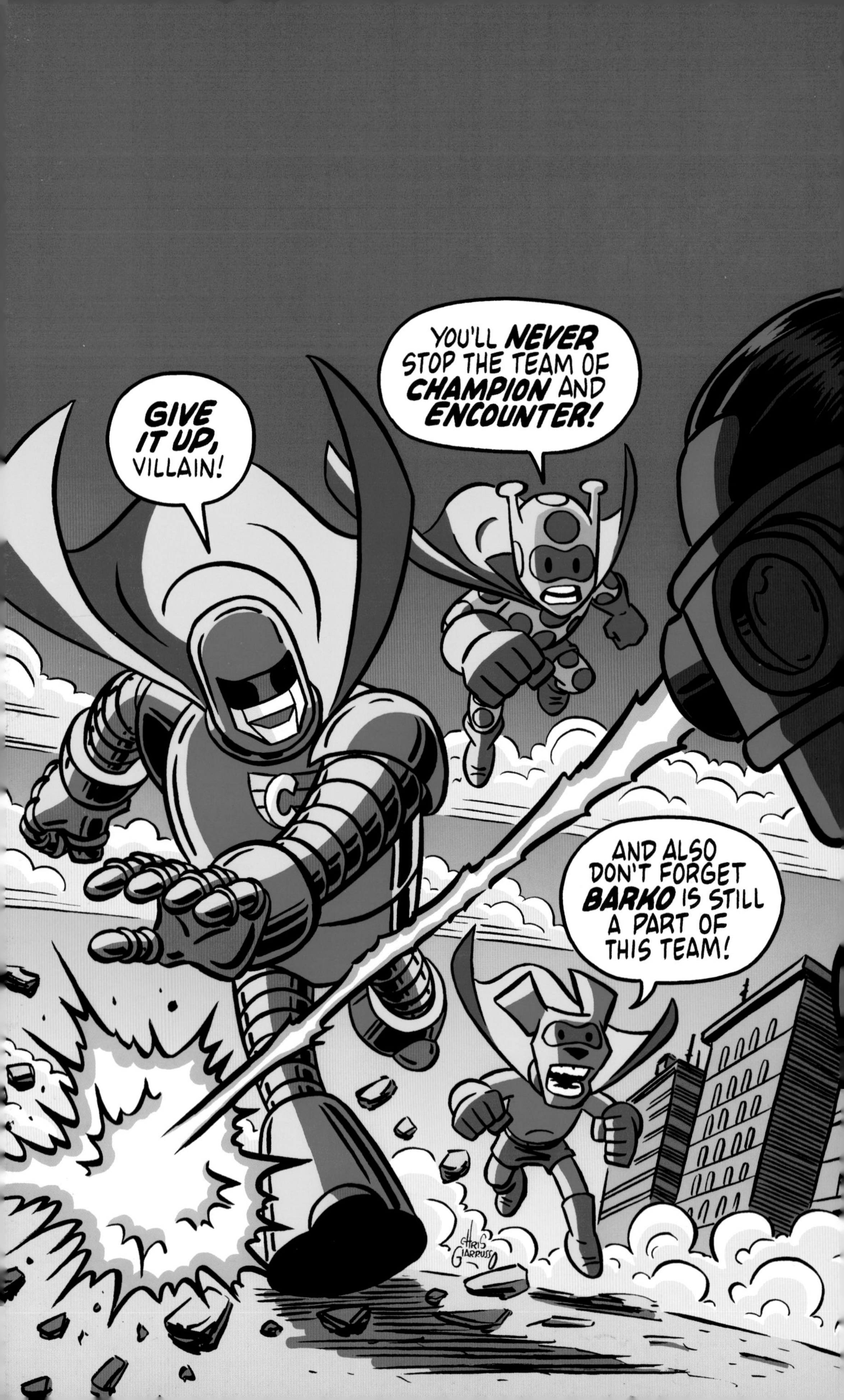
GIVE IT UP, VILLAIN!
YOU'LL NEVER STOP THE TEAM OF CHAMPION AND ENCOUNTER!
AND ALSO DON'T FORGET BARKO IS STILL A PART OF THIS TEAM!
CHRIS GIARRUSSO

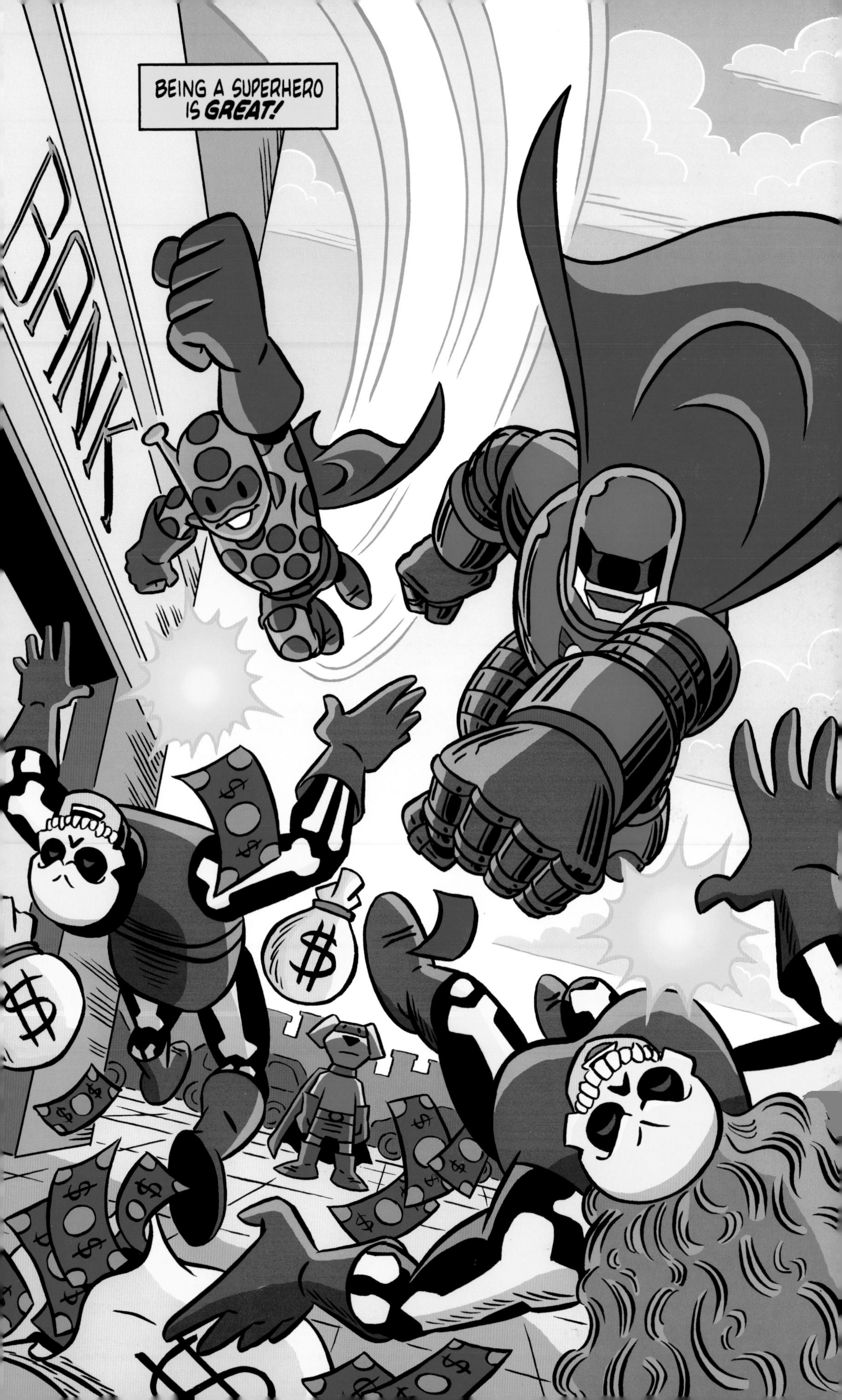
BEING A SUPERHERO IS GREAT!
BANK

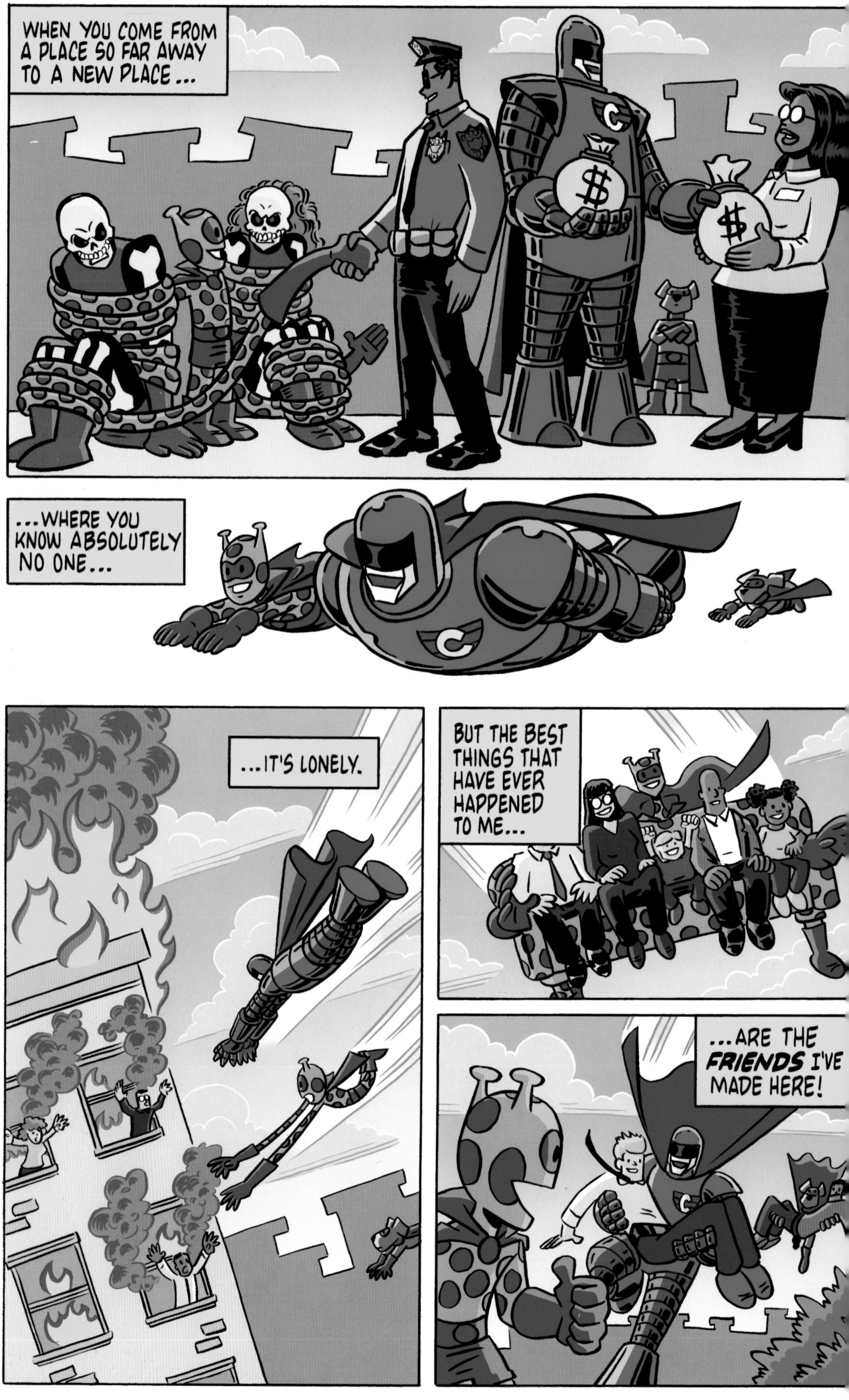
WHEN YOU COME FROM A PLACE SO FAR AWAY TO A NEW PLACE...
...WHERE YOU KNOW ABSOLUTELY NO ONE...
...IT'S LONELY.
BUT THE BEST THINGS THAT HAVE EVER HAPPENED TO ME...
...ARE THE FRIENDS I'VE MADE HERE!

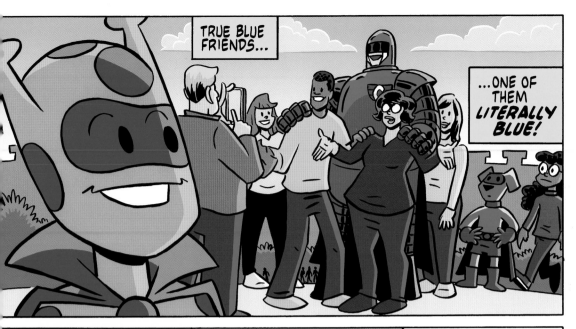

TRUE BLUE FRIENDS...

...ONE OF THEM *LITERALLY BLUE!*

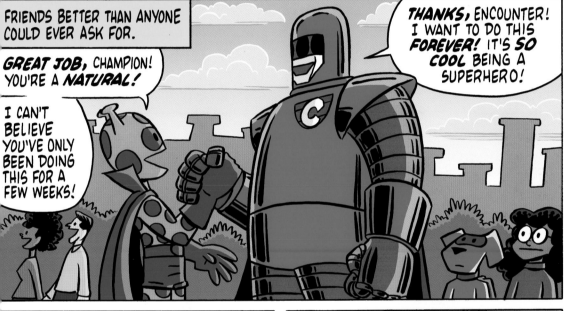

FRIENDS BETTER THAN ANYONE COULD EVER ASK FOR.

GREAT JOB, CHAMPION! YOU'RE A *NATURAL!*

I CAN'T BELIEVE YOU'VE ONLY BEEN DOING THIS FOR A FEW WEEKS!

THANKS, ENCOUNTER! I WANT TO DO THIS *FOREVER!* IT'S *SO COOL* BEING A SUPERHERO!

IT'S BEEN *GREAT* HAVING ANOTHER HERO THAT LOVES THIS AS MUCH AS *I* DO!

WE SHOULD START AN *OFFICIAL SUPERTEAM!*

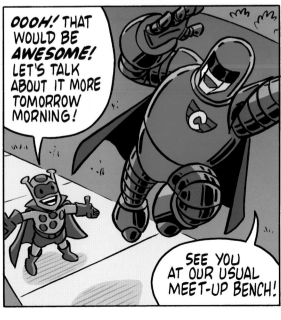

OOOH! THAT WOULD BE *AWESOME!* LET'S TALK ABOUT IT MORE TOMORROW MORNING!

SEE YOU AT OUR USUAL MEET-UP BENCH!

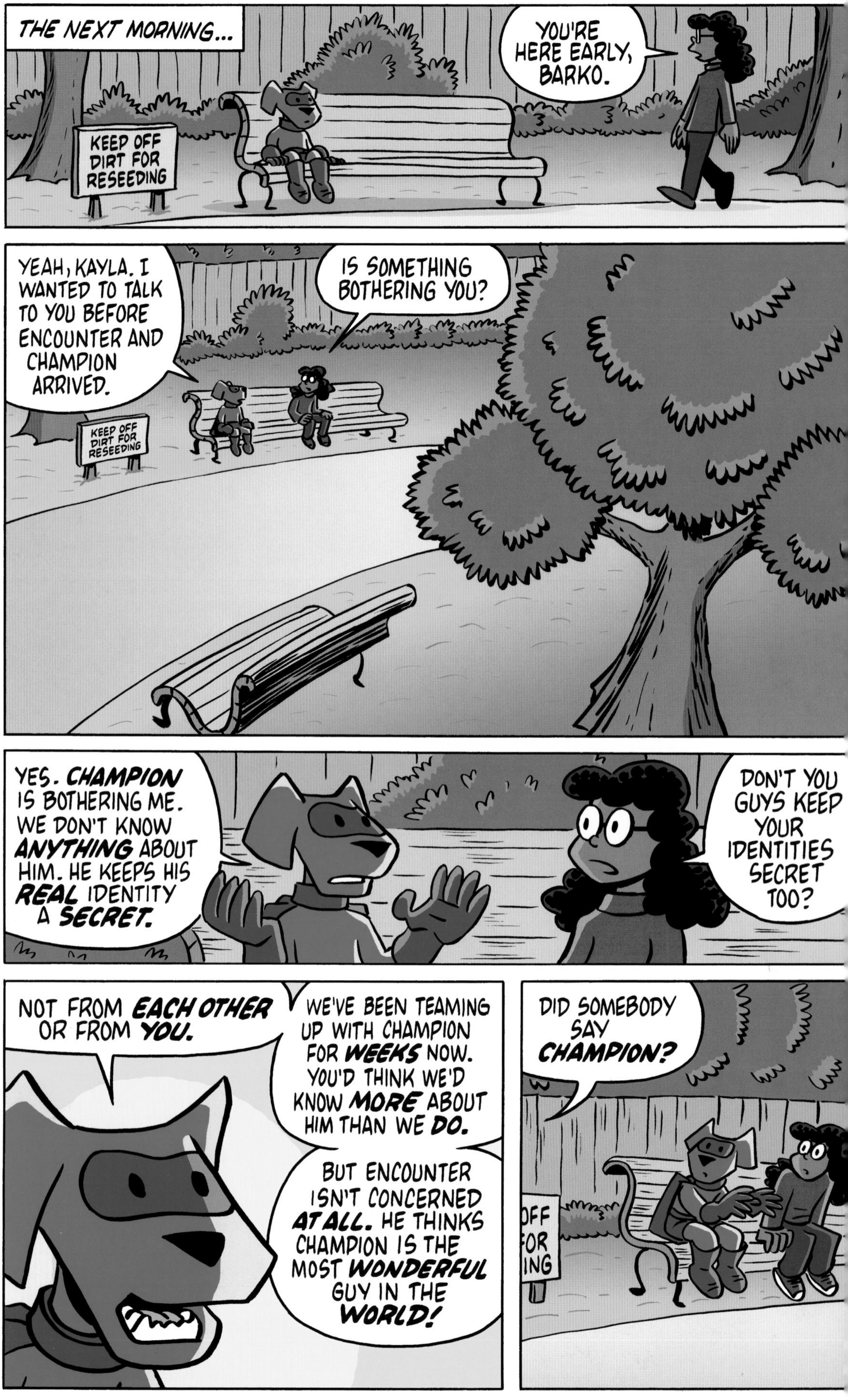
THE NEXT MORNING...
YOU'RE HERE EARLY, BARKO.
KEEP OFF DIRT FOR RESEEDING
YEAH, KAYLA. I WANTED TO TALK TO YOU BEFORE ENCOUNTER AND CHAMPION ARRIVED.
IS SOMETHING BOTHERING YOU?
KEEP OFF DIRT FOR RESEEDING
YES. CHAMPION IS BOTHERING ME. WE DON'T KNOW ANYTHING ABOUT HIM. HE KEEPS HIS REAL IDENTITY A SECRET.
DON'T YOU GUYS KEEP YOUR IDENTITIES SECRET TOO?
NOT FROM EACH OTHER OR FROM YOU.
WE'VE BEEN TEAMING UP WITH CHAMPION FOR WEEKS NOW. YOU'D THINK WE'D KNOW MORE ABOUT HIM THAN WE DO.
BUT ENCOUNTER ISN'T CONCERNED AT ALL. HE THINKS CHAMPION IS THE MOST WONDERFUL GUY IN THE WORLD!
DID SOMEBODY SAY CHAMPION?

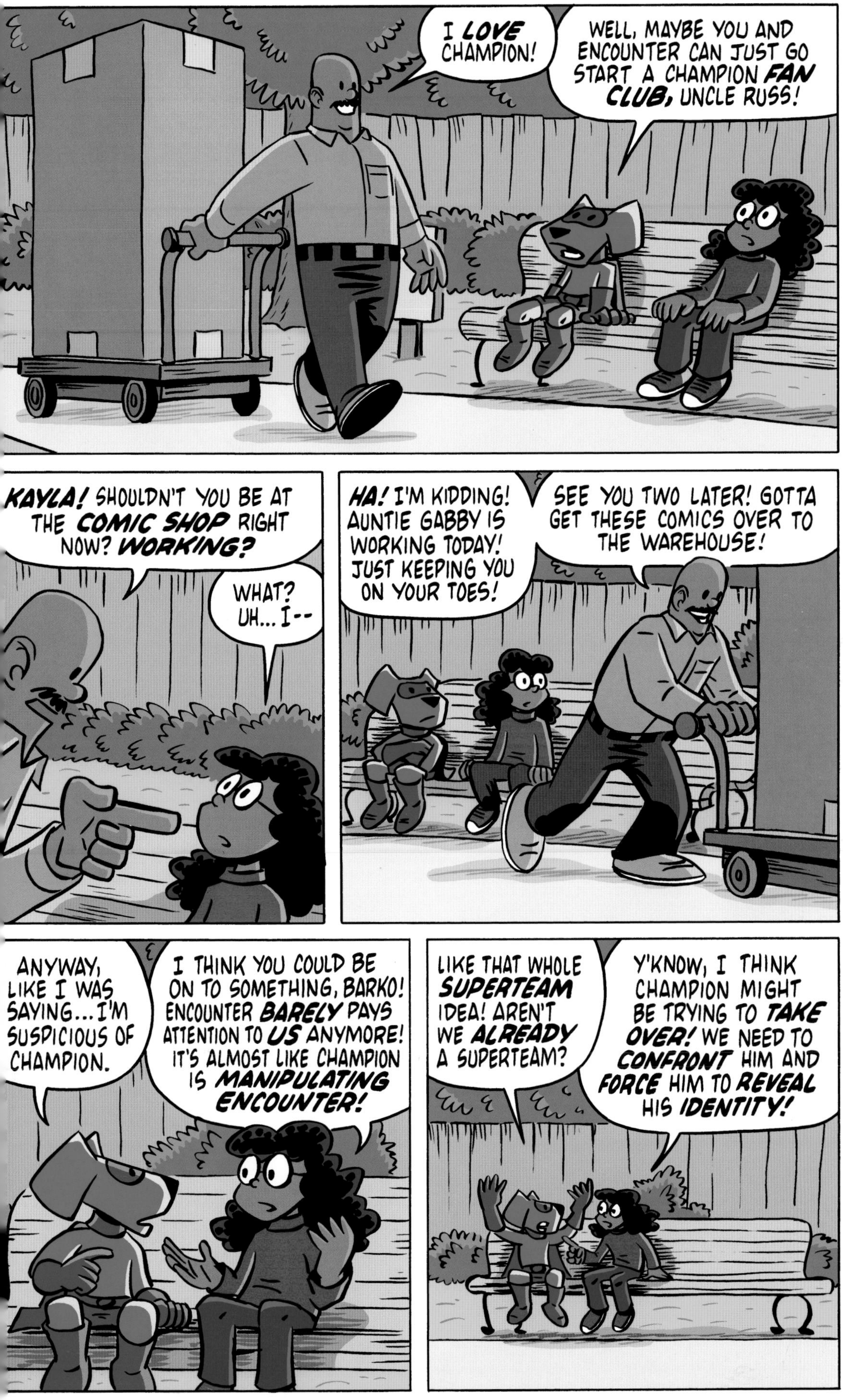

I LOVE CHAMPION!
WELL, MAYBE YOU AND ENCOUNTER CAN JUST GO START A CHAMPION FAN CLUB, UNCLE RUSS!
KAYLA! SHOULDN'T YOU BE AT THE COMIC SHOP RIGHT NOW? WORKING?
WHAT? UH... I--
HA! I'M KIDDING! AUNTIE GABBY IS WORKING TODAY! JUST KEEPING YOU ON YOUR TOES!
SEE YOU TWO LATER! GOTTA GET THESE COMICS OVER TO THE WAREHOUSE!
ANYWAY, LIKE I WAS SAYING... I'M SUSPICIOUS OF CHAMPION.
I THINK YOU COULD BE ON TO SOMETHING, BARKO! ENCOUNTER BARELY PAYS ATTENTION TO US ANYMORE! IT'S ALMOST LIKE CHAMPION IS MANIPULATING ENCOUNTER!
LIKE THAT WHOLE SUPERTEAM IDEA! AREN'T WE ALREADY A SUPERTEAM?
Y'KNOW, I THINK CHAMPION MIGHT BE TRYING TO TAKE OVER! WE NEED TO CONFRONT HIM AND FORCE HIM TO REVEAL HIS IDENTITY!

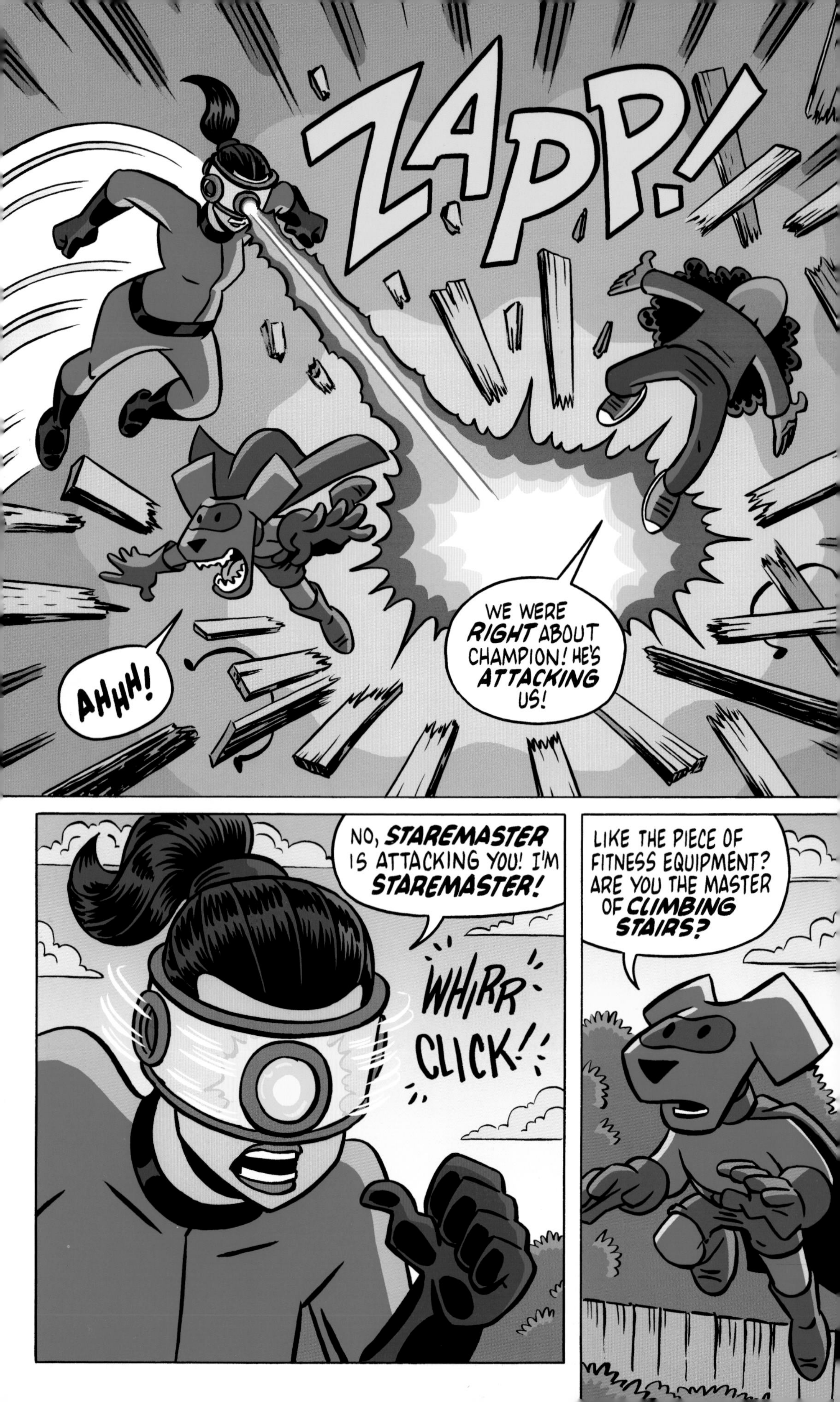

ZAPP!
AHHH!
WE WERE RIGHT ABOUT CHAMPION! HE'S ATTACKING US!
NO, STAREMASTER IS ATTACKING YOU! I'M STAREMASTER!
WHIRR
CLICK!
LIKE THE PIECE OF FITNESS EQUIPMENT? ARE YOU THE MASTER OF CLIMBING STAIRS?

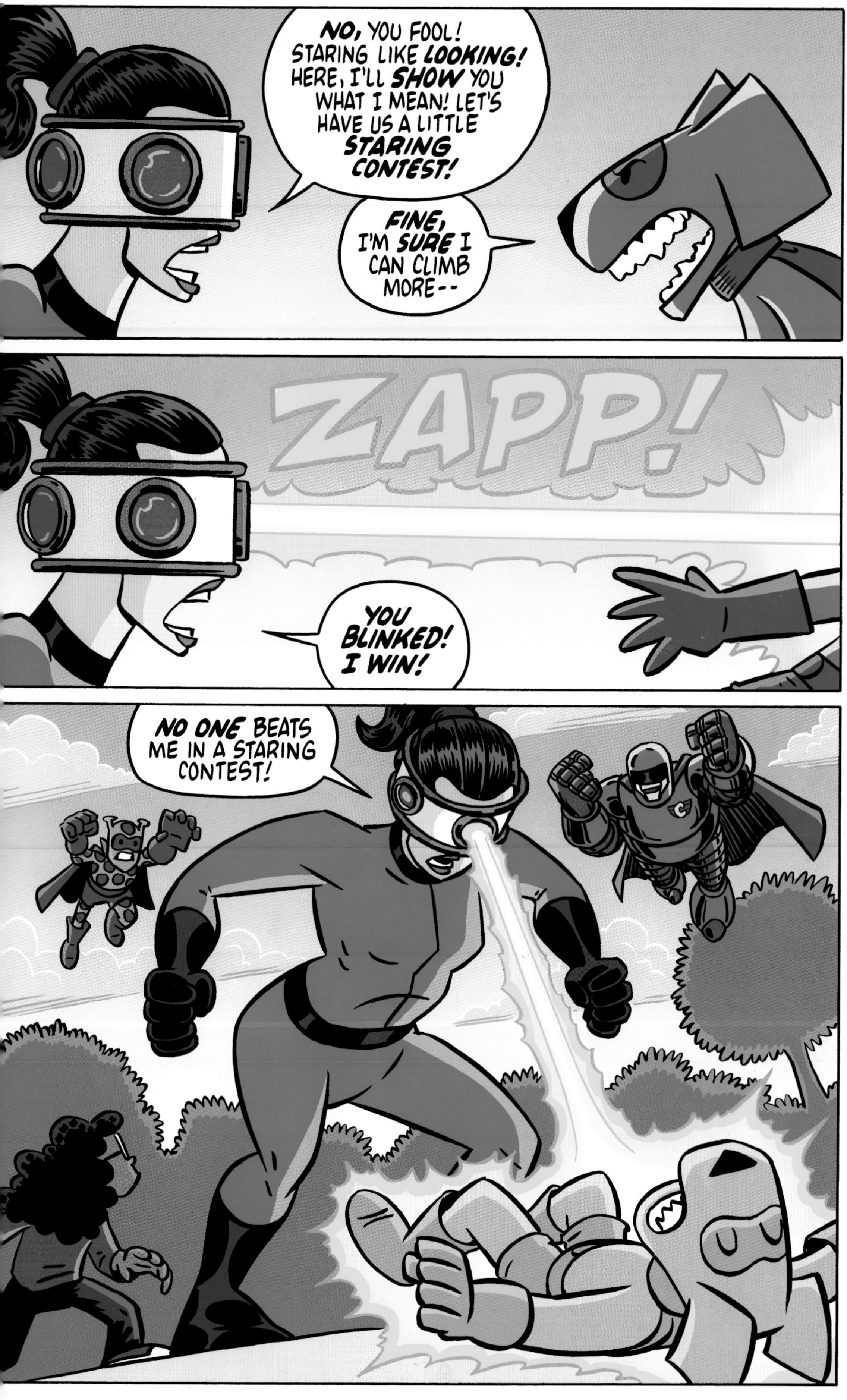
NO, YOU FOOL! STARING LIKE LOOKING! HERE, I'LL SHOW YOU WHAT I MEAN! LET'S HAVE US A LITTLE STARING CONTEST!
FINE, I'M SURE I CAN CLIMB MORE--
ZAPP!
YOU BLINKED! I WIN!
NO ONE BEATS ME IN A STARING CONTEST!

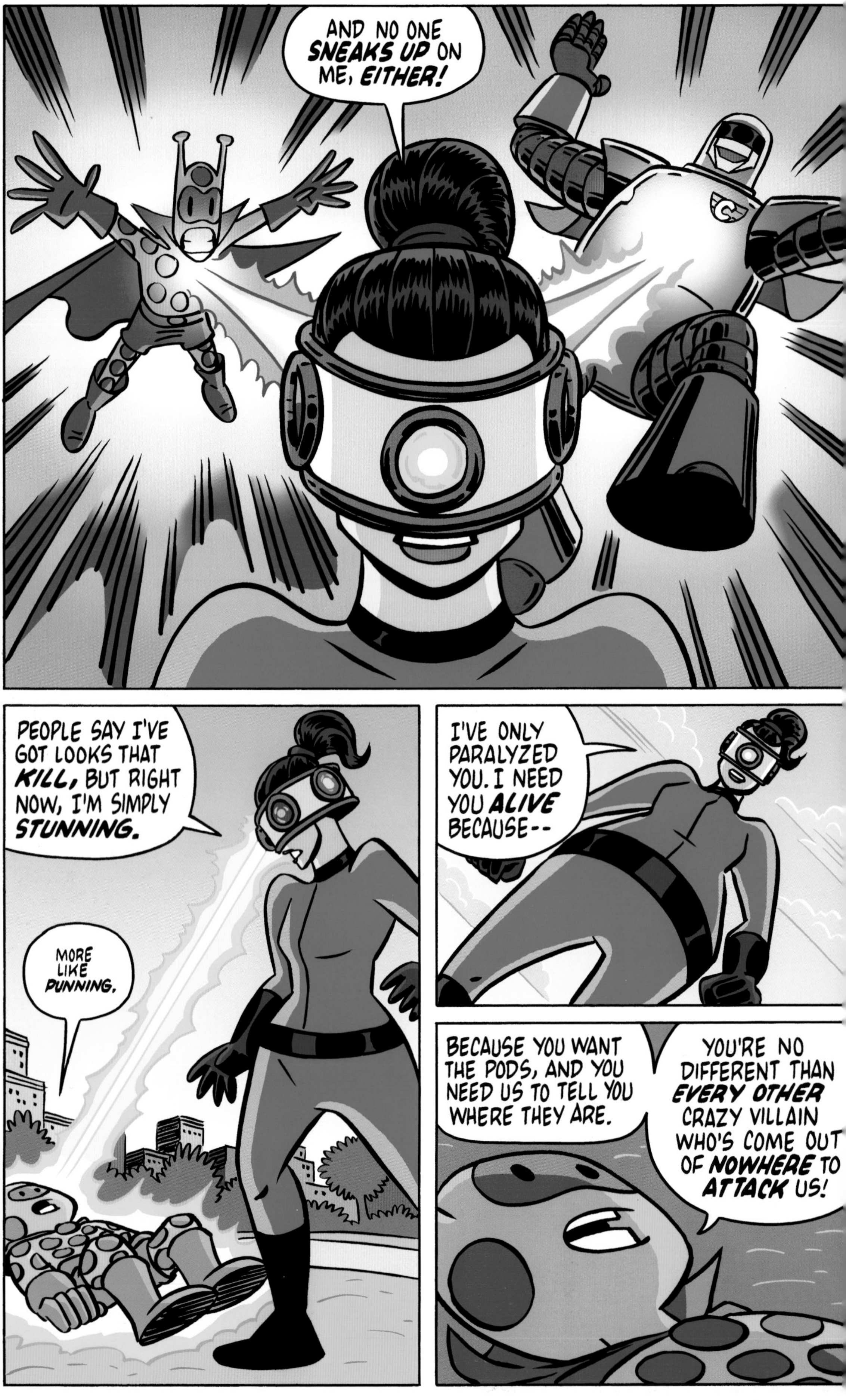
AND NO ONE SNEAKS UP ON ME, EITHER!
PEOPLE SAY I'VE GOT LOOKS THAT KILL, BUT RIGHT NOW, I'M SIMPLY STUNNING.
MORE LIKE PUNNING.
I'VE ONLY PARALYZED YOU. I NEED YOU ALIVE BECAUSE--
BECAUSE YOU WANT THE PODS, AND YOU NEED US TO TELL YOU WHERE THEY ARE.
YOU'RE NO DIFFERENT THAN EVERY OTHER CRAZY VILLAIN WHO'S COME OUT OF NOWHERE TO ATTACK US!

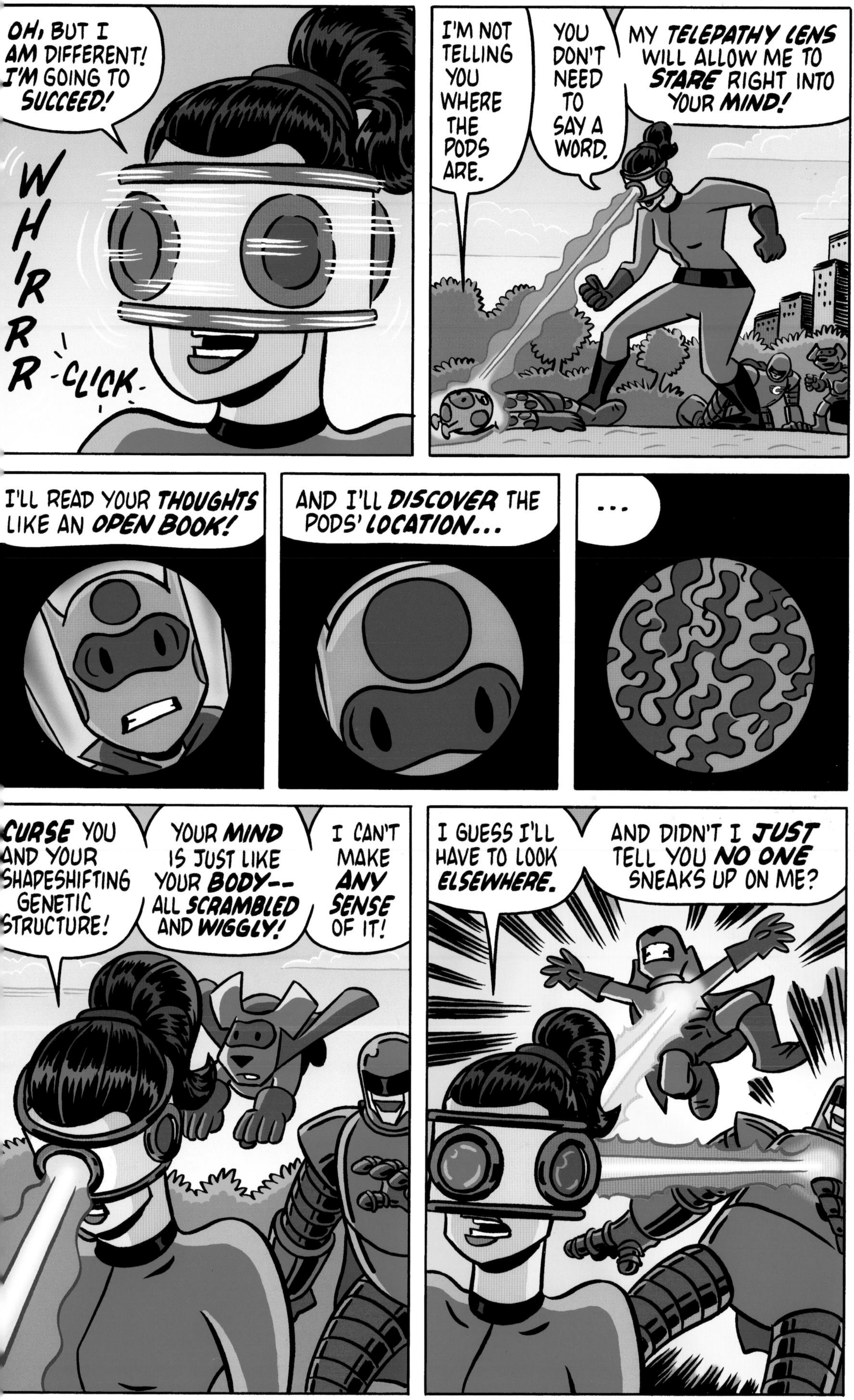
OH, BUT I AM DIFFERENT! I'M GOING TO SUCCEED!
WHIRRR
CLICK
I'M NOT TELLING YOU WHERE THE PODS ARE.
YOU DON'T NEED TO SAY A WORD.
MY TELEPATHY LENS WILL ALLOW ME TO STARE RIGHT INTO YOUR MIND!
I'LL READ YOUR THOUGHTS LIKE AN OPEN BOOK!
AND I'LL DISCOVER THE PODS' LOCATION...
...
CURSE YOU AND YOUR SHAPESHIFTING GENETIC STRUCTURE!
YOUR MIND IS JUST LIKE YOUR BODY-- ALL SCRAMBLED AND WIGGLY!
I CAN'T MAKE ANY SENSE OF IT!
I GUESS I'LL HAVE TO LOOK ELSEWHERE.
AND DIDN'T I JUST TELL YOU NO ONE SNEAKS UP ON ME?

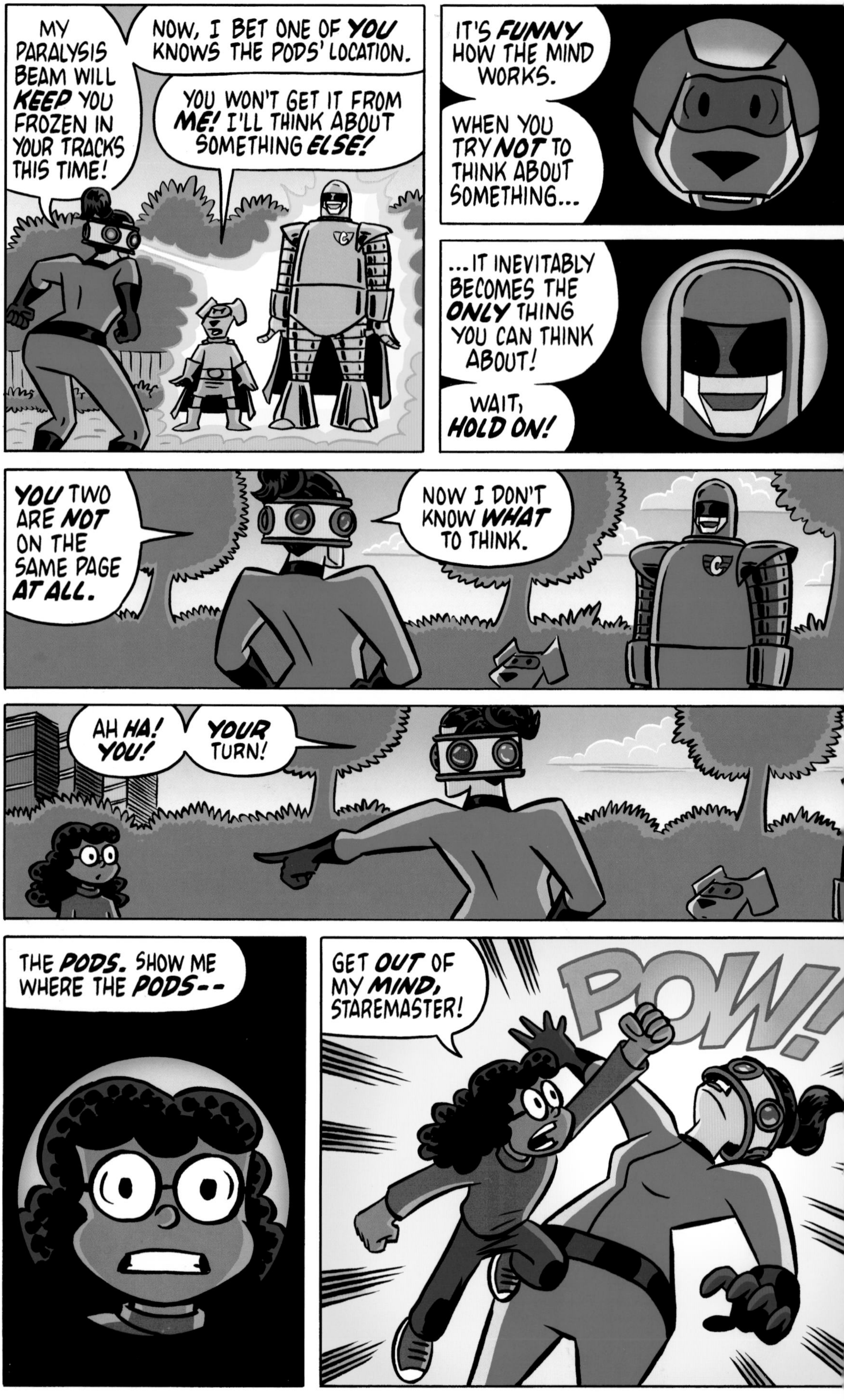
MY PARALYSIS BEAM WILL KEEP YOU FROZEN IN YOUR TRACKS THIS TIME!
NOW, I BET ONE OF YOU KNOWS THE PODS' LOCATION.
YOU WON'T GET IT FROM ME! I'LL THINK ABOUT SOMETHING ELSE!
IT'S FUNNY HOW THE MIND WORKS.
WHEN YOU TRY NOT TO THINK ABOUT SOMETHING...
...IT INEVITABLY BECOMES THE ONLY THING YOU CAN THINK ABOUT!
WAIT, HOLD ON!
YOU TWO ARE NOT ON THE SAME PAGE AT ALL.
NOW I DON'T KNOW WHAT TO THINK.
AH HA! YOU!
YOUR TURN!
THE PODS. SHOW ME WHERE THE PODS--
GET OUT OF MY MIND, STAREMASTER!
POW!

?
ARE YOU KIDDING ME?
DIDN'T YOU SEE HOW EASILY I DEFEATED YOUR SUPERPOWERED FRIENDS?
I WAS GOING EASY ON YOU BECAUSE YOU'RE JUST A POWERLESS KID...
...BUT NOW I HAVE TO GET TOUGH WITH YOU!
DON'T YOU TOUCH HER!
AAAGH!
HOW?

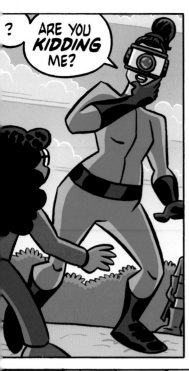

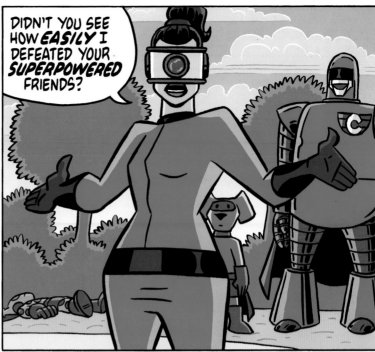

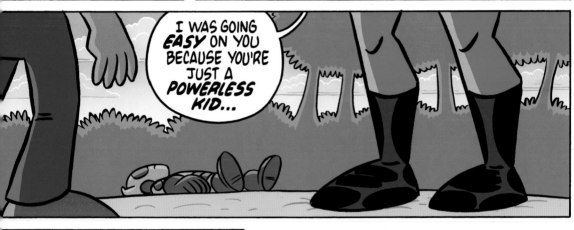

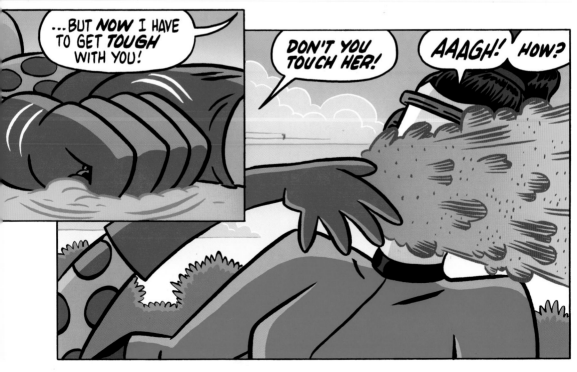

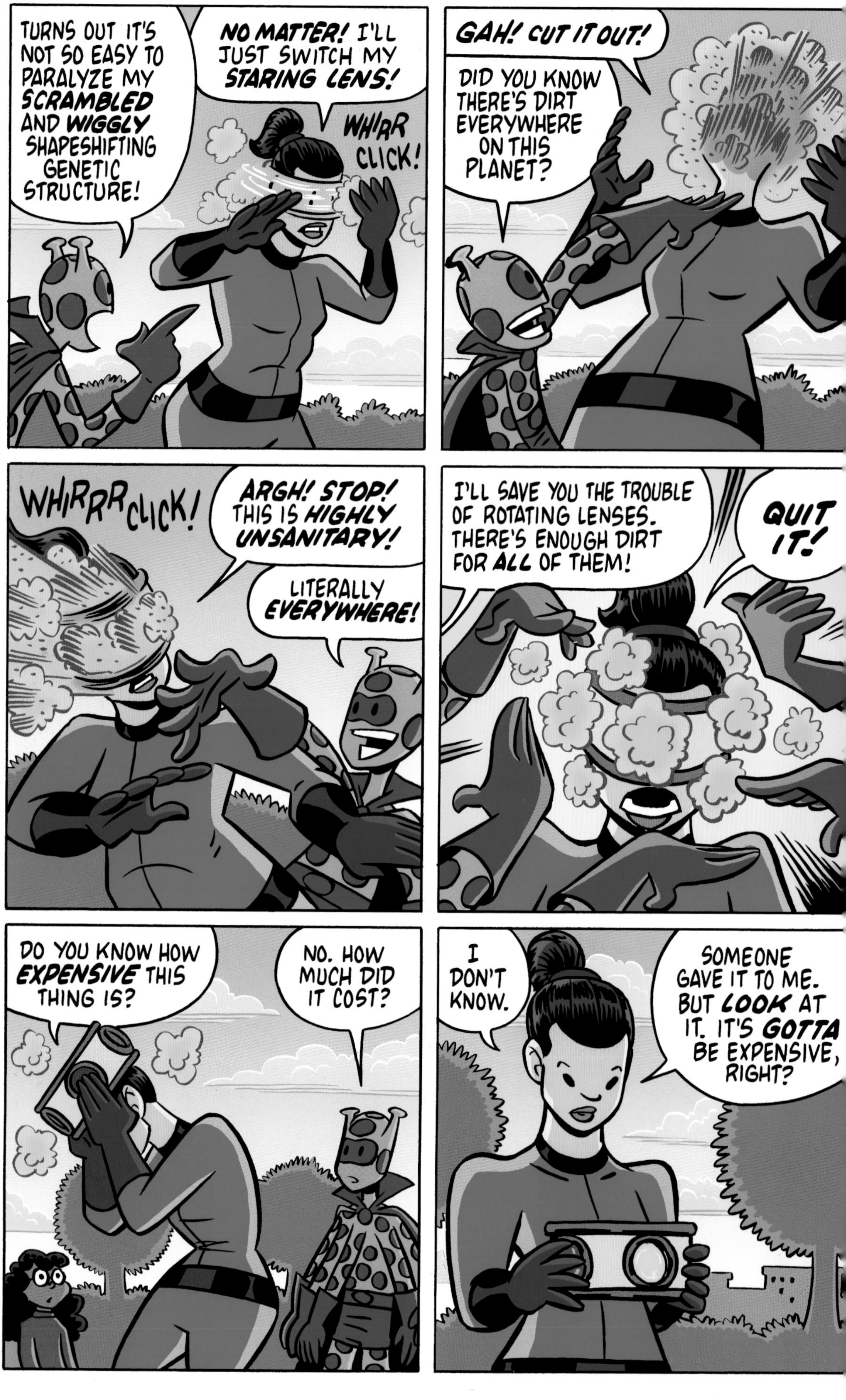
TURNS OUT IT'S NOT SO EASY TO PARALYZE MY SCRAMBLED AND WIGGLY SHAPESHIFTING GENETIC STRUCTURE!
NO MATTER! I'LL JUST SWITCH MY STARING LENS!
WHIRR CLICK!
GAH! CUT IT OUT!
DID YOU KNOW THERE'S DIRT EVERYWHERE ON THIS PLANET?
WHIRRR CLICK!
ARGH! STOP! THIS IS HIGHLY UNSANITARY!
LITERALLY EVERYWHERE!
I'LL SAVE YOU THE TROUBLE OF ROTATING LENSES. THERE'S ENOUGH DIRT FOR ALL OF THEM!
QUIT IT!
DO YOU KNOW HOW EXPENSIVE THIS THING IS?
NO. HOW MUCH DID IT COST?
I DON'T KNOW.
SOMEONE GAVE IT TO ME. BUT LOOK AT IT. IT'S GOTTA BE EXPENSIVE, RIGHT?

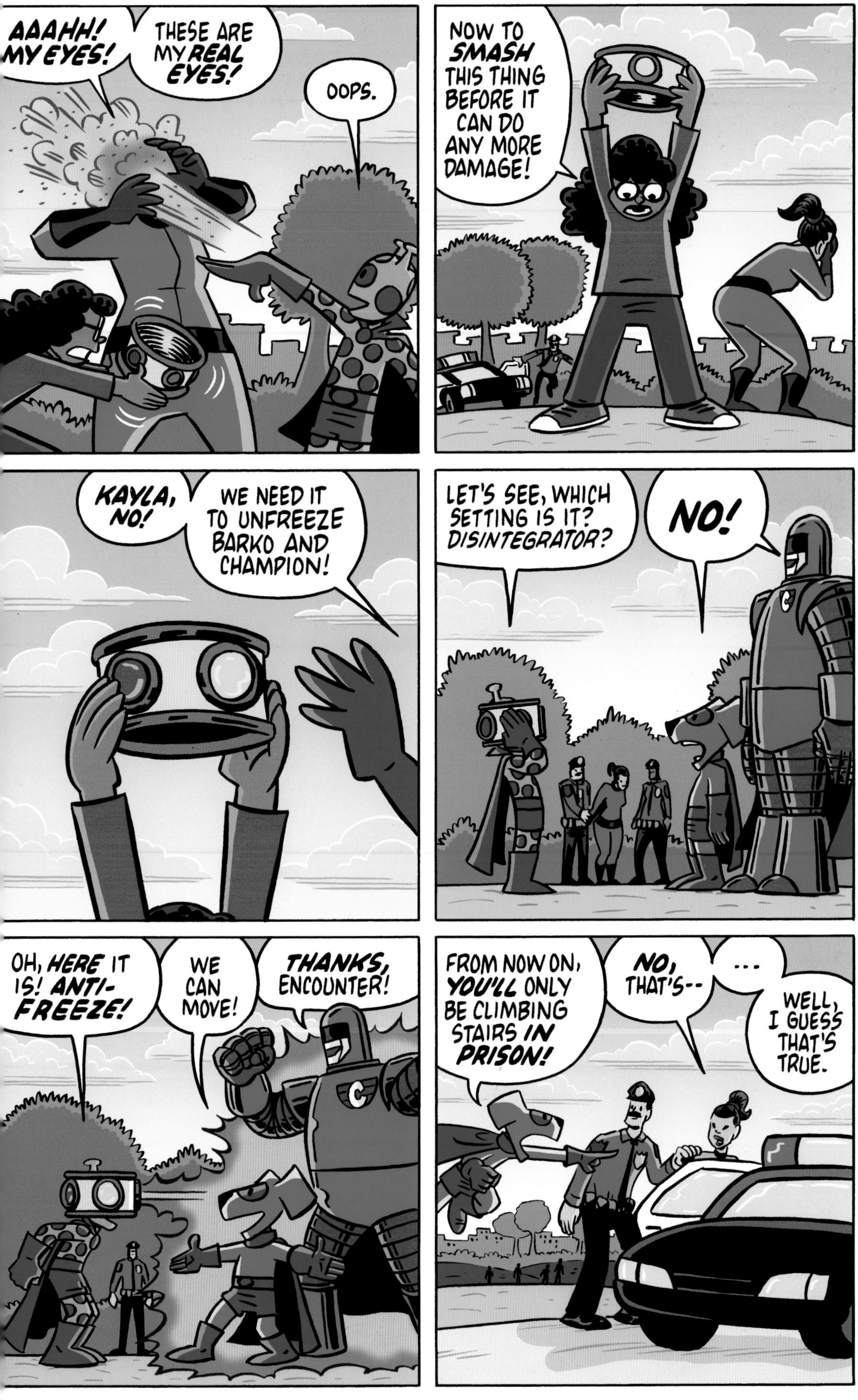
AAAHH! MY EYES!
THESE ARE MY REAL EYES!
OOPS.
NOW TO SMASH THIS THING BEFORE IT CAN DO ANY MORE DAMAGE!
KAYLA, NO!
WE NEED IT TO UNFREEZE BARKO AND CHAMPION!
LET'S SEE, WHICH SETTING IS IT? DISINTEGRATOR?
NO!
OH, HERE IT IS! ANTI-FREEZE!
WE CAN MOVE!
THANKS, ENCOUNTER!
FROM NOW ON, YOU'LL ONLY BE CLIMBING STAIRS IN PRISON!
NO, THAT'S--
...
WELL, I GUESS THAT'S TRUE.

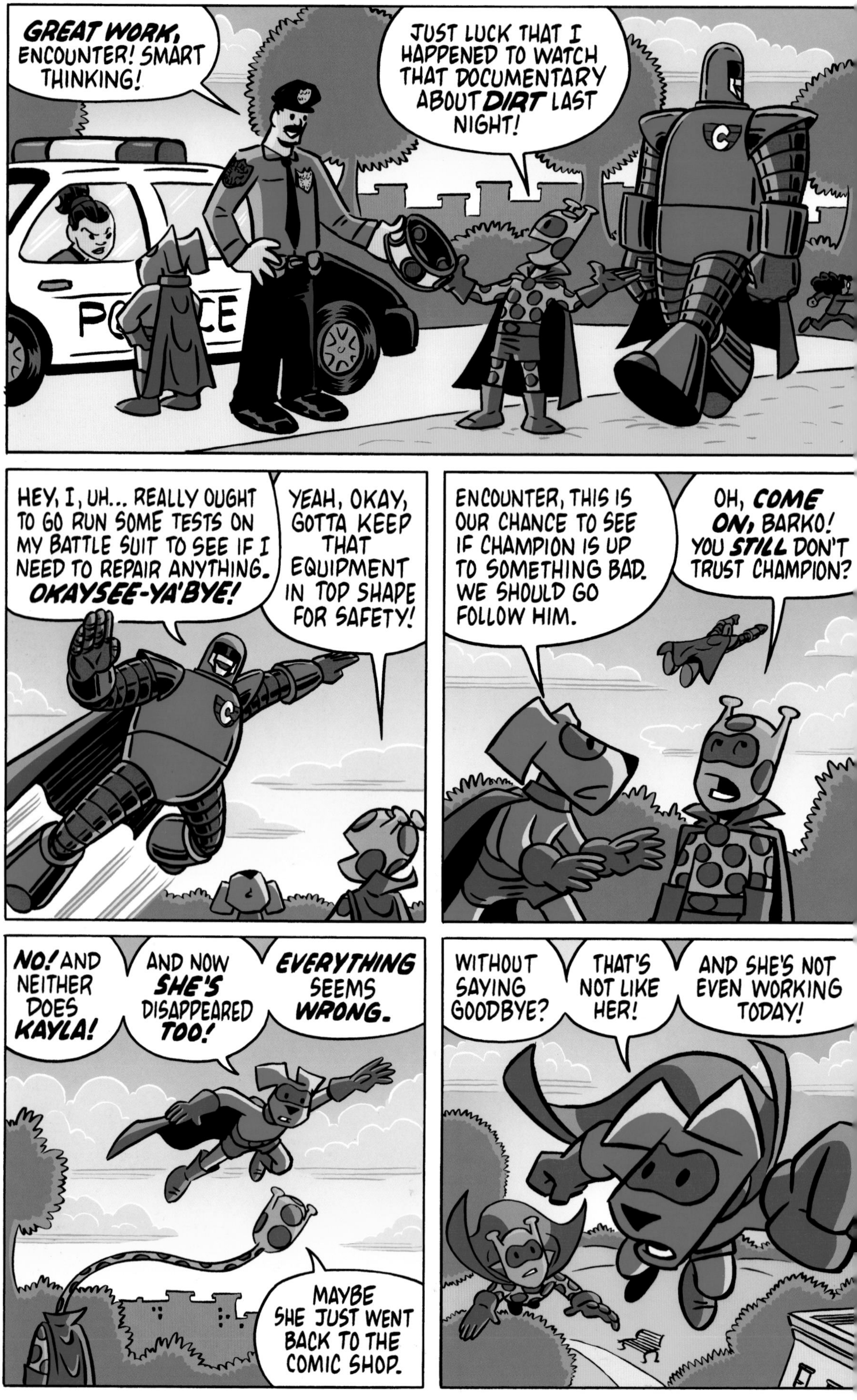
GREAT WORK, ENCOUNTER! SMART THINKING!
JUST LUCK THAT I HAPPENED TO WATCH THAT DOCUMENTARY ABOUT DIRT LAST NIGHT!
POLICE
HEY, I, UH... REALLY OUGHT TO GO RUN SOME TESTS ON MY BATTLE SUIT TO SEE IF I NEED TO REPAIR ANYTHING. OKAYSEE-YA'BYE!
YEAH, OKAY, GOTTA KEEP THAT EQUIPMENT IN TOP SHAPE FOR SAFETY!
ENCOUNTER, THIS IS OUR CHANCE TO SEE IF CHAMPION IS UP TO SOMETHING BAD. WE SHOULD GO FOLLOW HIM.
OH, COME ON, BARKO! YOU STILL DON'T TRUST CHAMPION?
NO! AND NEITHER DOES KAYLA!
AND NOW SHE'S DISAPPEARED TOO!
EVERYTHING SEEMS WRONG.
MAYBE SHE JUST WENT BACK TO THE COMIC SHOP.
WITHOUT SAYING GOODBYE?
THAT'S NOT LIKE HER!
AND SHE'S NOT EVEN WORKING TODAY!

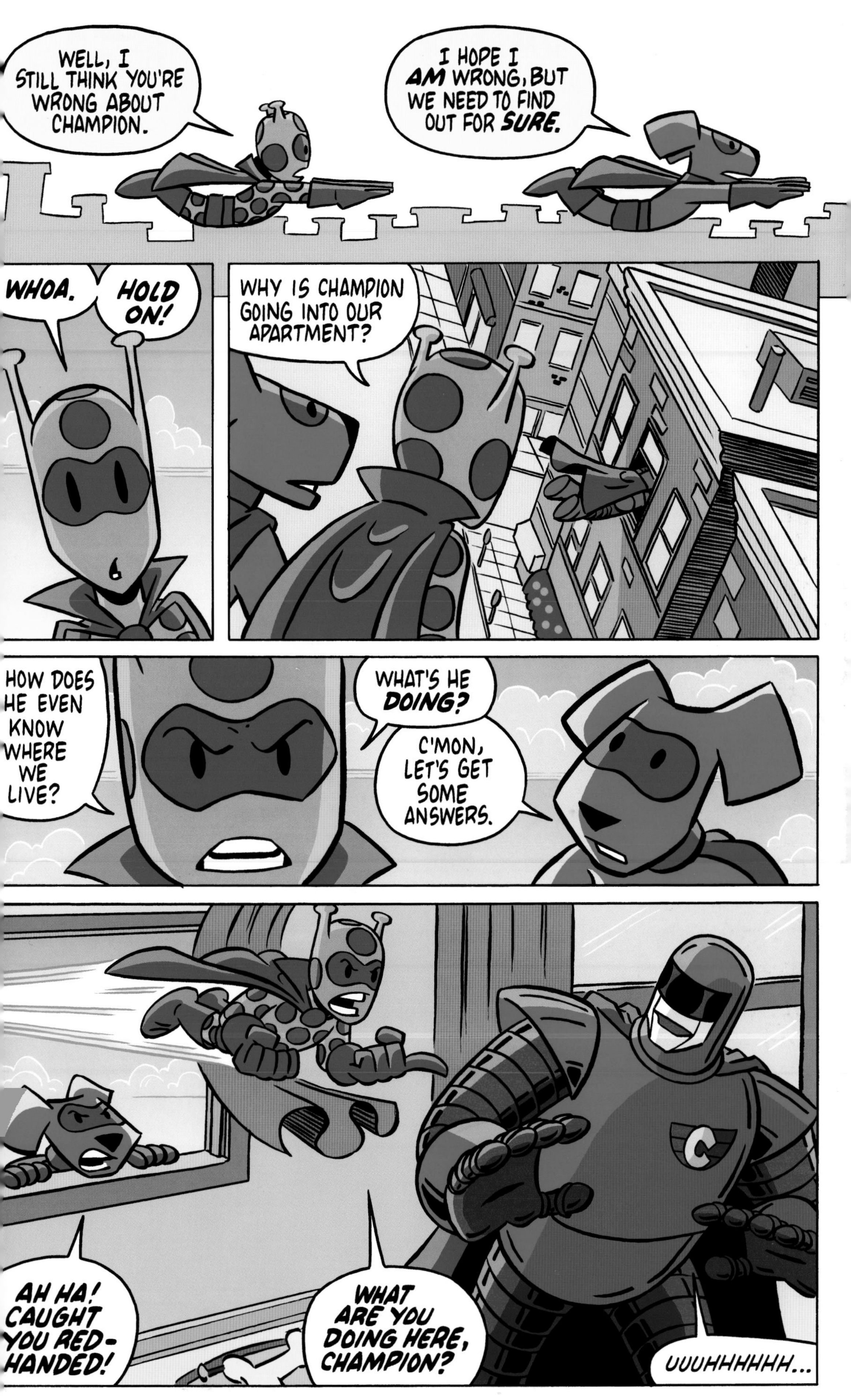
WELL, I STILL THINK YOU'RE WRONG ABOUT CHAMPION.
I HOPE I AM WRONG, BUT WE NEED TO FIND OUT FOR SURE.
WHOA.
HOLD ON!
WHY IS CHAMPION GOING INTO OUR APARTMENT?
HOW DOES HE EVEN KNOW WHERE WE LIVE?
WHAT'S HE DOING?
C'MON, LET'S GET SOME ANSWERS.
AH HA! CAUGHT YOU RED-HANDED!
WHAT ARE YOU DOING HERE, CHAMPION?
UUUHHHHHH...

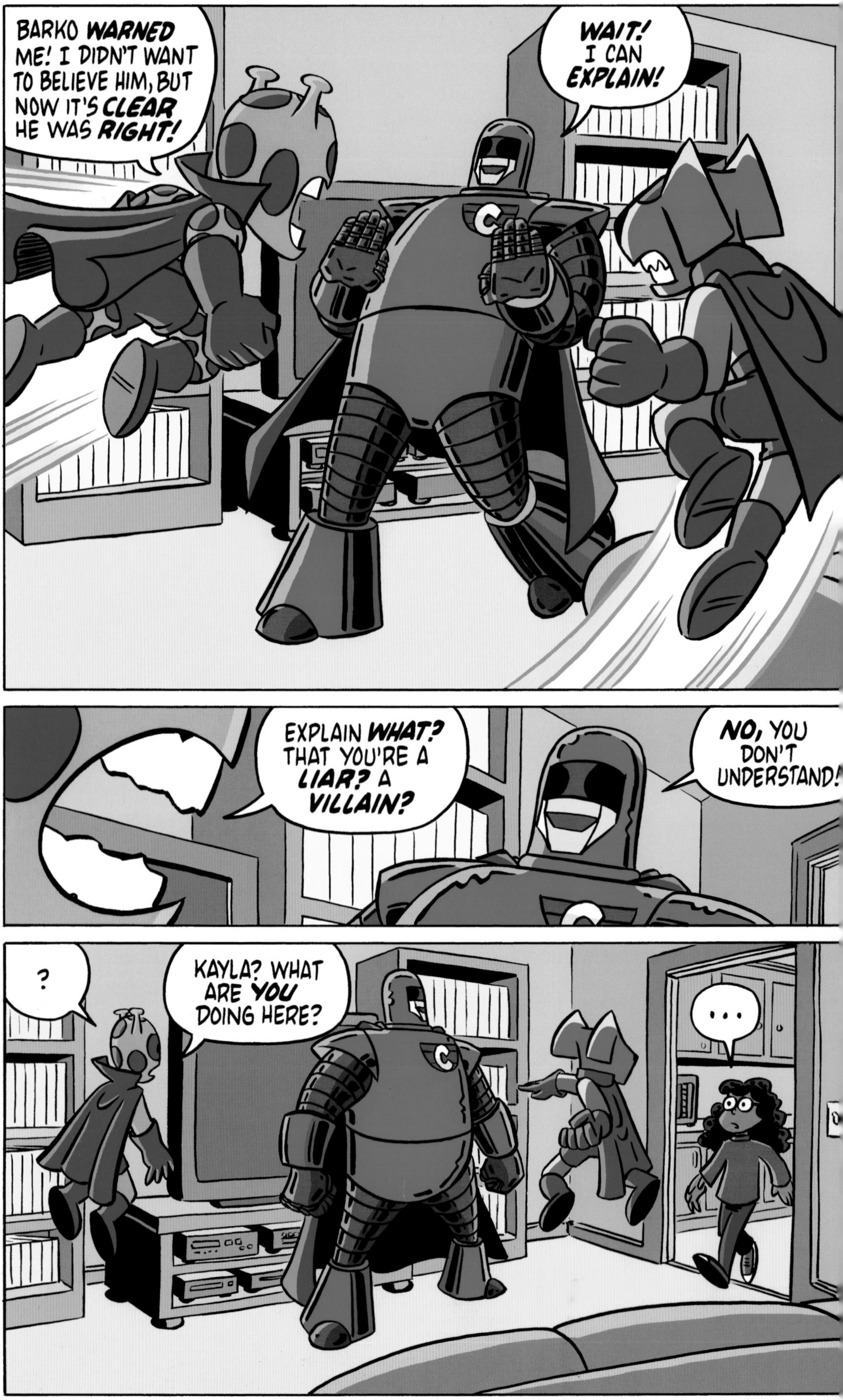
BARKO WARNED ME! I DIDN'T WANT TO BELIEVE HIM, BUT NOW IT'S CLEAR HE WAS RIGHT!
WAIT! I CAN EXPLAIN!
EXPLAIN WHAT? THAT YOU'RE A LIAR? A VILLAIN?
NO, YOU DON'T UNDERSTAND!
?
KAYLA? WHAT ARE YOU DOING HERE?
...

AFTER TALKING TO BARKO EARLIER, I BECAME WORRIED THAT *CHAMPION* MIGHT TRY TO *STEAL* THE PODS. I RACED HERE AS SOON AS I COULD TO *HIDE* THEM!

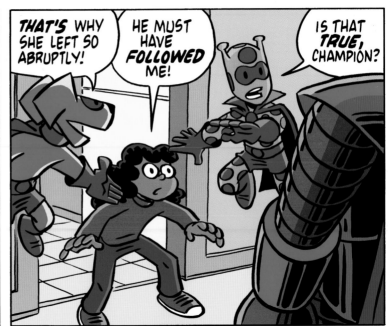

THAT'S WHY SHE LEFT SO ABRUPTLY!

HE MUST HAVE *FOLLOWED* ME!

IS THAT *TRUE*, CHAMPION?

YES, I *DID* FOLLOW HER HERE, BUT--

YOU'VE BEEN AFTER MY PODS *ALL ALONG*, HAVEN'T YOU?

YOU SENT ALL THOSE VILLAINS AFTER US!

GADGET MAN! COLD BLAZE! RIBBON RHONDA! DECONSTRUCTINATOR! STAREMASTER!

WERE THEY REALLY EVEN *VILLAINS* AT ALL? OR JUST MORE INNOCENT PEOPLE YOU *MANIPULATED* THE WAY YOU'RE TRYING TO MANIPULATE *US*?

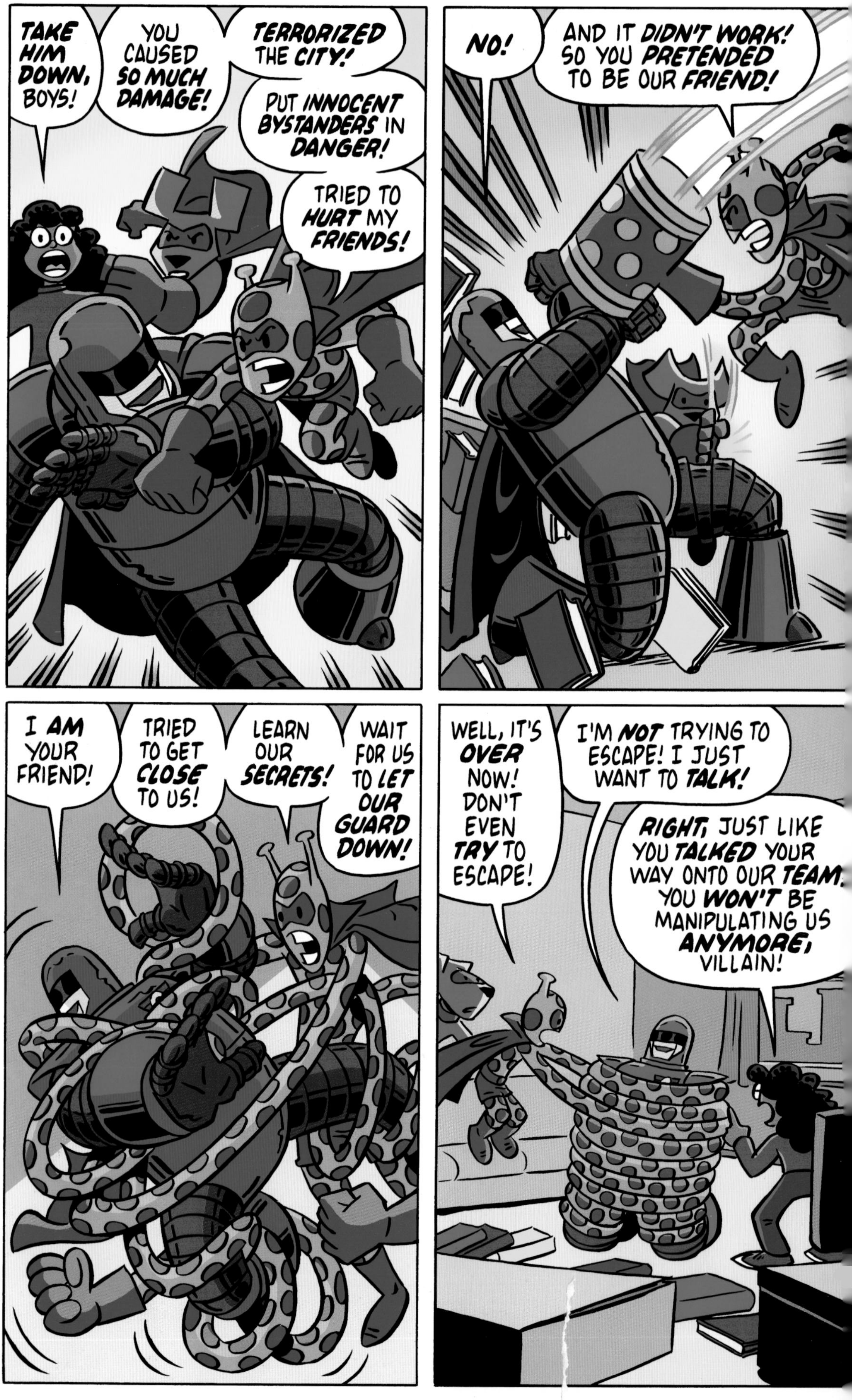
TAKE HIM DOWN, BOYS!
YOU CAUSED SO MUCH DAMAGE!
TERRORIZED THE CITY!
PUT INNOCENT BYSTANDERS IN DANGER!
TRIED TO HURT MY FRIENDS!
NO!
AND IT DIDN'T WORK! SO YOU PRETENDED TO BE OUR FRIEND!
I AM YOUR FRIEND!
TRIED TO GET CLOSE TO US!
LEARN OUR SECRETS!
WAIT FOR US TO LET OUR GUARD DOWN!
WELL, IT'S OVER NOW! DON'T EVEN TRY TO ESCAPE!
I'M NOT TRYING TO ESCAPE! I JUST WANT TO TALK!
RIGHT, JUST LIKE YOU TALKED YOUR WAY ONTO OUR TEAM. YOU WON'T BE MANIPULATING US ANYMORE, VILLAIN!

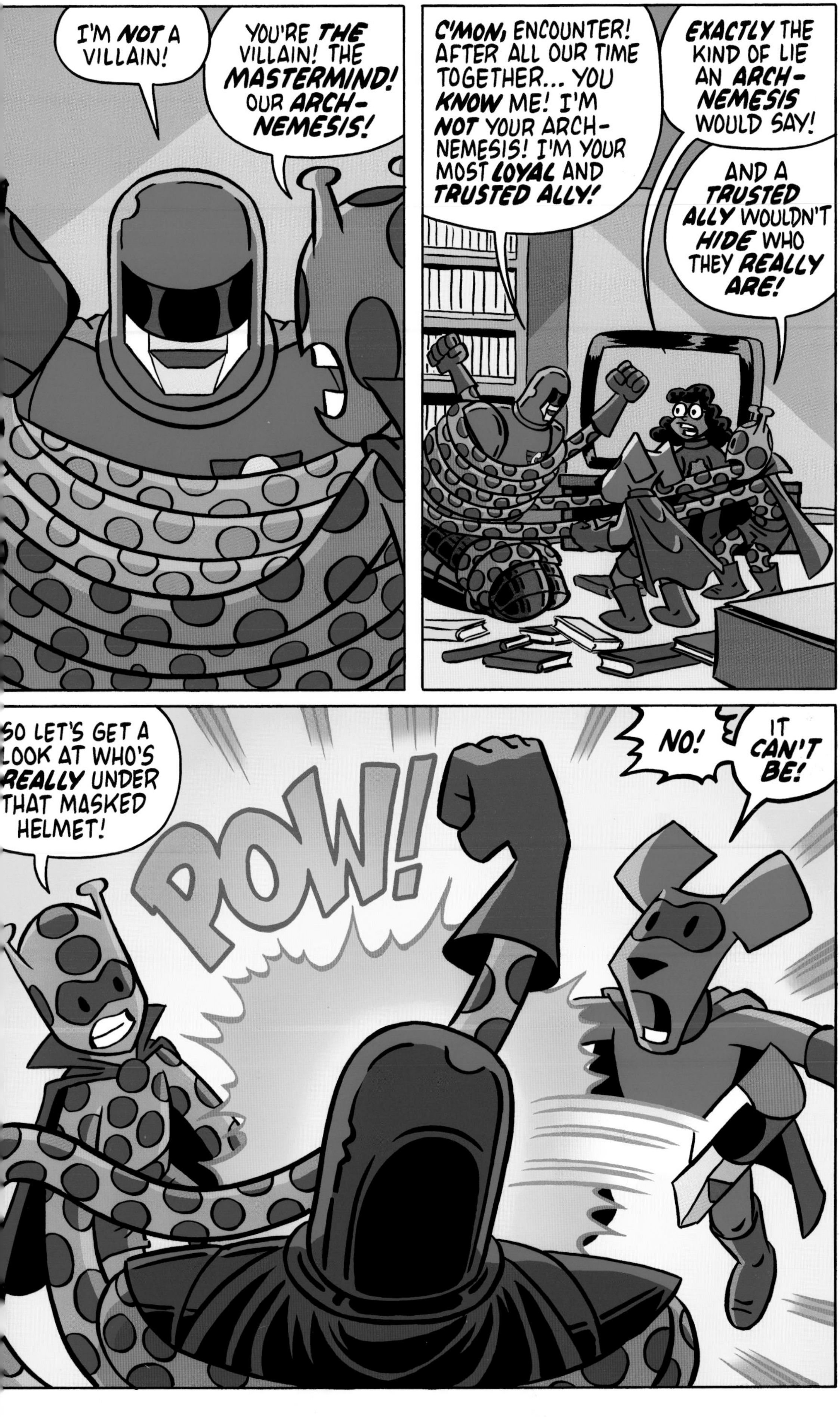

I'M *NOT* A VILLAIN!
YOU'RE *THE* VILLAIN! THE *MASTERMIND!* OUR *ARCH-NEMESIS!*
C'MON, ENCOUNTER! AFTER ALL OUR TIME TOGETHER... YOU *KNOW* ME! I'M *NOT* YOUR ARCH-NEMESIS! I'M YOUR MOST *LOYAL* AND *TRUSTED ALLY!*
EXACTLY THE KIND OF LIE AN *ARCH-NEMESIS* WOULD SAY!
AND A *TRUSTED ALLY* WOULDN'T *HIDE* WHO THEY *REALLY ARE!*
SO LET'S GET A LOOK AT WHO'S *REALLY* UNDER THAT MASKED HELMET!
POW!
NO!
IT *CAN'T BE!*

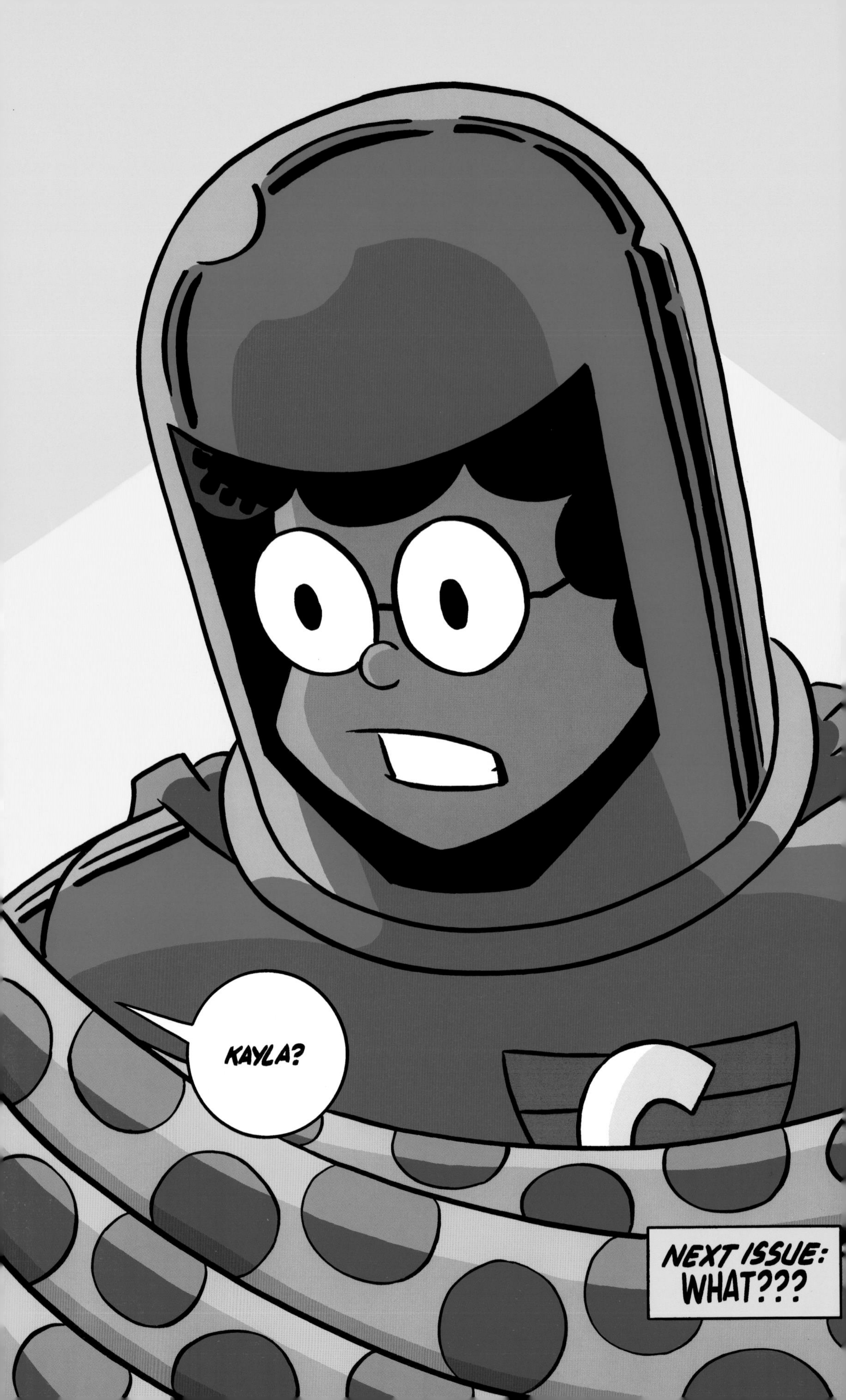
KAYLA?
NEXT ISSUE:
WHAT???

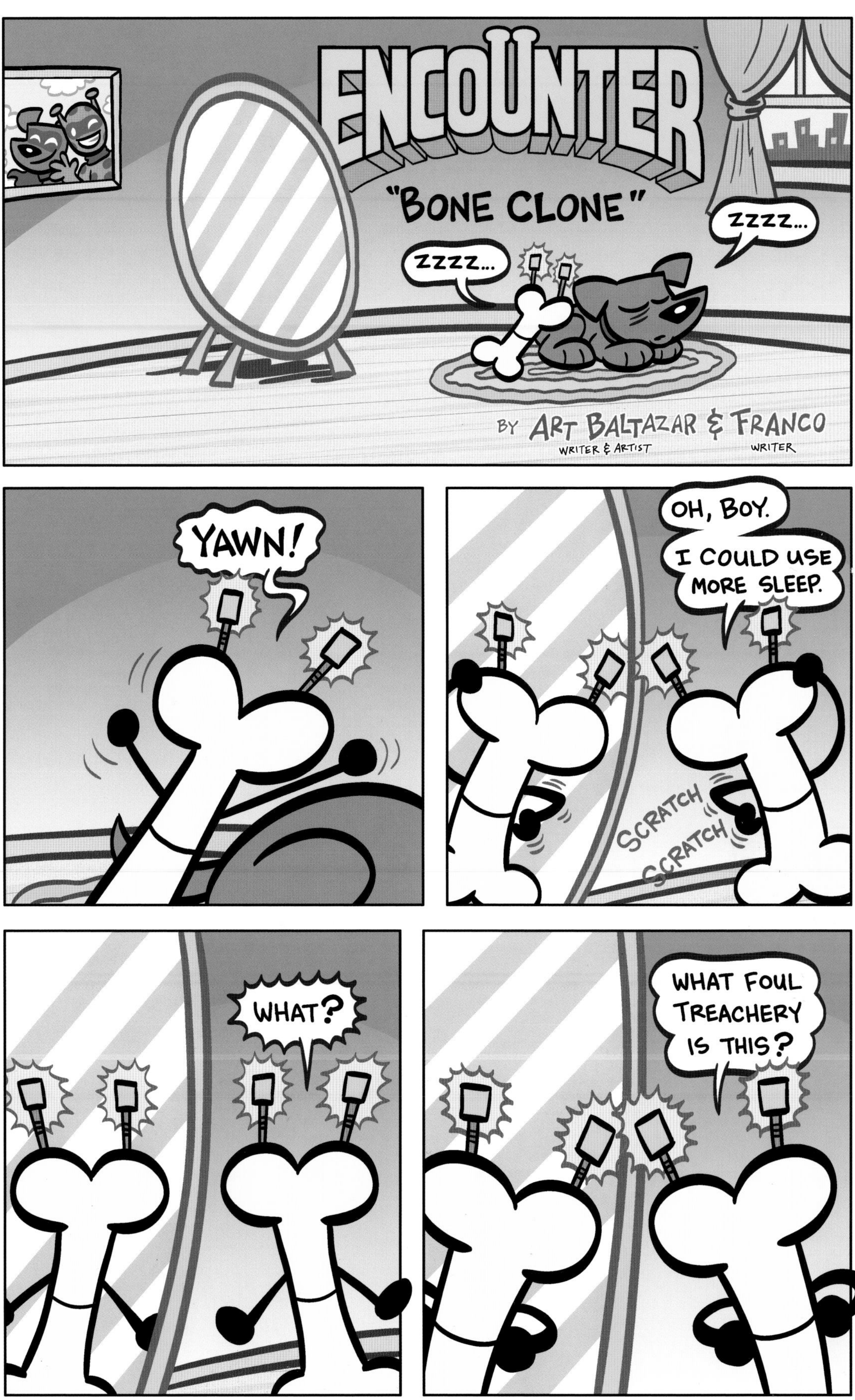
ENCOUNTER™
"BONE CLONE"
ZZZZ...
ZZZZ...
BY ART BALTAZAR & FRANCO
WRITER & ARTIST
WRITER
YAWN!
OH, BOY.
I COULD USE MORE SLEEP.
SCRATCH
SCRATCH
WHAT?
WHAT FOUL TREACHERY IS THIS?

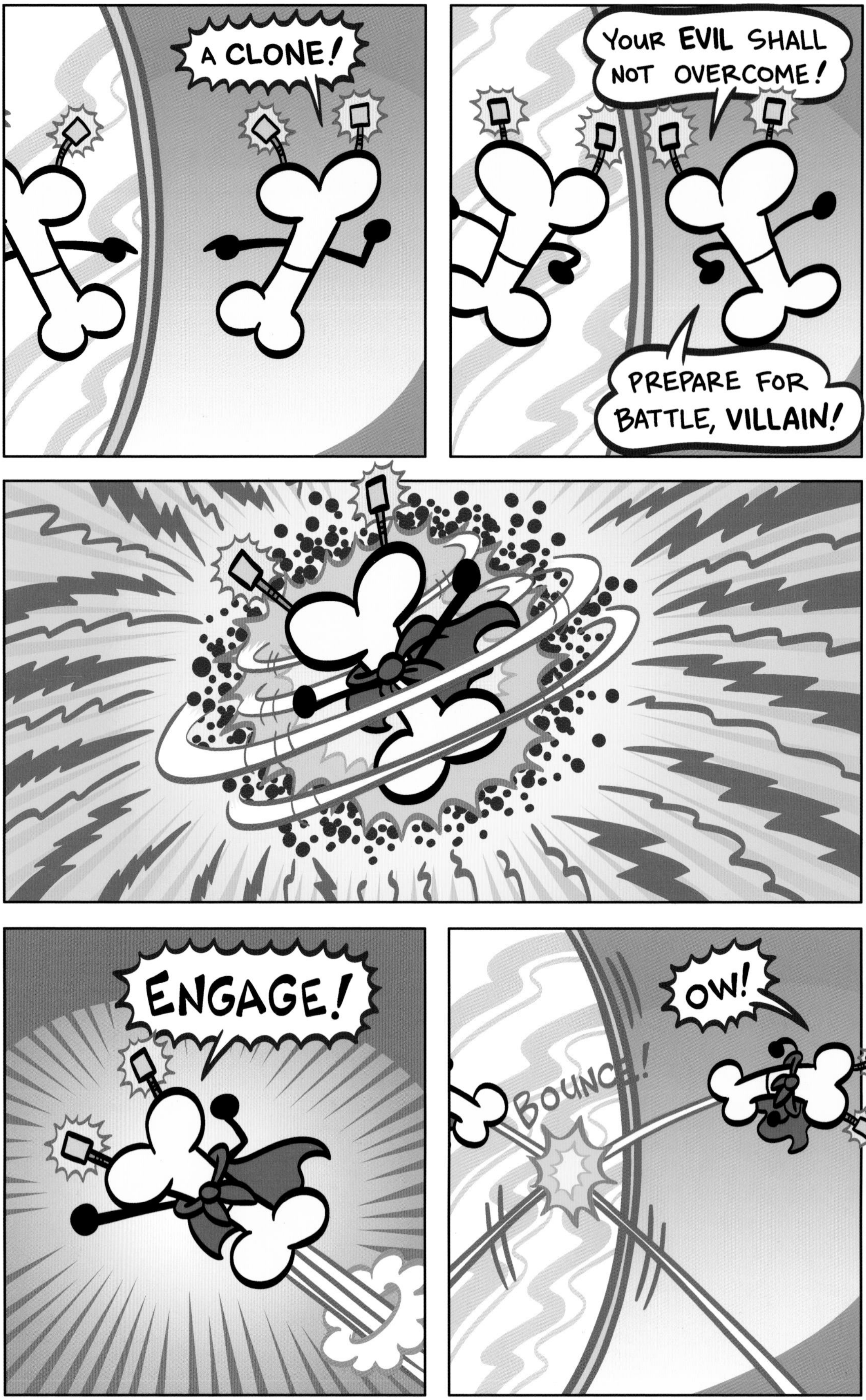

A CLONE!
YOUR EVIL SHALL NOT OVERCOME!
PREPARE FOR BATTLE, VILLAIN!
ENGAGE!
BOUNCE!
OW!

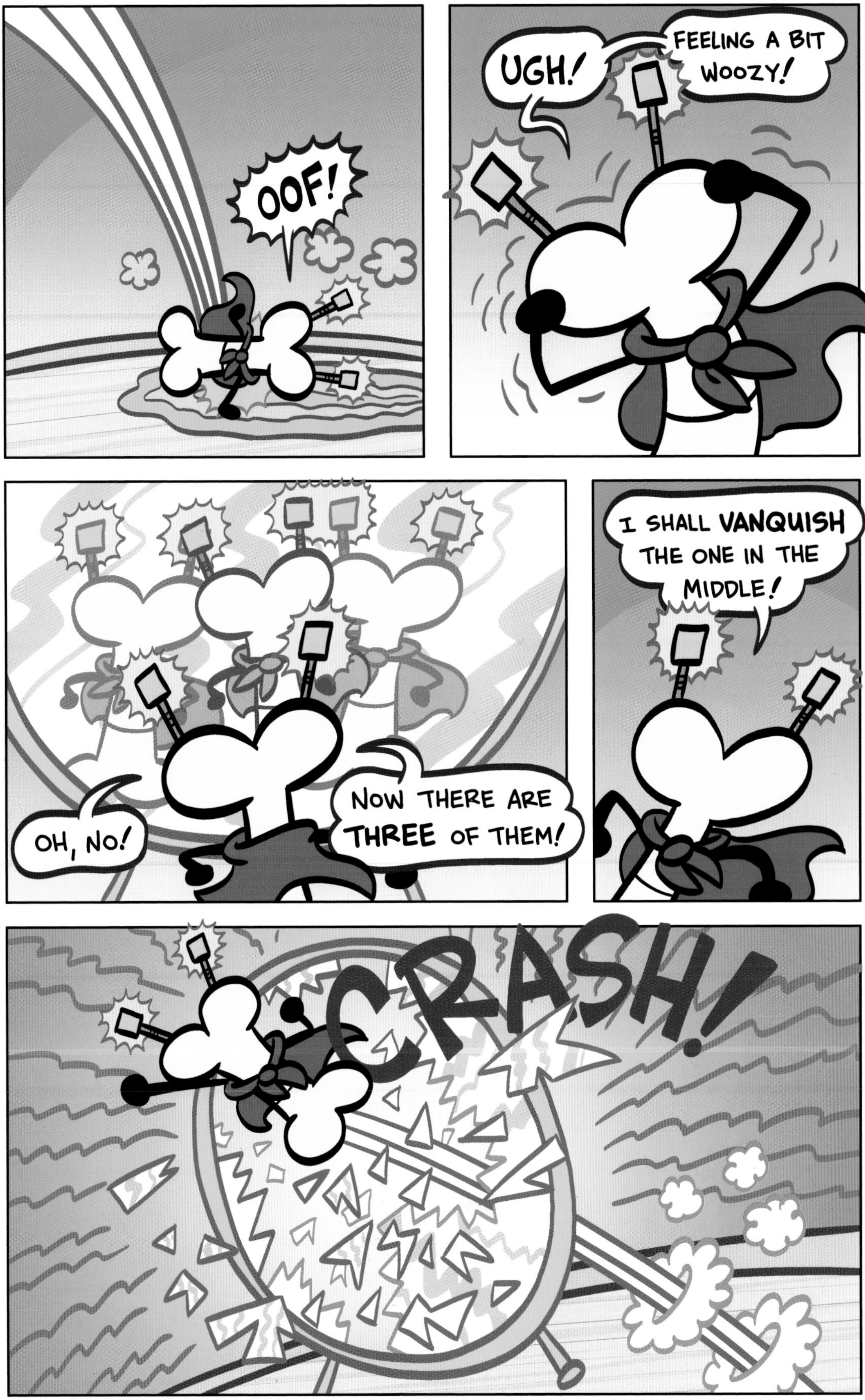
OOF!
UGH!
FEELING A BIT WOOZY!
OH, NO!
NOW THERE ARE THREE OF THEM!
I SHALL VANQUISH THE ONE IN THE MIDDLE!
CRASH!

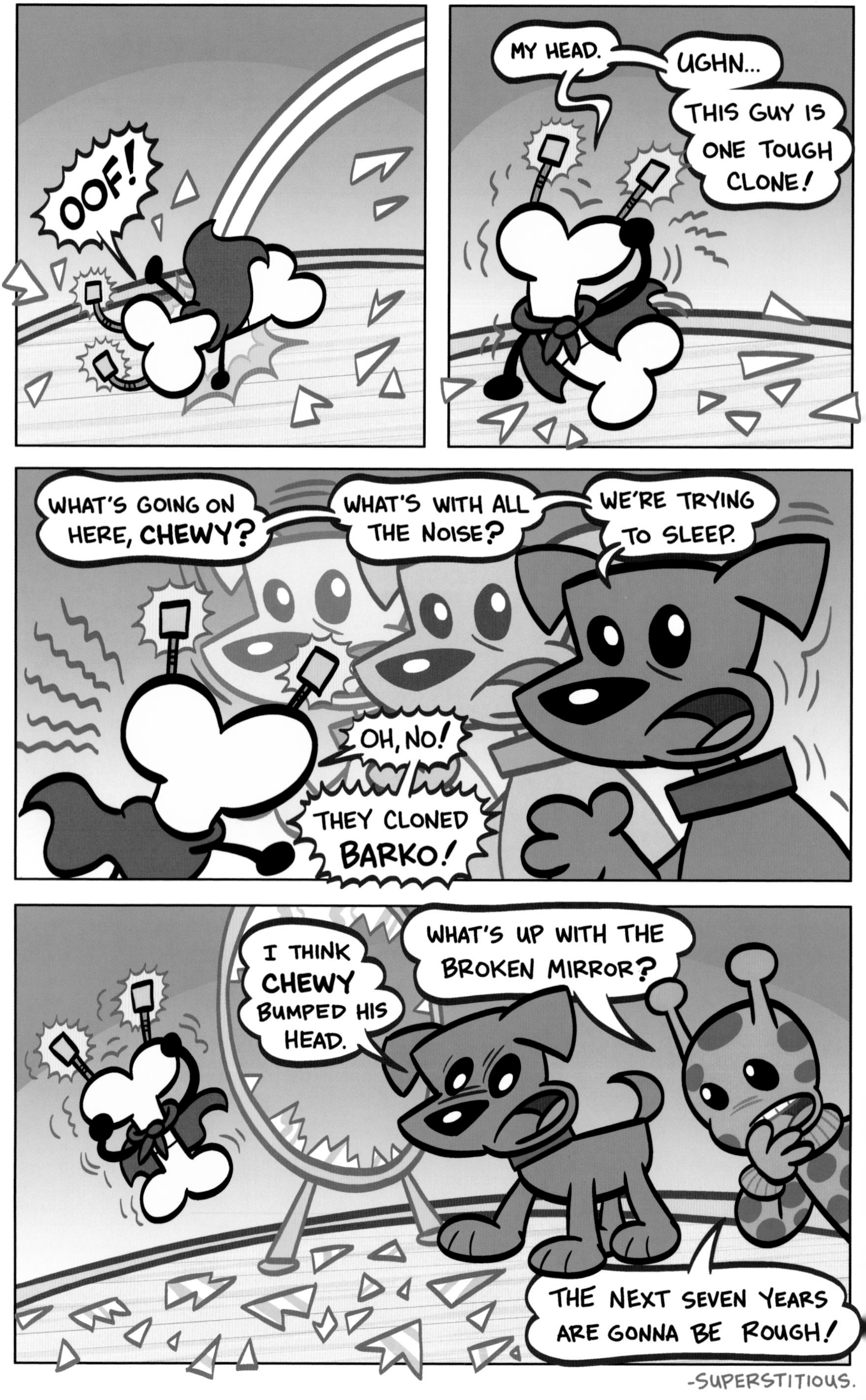
OOF!
MY HEAD.
UGHN...
THIS GUY IS ONE TOUGH CLONE!
WHAT'S GOING ON HERE, CHEWY?
WHAT'S WITH ALL THE NOISE?
WE'RE TRYING TO SLEEP.
OH, NO!
THEY CLONED BARKO!
I THINK CHEWY BUMPED HIS HEAD.
WHAT'S UP WITH THE BROKEN MIRROR?
THE NEXT SEVEN YEARS ARE GONNA BE ROUGH!

-SUPERSTITIOUS.

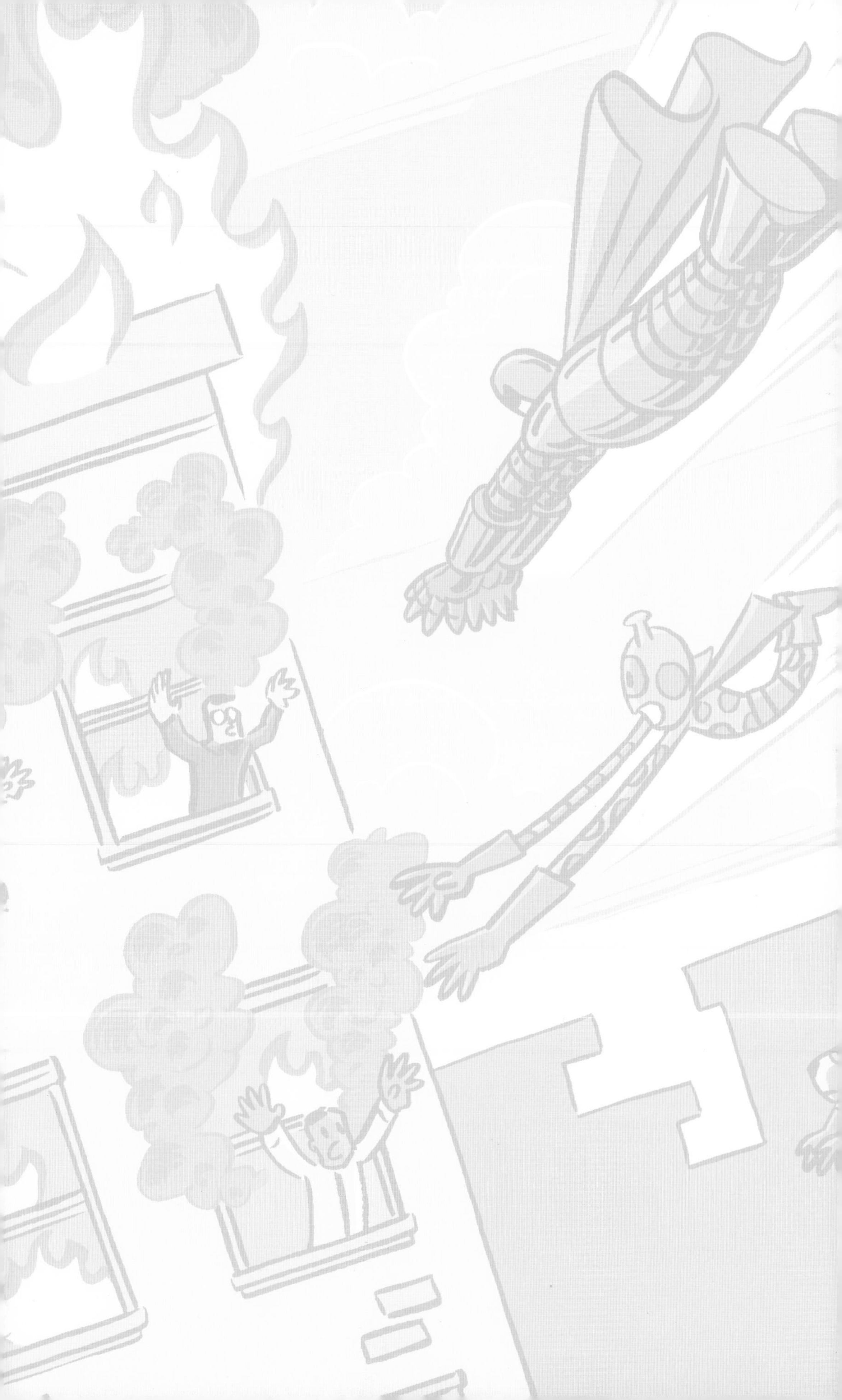

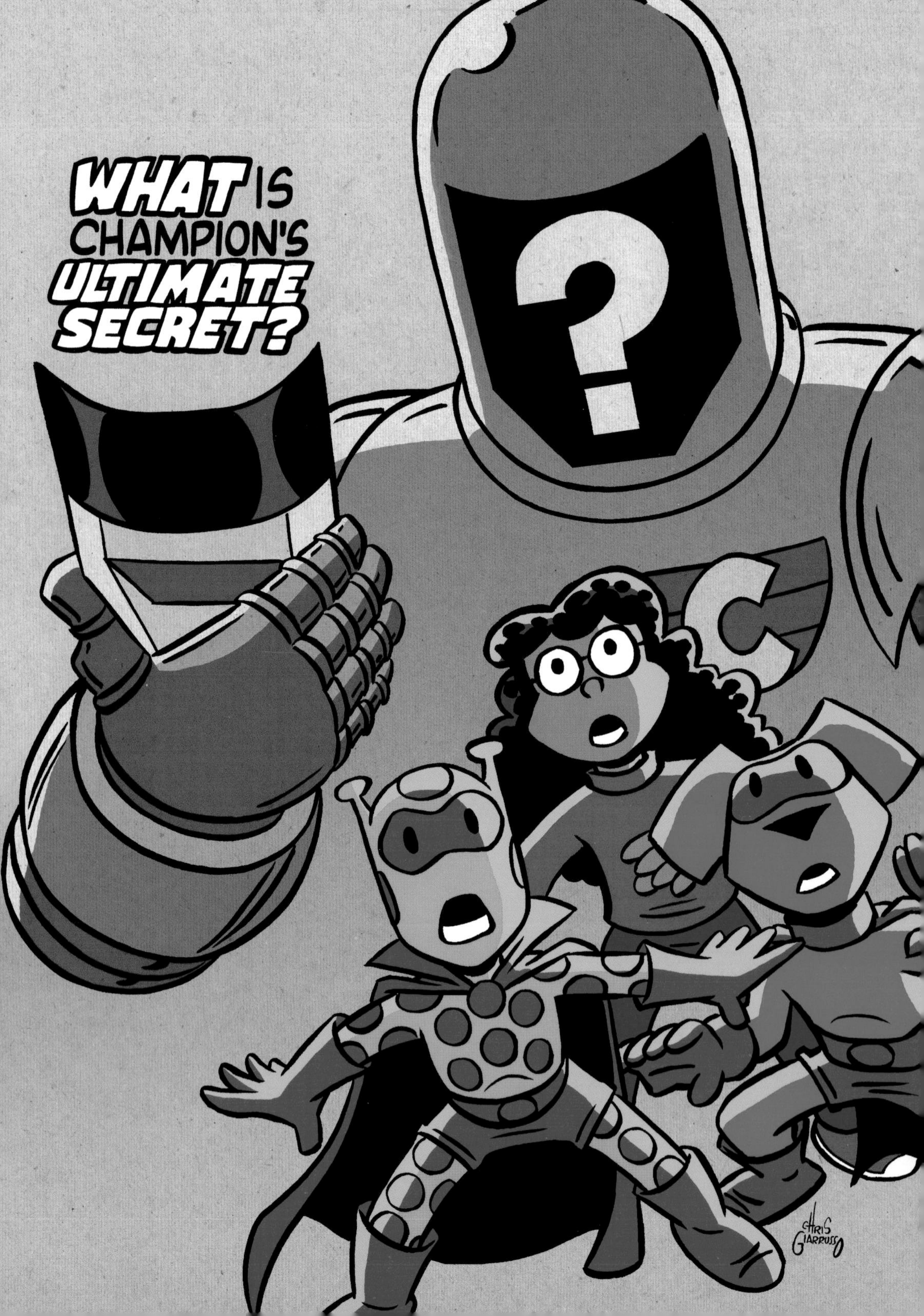
WHAT IS
CHAMPION'S
ULTIMATE
SECRET?
CHRIS GIARRUSSO

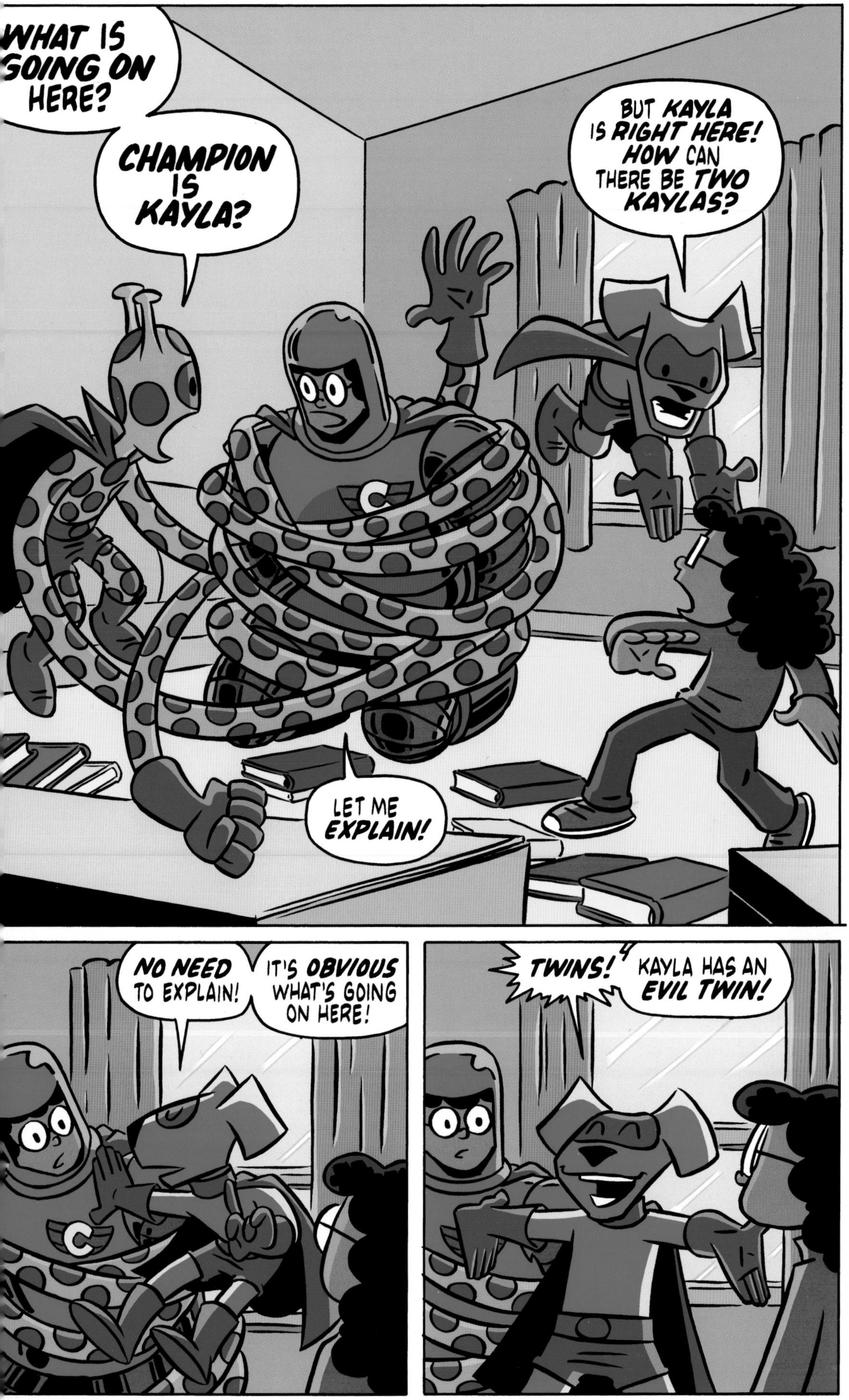
WHAT IS GOING ON HERE?
CHAMPION IS KAYLA?
BUT KAYLA IS RIGHT HERE! HOW CAN THERE BE TWO KAYLAS?
LET ME EXPLAIN!
NO NEED TO EXPLAIN!
IT'S OBVIOUS WHAT'S GOING ON HERE!
TWINS!
KAYLA HAS AN EVIL TWIN!

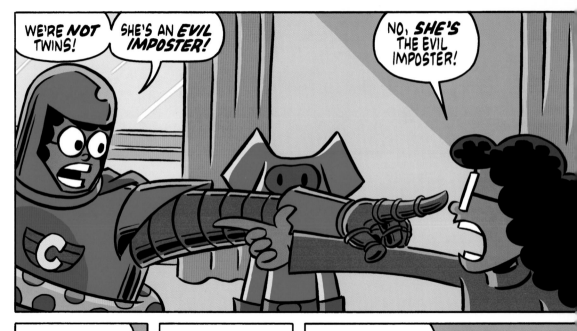

WE'RE **NOT** TWINS!

SHE'S AN **EVIL IMPOSTER!**

NO, **SHE'S** THE EVIL IMPOSTER!

SO, HOW DO WE KNOW **WHICH** KAYLA IS THE **REAL** KAYLA?

OBVIOUSLY, **SHE'S** THE FAKE KAYLA!

BARKO, YOU DIDN'T TRUST CHAMPION **BEFORE,** AND NOW YOU'VE **JUST** CAUGHT HER BREAKING INTO YOUR HOME.

SHE'S CLEARLY THE VILLAIN WHO'S BEEN TRYING TO STEAL ENCOUNTER'S PODS!

I ONLY **CAME** HERE BECAUSE I WAS FOLLOWING **HER!**

DID YOU GUYS HEAR THAT CONFESSION? **FAKE KAYLA** HAS BEEN **STALKING** ME!

I'M GETTING **OUT** OF HERE BEFORE SHE USES THAT DANGEROUS POWER SUIT TO **ELIMINATE** ME!

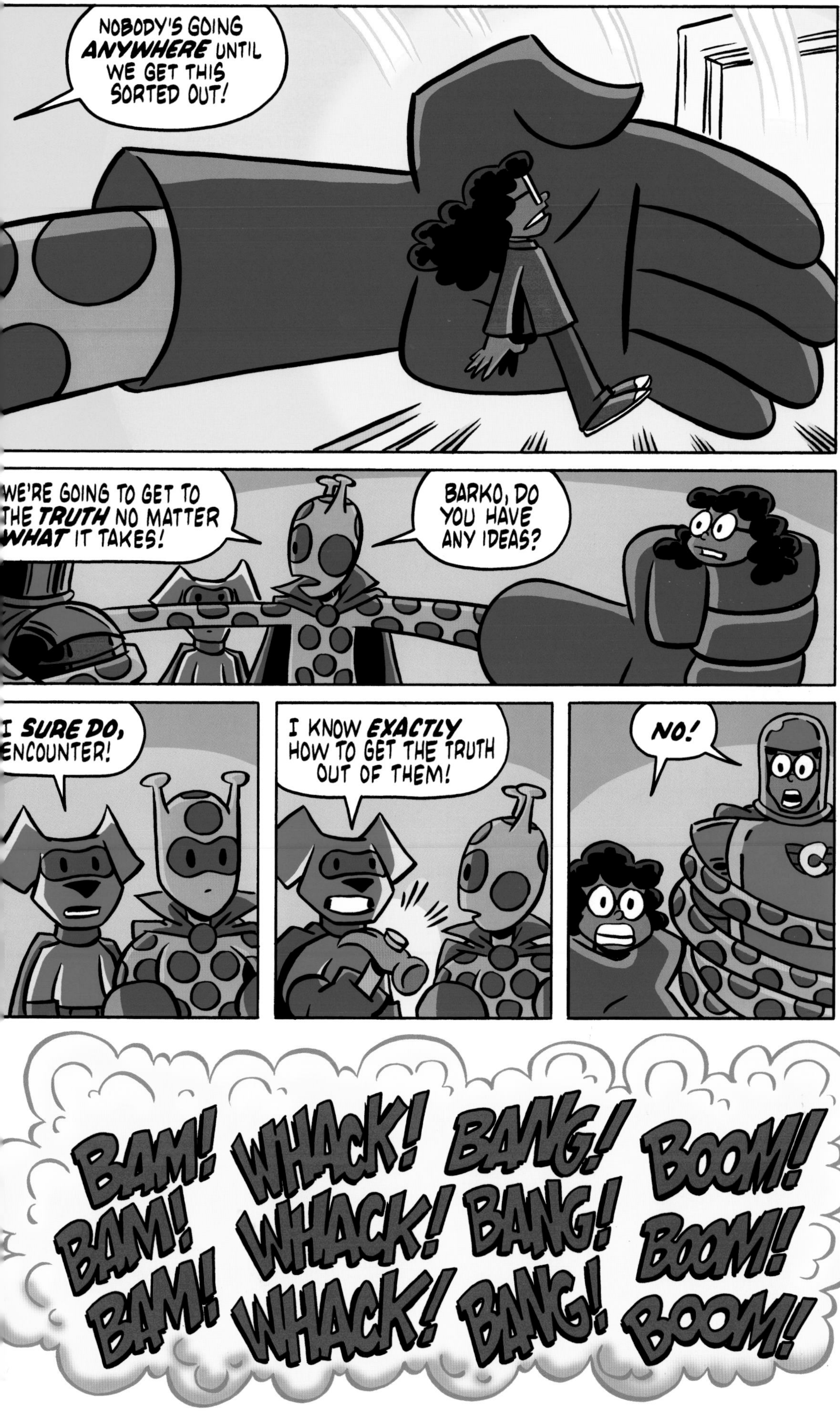

NOBODY'S GOING **ANYWHERE** UNTIL WE GET THIS SORTED OUT!
WE'RE GOING TO GET TO THE **TRUTH** NO MATTER **WHAT** IT TAKES!
BARKO, DO YOU HAVE ANY IDEAS?
I **SURE DO,** ENCOUNTER!
I KNOW **EXACTLY** HOW TO GET THE TRUTH OUT OF THEM!
NO!
BAM! WHACK! BANG! BOOM!
BAM! WHACK! BANG! BOOM!
BAM! WHACK! BANG! BOOM!

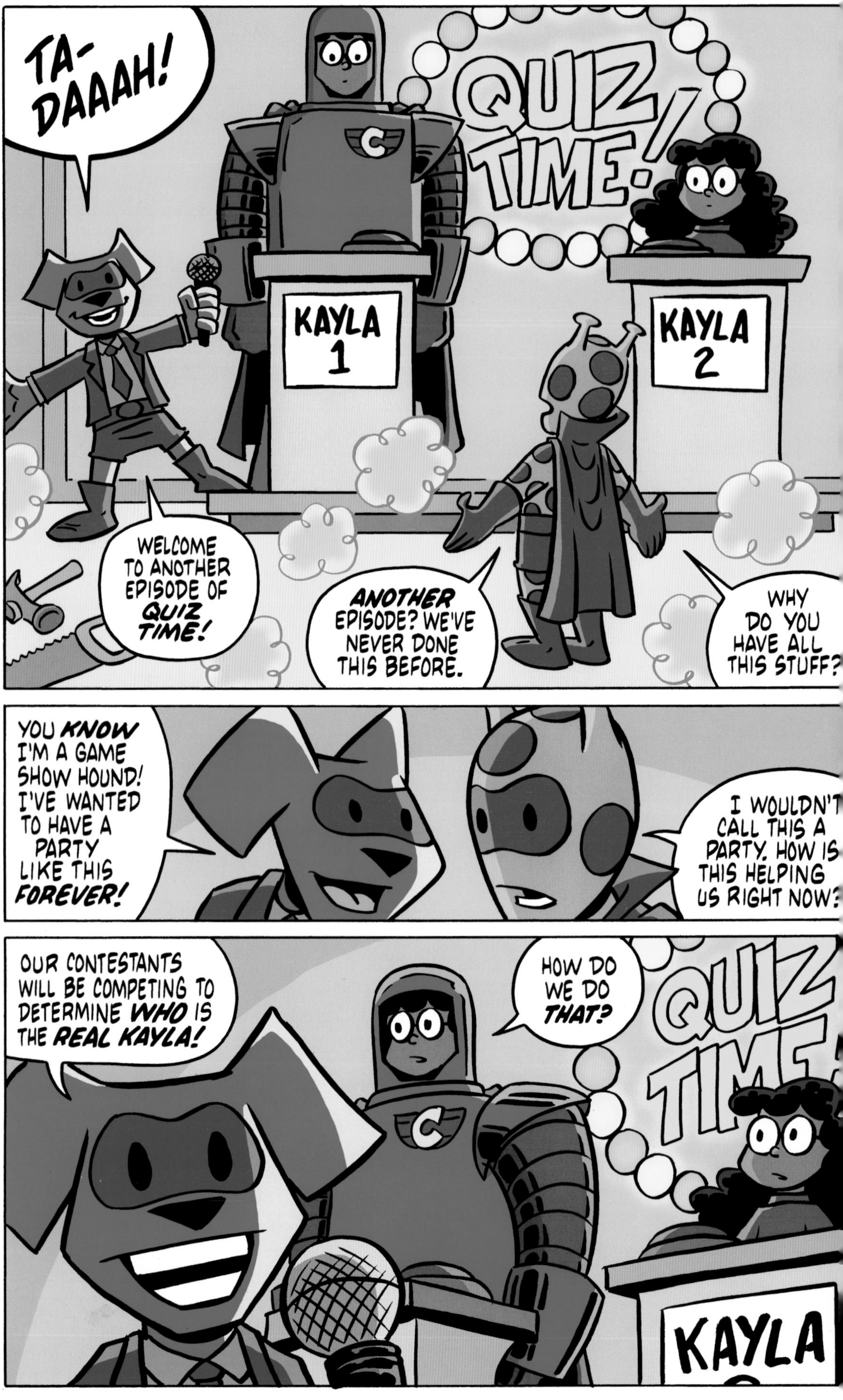
TA-DAAAH!
QUIZ TIME!
KAYLA 1
KAYLA 2
WELCOME TO ANOTHER EPISODE OF QUIZ TIME!
ANOTHER EPISODE? WE'VE NEVER DONE THIS BEFORE.
WHY DO YOU HAVE ALL THIS STUFF?
YOU KNOW I'M A GAME SHOW HOUND! I'VE WANTED TO HAVE A PARTY LIKE THIS FOREVER!
I WOULDN'T CALL THIS A PARTY. HOW IS THIS HELPING US RIGHT NOW?
OUR CONTESTANTS WILL BE COMPETING TO DETERMINE WHO IS THE REAL KAYLA!
HOW DO WE DO THAT?
KAYLA

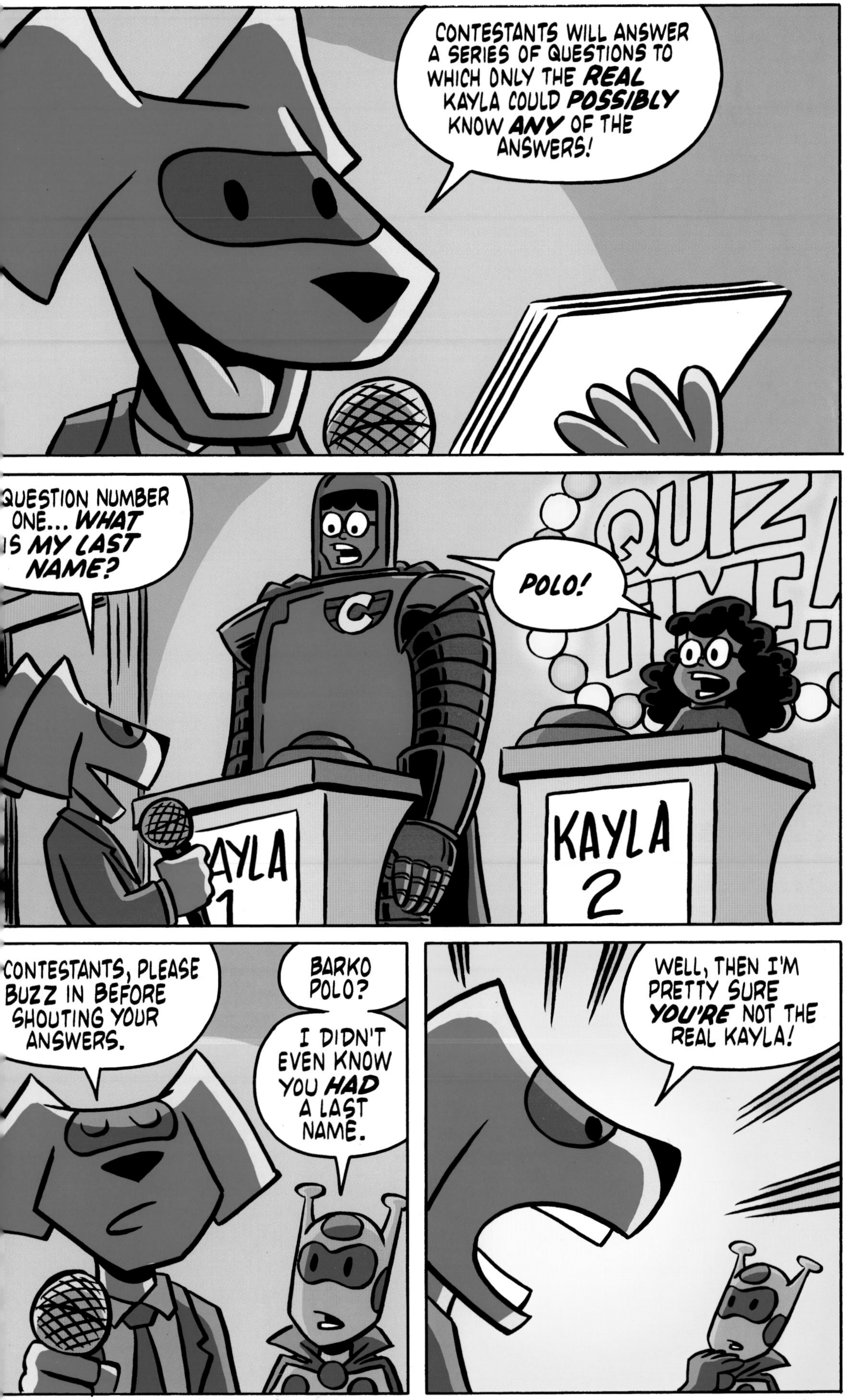
CONTESTANTS WILL ANSWER A SERIES OF QUESTIONS TO WHICH ONLY THE REAL KAYLA COULD POSSIBLY KNOW ANY OF THE ANSWERS!
QUESTION NUMBER ONE... WHAT IS MY LAST NAME?
POLO!
QUIZ TIME!
AYLA 1
KAYLA 2
CONTESTANTS, PLEASE BUZZ IN BEFORE SHOUTING YOUR ANSWERS.
BARKO POLO?
I DIDN'T EVEN KNOW YOU HAD A LAST NAME.
WELL, THEN I'M PRETTY SURE YOU'RE NOT THE REAL KAYLA!

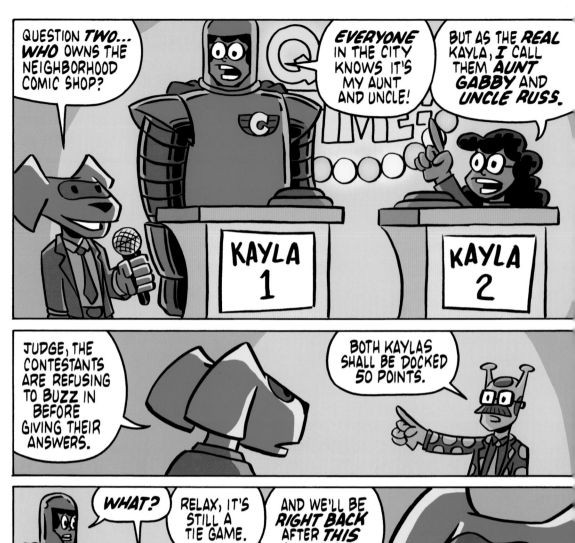

QUESTION *TWO*... *WHO* OWNS THE NEIGHBORHOOD COMIC SHOP?

EVERYONE IN THE CITY KNOWS IT'S MY AUNT AND UNCLE!

BUT AS THE *REAL* KAYLA, *I* CALL THEM *AUNT GABBY* AND *UNCLE RUSS.*

KAYLA 1

KAYLA 2

JUDGE, THE CONTESTANTS ARE REFUSING TO BUZZ IN BEFORE GIVING THEIR ANSWERS.

BOTH KAYLAS SHALL BE DOCKED 50 POINTS.

WHAT?

RELAX, IT'S STILL A TIE GAME.

AND WE'LL BE *RIGHT BACK* AFTER *THIS* COMMERCIAL BREAK!

JUDGE, A WORD IN PRIVATE, PLEASE?

THIS IS *NOT* HOW I IMAGINED MY FIRST GAME SHOW WOULD GO.

THEY *AREN'T* USING THEIR *BUZZERS.*

WE NEED TO TAKE *CONTROL.*

WAIT... YES, THAT'S IT, *CONTROL!*

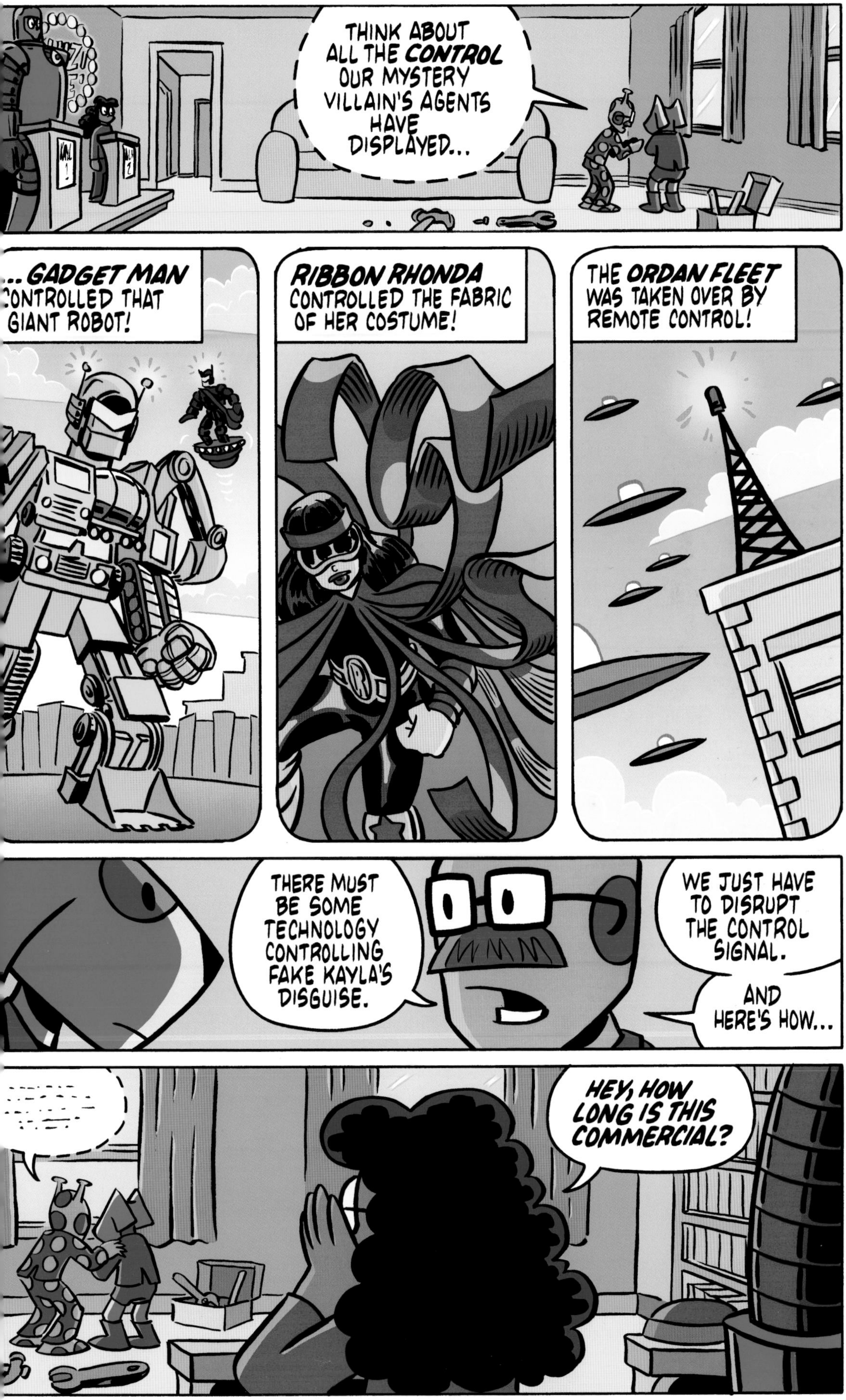
THINK ABOUT ALL THE CONTROL OUR MYSTERY VILLAIN'S AGENTS HAVE DISPLAYED...
...GADGET MAN CONTROLLED THAT GIANT ROBOT!
RIBBON RHONDA CONTROLLED THE FABRIC OF HER COSTUME!
THE ORDAN FLEET WAS TAKEN OVER BY REMOTE CONTROL!
THERE MUST BE SOME TECHNOLOGY CONTROLLING FAKE KAYLA'S DISGUISE.
WE JUST HAVE TO DISRUPT THE CONTROL SIGNAL.
AND HERE'S HOW...
HEY, HOW LONG IS THIS COMMERCIAL?

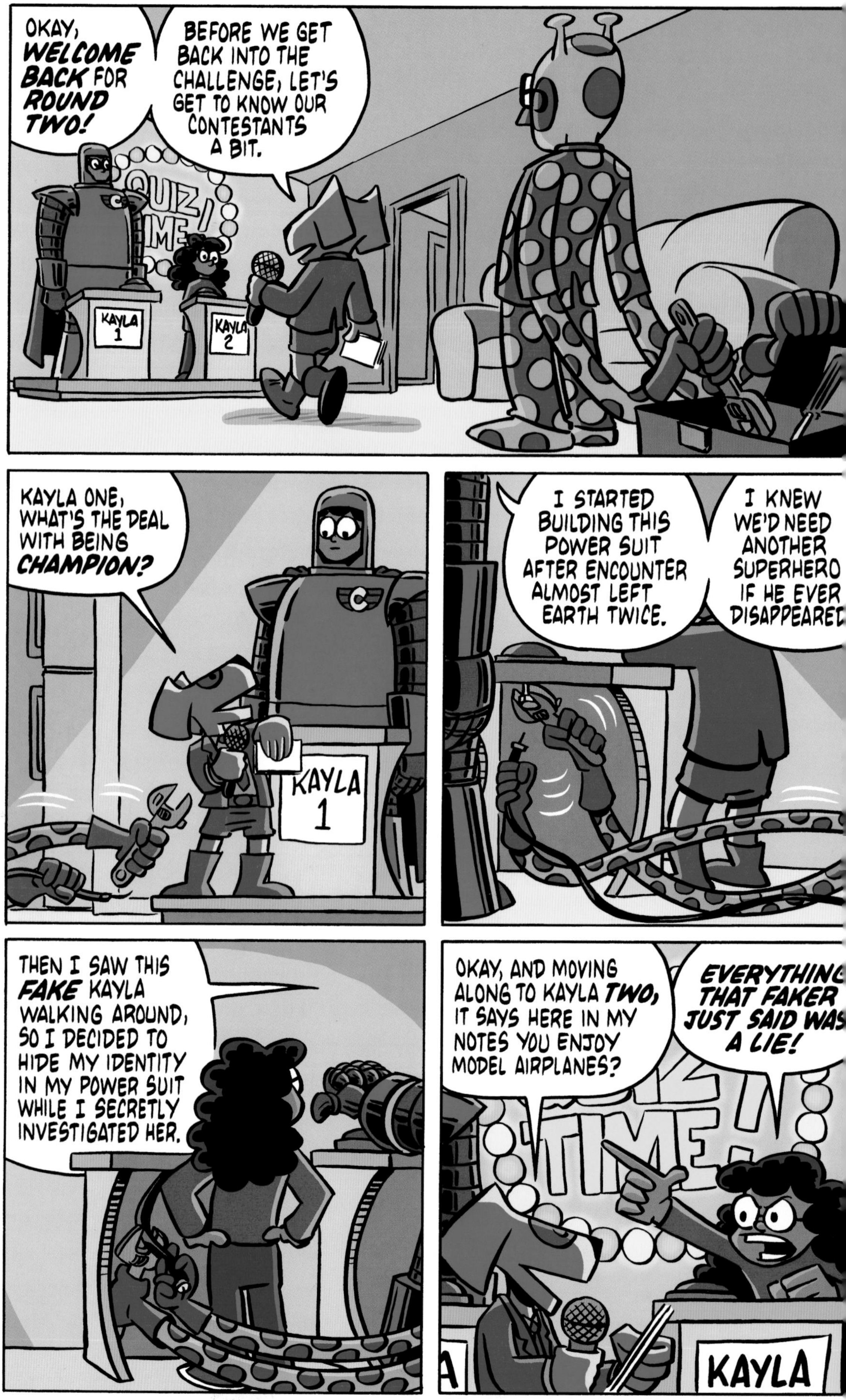

OKAY, WELCOME BACK FOR ROUND TWO!
BEFORE WE GET BACK INTO THE CHALLENGE, LET'S GET TO KNOW OUR CONTESTANTS A BIT.
QUIZ TIME
KAYLA 1
KAYLA 2
KAYLA ONE, WHAT'S THE DEAL WITH BEING CHAMPION?
KAYLA 1
I STARTED BUILDING THIS POWER SUIT AFTER ENCOUNTER ALMOST LEFT EARTH TWICE.
I KNEW WE'D NEED ANOTHER SUPERHERO IF HE EVER DISAPPEARED
THEN I SAW THIS FAKE KAYLA WALKING AROUND, SO I DECIDED TO HIDE MY IDENTITY IN MY POWER SUIT WHILE I SECRETLY INVESTIGATED HER.
OKAY, AND MOVING ALONG TO KAYLA TWO, IT SAYS HERE IN MY NOTES YOU ENJOY MODEL AIRPLANES?
EVERYTHING THAT FAKER JUST SAID WAS A LIE!
TIME
KAYLA

AND I'M GETTING THE SIGNAL FROM OUR JUDGE THAT IT'S TIME TO MOVE ON.
GET READY FOR THE *TOUGH* QUESTIONS!
WHAT IS YOUR *FAVORITE COLOR?*
RED!
KAYLA
PLEASE REMEMBER, YOU *MUST* BUZZ IN BEFORE YOU ANSWER.
NEXT QUESTION...
...DO YOU LIKE *CUPCAKES?*
YES!
KAYLA
OKAY, *NEITHER ONE* OF YOU SEEMS TO BE GETTING THIS *BUZZER* RULE... WHICH IS *ASTONISHING* CONSIDERING *ONE* OF YOU *MUST* BE THE REAL KAYLA.
ALRIGHT, HERE WE GO.
LET'S MAKE THIS AS *EASY* AS POSSIBLE.
WHOEVER HITS THE BUZZER FIRST WINS RIGHT NOW!
WHACK! WHACK!
BUZZ! BUZZ!

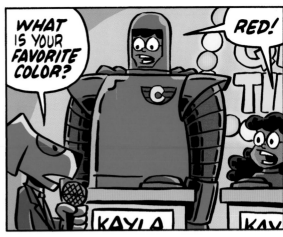

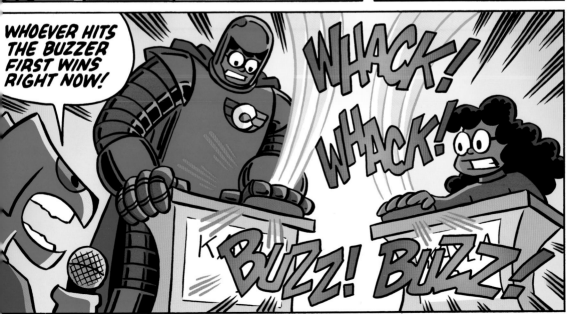

ENCOUNTER, DID YOU RIG THE BUZZER TO DEACTIVATE MY POWER SUIT?
CORRECT ANSWER! THAT MEANS YOU MUST BE THE FAKE KAYLA!
NO, BARKO, LOOK!
HUH?
AARGH! YOU'VE DEACTIVATED MY MATTER DISPLACEMENT HARNESS...
...AND MY HOLOGRAPHIC EXO-IMAGE PROJECTOR!
CURSE YOU, KRESTON ROH!
THAT GUY KIND OF LOOKS LIKE YOU, ENCOUNTER!
NO! IT... IT CAN'T BE!
OH, I SEE WHAT'S GOING ON HERE! TWINS!
ENCOUNTER HAS AN EVIL TWIN!

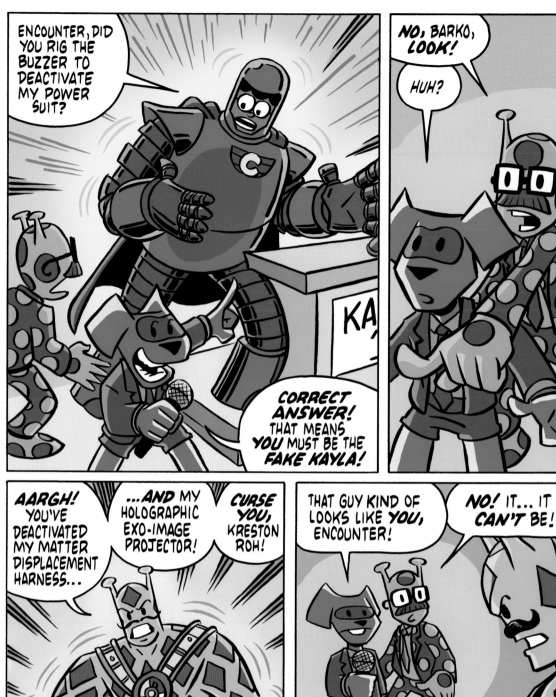

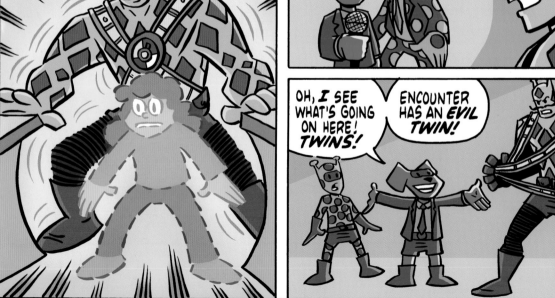

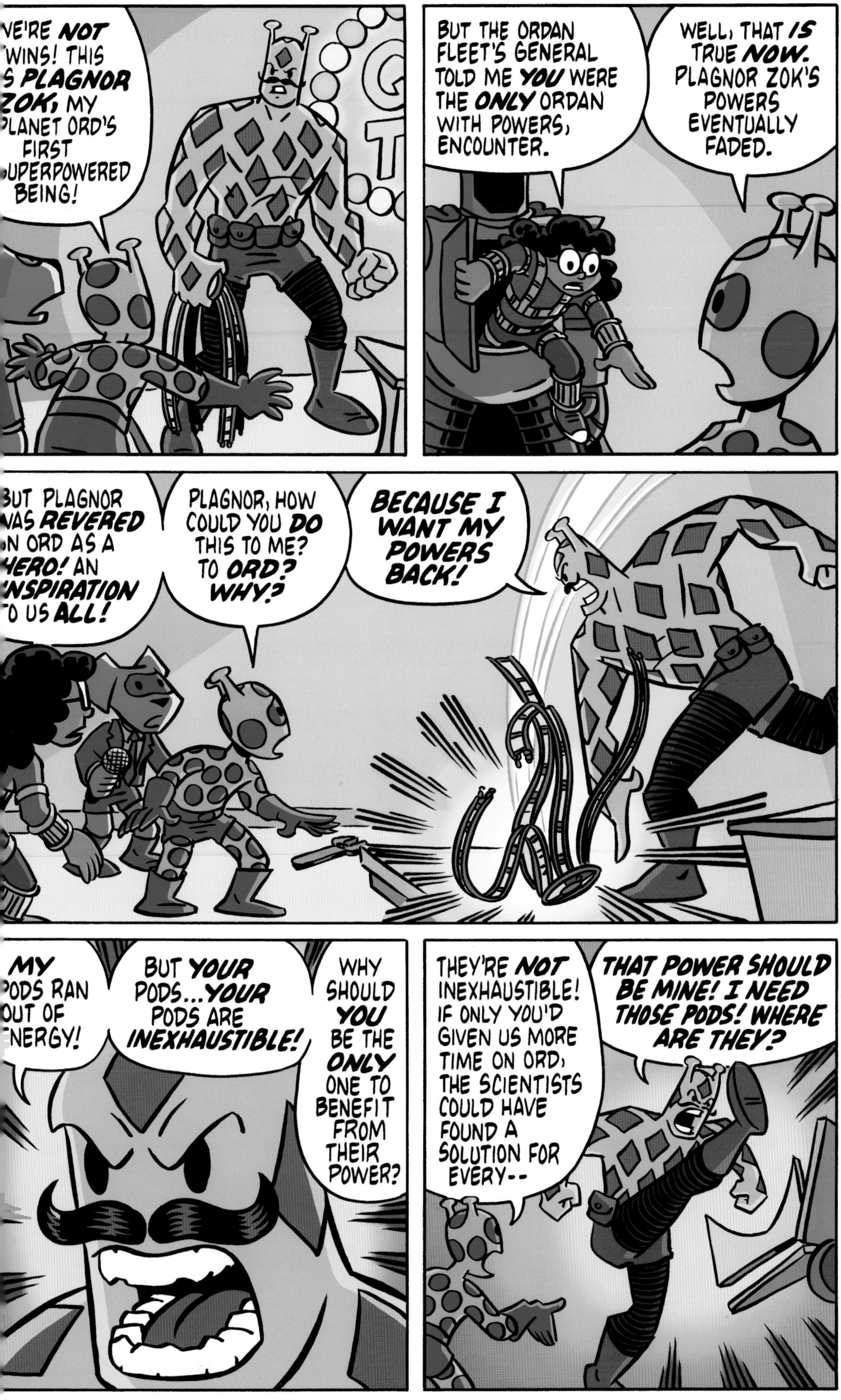

VE'RE NOT 'WINS! THIS S PLAGNOR ZOK, MY PLANET ORD'S FIRST UPERPOWERED BEING!
BUT THE ORDAN FLEET'S GENERAL TOLD ME YOU WERE THE ONLY ORDAN WITH POWERS, ENCOUNTER.
WELL, THAT IS TRUE NOW. PLAGNOR ZOK'S POWERS EVENTUALLY FADED.
BUT PLAGNOR VAS REVERED N ORD AS A HERO! AN NSPIRATION O US ALL!
PLAGNOR, HOW COULD YOU DO THIS TO ME? TO ORD? WHY?
BECAUSE I WANT MY POWERS BACK!
MY PODS RAN OUT OF NERGY!
BUT YOUR PODS... YOUR PODS ARE INEXHAUSTIBLE!
WHY SHOULD YOU BE THE ONLY ONE TO BENEFIT FROM THEIR POWER?
THEY'RE NOT INEXHAUSTIBLE! IF ONLY YOU'D GIVEN US MORE TIME ON ORD, THE SCIENTISTS COULD HAVE FOUND A SOLUTION FOR EVERY--
THAT POWER SHOULD BE MINE! I NEED THOSE PODS! WHERE ARE THEY?

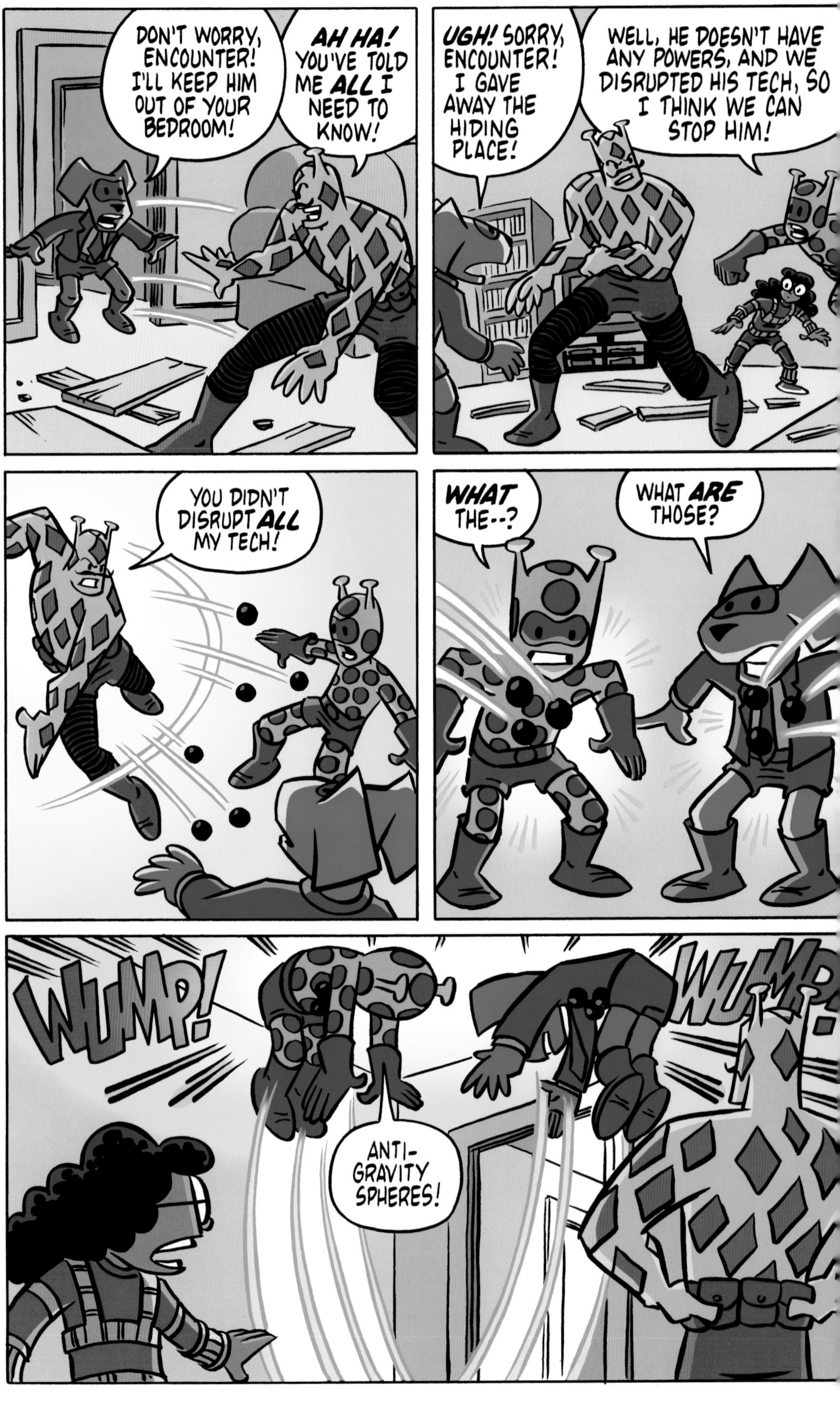
DON'T WORRY, ENCOUNTER! I'LL KEEP HIM OUT OF YOUR BEDROOM!
AH HA! YOU'VE TOLD ME ALL I NEED TO KNOW!
UGH! SORRY, ENCOUNTER! I GAVE AWAY THE HIDING PLACE!
WELL, HE DOESN'T HAVE ANY POWERS, AND WE DISRUPTED HIS TECH, SO I THINK WE CAN STOP HIM!
YOU DIDN'T DISRUPT ALL MY TECH!
WHAT THE--?
WHAT ARE THOSE?
WUMP!
ANTI-GRAVITY SPHERES!

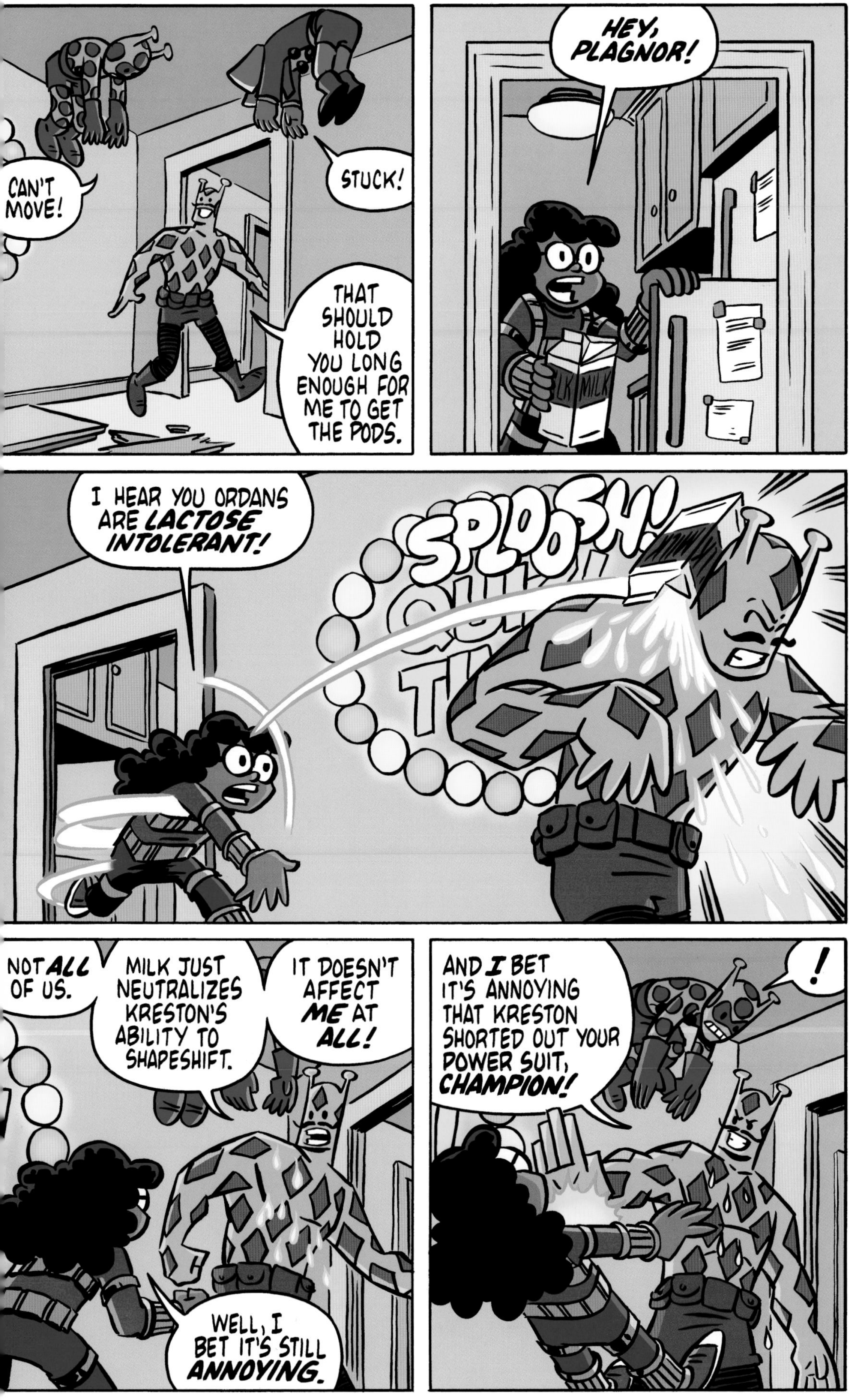
CAN'T MOVE!
STUCK!
THAT SHOULD HOLD YOU LONG ENOUGH FOR ME TO GET THE PODS.
HEY, PLAGNOR!
MILK
I HEAR YOU ORDANS ARE LACTOSE INTOLERANT!
SPLOOSH!
NOT ALL OF US.
MILK JUST NEUTRALIZES KRESTON'S ABILITY TO SHAPESHIFT.
IT DOESN'T AFFECT ME AT ALL!
WELL, I BET IT'S STILL ANNOYING.
AND I BET IT'S ANNOYING THAT KRESTON SHORTED OUT YOUR POWER SUIT, CHAMPION!
!

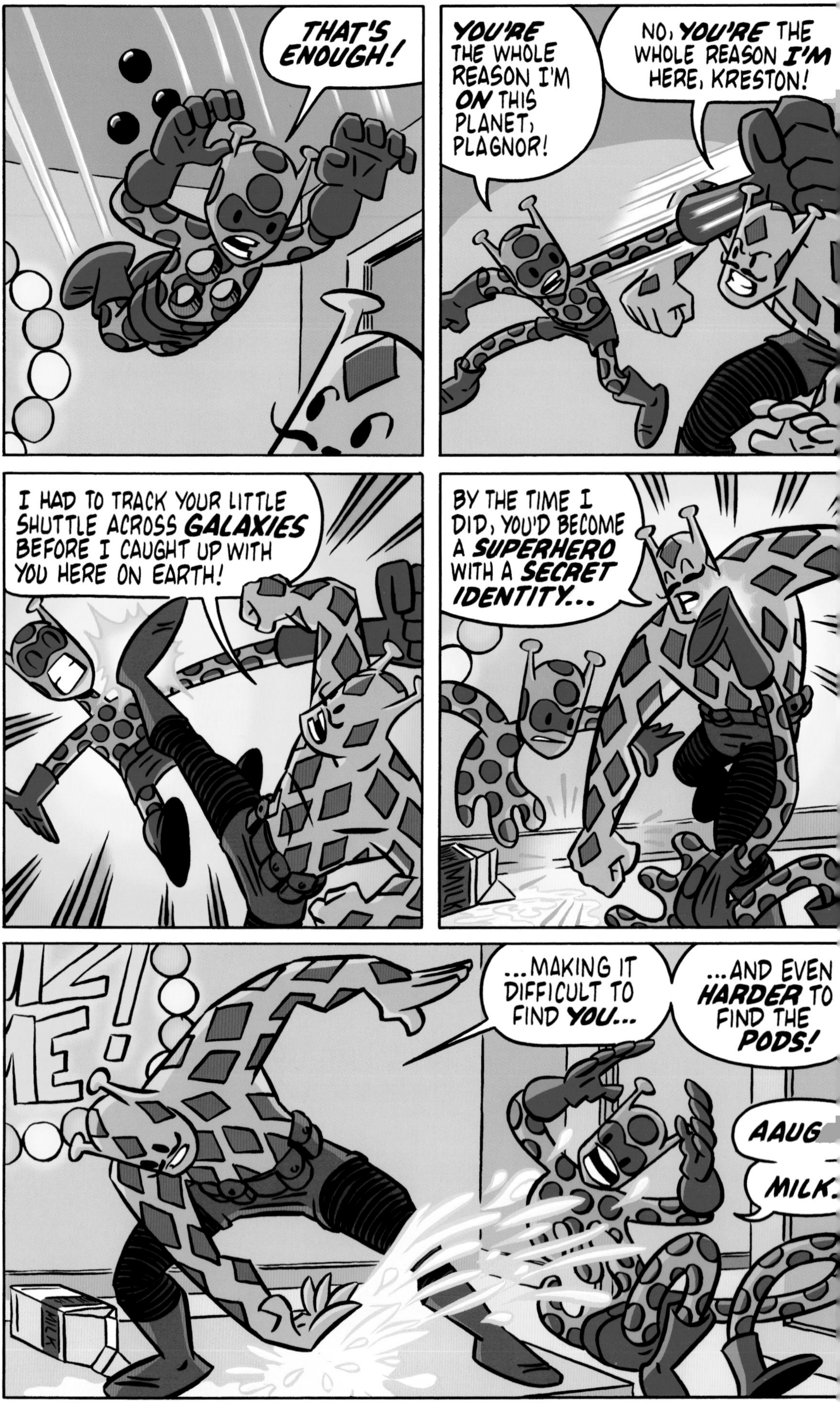
THAT'S ENOUGH!
YOU'RE THE WHOLE REASON I'M ON THIS PLANET, PLAGNOR!
NO, YOU'RE THE WHOLE REASON I'M HERE, KRESTON!
I HAD TO TRACK YOUR LITTLE SHUTTLE ACROSS GALAXIES BEFORE I CAUGHT UP WITH YOU HERE ON EARTH!
BY THE TIME I DID, YOU'D BECOME A SUPERHERO WITH A SECRET IDENTITY...
...MAKING IT DIFFICULT TO FIND YOU...
...AND EVEN HARDER TO FIND THE PODS!
AAUG
MILK.

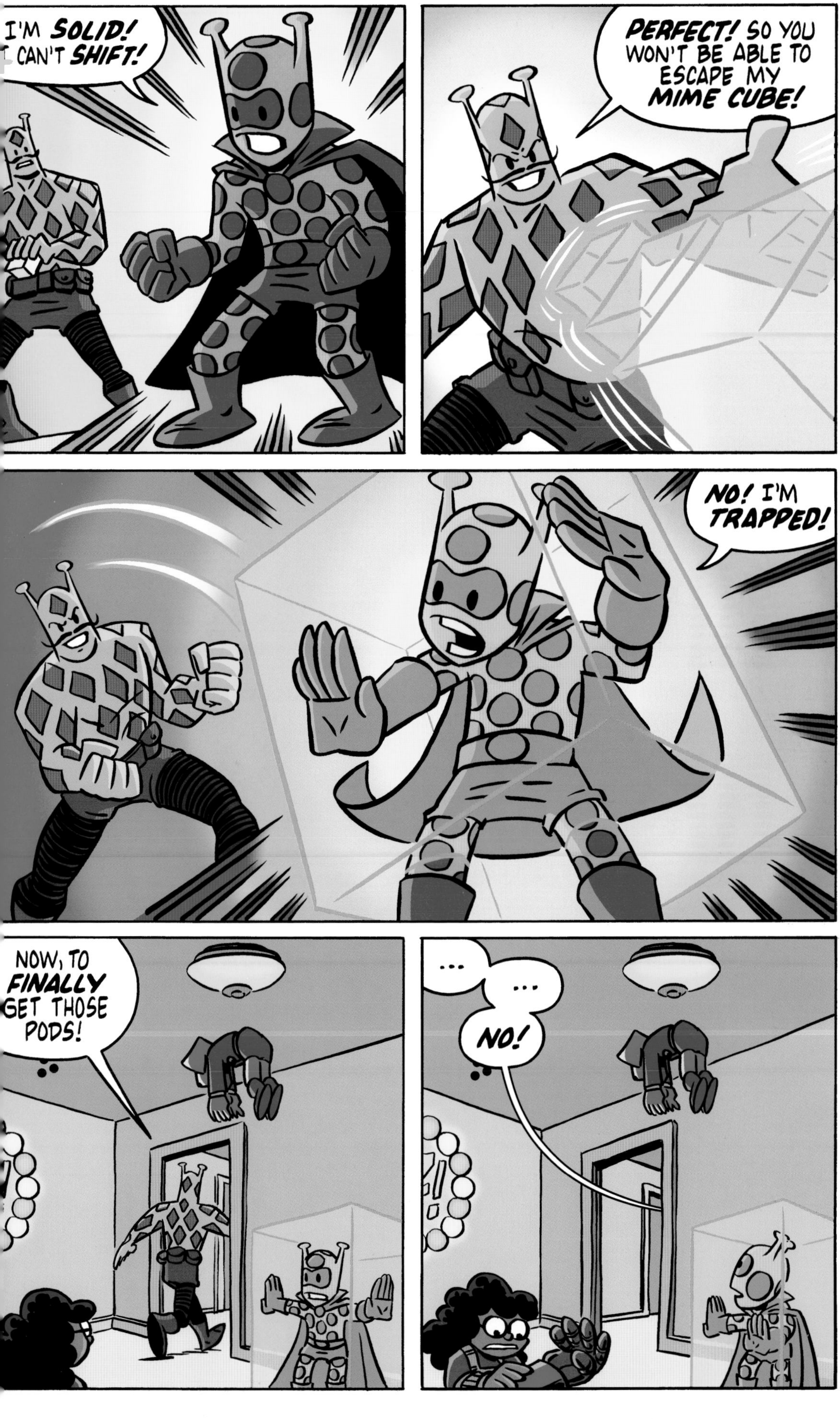

I'M SOLID! I CAN'T SHIFT!
PERFECT! SO YOU WON'T BE ABLE TO ESCAPE MY MIME CUBE!
NO! I'M TRAPPED!
NOW, TO FINALLY GET THOSE PODS!
...
...
NO!

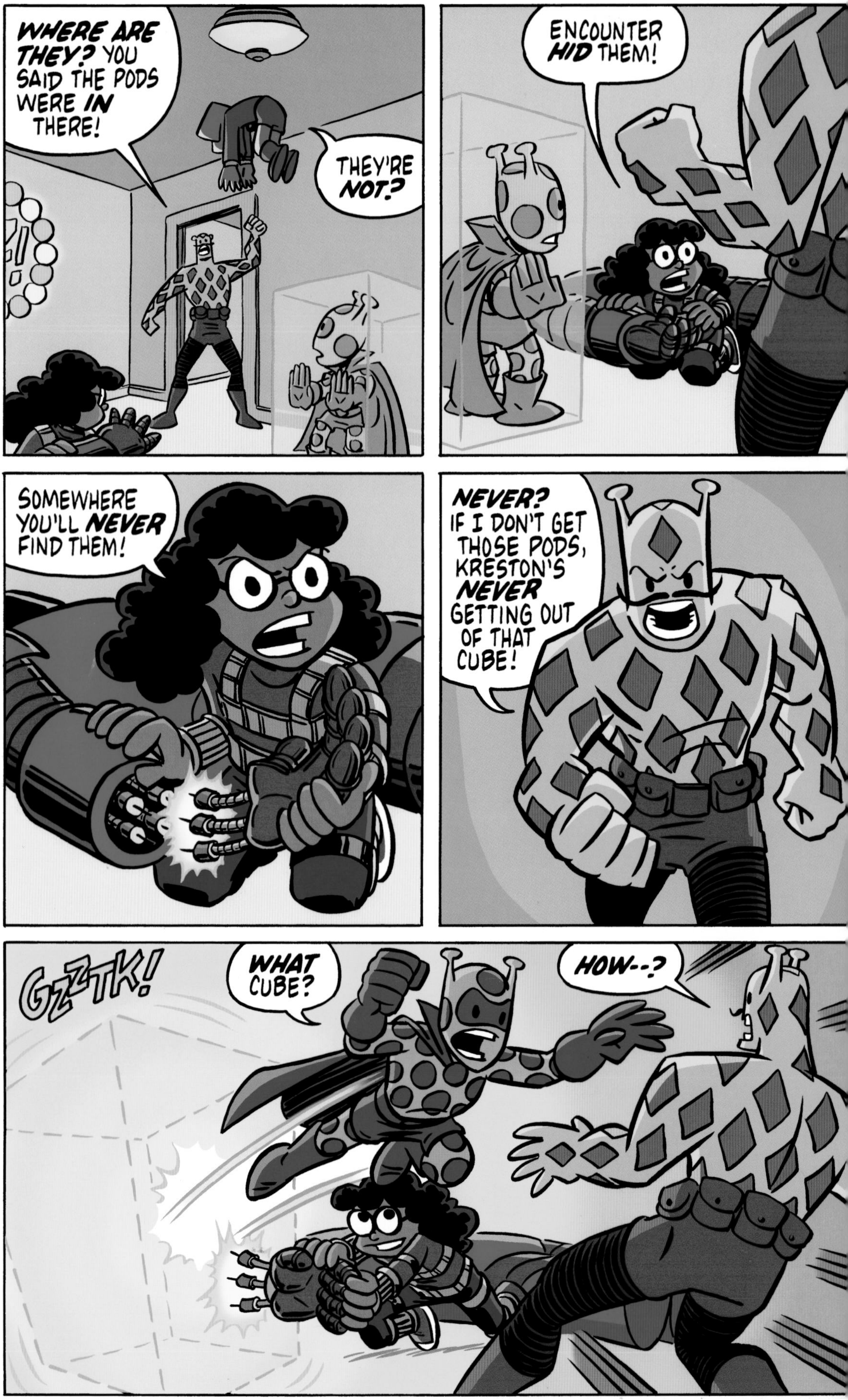
WHERE ARE THEY? YOU SAID THE PODS WERE IN THERE!
THEY'RE NOT?
ENCOUNTER HID THEM!
SOMEWHERE YOU'LL NEVER FIND THEM!
NEVER? IF I DON'T GET THOSE PODS, KRESTON'S NEVER GETTING OUT OF THAT CUBE!
GZZTK!
WHAT CUBE?
HOW--?

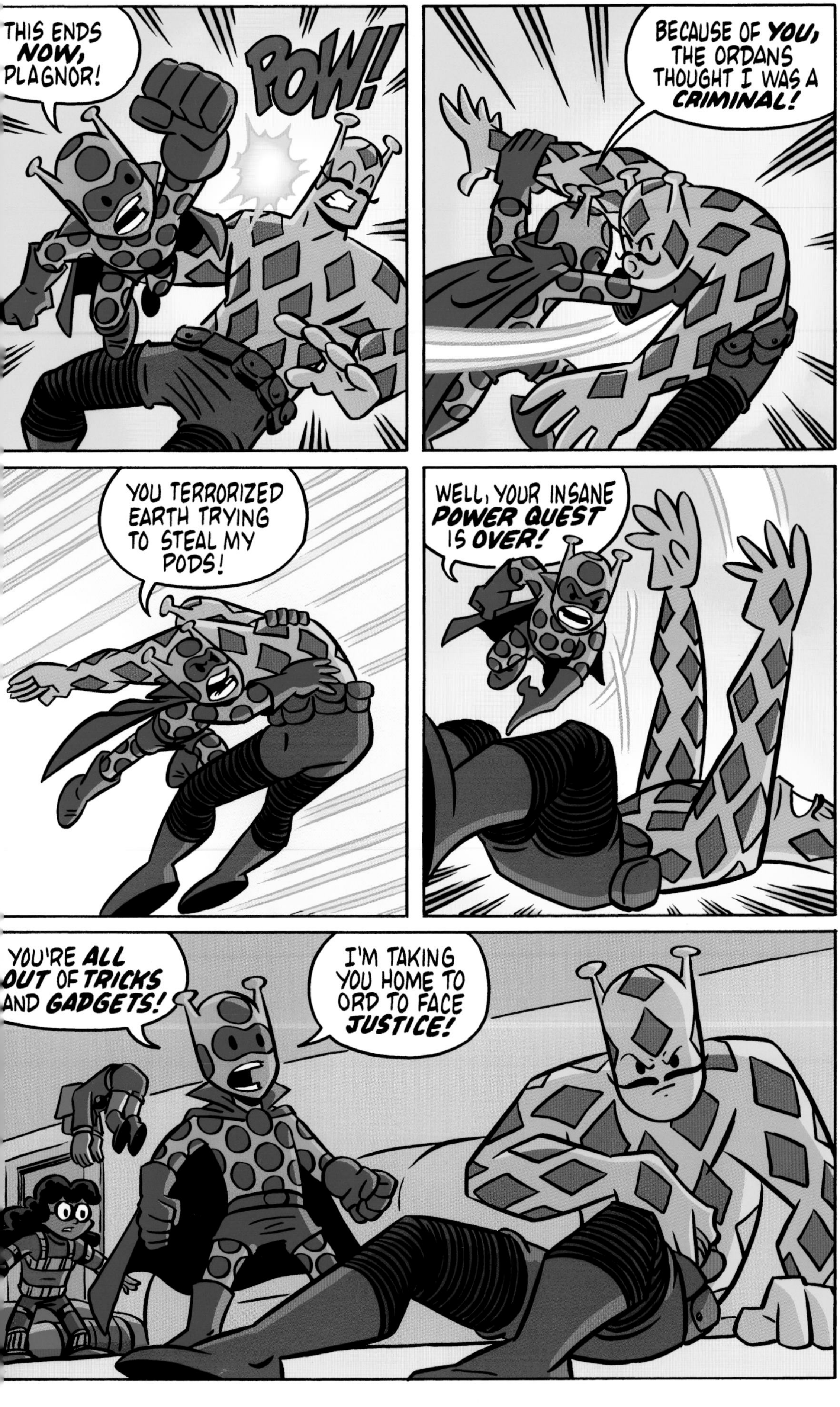
THIS ENDS NOW, PLAGNOR!
POW!
BECAUSE OF YOU, THE ORDANS THOUGHT I WAS A CRIMINAL!
YOU TERRORIZED EARTH TRYING TO STEAL MY PODS!
WELL, YOUR INSANE POWER QUEST IS OVER!
YOU'RE ALL OUT OF TRICKS AND GADGETS!
I'M TAKING YOU HOME TO ORD TO FACE JUSTICE!

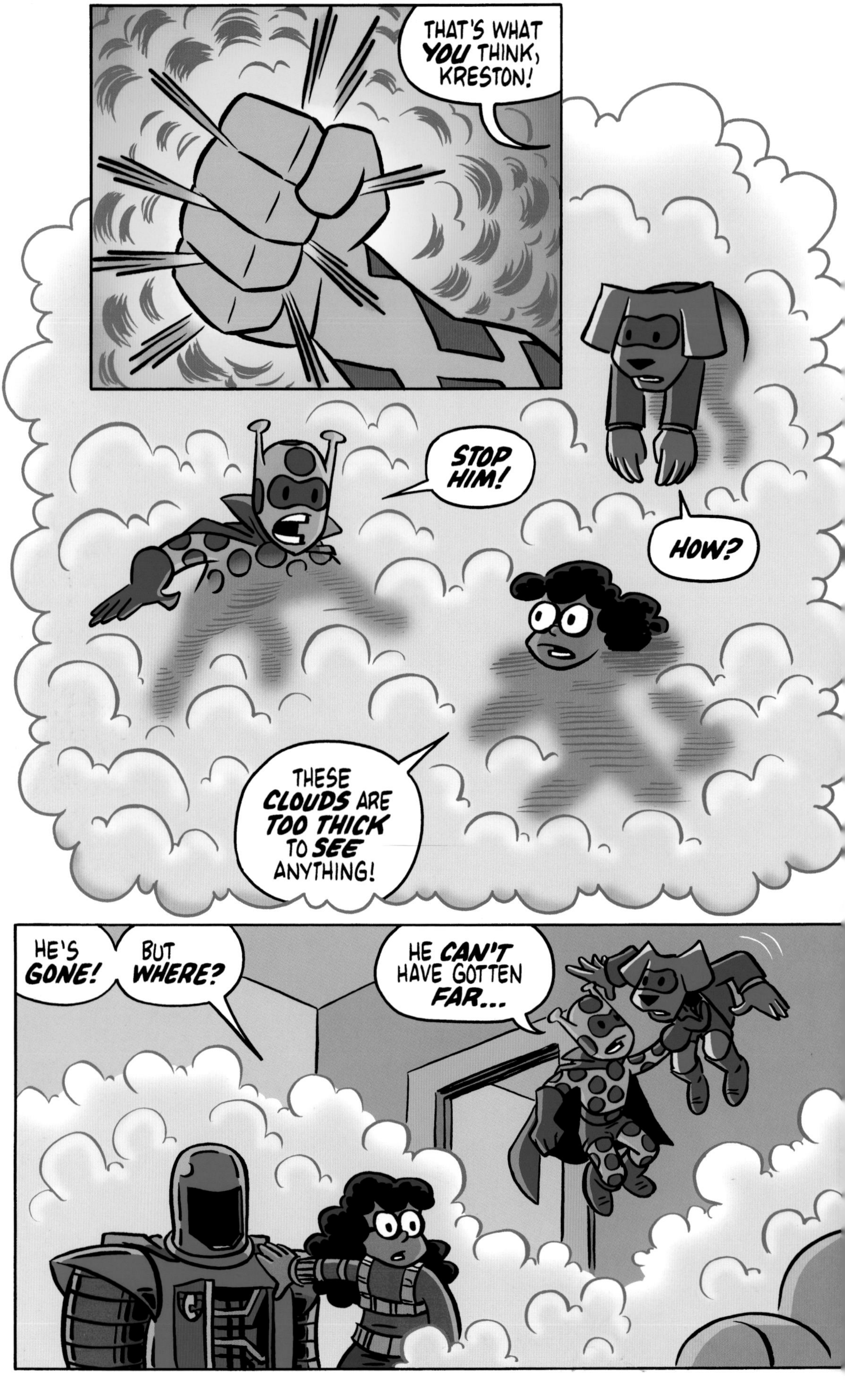
THAT'S WHAT YOU THINK, KRESTON!
STOP HIM!
HOW?
THESE CLOUDS ARE TOO THICK TO SEE ANYTHING!
HE'S GONE!
BUT WHERE?
HE CAN'T HAVE GOTTEN FAR...

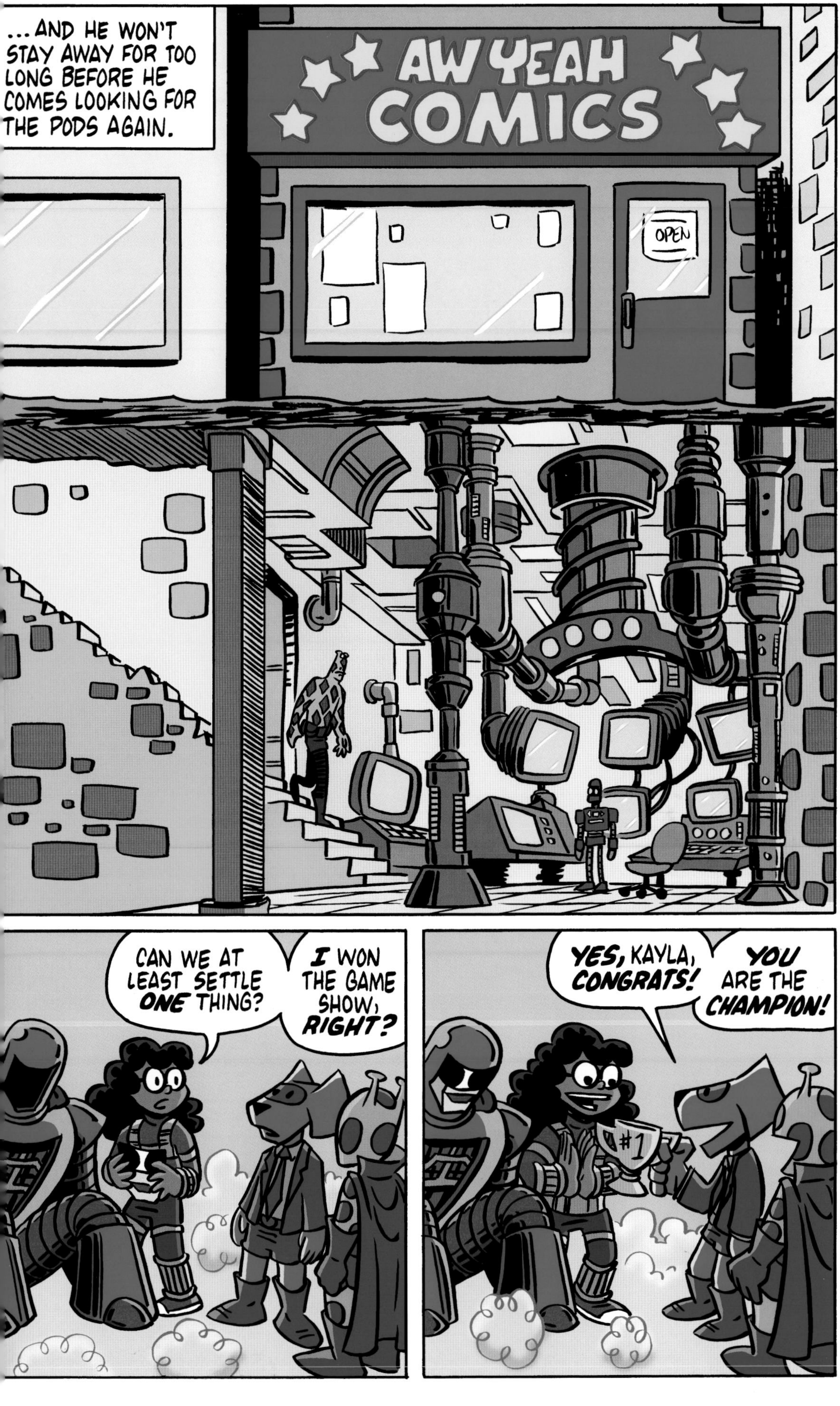

...AND HE WON'T STAY AWAY FOR TOO LONG BEFORE HE COMES LOOKING FOR THE PODS AGAIN.
AW YEAH COMICS
OPEN
CAN WE AT LEAST SETTLE ONE THING?
I WON THE GAME SHOW, RIGHT?
YES, KAYLA, CONGRATS!
YOU ARE THE CHAMPION!
#1

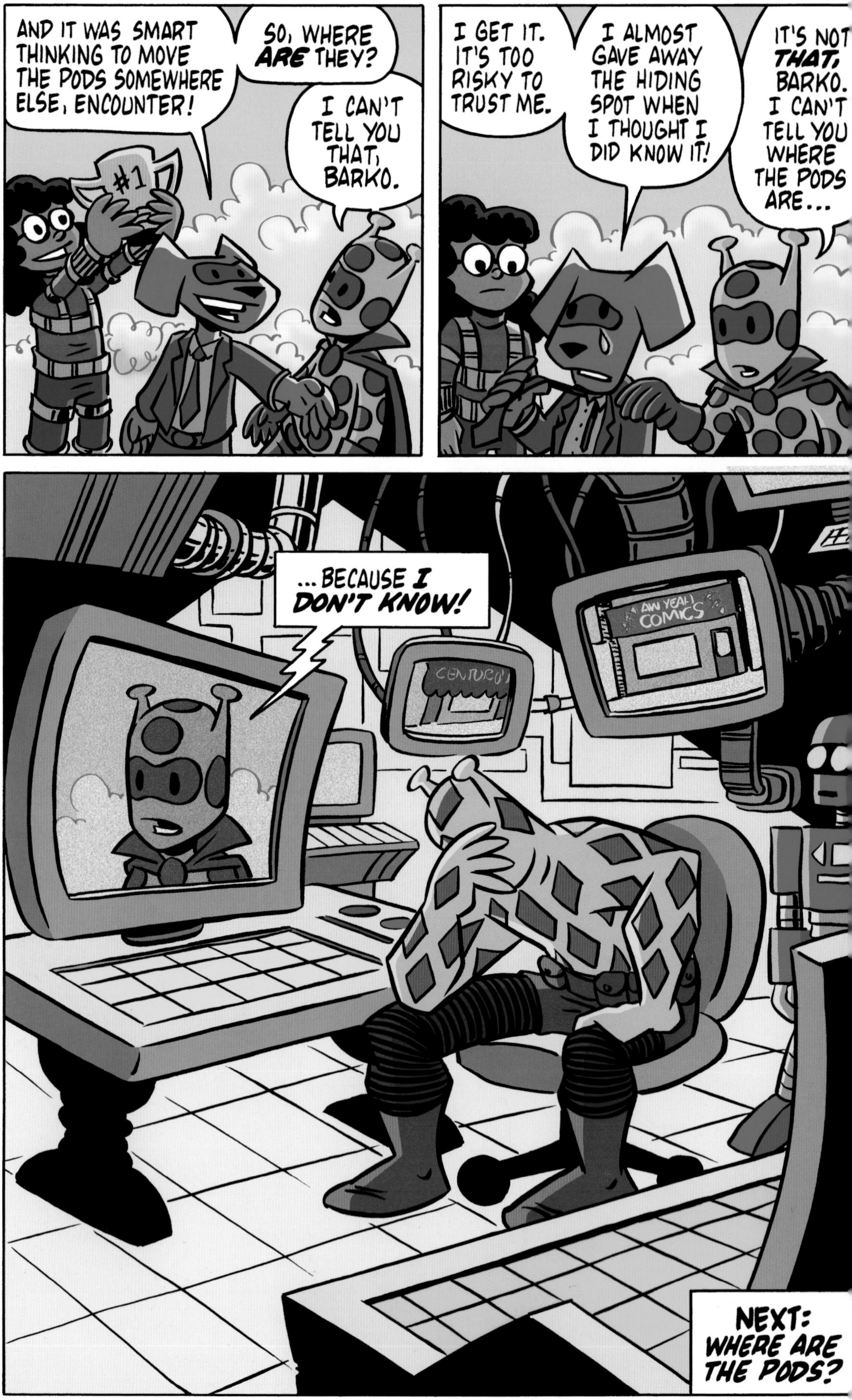
AND IT WAS SMART THINKING TO MOVE THE PODS SOMEWHERE ELSE, ENCOUNTER!
SO, WHERE ARE THEY?
I CAN'T TELL YOU THAT, BARKO.
#1
I GET IT. IT'S TOO RISKY TO TRUST ME.
I ALMOST GAVE AWAY THE HIDING SPOT WHEN I THOUGHT I DID KNOW IT!
IT'S NOT THAT, BARKO. I CAN'T TELL YOU WHERE THE PODS ARE...
...BECAUSE I DON'T KNOW!
AW YEAH COMICS
NEXT: WHERE ARE THE PODS?

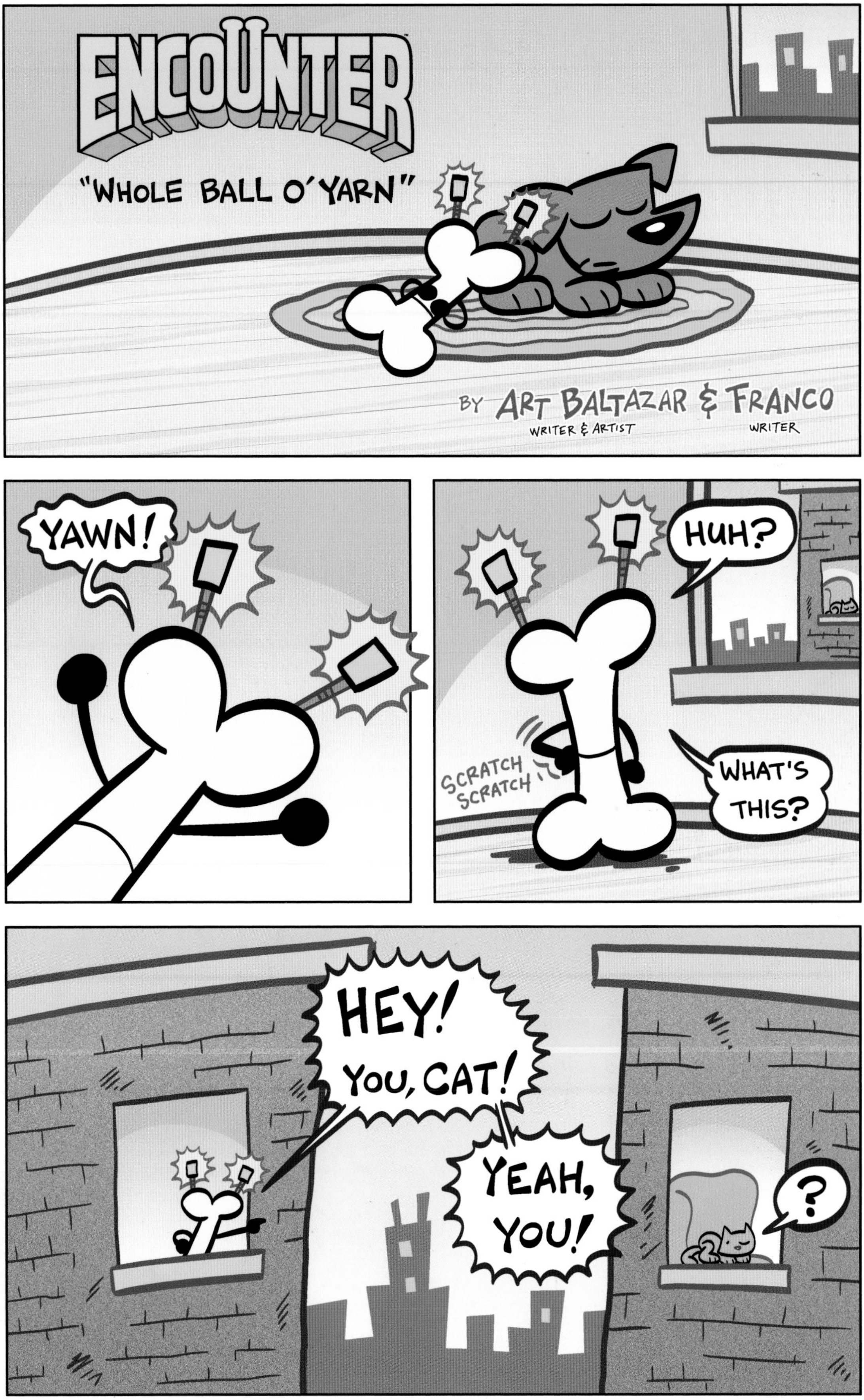
ENCOUNTER
"WHOLE BALL O'YARN"
BY ART BALTAZAR & FRANCO
WRITER & ARTIST
WRITER
YAWN!
HUH?
SCRATCH SCRATCH
WHAT'S THIS?
HEY! YOU, CAT!
YEAH, YOU!
?

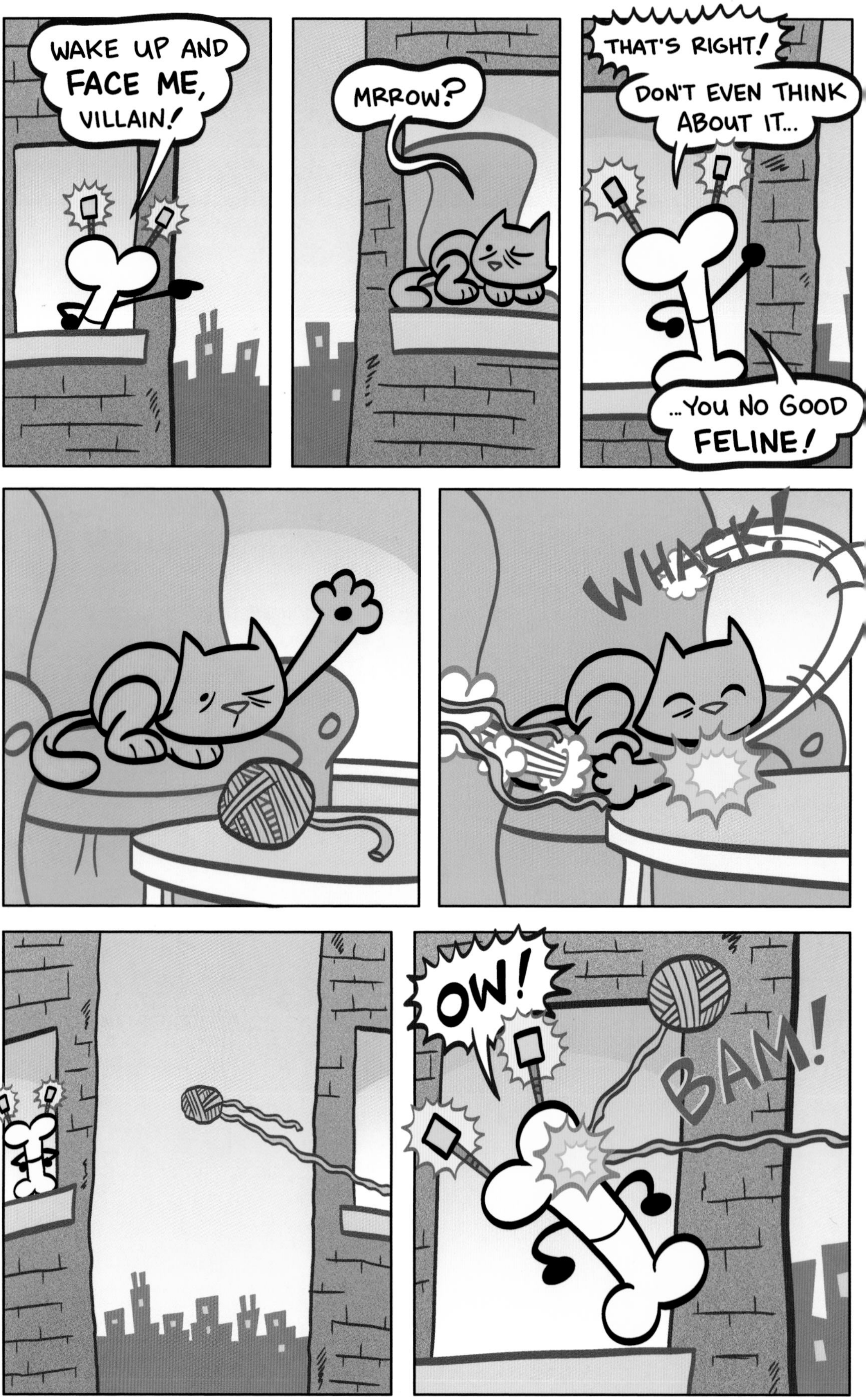

WAKE UP AND FACE ME, VILLAIN!
MRROW?
THAT'S RIGHT!
DON'T EVEN THINK ABOUT IT...
...YOU NO GOOD FELINE!
WHACK!
OW!
BAM!

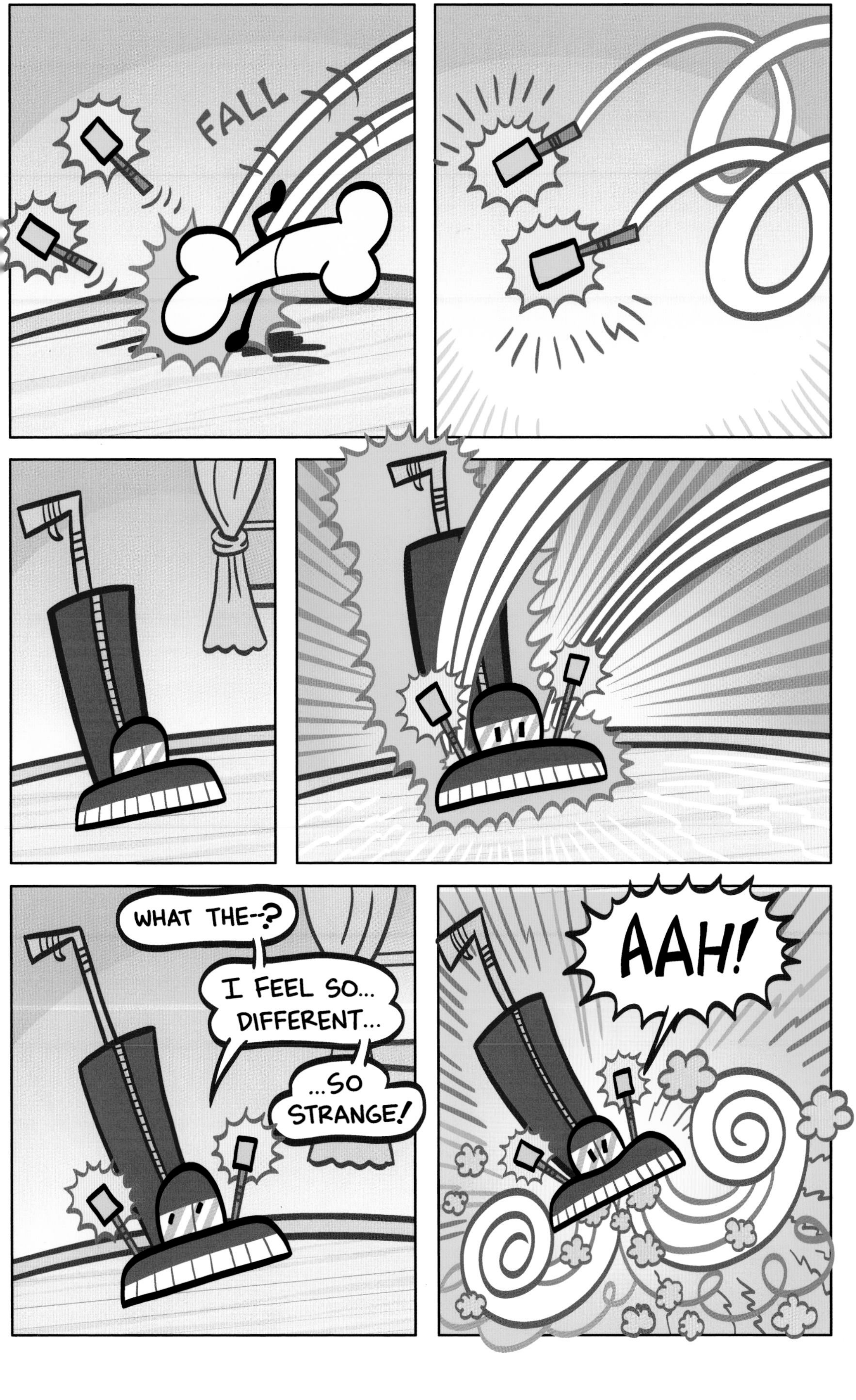
FALL
WHAT THE--?
I FEEL SO... DIFFERENT...
...SO STRANGE!
AAH!

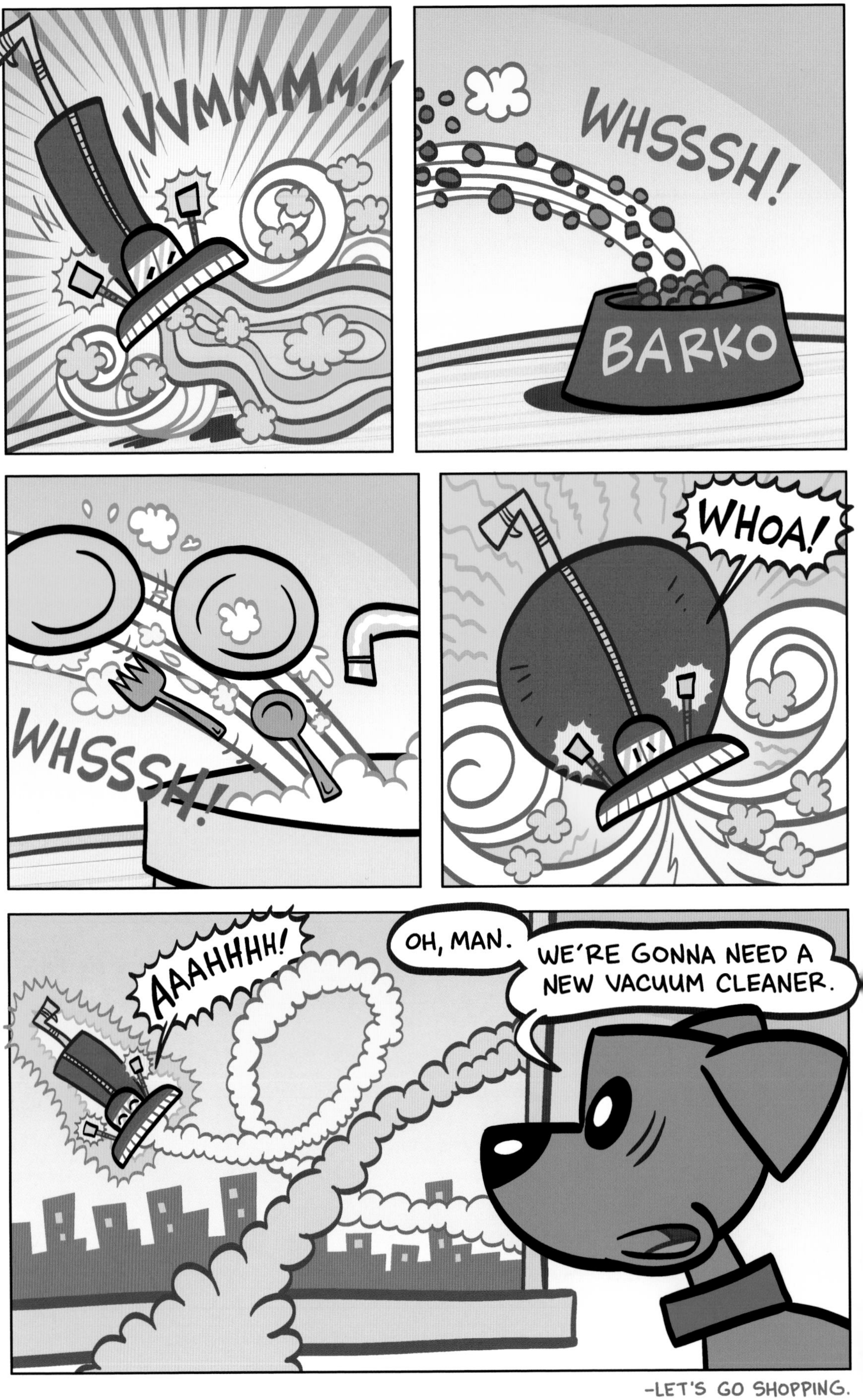
VVMMMMM!!
WHSSSSH!
BARKO
WHSSSH!
WHOA!
AAAHHHH!
OH, MAN.
WE'RE GONNA NEED A NEW VACUUM CLEANER.

-LET'S GO SHOPPING.

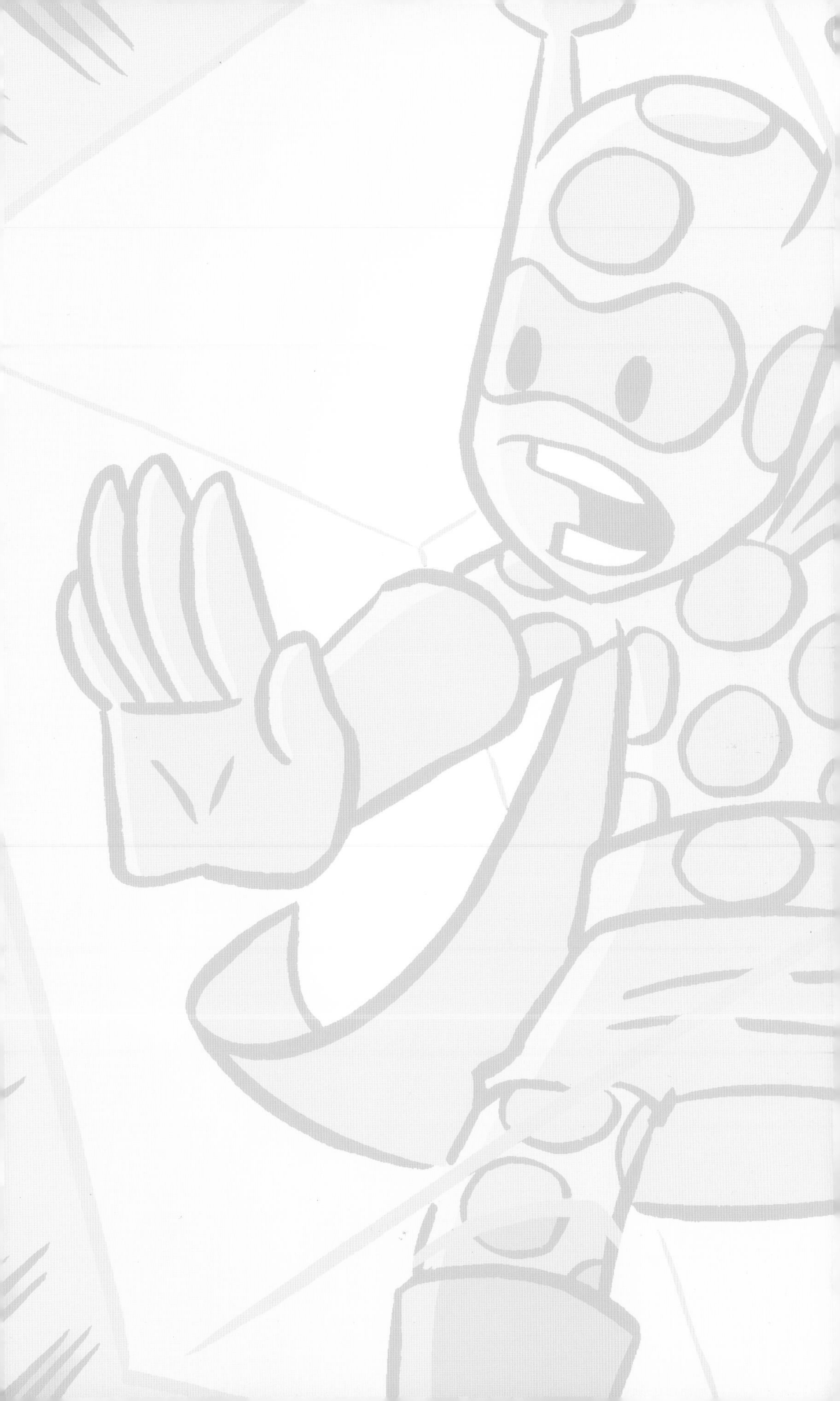

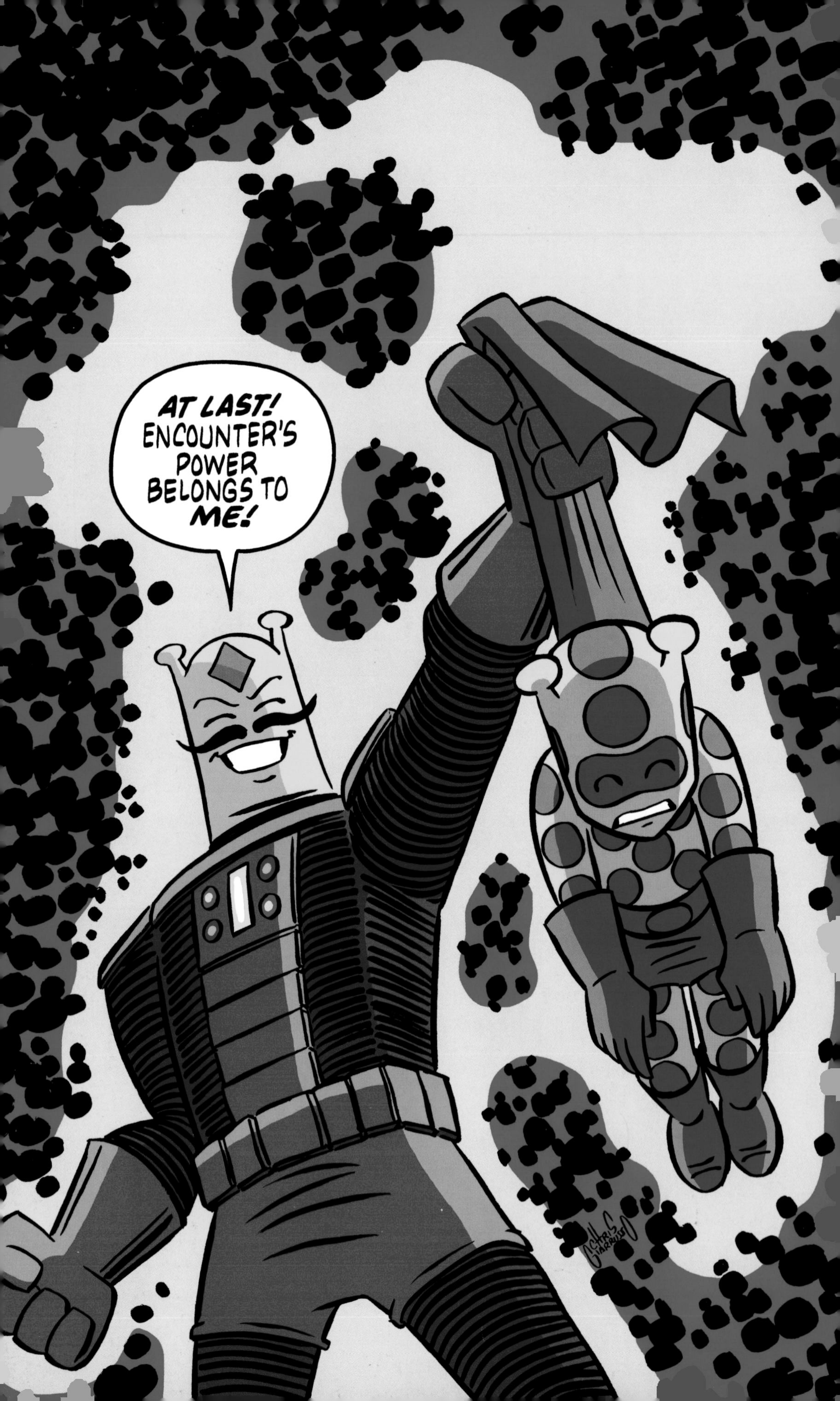
AT LAST! ENCOUNTER'S POWER BELONGS TO ME!

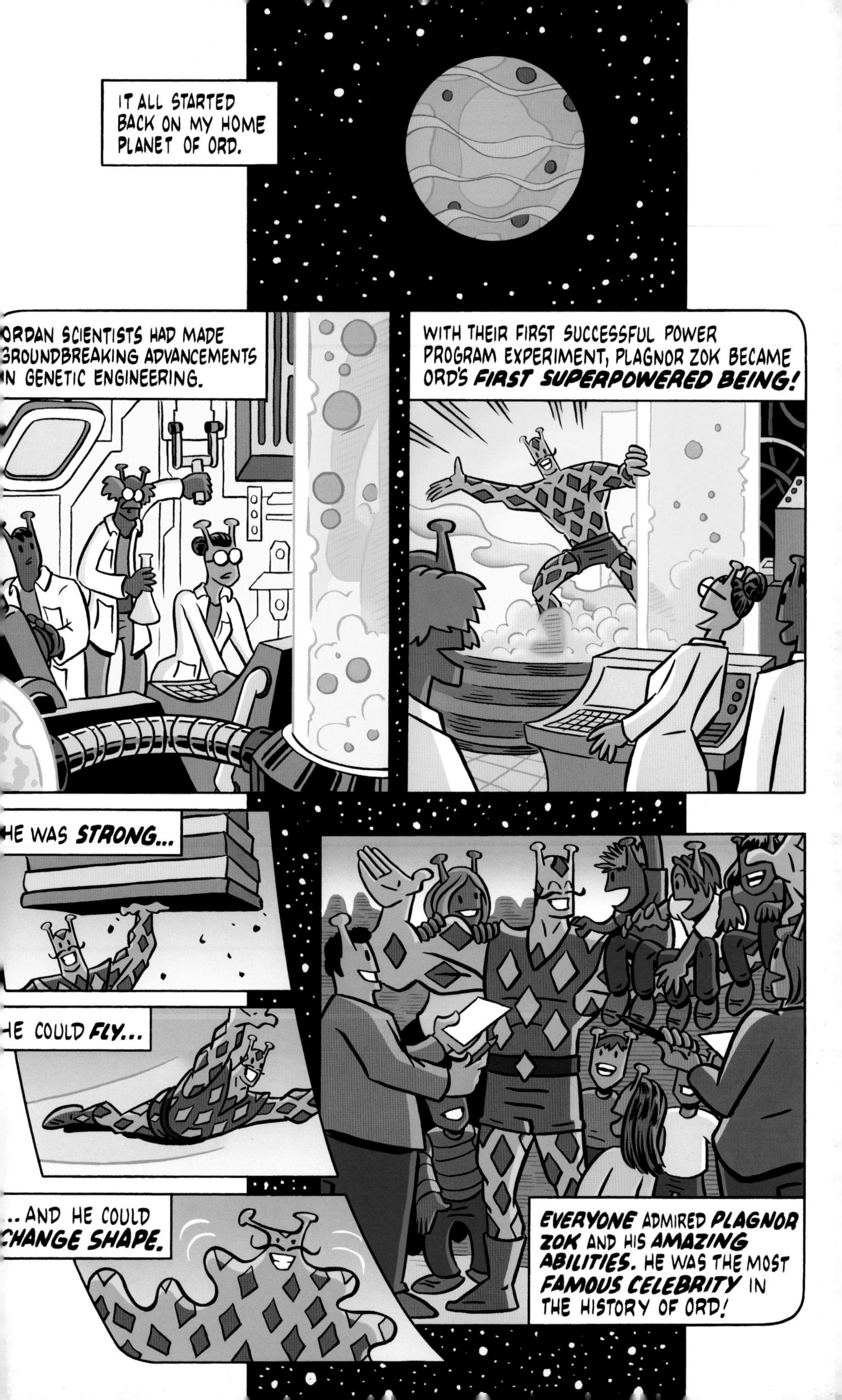
IT ALL STARTED BACK ON MY HOME PLANET OF ORD.
ORDAN SCIENTISTS HAD MADE GROUNDBREAKING ADVANCEMENTS IN GENETIC ENGINEERING.
WITH THEIR FIRST SUCCESSFUL POWER PROGRAM EXPERIMENT, PLAGNOR ZOK BECAME ORD'S FIRST SUPERPOWERED BEING!
HE WAS STRONG...
HE COULD FLY...
...AND HE COULD CHANGE SHAPE.
EVERYONE ADMIRED PLAGNOR ZOK AND HIS AMAZING ABILITIES. HE WAS THE MOST FAMOUS CELEBRITY IN THE HISTORY OF ORD!

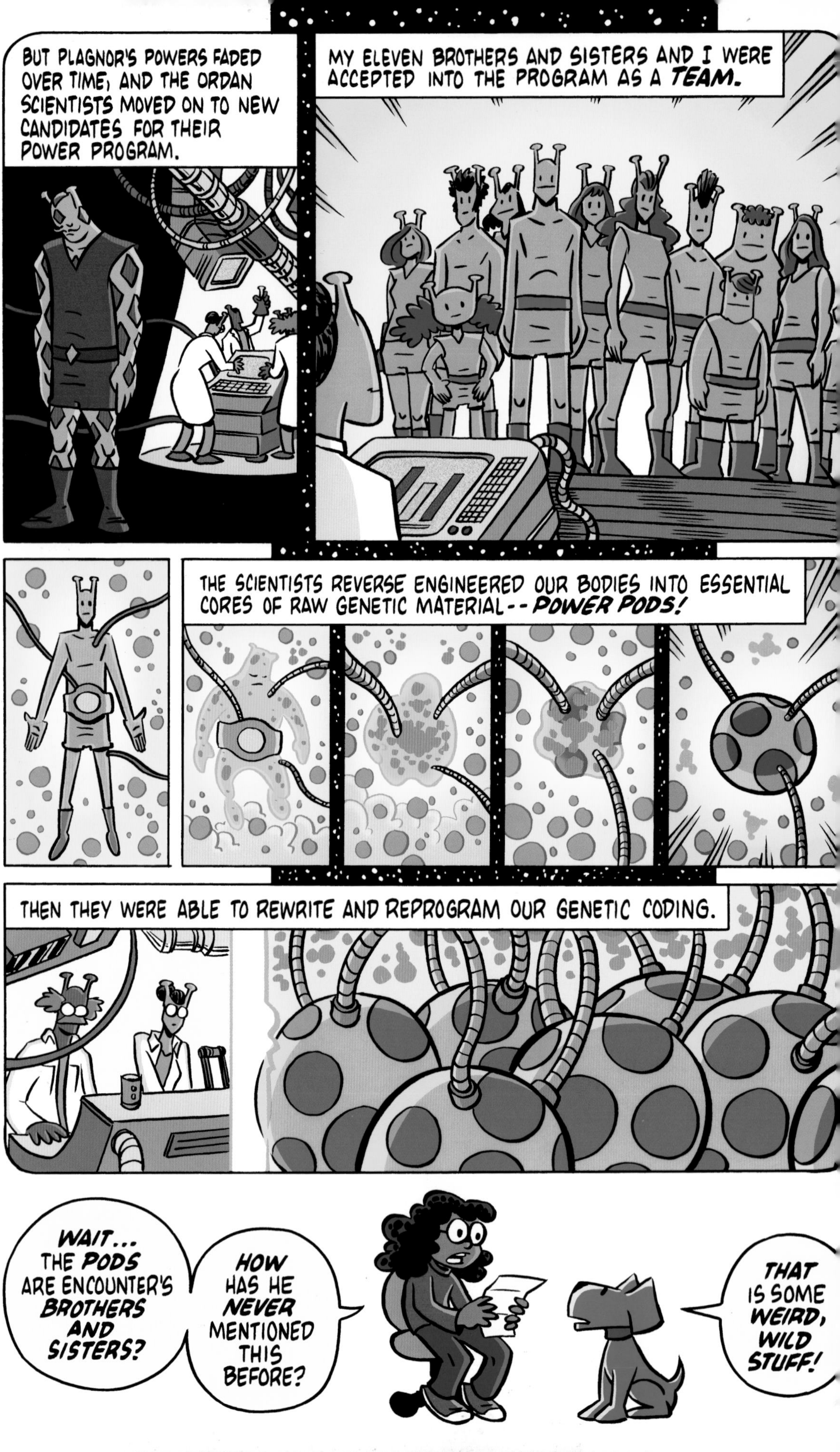

BUT PLAGNOR'S POWERS FADED OVER TIME, AND THE ORDAN SCIENTISTS MOVED ON TO NEW CANDIDATES FOR THEIR POWER PROGRAM.
MY ELEVEN BROTHERS AND SISTERS AND I WERE ACCEPTED INTO THE PROGRAM AS A TEAM.
THE SCIENTISTS REVERSE ENGINEERED OUR BODIES INTO ESSENTIAL CORES OF RAW GENETIC MATERIAL--POWER PODS!
THEN THEY WERE ABLE TO REWRITE AND REPROGRAM OUR GENETIC CODING.
WAIT... THE PODS ARE ENCOUNTER'S BROTHERS AND SISTERS?
HOW HAS HE NEVER MENTIONED THIS BEFORE?
THAT IS SOME WEIRD, WILD STUFF!

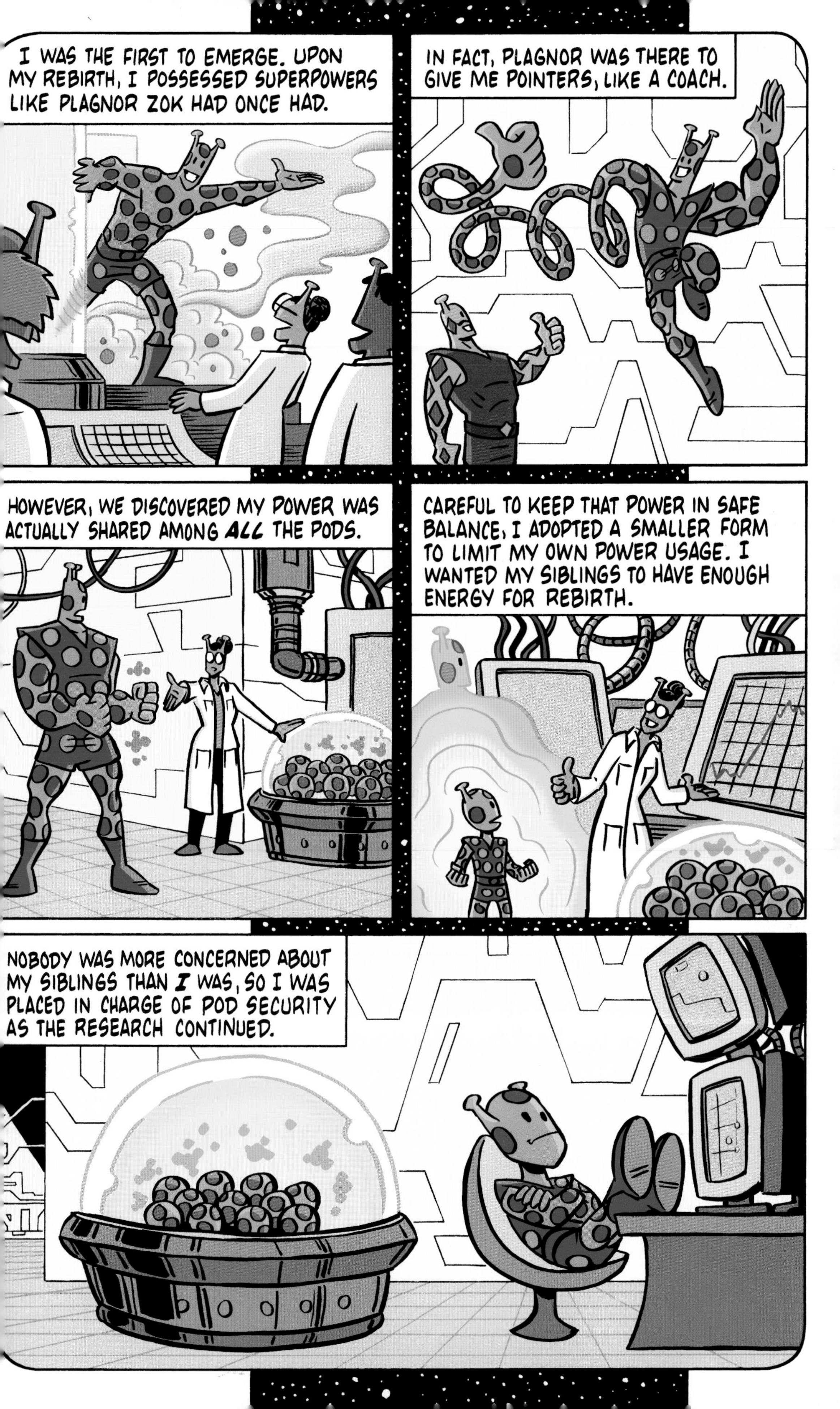
I WAS THE FIRST TO EMERGE. UPON MY REBIRTH, I POSSESSED SUPERPOWERS LIKE PLAGNOR ZOK HAD ONCE HAD.
IN FACT, PLAGNOR WAS THERE TO GIVE ME POINTERS, LIKE A COACH.
HOWEVER, WE DISCOVERED MY POWER WAS ACTUALLY SHARED AMONG ALL THE PODS.
CAREFUL TO KEEP THAT POWER IN SAFE BALANCE, I ADOPTED A SMALLER FORM TO LIMIT MY OWN POWER USAGE. I WANTED MY SIBLINGS TO HAVE ENOUGH ENERGY FOR REBIRTH.
NOBODY WAS MORE CONCERNED ABOUT MY SIBLINGS THAN I WAS, SO I WAS PLACED IN CHARGE OF POD SECURITY AS THE RESEARCH CONTINUED.

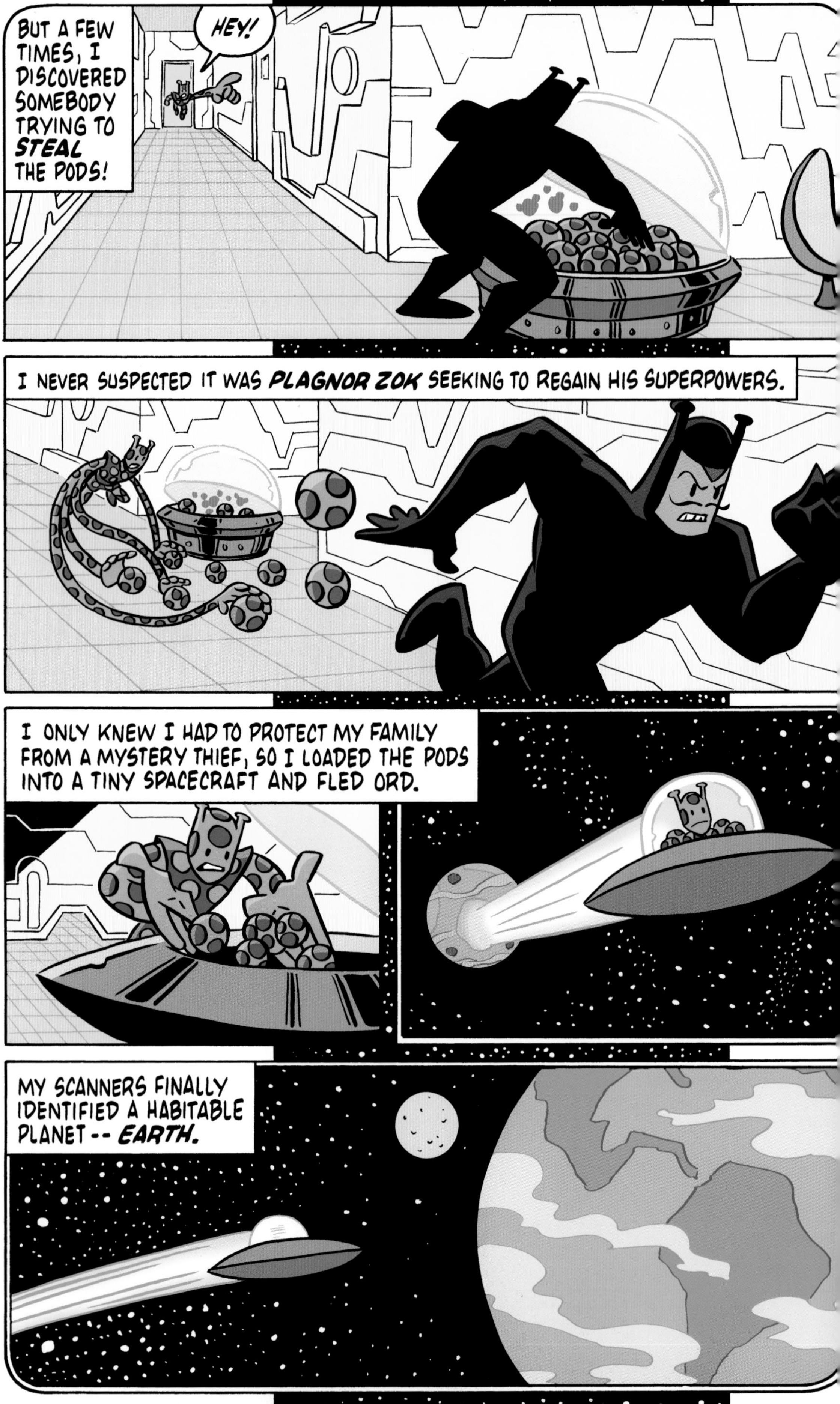
BUT A FEW TIMES, I DISCOVERED SOMEBODY TRYING TO STEAL THE PODS!
HEY!
I NEVER SUSPECTED IT WAS PLAGNOR ZOK SEEKING TO REGAIN HIS SUPERPOWERS.
I ONLY KNEW I HAD TO PROTECT MY FAMILY FROM A MYSTERY THIEF, SO I LOADED THE PODS INTO A TINY SPACECRAFT AND FLED ORD.
MY SCANNERS FINALLY IDENTIFIED A HABITABLE PLANET -- EARTH.

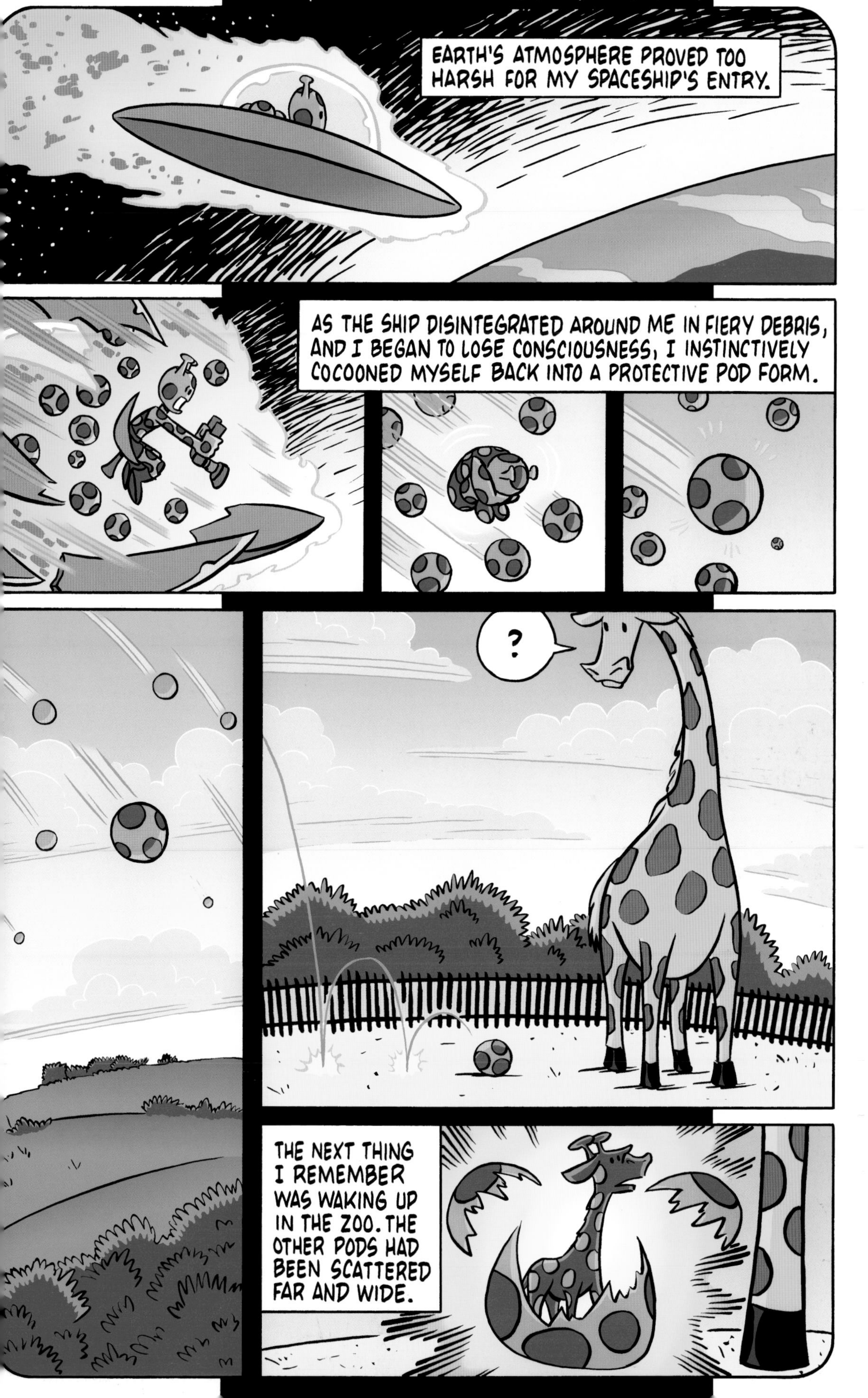
EARTH'S ATMOSPHERE PROVED TOO HARSH FOR MY SPACESHIP'S ENTRY.
AS THE SHIP DISINTEGRATED AROUND ME IN FIERY DEBRIS, AND I BEGAN TO LOSE CONSCIOUSNESS, I INSTINCTIVELY COCOONED MYSELF BACK INTO A PROTECTIVE POD FORM.
?
THE NEXT THING I REMEMBER WAS WAKING UP IN THE ZOO. THE OTHER PODS HAD BEEN SCATTERED FAR AND WIDE.

SOON AFTER, I MET THE TWO OF YOU.

AS YOU NO DOUBT RECALL, MY FIRST MISSION WAS TO GATHER UP THE PODS.

YES, THAT SOUNDS FAMILIAR.

I DON'T REMEMBER THAT *AT ALL.*

USING A MEDITATION TECHNIQUE THAT LINKS ME TO MY SIBLINGS, I WAS ABLE TO LOCATE AND RETRIEVE THE PODS WITH BARKO'S HELP.

OH, YEAH, I *DO* KINDA REMEMBER THAT.

NOW THAT THE PODS HAVE GONE MISSING, I MUST ONCE AGAIN RELY ON MY FOCUSED MEDITATION TECHNIQUE TO FIND THEM.

I KNOW YOU WANT TO HELP ME, BUT WITH PLAGNOR STILL DETERMINED TO STEAL THE PODS, I THOUGHT I SHOULD GATHER THEM AS COVERTLY AS POSSIBLE.

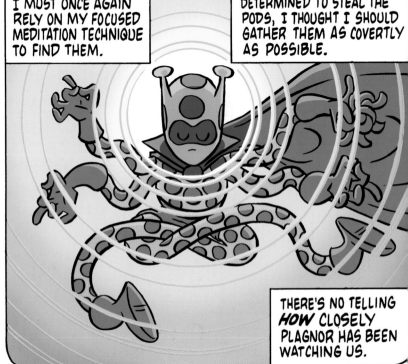

THERE'S NO TELLING *HOW* CLOSELY PLAGNOR HAS BEEN WATCHING US.

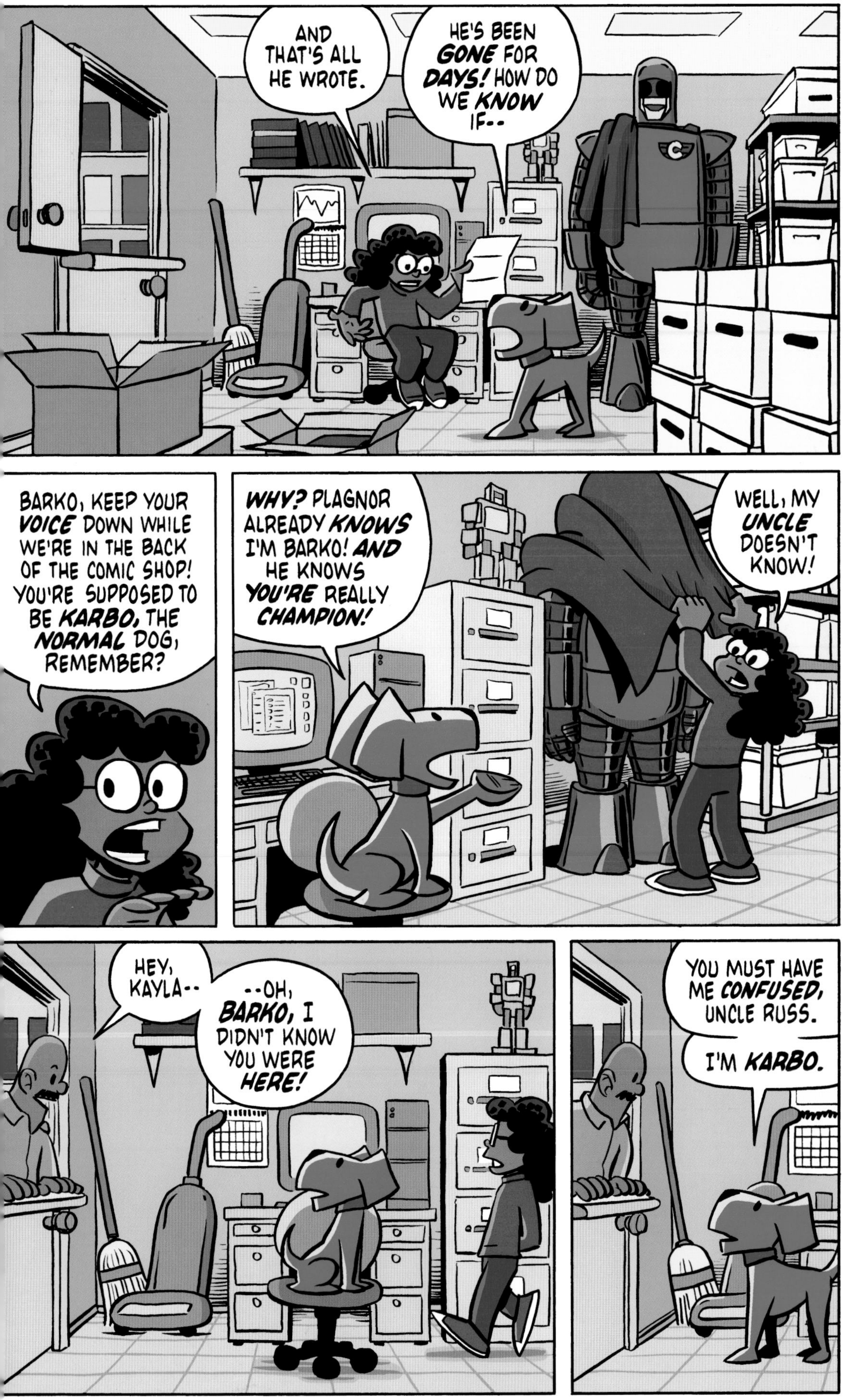
AND THAT'S ALL HE WROTE.
HE'S BEEN GONE FOR DAYS! HOW DO WE KNOW IF--
BARKO, KEEP YOUR VOICE DOWN WHILE WE'RE IN THE BACK OF THE COMIC SHOP! YOU'RE SUPPOSED TO BE KARBO, THE NORMAL DOG, REMEMBER?
WHY? PLAGNOR ALREADY KNOWS I'M BARKO! AND HE KNOWS YOU'RE REALLY CHAMPION!
WELL, MY UNCLE DOESN'T KNOW!
HEY, KAYLA--
--OH, BARKO, I DIDN'T KNOW YOU WERE HERE!
YOU MUST HAVE ME CONFUSED, UNCLE RUSS.
I'M KARBO.

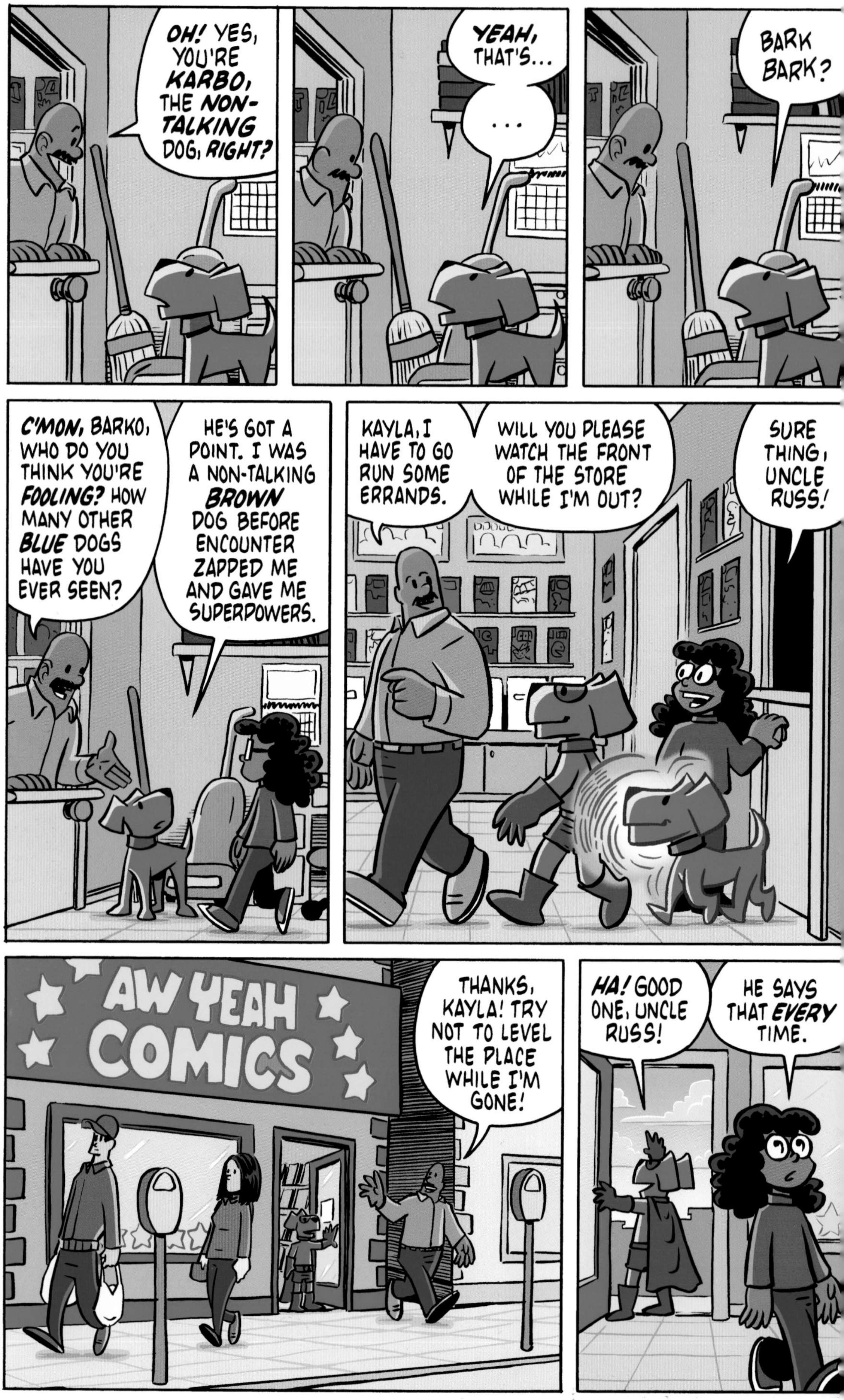
OH! YES, YOU'RE KARBO, THE NON-TALKING DOG, RIGHT?
YEAH, THAT'S...
...
BARK BARK?
C'MON, BARKO, WHO DO YOU THINK YOU'RE FOOLING? HOW MANY OTHER BLUE DOGS HAVE YOU EVER SEEN?
HE'S GOT A POINT. I WAS A NON-TALKING BROWN DOG BEFORE ENCOUNTER ZAPPED ME AND GAVE ME SUPERPOWERS.
KAYLA, I HAVE TO GO RUN SOME ERRANDS.
WILL YOU PLEASE WATCH THE FRONT OF THE STORE WHILE I'M OUT?
SURE THING, UNCLE RUSS!
AW YEAH COMICS
THANKS, KAYLA! TRY NOT TO LEVEL THE PLACE WHILE I'M GONE!
HA! GOOD ONE, UNCLE RUSS!
HE SAYS THAT EVERY TIME.

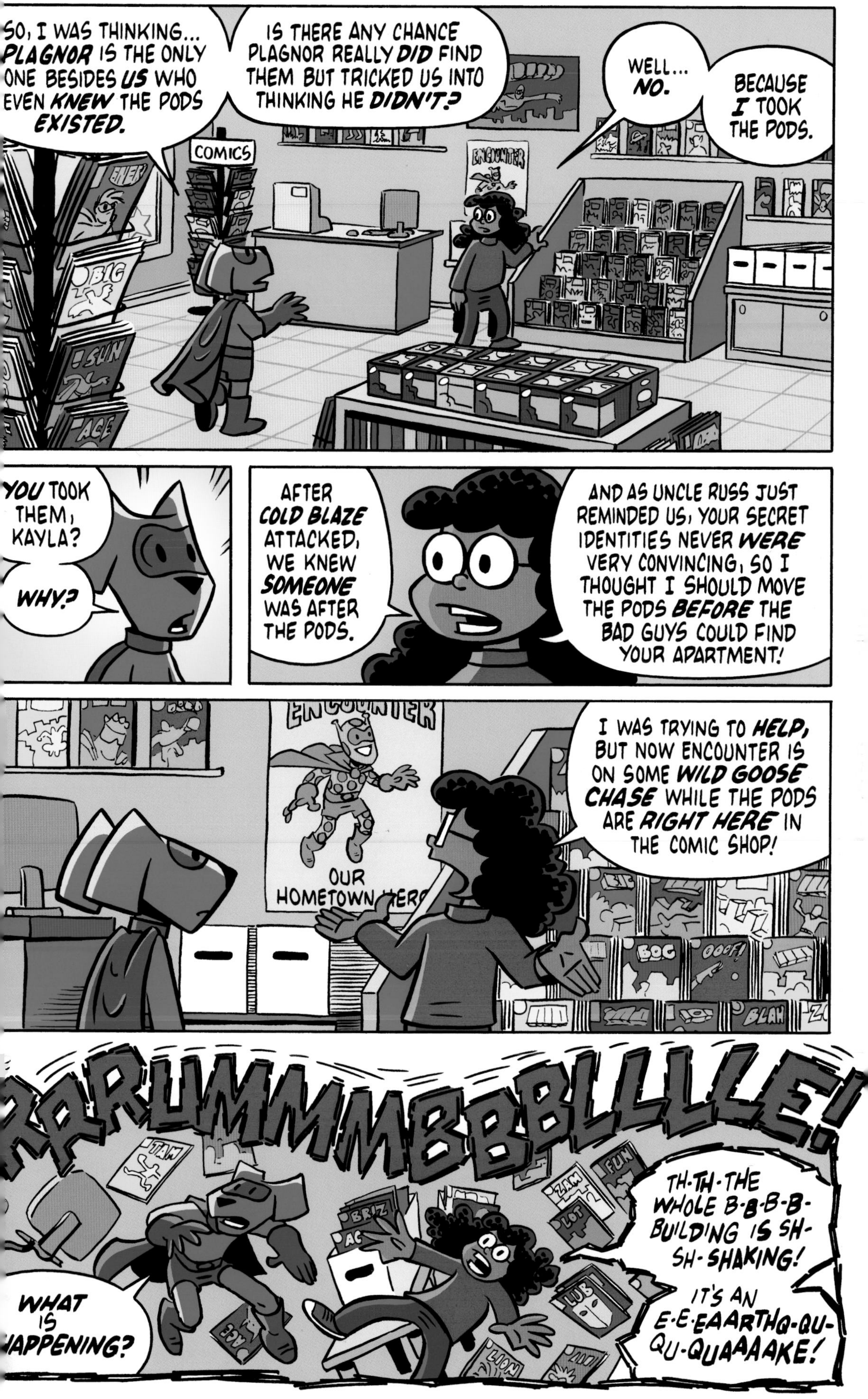

SO, I WAS THINKING... PLAGNOR IS THE ONLY ONE BESIDES US WHO EVEN KNEW THE PODS EXISTED.
IS THERE ANY CHANCE PLAGNOR REALLY DID FIND THEM BUT TRICKED US INTO THINKING HE DIDN'T?
WELL... NO.
BECAUSE I TOOK THE PODS.
COMICS
ENCOUNTER
YOU TOOK THEM, KAYLA?
WHY?
AFTER COLD BLAZE ATTACKED, WE KNEW SOMEONE WAS AFTER THE PODS.
AND AS UNCLE RUSS JUST REMINDED US, YOUR SECRET IDENTITIES NEVER WERE VERY CONVINCING, SO I THOUGHT I SHOULD MOVE THE PODS BEFORE THE BAD GUYS COULD FIND YOUR APARTMENT!
ENCOUNTER
OUR HOMETOWN HERO
I WAS TRYING TO HELP, BUT NOW ENCOUNTER IS ON SOME WILD GOOSE CHASE WHILE THE PODS ARE RIGHT HERE IN THE COMIC SHOP!
RRRUMMMMBBBLLLLE!
WHAT IS HAPPENING?
TH-TH-THE WHOLE B-B-B-B-BUILDING IS SH-SH-SHAKING!
IT'S AN E-E-EAARTHQ-QU-QU-QUAAAAKE!

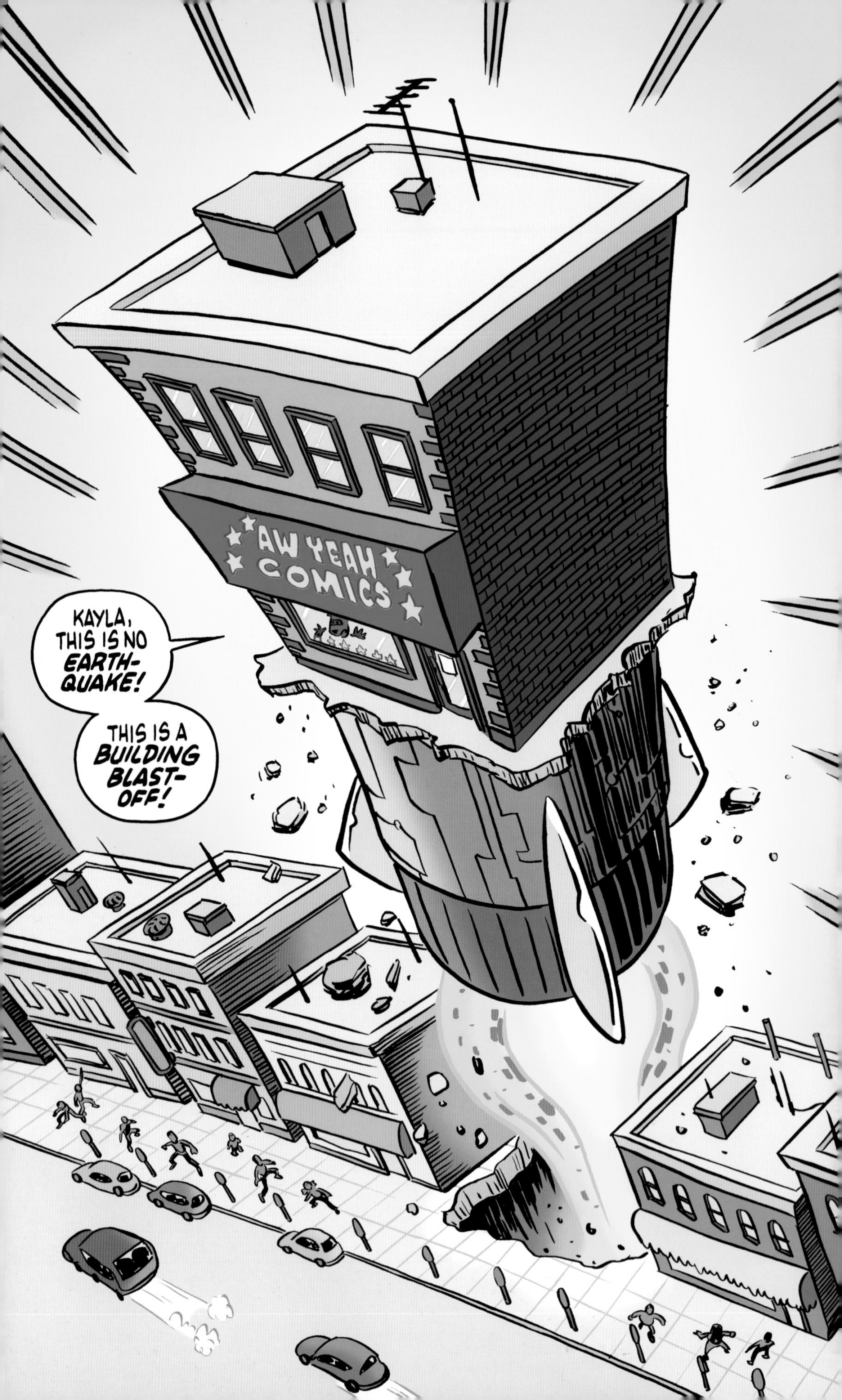
AW YEAH COMICS
KAYLA, THIS IS NO EARTH-QUAKE!
THIS IS A BUILDING BLAST-OFF!

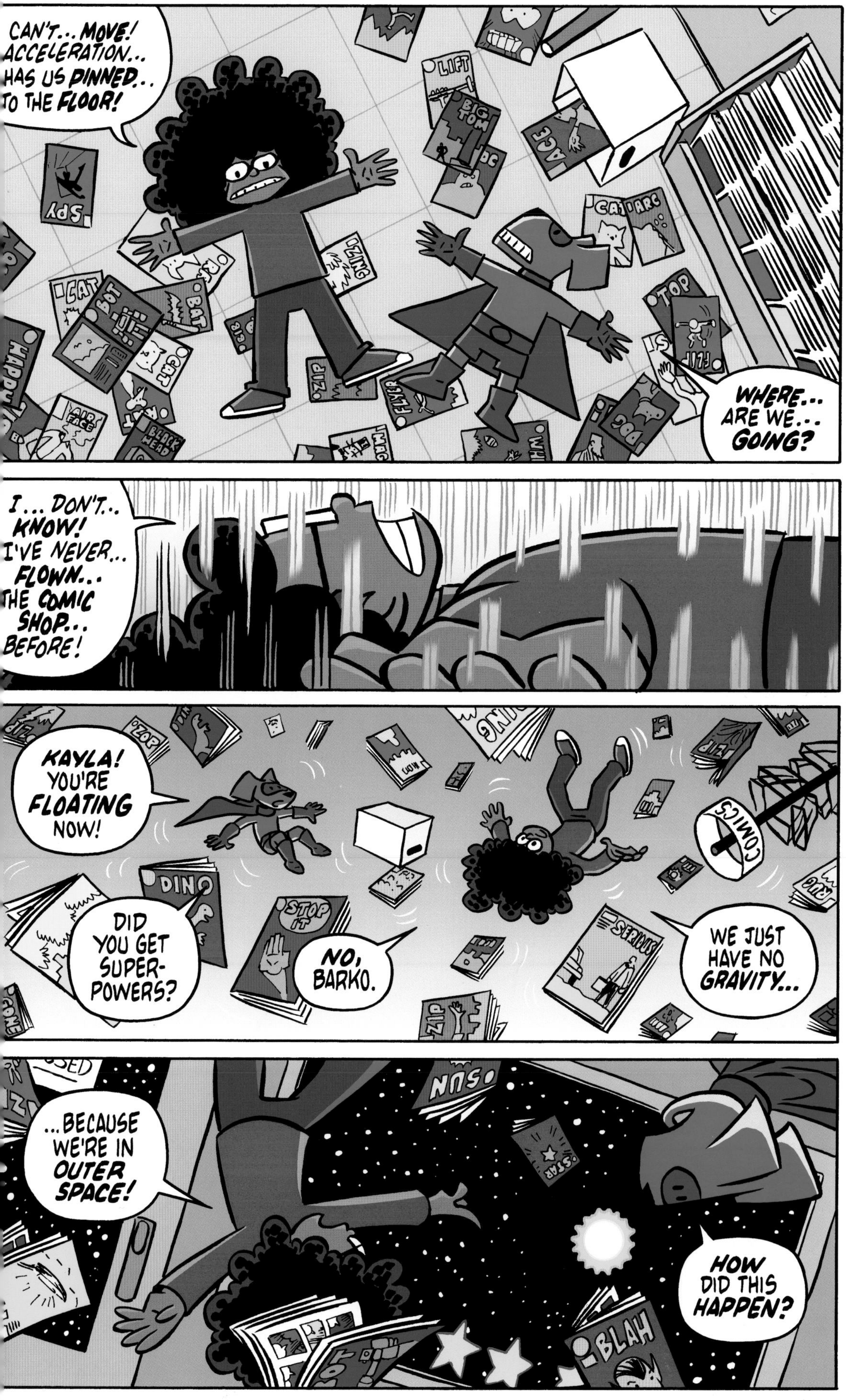
CAN'T... MOVE! ACCELERATION... HAS US PINNED... TO THE FLOOR!
WHERE... ARE WE... GOING?
I... DON'T... KNOW! I'VE NEVER... FLOWN... THE COMIC SHOP... BEFORE!
KAYLA! YOU'RE FLOATING NOW!
DID YOU GET SUPER-POWERS?
NO, BARKO.
WE JUST HAVE NO GRAVITY...
...BECAUSE WE'RE IN OUTER SPACE!
HOW DID THIS HAPPEN?

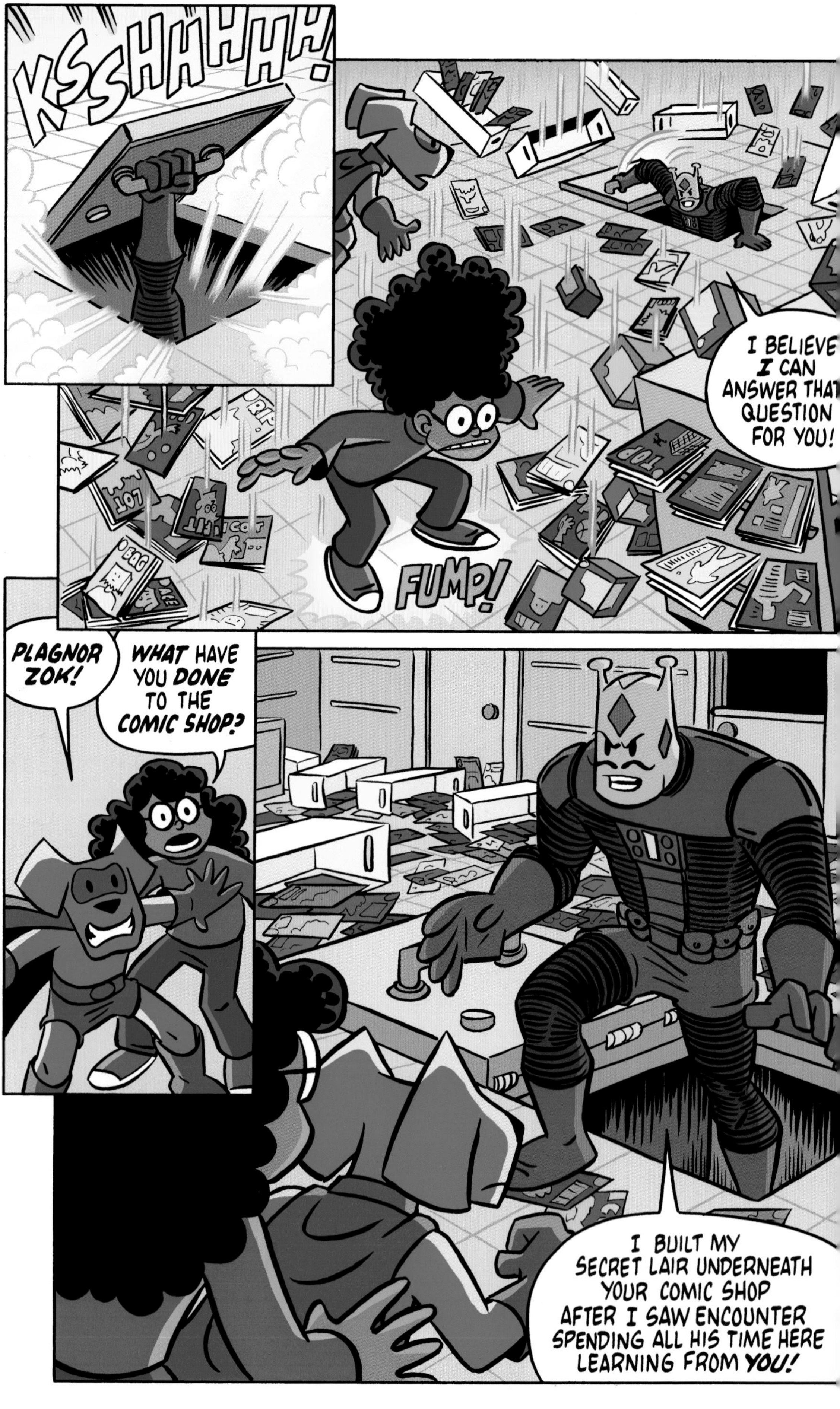

KSSHHHHH!
I BELIEVE I CAN ANSWER THAT QUESTION FOR YOU!
FUMP!
PLAGNOR ZOK!
WHAT HAVE YOU DONE TO THE COMIC SHOP?
I BUILT MY SECRET LAIR UNDERNEATH YOUR COMIC SHOP AFTER I SAW ENCOUNTER SPENDING ALL HIS TIME HERE LEARNING FROM YOU!

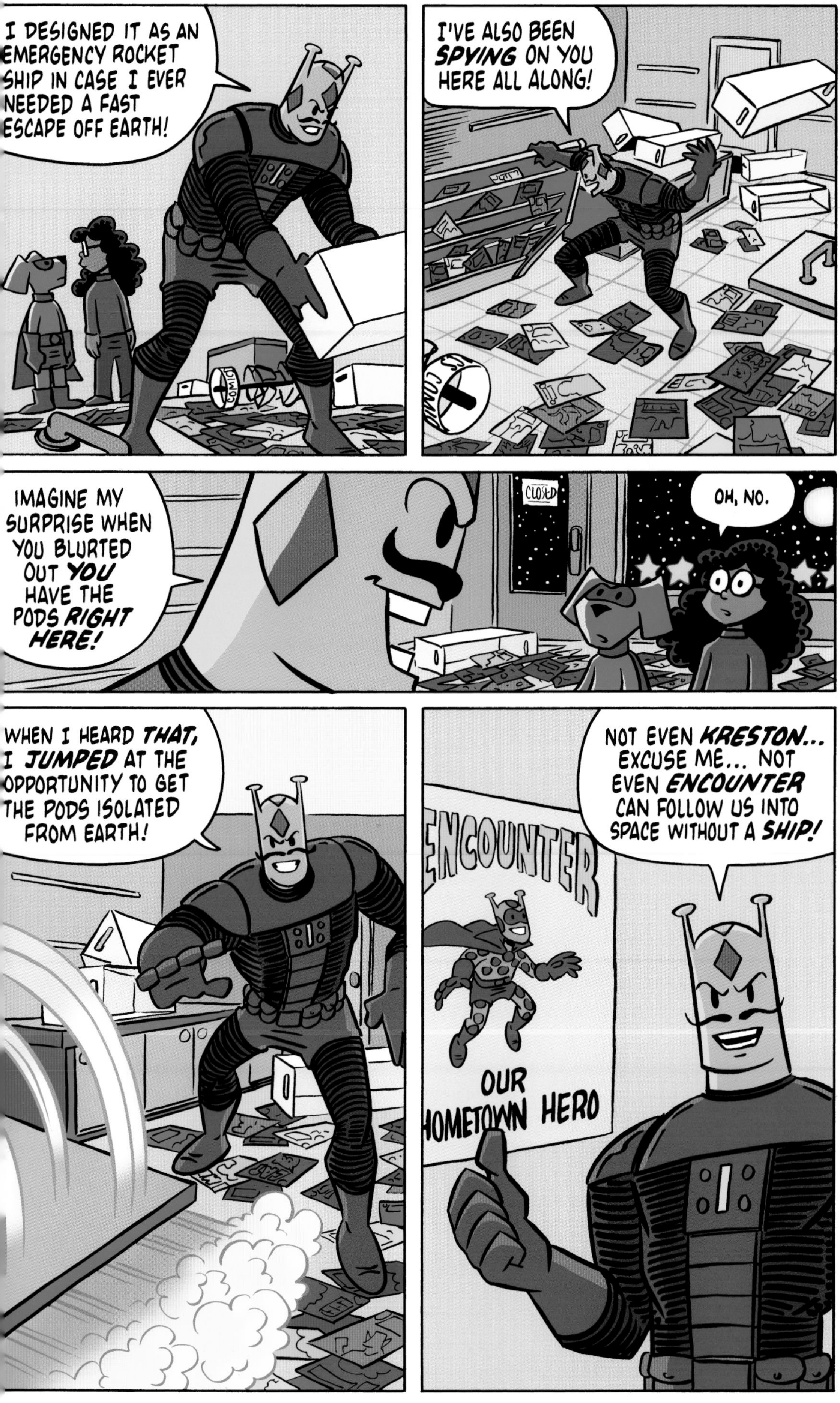
I DESIGNED IT AS AN EMERGENCY ROCKET SHIP IN CASE I EVER NEEDED A FAST ESCAPE OFF EARTH!
COMICS
I'VE ALSO BEEN SPYING ON YOU HERE ALL ALONG!
IMAGINE MY SURPRISE WHEN YOU BLURTED OUT YOU HAVE THE PODS RIGHT HERE!
CLOSED
OH, NO.
WHEN I HEARD THAT, I JUMPED AT THE OPPORTUNITY TO GET THE PODS ISOLATED FROM EARTH!
NOT EVEN KRESTON... EXCUSE ME... NOT EVEN ENCOUNTER CAN FOLLOW US INTO SPACE WITHOUT A SHIP!
ENCOUNTER
OUR HOMETOWN HERO

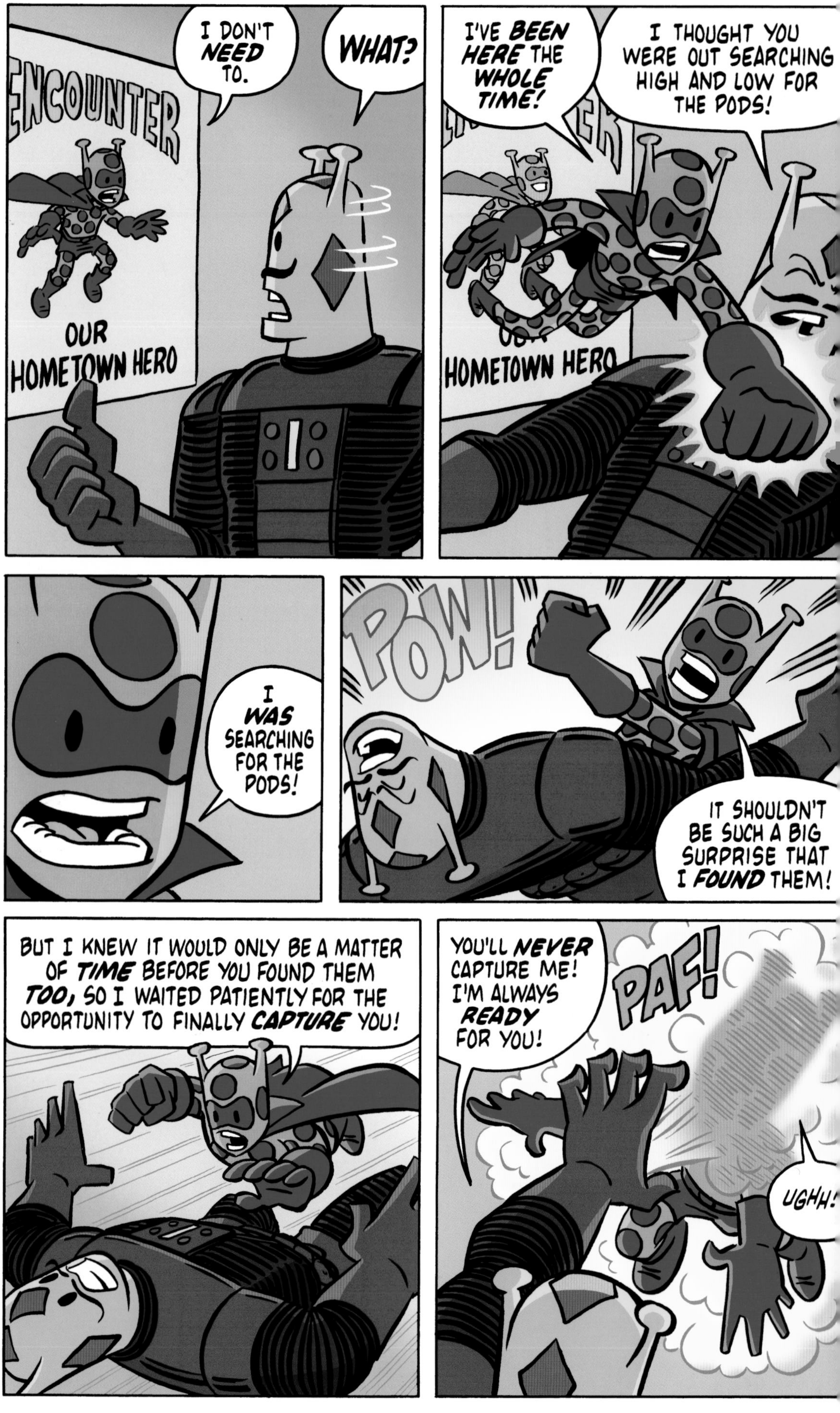

ENCOUNTER
OUR HOMETOWN HERO
I DON'T NEED TO.
WHAT?
I'VE BEEN HERE THE WHOLE TIME!
I THOUGHT YOU WERE OUT SEARCHING HIGH AND LOW FOR THE PODS!
HOMETOWN HERO
I WAS SEARCHING FOR THE PODS!
POW!
IT SHOULDN'T BE SUCH A BIG SURPRISE THAT I FOUND THEM!
BUT I KNEW IT WOULD ONLY BE A MATTER OF TIME BEFORE YOU FOUND THEM TOO, SO I WAITED PATIENTLY FOR THE OPPORTUNITY TO FINALLY CAPTURE YOU!
YOU'LL NEVER CAPTURE ME! I'M ALWAYS READY FOR YOU!
PAF!
UGHH!

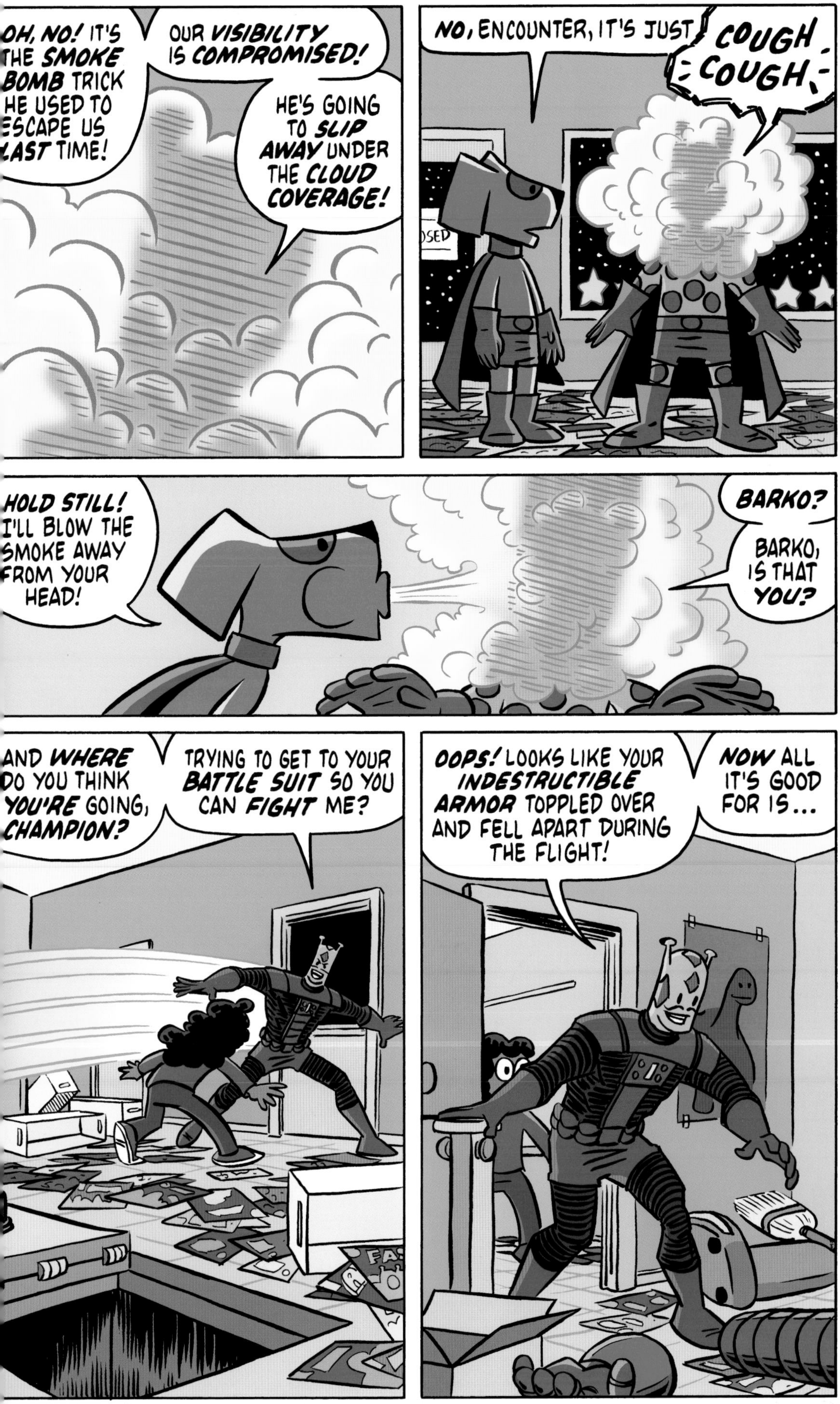

OH, NO! IT'S THE SMOKE BOMB TRICK HE USED TO ESCAPE US LAST TIME!
OUR VISIBILITY IS COMPROMISED!
HE'S GOING TO SLIP AWAY UNDER THE CLOUD COVERAGE!
NO, ENCOUNTER, IT'S JUST
COUGH COUGH
HOLD STILL! I'LL BLOW THE SMOKE AWAY FROM YOUR HEAD!
BARKO?
BARKO, IS THAT YOU?
AND WHERE DO YOU THINK YOU'RE GOING, CHAMPION?
TRYING TO GET TO YOUR BATTLE SUIT SO YOU CAN FIGHT ME?
OOPS! LOOKS LIKE YOUR INDESTRUCTIBLE ARMOR TOPPLED OVER AND FELL APART DURING THE FLIGHT!
NOW ALL IT'S GOOD FOR IS...

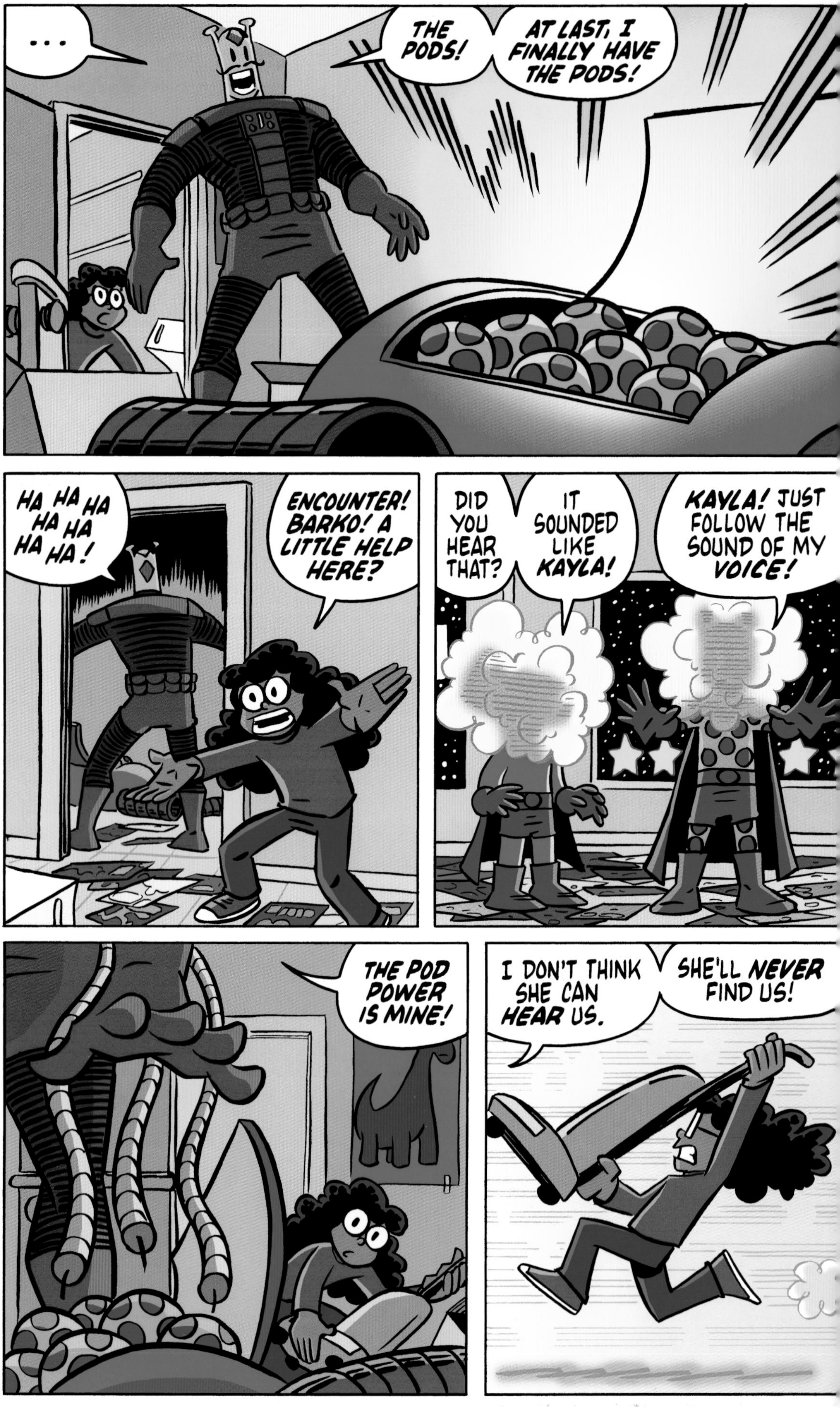
...
THE PODS!
AT LAST, I FINALLY HAVE THE PODS!
HA HA HA HA HA HA HA!
ENCOUNTER! BARKO! A LITTLE HELP HERE?
DID YOU HEAR THAT?
IT SOUNDED LIKE KAYLA!
KAYLA! JUST FOLLOW THE SOUND OF MY VOICE!
THE POD POWER IS MINE!
I DON'T THINK SHE CAN HEAR US.
SHE'LL NEVER FIND US!

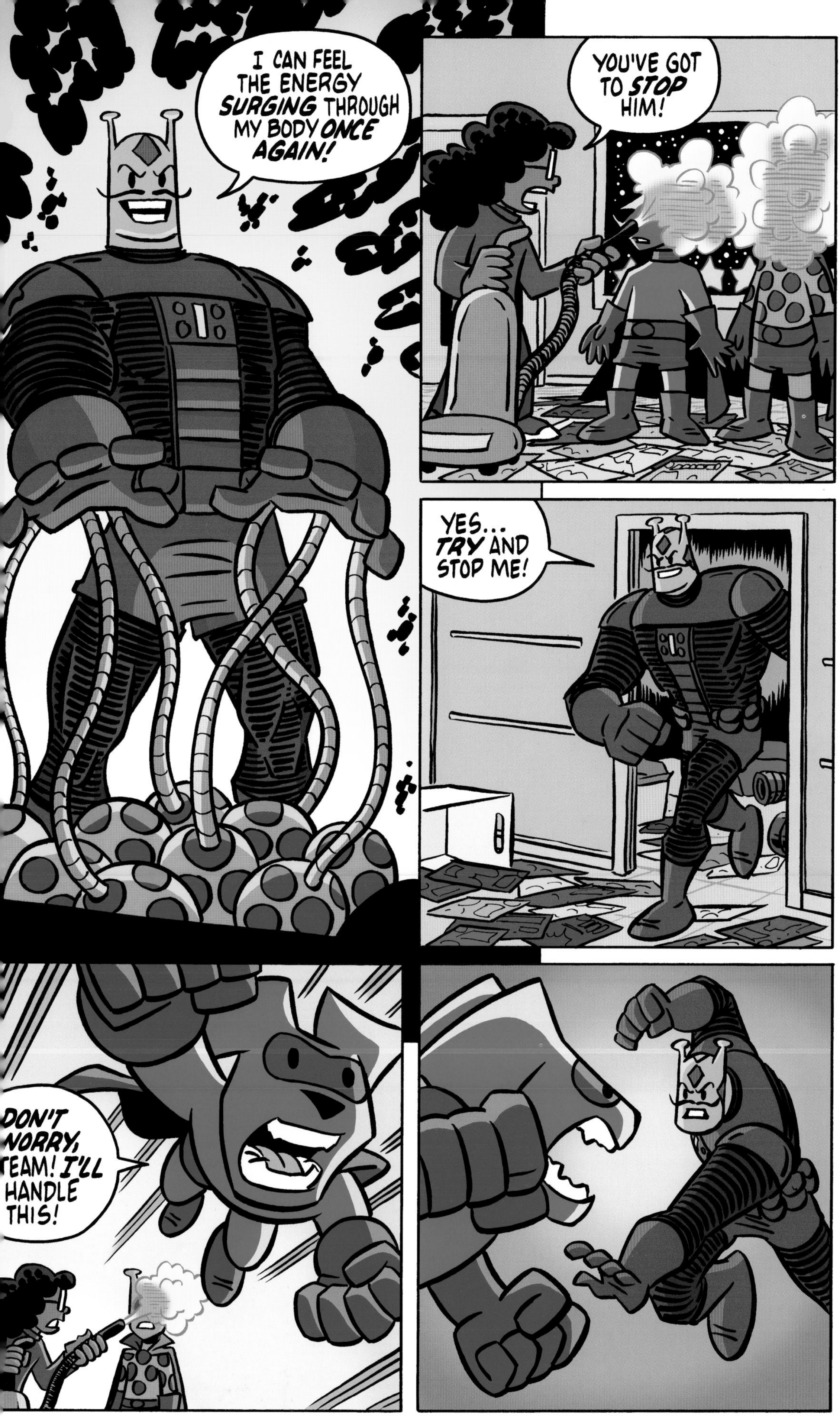
I CAN FEEL THE ENERGY SURGING THROUGH MY BODY ONCE AGAIN!
YOU'VE GOT TO STOP HIM!
YES... TRY AND STOP ME!
DON'T WORRY, TEAM! I'LL HANDLE THIS!

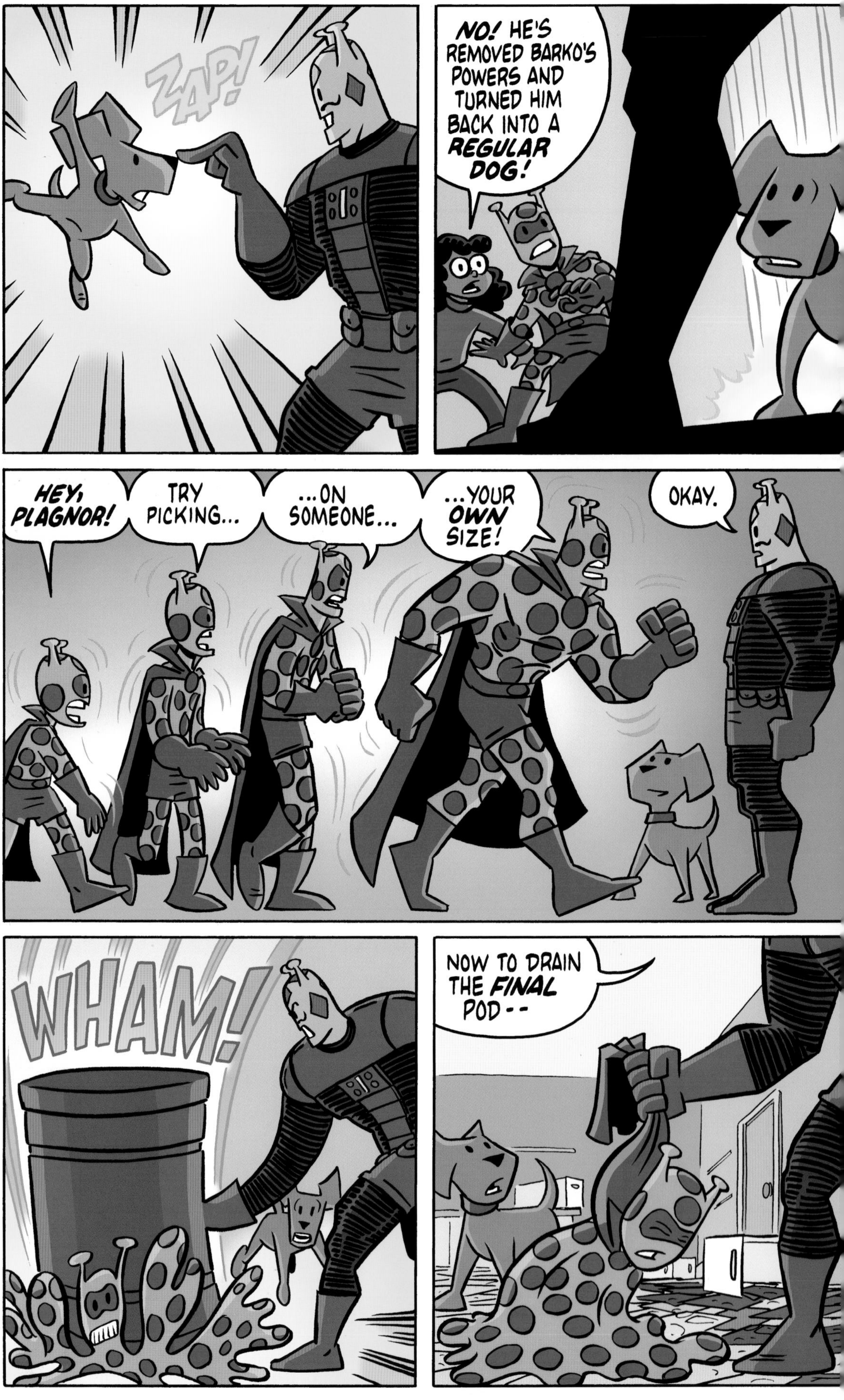

ZAP!
NO! HE'S REMOVED BARKO'S POWERS AND TURNED HIM BACK INTO A REGULAR DOG!
HEY, PLAGNOR!
TRY PICKING...
...ON SOMEONE...
...YOUR OWN SIZE!
OKAY.
WHAM!
NOW TO DRAIN THE FINAL POD--

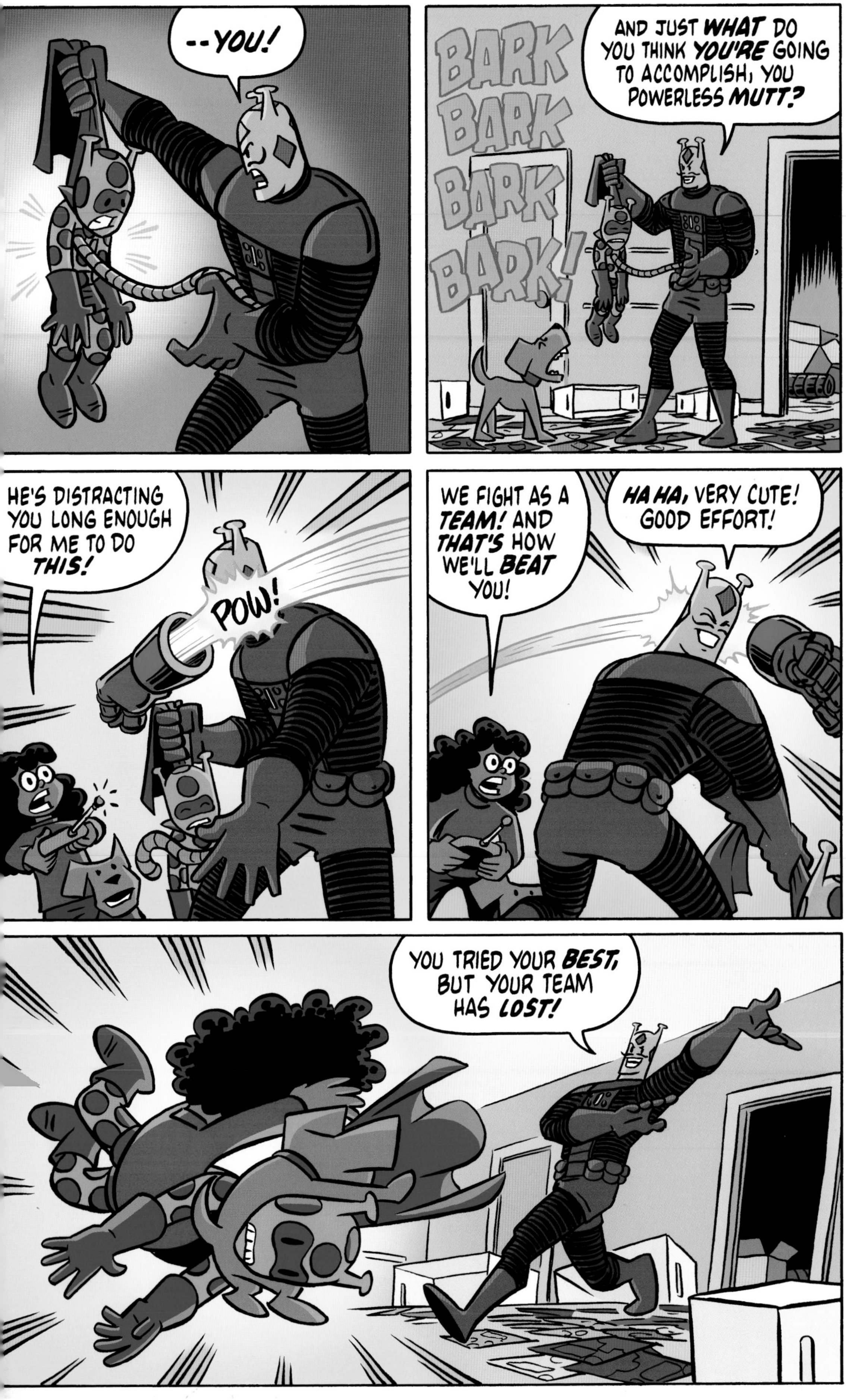

--YOU!
BARK BARK BARK BARK!
AND JUST WHAT DO YOU THINK YOU'RE GOING TO ACCOMPLISH, YOU POWERLESS MUTT?
HE'S DISTRACTING YOU LONG ENOUGH FOR ME TO DO THIS!
POW!
WE FIGHT AS A TEAM! AND THAT'S HOW WE'LL BEAT YOU!
HA HA, VERY CUTE! GOOD EFFORT!
YOU TRIED YOUR BEST, BUT YOUR TEAM HAS LOST!

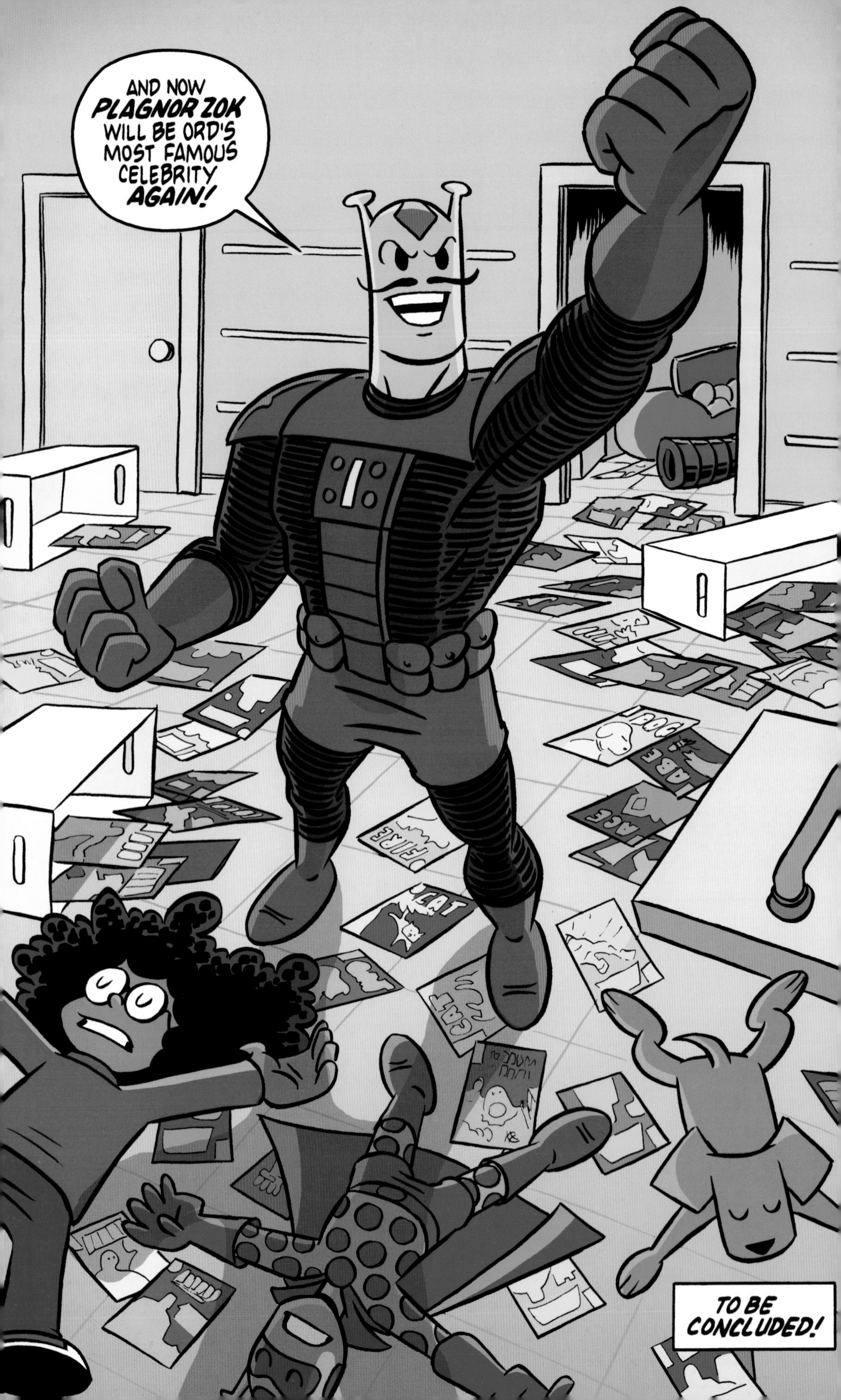
AND NOW PLAGNOR ZOK WILL BE ORD'S MOST FAMOUS CELEBRITY AGAIN!
TO BE CONCLUDED!

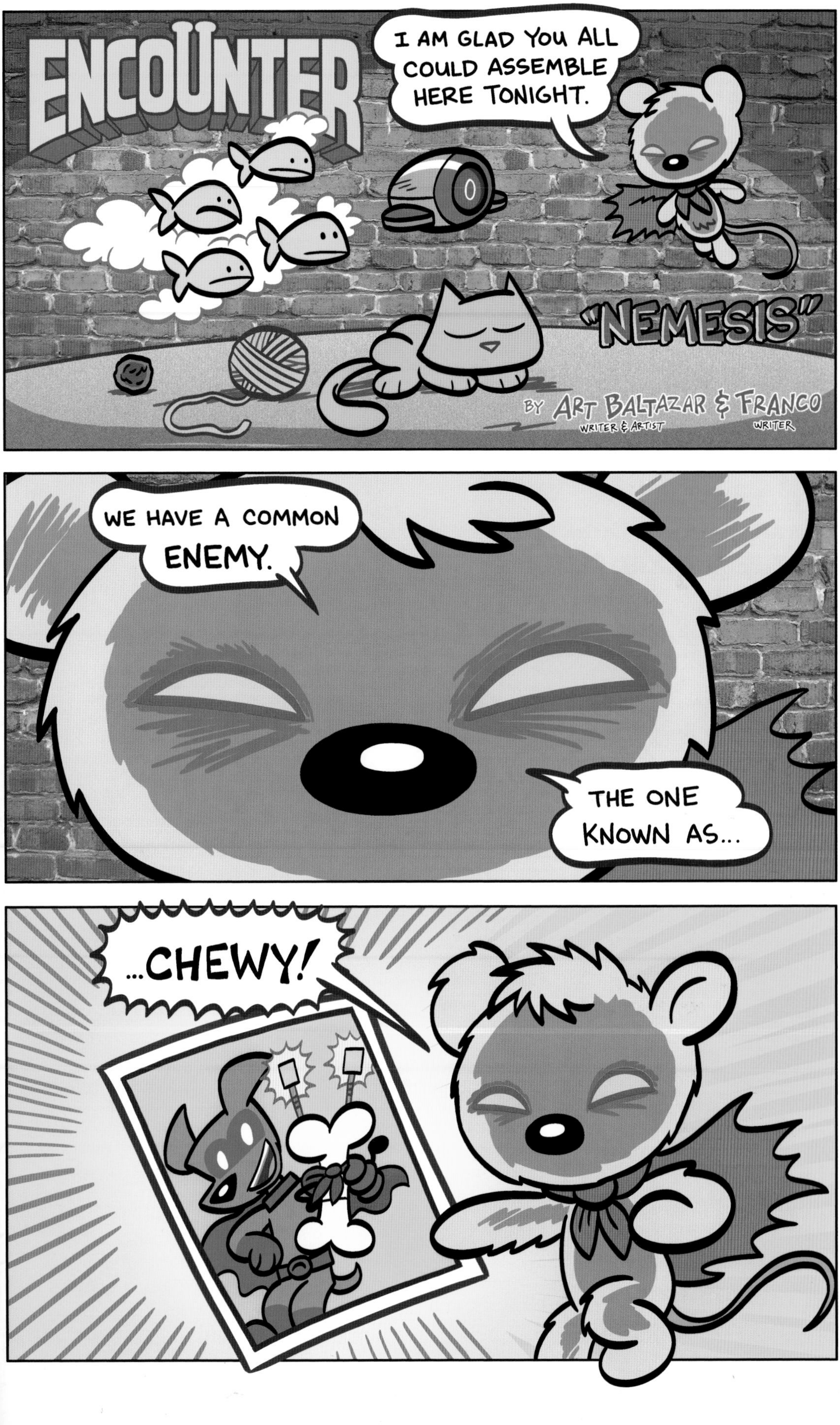
ENCOUNTER
I AM GLAD YOU ALL COULD ASSEMBLE HERE TONIGHT.
"NEMESIS"
BY ART BALTAZAR WRITER & ARTIST & FRANCO WRITER
WE HAVE A COMMON ENEMY.
THE ONE KNOWN AS...
...CHEWY!

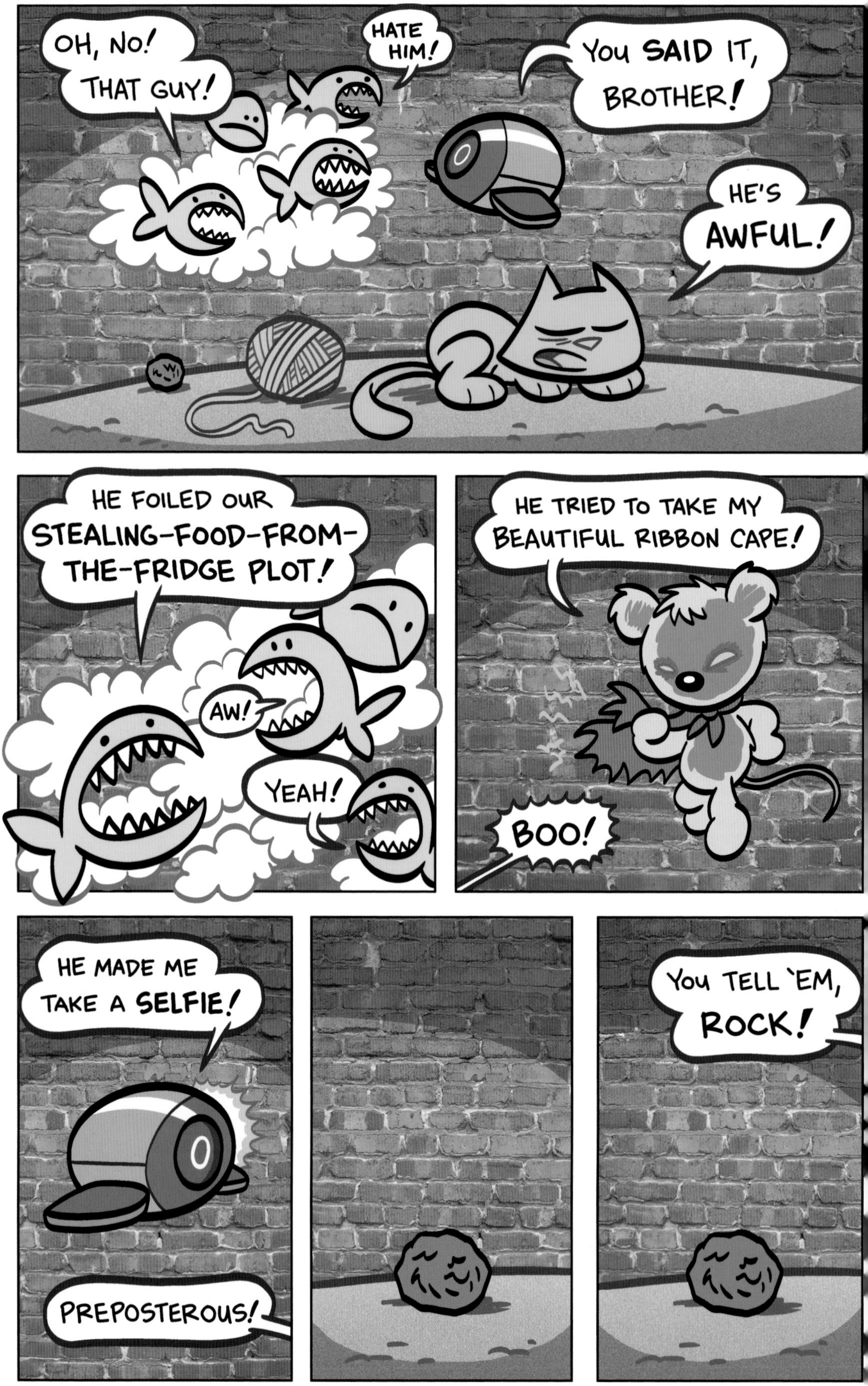

OH, NO! THAT GUY!
HATE HIM!
YOU SAID IT, BROTHER!
HE'S AWFUL!
HE FOILED OUR STEALING-FOOD-FROM-THE-FRIDGE PLOT!
AW!
YEAH!
HE TRIED TO TAKE MY BEAUTIFUL RIBBON CAPE!
BOO!
HE MADE ME TAKE A SELFIE!
PREPOSTEROUS!
YOU TELL 'EM, ROCK!

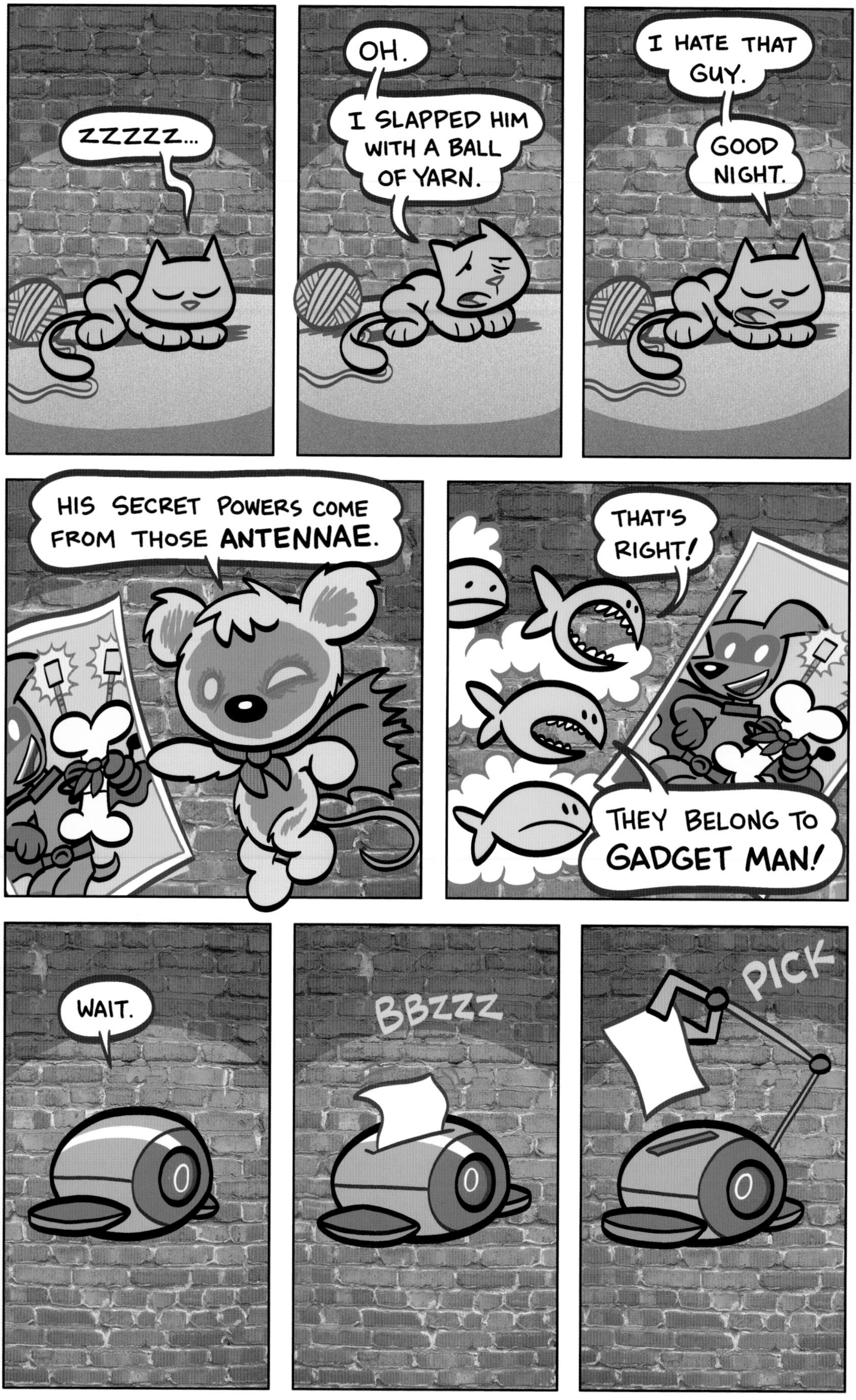
ZZZZZ...
OH.
I SLAPPED HIM WITH A BALL OF YARN.
I HATE THAT GUY.
GOOD NIGHT.
HIS SECRET POWERS COME FROM THOSE ANTENNAE.
THAT'S RIGHT!
THEY BELONG TO GADGET MAN!
WAIT.
BBZZZ
PICK

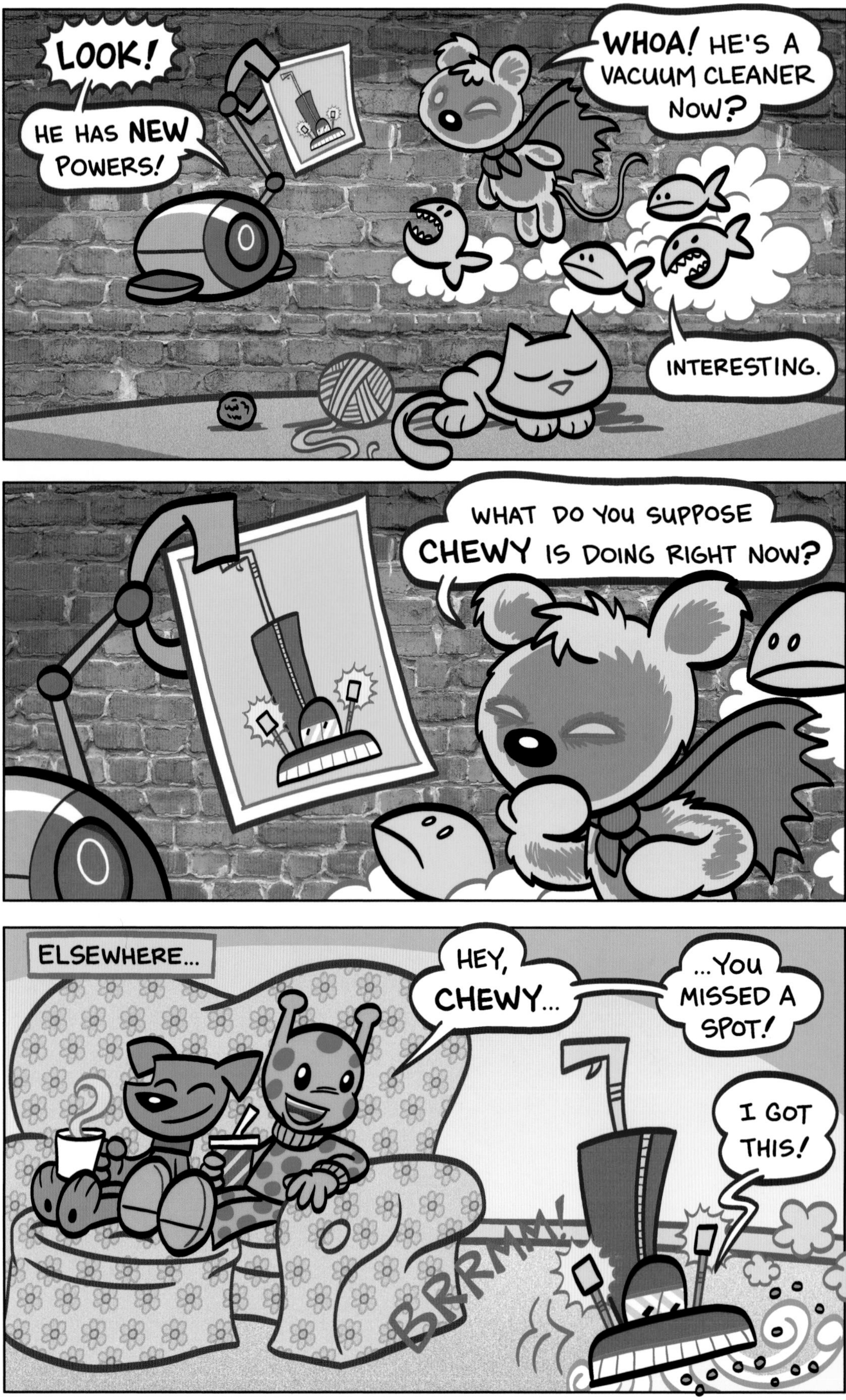
LOOK!
HE HAS NEW POWERS!
WHOA! HE'S A VACUUM CLEANER NOW?
INTERESTING.
WHAT DO YOU SUPPOSE CHEWY IS DOING RIGHT NOW?
ELSEWHERE...
HEY, CHEWY...
...YOU MISSED A SPOT!
I GOT THIS!
BRRMM!

–CLEAN UP TIME!

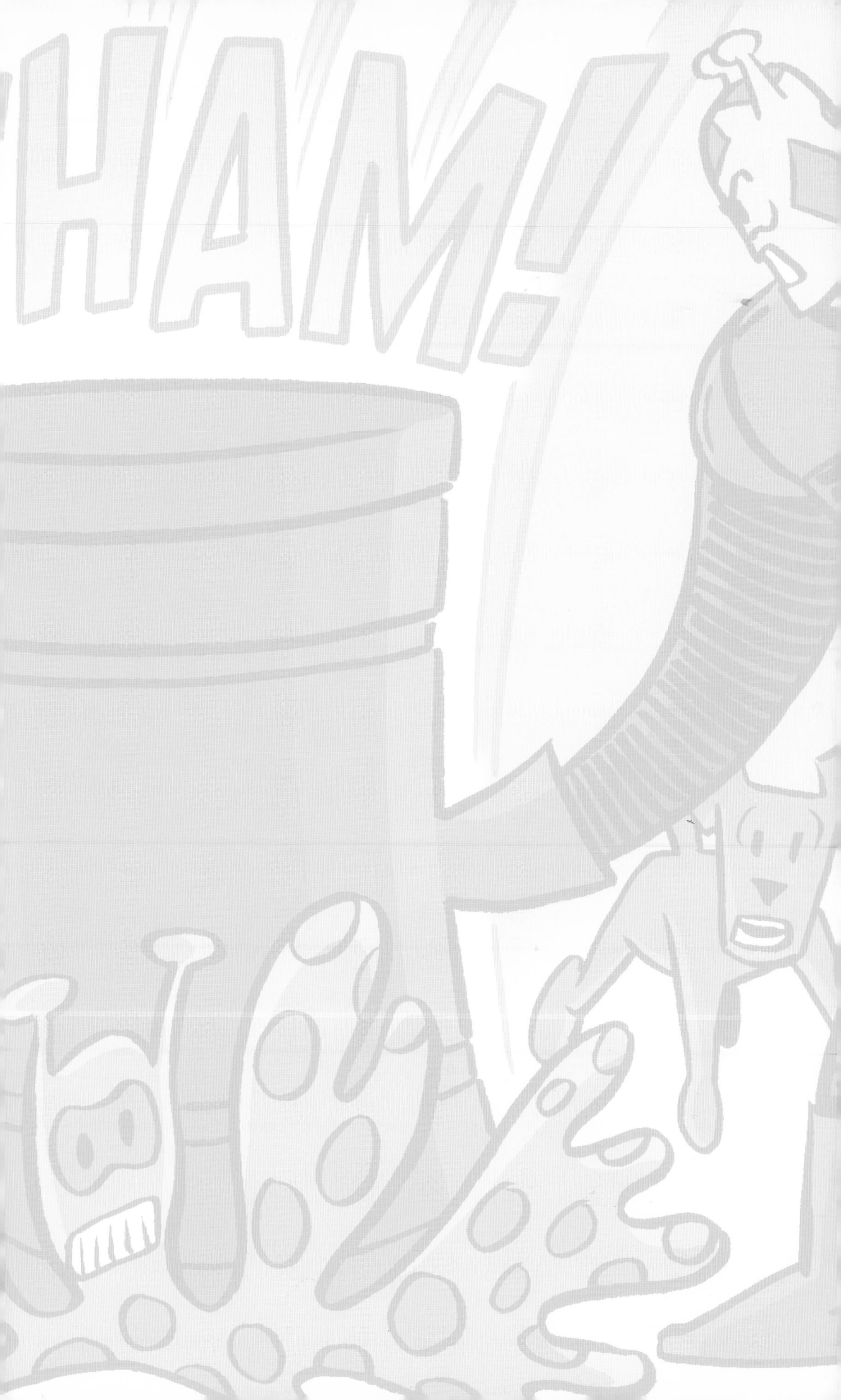
HAM!

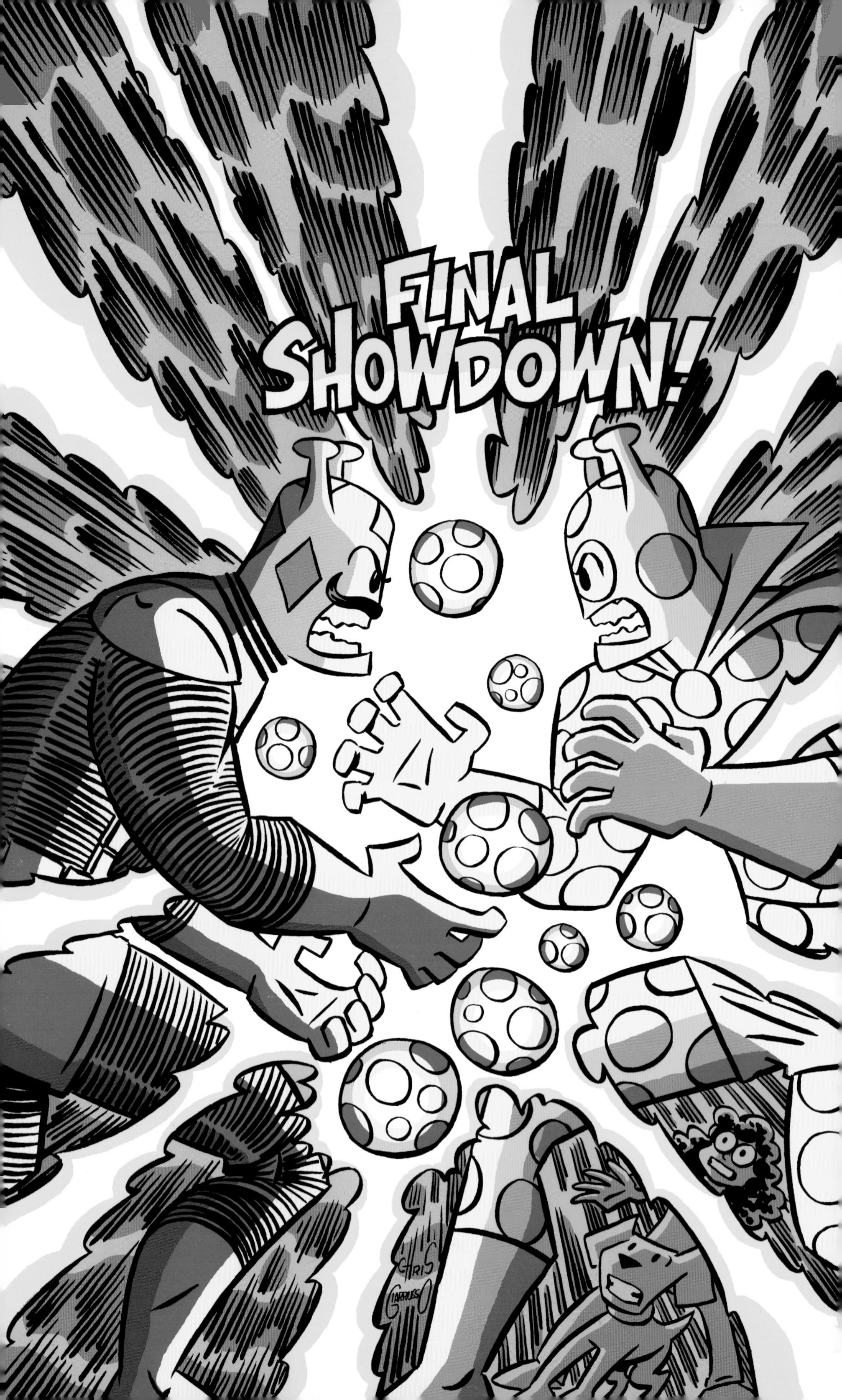
FINAL SHOWDOWN!

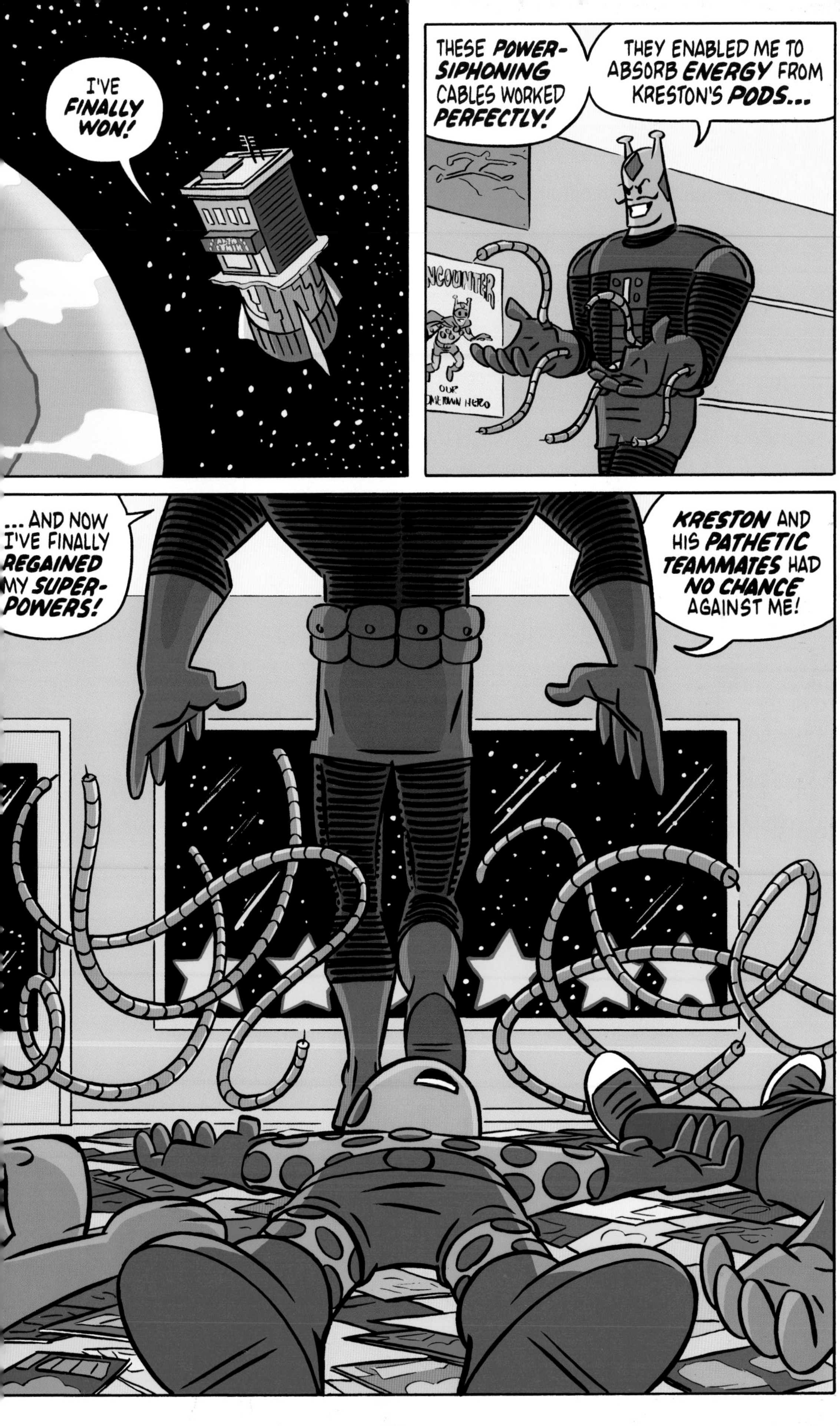
I'VE FINALLY WON!
THESE POWER-SIPHONING CABLES WORKED PERFECTLY!
THEY ENABLED ME TO ABSORB ENERGY FROM KRESTON'S PODS...
... AND NOW I'VE FINALLY REGAINED MY SUPER-POWERS!
KRESTON AND HIS PATHETIC TEAMMATES HAD NO CHANCE AGAINST ME!

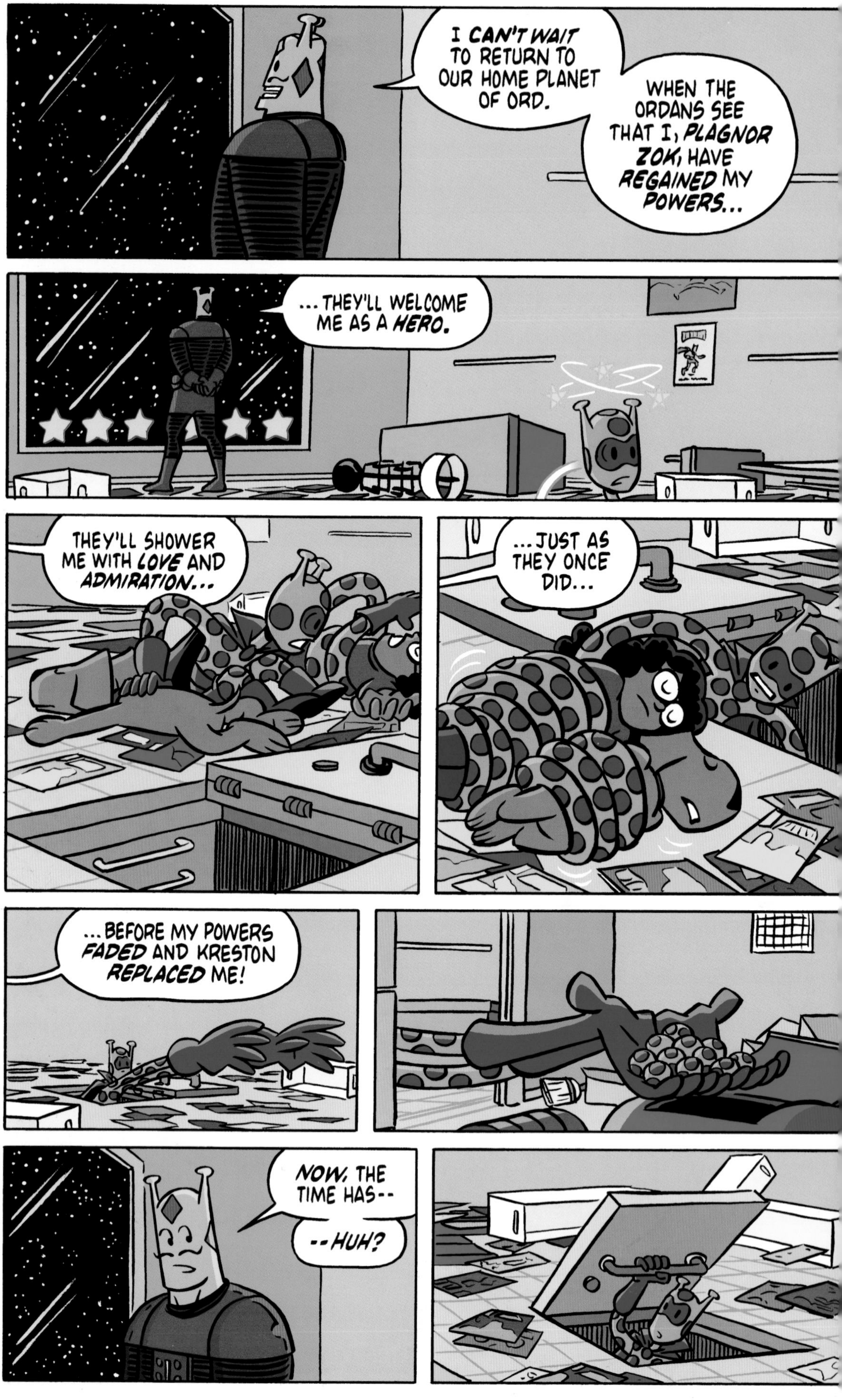
I CAN'T WAIT TO RETURN TO OUR HOME PLANET OF ORD.
WHEN THE ORDANS SEE THAT I, PLAGNOR ZOK, HAVE REGAINED MY POWERS...
...THEY'LL WELCOME ME AS A HERO.
THEY'LL SHOWER ME WITH LOVE AND ADMIRATION...
...JUST AS THEY ONCE DID...
...BEFORE MY POWERS FADED AND KRESTON REPLACED ME!
NOW, THE TIME HAS--
--HUH?

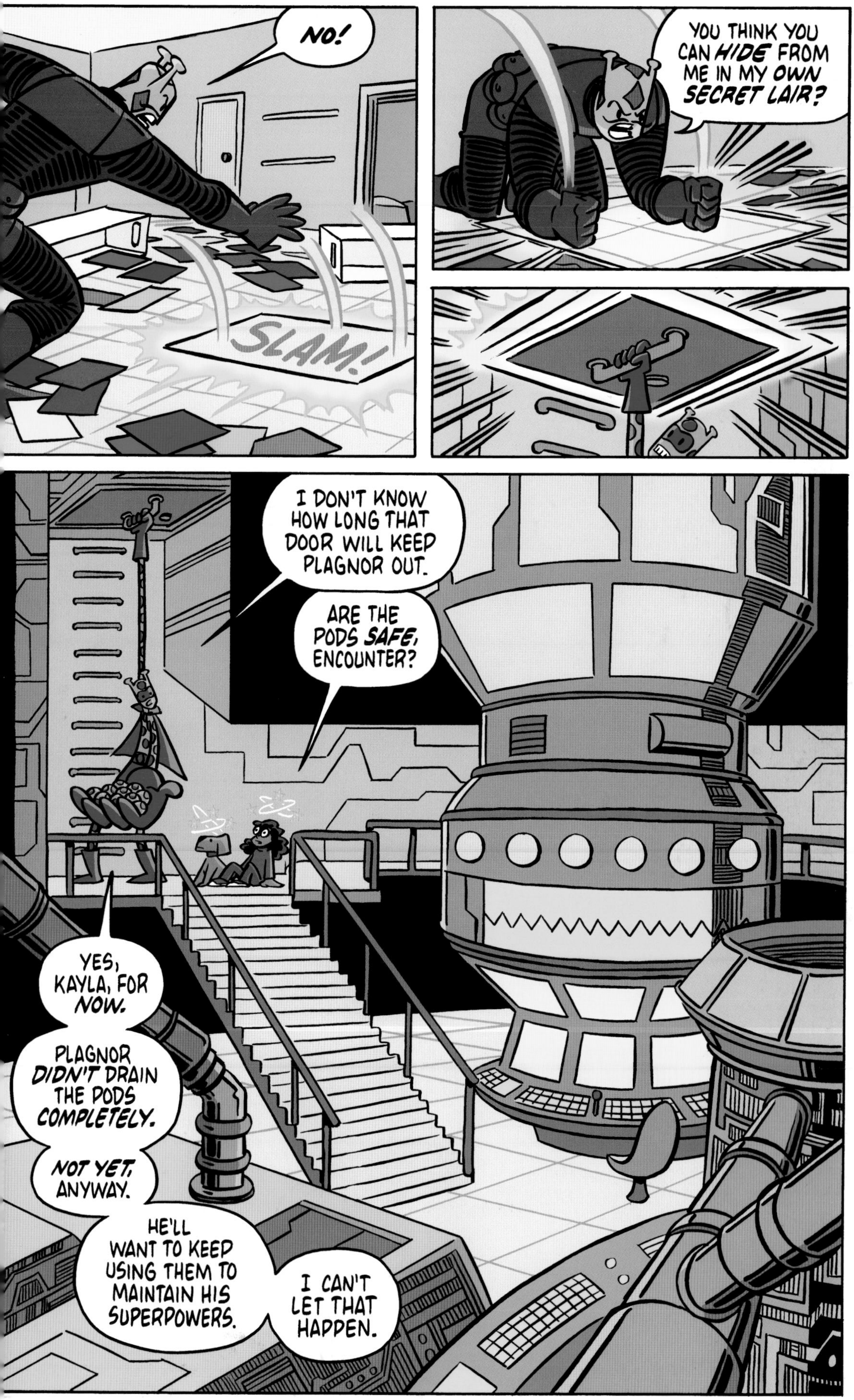
NO!
SLAM!
YOU THINK YOU CAN HIDE FROM ME IN MY OWN SECRET LAIR?
I DON'T KNOW HOW LONG THAT DOOR WILL KEEP PLAGNOR OUT.
ARE THE PODS SAFE, ENCOUNTER?
YES, KAYLA, FOR NOW.
PLAGNOR DIDN'T DRAIN THE PODS COMPLETELY.
NOT YET, ANYWAY.
HE'LL WANT TO KEEP USING THEM TO MAINTAIN HIS SUPERPOWERS.
I CAN'T LET THAT HAPPEN.

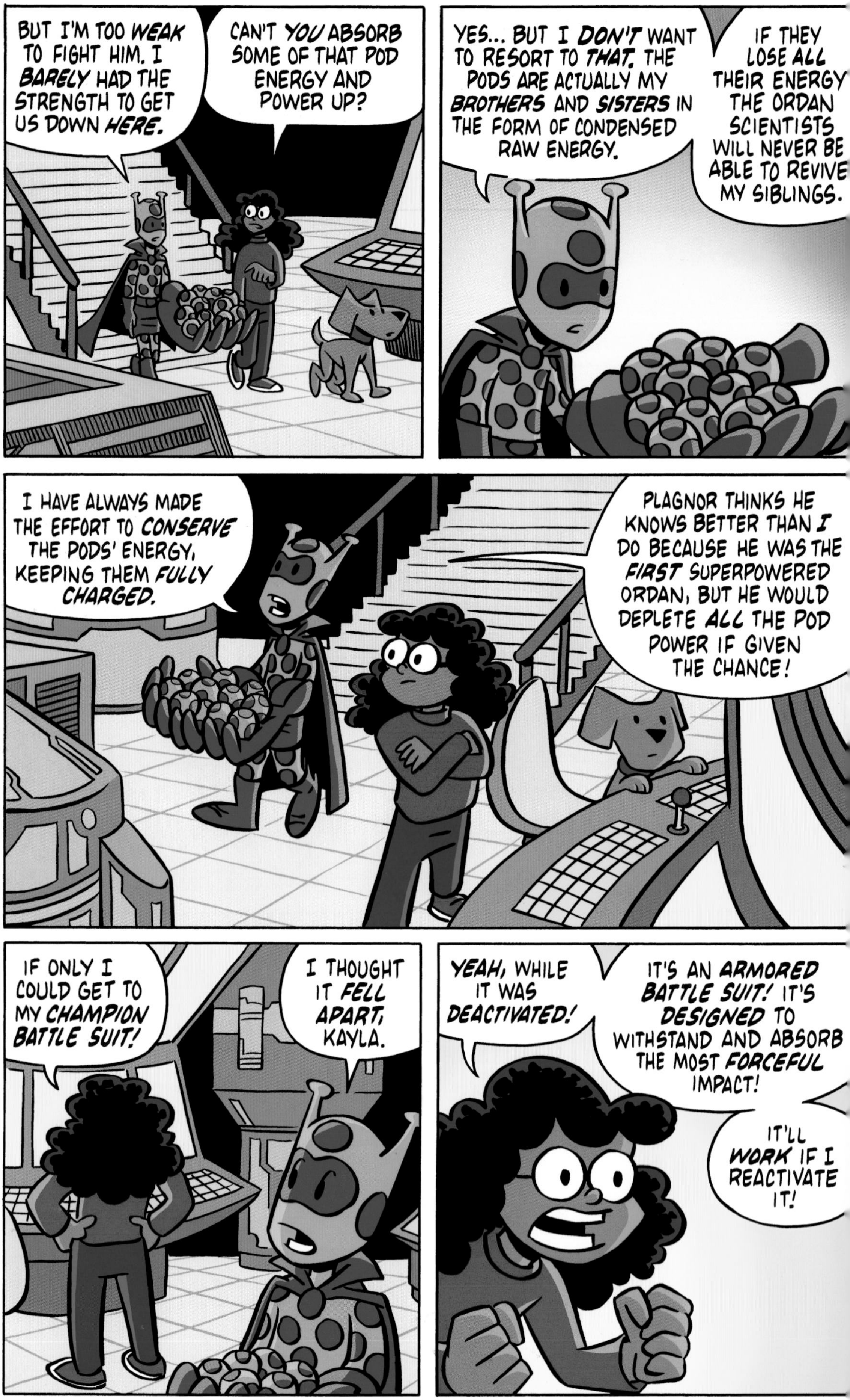

BUT I'M TOO WEAK TO FIGHT HIM. I BARELY HAD THE STRENGTH TO GET US DOWN HERE.
CAN'T YOU ABSORB SOME OF THAT POD ENERGY AND POWER UP?
YES... BUT I DON'T WANT TO RESORT TO THAT. THE PODS ARE ACTUALLY MY BROTHERS AND SISTERS IN THE FORM OF CONDENSED RAW ENERGY.
IF THEY LOSE ALL THEIR ENERGY THE ORDAN SCIENTISTS WILL NEVER BE ABLE TO REVIVE MY SIBLINGS.
I HAVE ALWAYS MADE THE EFFORT TO CONSERVE THE PODS' ENERGY, KEEPING THEM FULLY CHARGED.
PLAGNOR THINKS HE KNOWS BETTER THAN I DO BECAUSE HE WAS THE FIRST SUPERPOWERED ORDAN, BUT HE WOULD DEPLETE ALL THE POD POWER IF GIVEN THE CHANCE!
IF ONLY I COULD GET TO MY CHAMPION BATTLE SUIT!
I THOUGHT IT FELL APART, KAYLA.
YEAH, WHILE IT WAS DEACTIVATED!
IT'S AN ARMORED BATTLE SUIT! IT'S DESIGNED TO WITHSTAND AND ABSORB THE MOST FORCEFUL IMPACT!
IT'LL WORK IF I REACTIVATE IT!

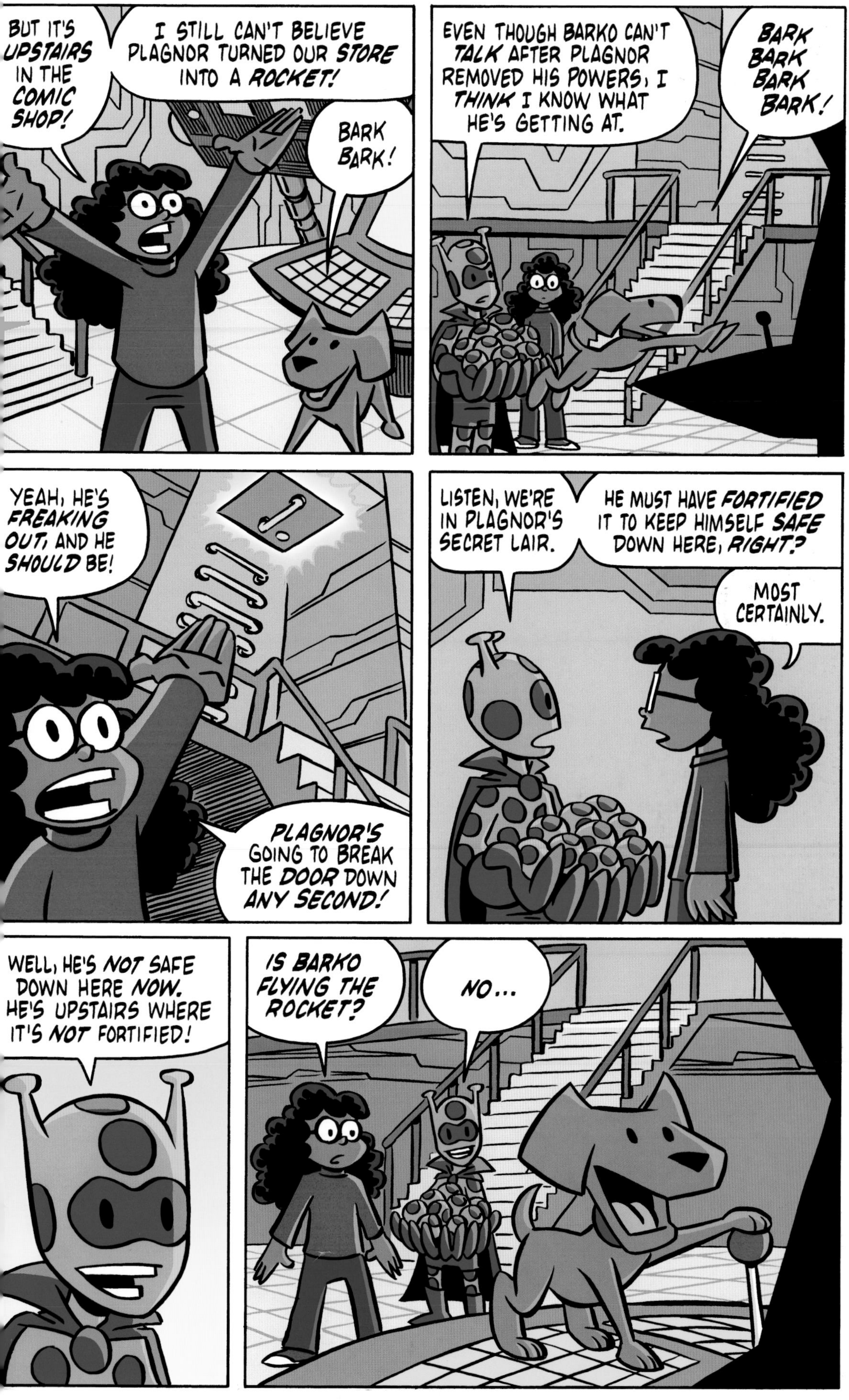

I STILL CAN'T BELIEVE PLAGNOR TURNED OUR STORE INTO A ROCKET!
BUT IT'S UPSTAIRS IN THE COMIC SHOP!
BARK BARK!
EVEN THOUGH BARKO CAN'T TALK AFTER PLAGNOR REMOVED HIS POWERS, I THINK I KNOW WHAT HE'S GETTING AT.
BARK BARK BARK BARK!
YEAH, HE'S FREAKING OUT, AND HE SHOULD BE!
PLAGNOR'S GOING TO BREAK THE DOOR DOWN ANY SECOND!
LISTEN, WE'RE IN PLAGNOR'S SECRET LAIR.
HE MUST HAVE FORTIFIED IT TO KEEP HIMSELF SAFE DOWN HERE, RIGHT?
MOST CERTAINLY.
WELL, HE'S NOT SAFE DOWN HERE NOW. HE'S UPSTAIRS WHERE IT'S NOT FORTIFIED!
IS BARKO FLYING THE ROCKET?
NO...

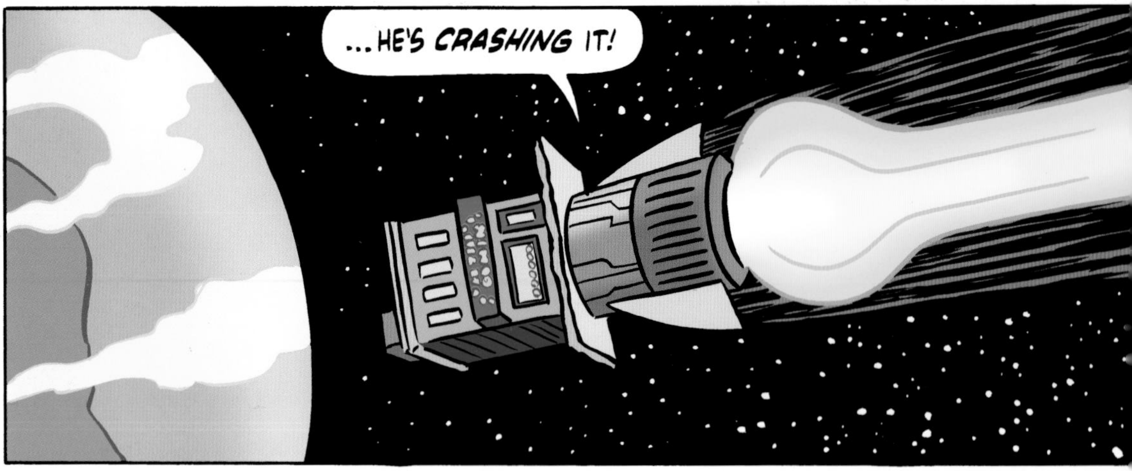
...HE'S CRASHING IT!

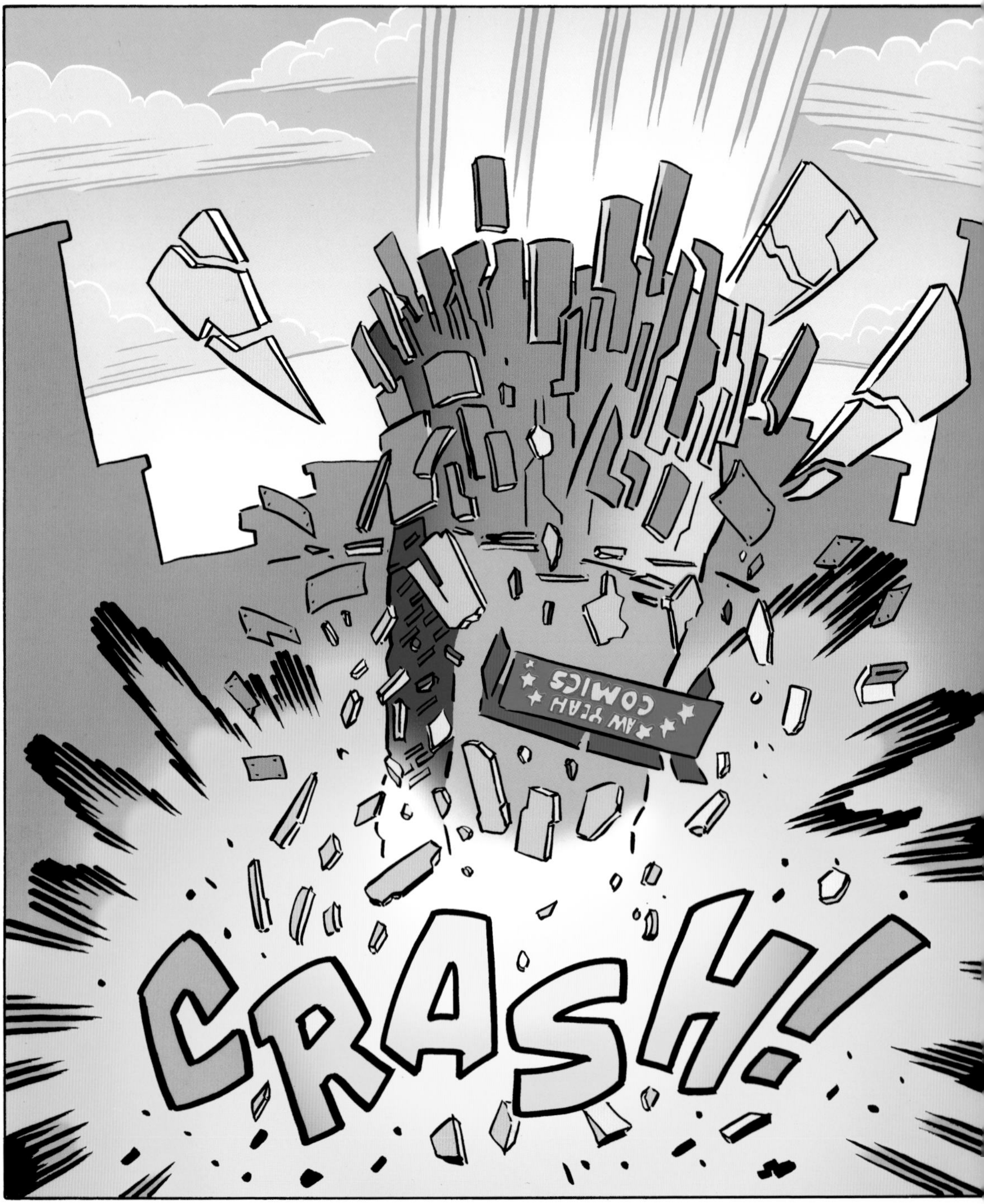
AW YEAH COMICS
CRASH!

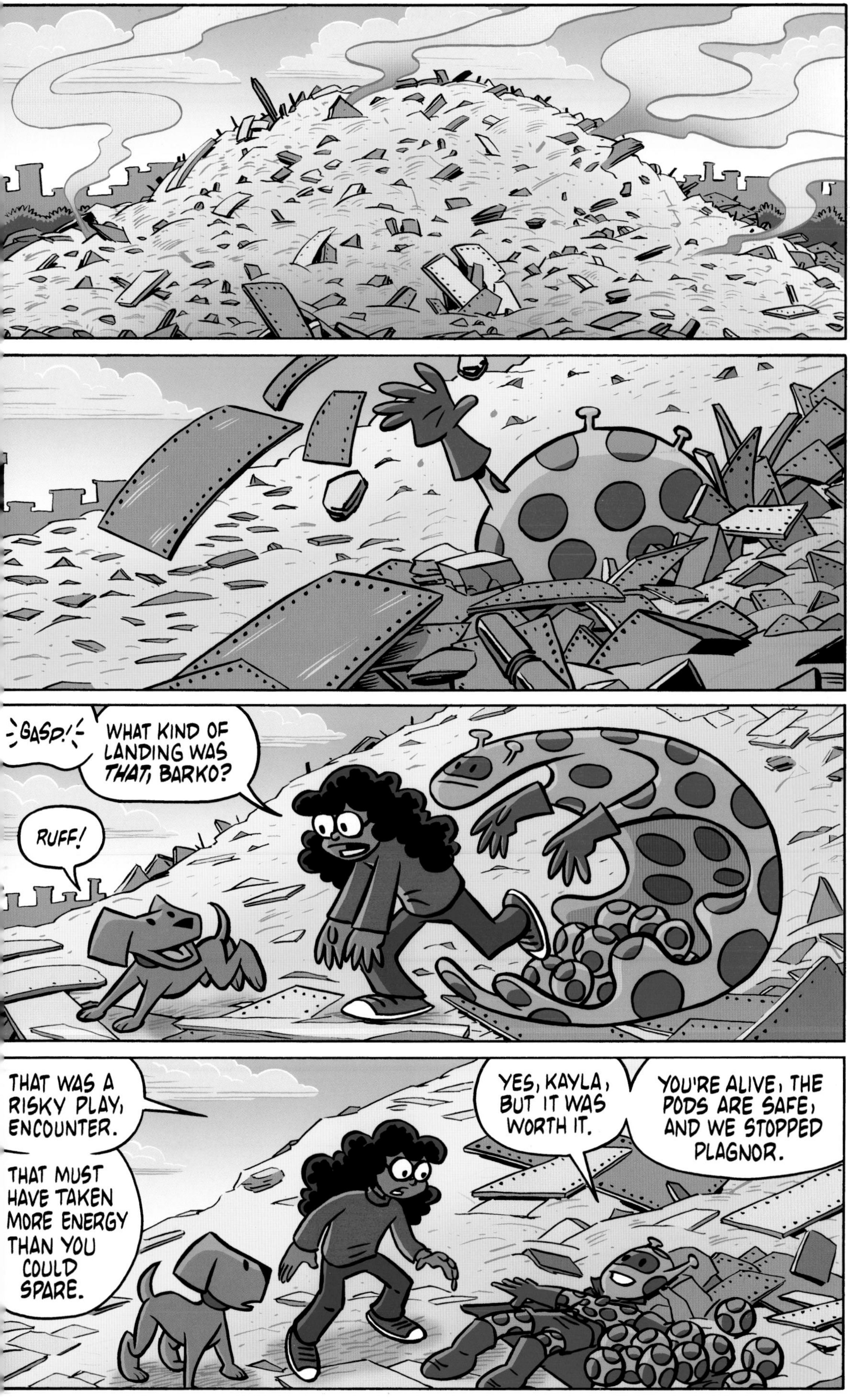
GASP!
WHAT KIND OF LANDING WAS THAT, BARKO?
RUFF!
THAT WAS A RISKY PLAY, ENCOUNTER.
THAT MUST HAVE TAKEN MORE ENERGY THAN YOU COULD SPARE.
YES, KAYLA, BUT IT WAS WORTH IT.
YOU'RE ALIVE, THE PODS ARE SAFE, AND WE STOPPED PLAGNOR.

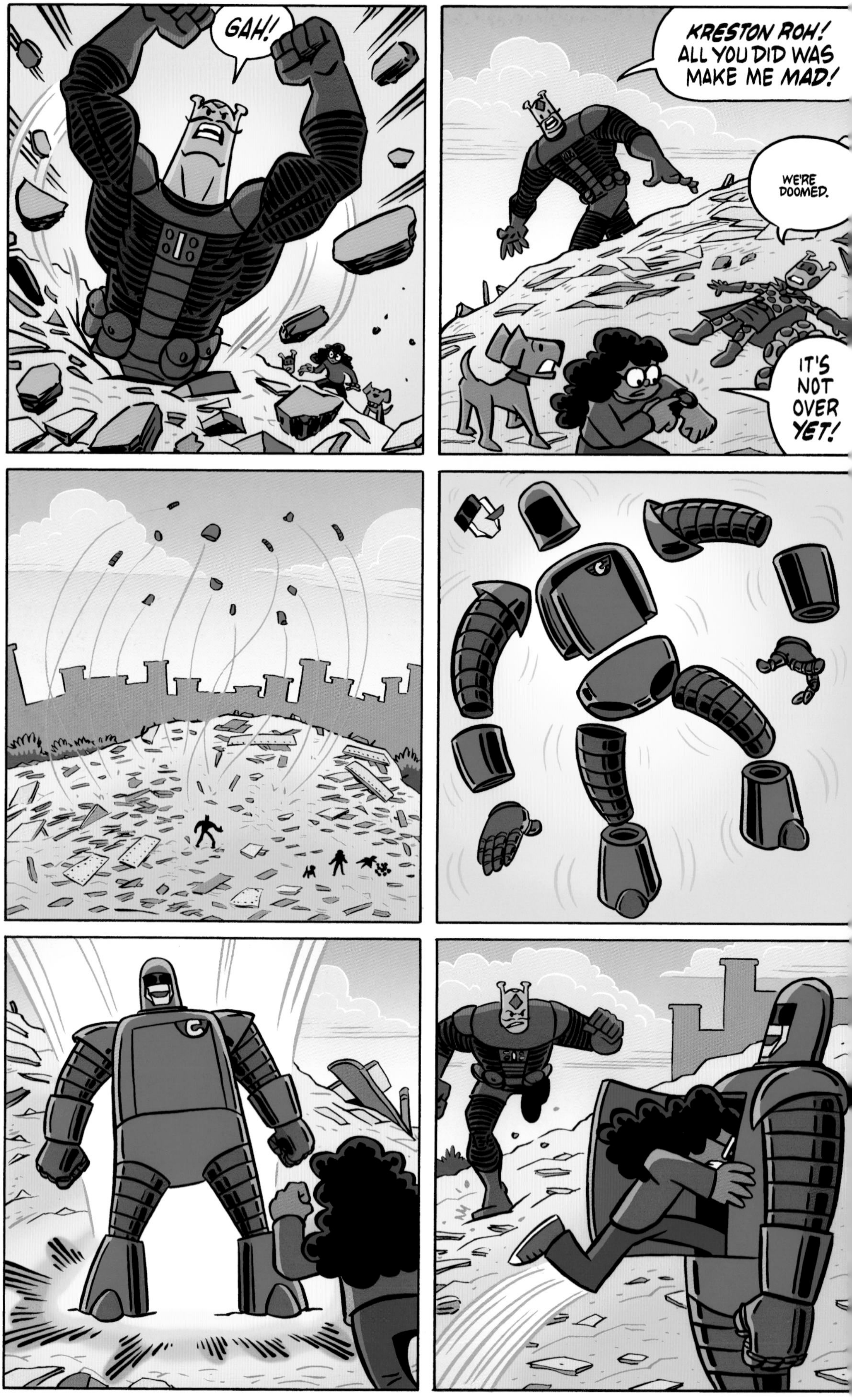

GAH!
KRESTON ROH! ALL YOU DID WAS MAKE ME MAD!
WE'RE DOOMED.
IT'S NOT OVER YET!

GIVE IT UP, CHAMPION! I'VE ALREADY WON!
YOU'RE RIGHT! SO WHY NOT JUST LEAVE US ALONE AND GO HOME?
NOT WITHOUT THE PODS!
YOU'RE TOUGHER THAN YOU LOOK!
MY ARMOR CAN WITHSTAND THE MOST FORCEFUL IMPACT!
IS THAT RIGHT?
OR WOULD YOU CARE TO REVISE YOUR STATEMENT?

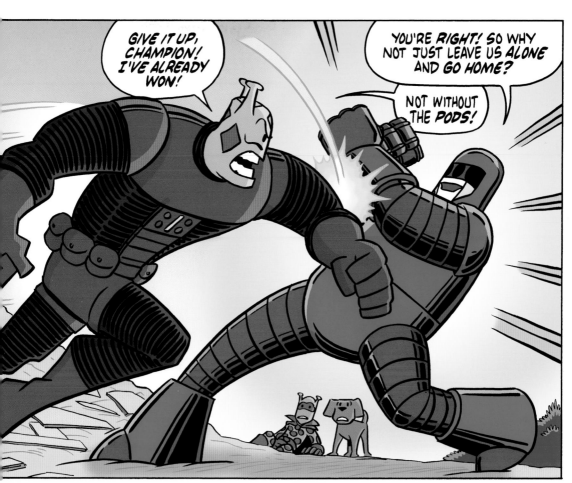

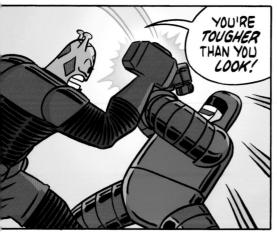

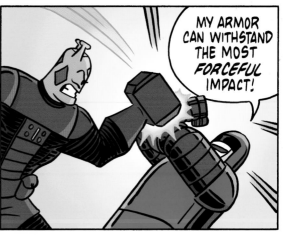

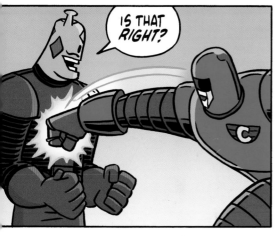

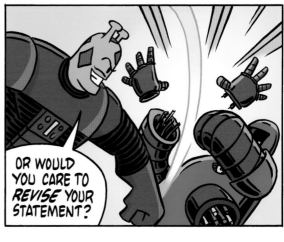

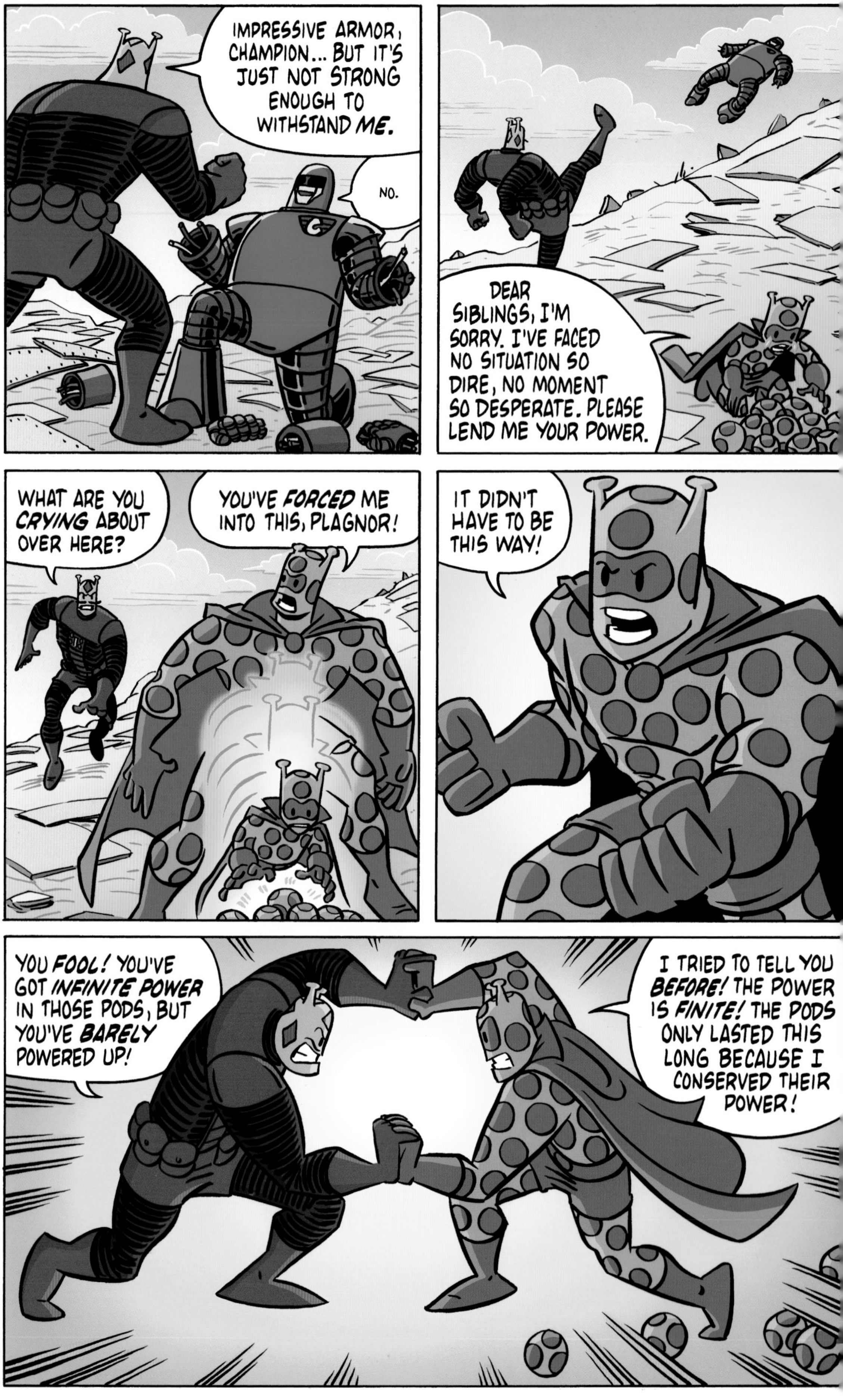
IMPRESSIVE ARMOR, CHAMPION... BUT IT'S JUST NOT STRONG ENOUGH TO WITHSTAND *ME.*
NO.
DEAR SIBLINGS, I'M SORRY. I'VE FACED NO SITUATION SO DIRE, NO MOMENT SO DESPERATE. PLEASE LEND ME YOUR POWER.
WHAT ARE YOU *CRYING* ABOUT OVER HERE?
YOU'VE *FORCED* ME INTO THIS, PLAGNOR!
IT DIDN'T HAVE TO BE THIS WAY!
YOU *FOOL!* YOU'VE GOT *INFINITE POWER* IN THOSE PODS, BUT YOU'VE *BARELY* POWERED UP!
I TRIED TO TELL YOU *BEFORE!* THE POWER IS *FINITE!* THE PODS ONLY LASTED THIS LONG BECAUSE I CONSERVED THEIR POWER!

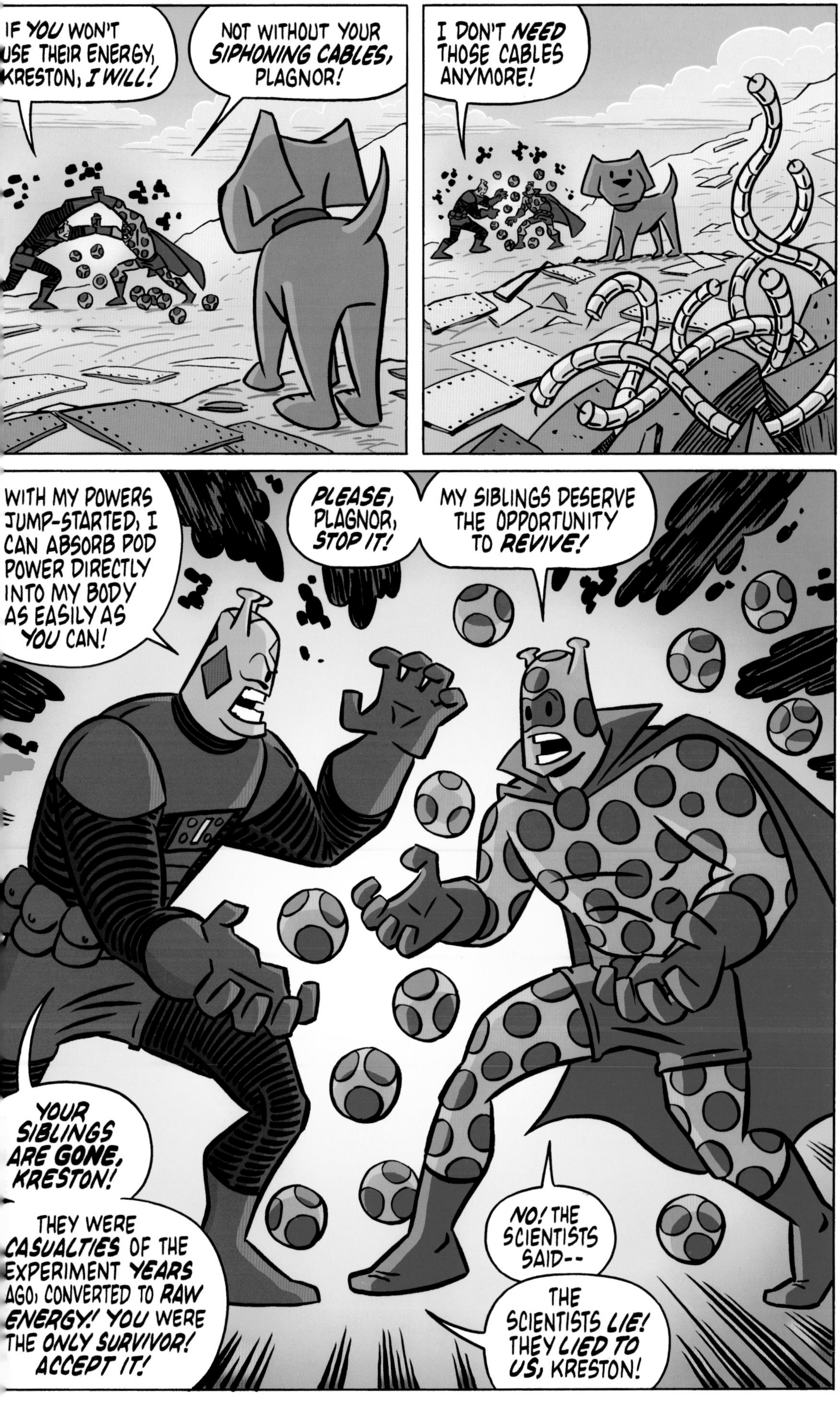
IF YOU WON'T USE THEIR ENERGY, KRESTON, I WILL!
NOT WITHOUT YOUR SIPHONING CABLES, PLAGNOR!
I DON'T NEED THOSE CABLES ANYMORE!
WITH MY POWERS JUMP-STARTED, I CAN ABSORB POD POWER DIRECTLY INTO MY BODY AS EASILY AS YOU CAN!
PLEASE, PLAGNOR, STOP IT!
MY SIBLINGS DESERVE THE OPPORTUNITY TO REVIVE!
YOUR SIBLINGS ARE GONE, KRESTON!
THEY WERE CASUALTIES OF THE EXPERIMENT YEARS AGO, CONVERTED TO RAW ENERGY! YOU WERE THE ONLY SURVIVOR! ACCEPT IT!
NO! THE SCIENTISTS SAID--
THE SCIENTISTS LIE! THEY LIED TO US, KRESTON!

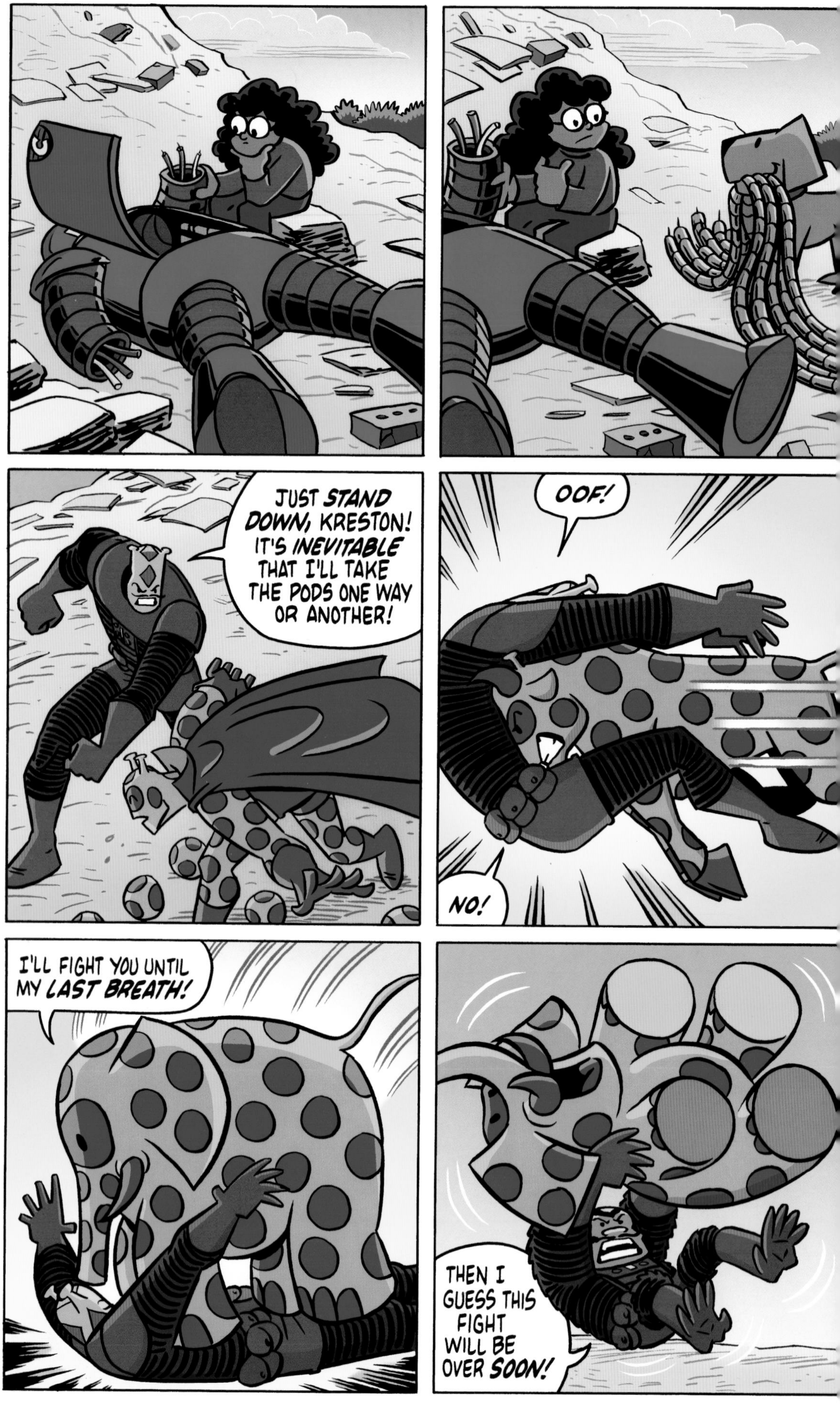
JUST STAND DOWN, KRESTON! IT'S INEVITABLE THAT I'LL TAKE THE PODS ONE WAY OR ANOTHER!
OOF!
NO!
I'LL FIGHT YOU UNTIL MY LAST BREATH!
THEN I GUESS THIS FIGHT WILL BE OVER SOON!

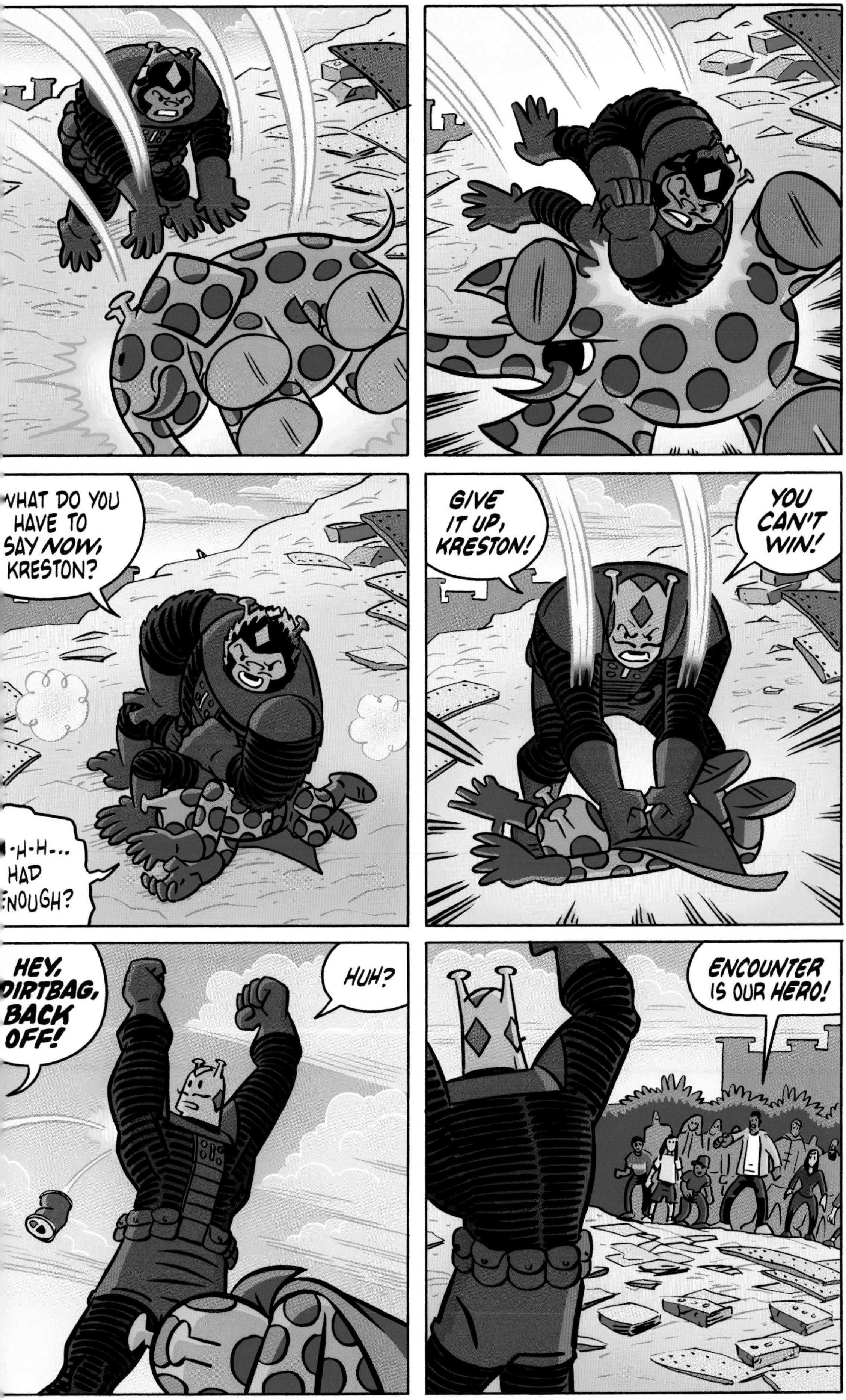
WHAT DO YOU HAVE TO SAY *NOW*, KRESTON?
-H-H... HAD ENOUGH?
GIVE IT UP, KRESTON!
YOU CAN'T WIN!
HEY, DIRTBAG, BACK OFF!
HUH?
ENCOUNTER IS OUR *HERO*!

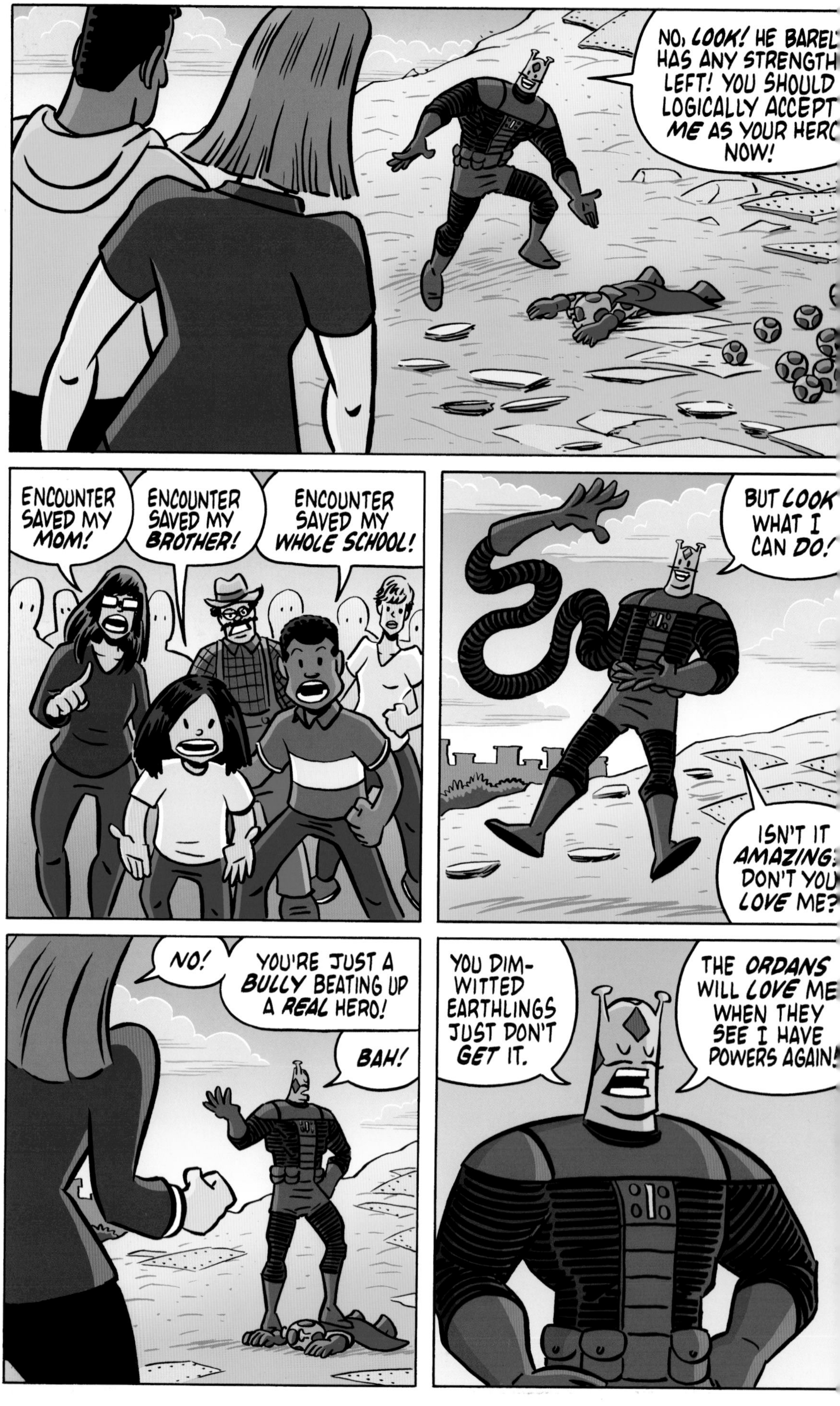

NO, LOOK! HE BAREL
HAS ANY STRENGTH
LEFT! YOU SHOULD
LOGICALLY ACCEPT
ME AS YOUR HERC
NOW!
ENCOUNTER SAVED MY MOM!
ENCOUNTER SAVED MY BROTHER!
ENCOUNTER SAVED MY WHOLE SCHOOL!
BUT LOOK WHAT I CAN DO!
ISN'T IT AMAZING! DON'T YOU LOVE ME?
NO!
YOU'RE JUST A BULLY BEATING UP A REAL HERO!
BAH!
YOU DIM-WITTED EARTHLINGS JUST DON'T GET IT.
THE ORDANS WILL LOVE ME WHEN THEY SEE I HAVE POWERS AGAIN!

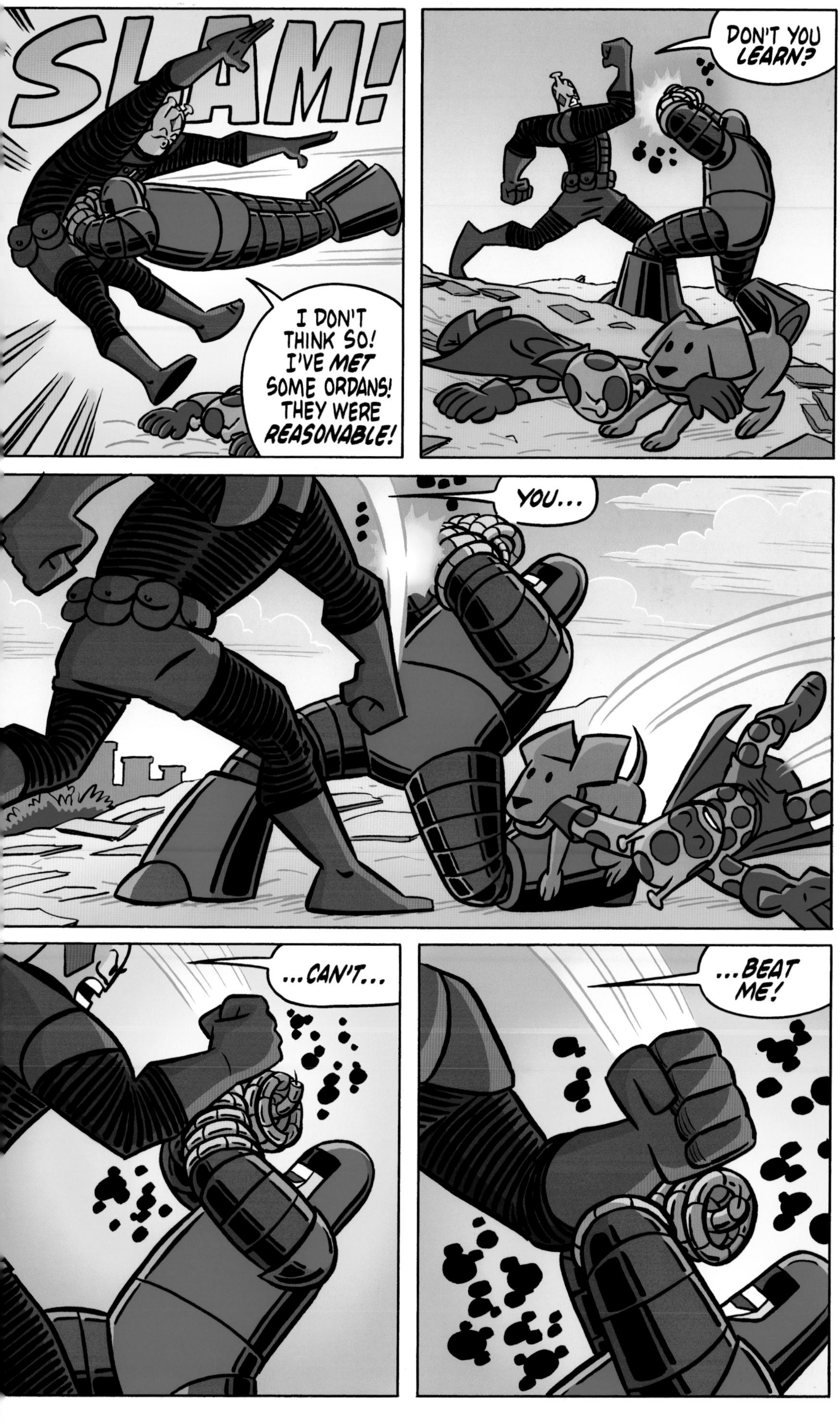
SLAM!
I DON'T THINK SO! I'VE MET SOME ORDANS! THEY WERE REASONABLE!
DON'T YOU LEARN?
YOU...
...CAN'T...
...BEAT ME!

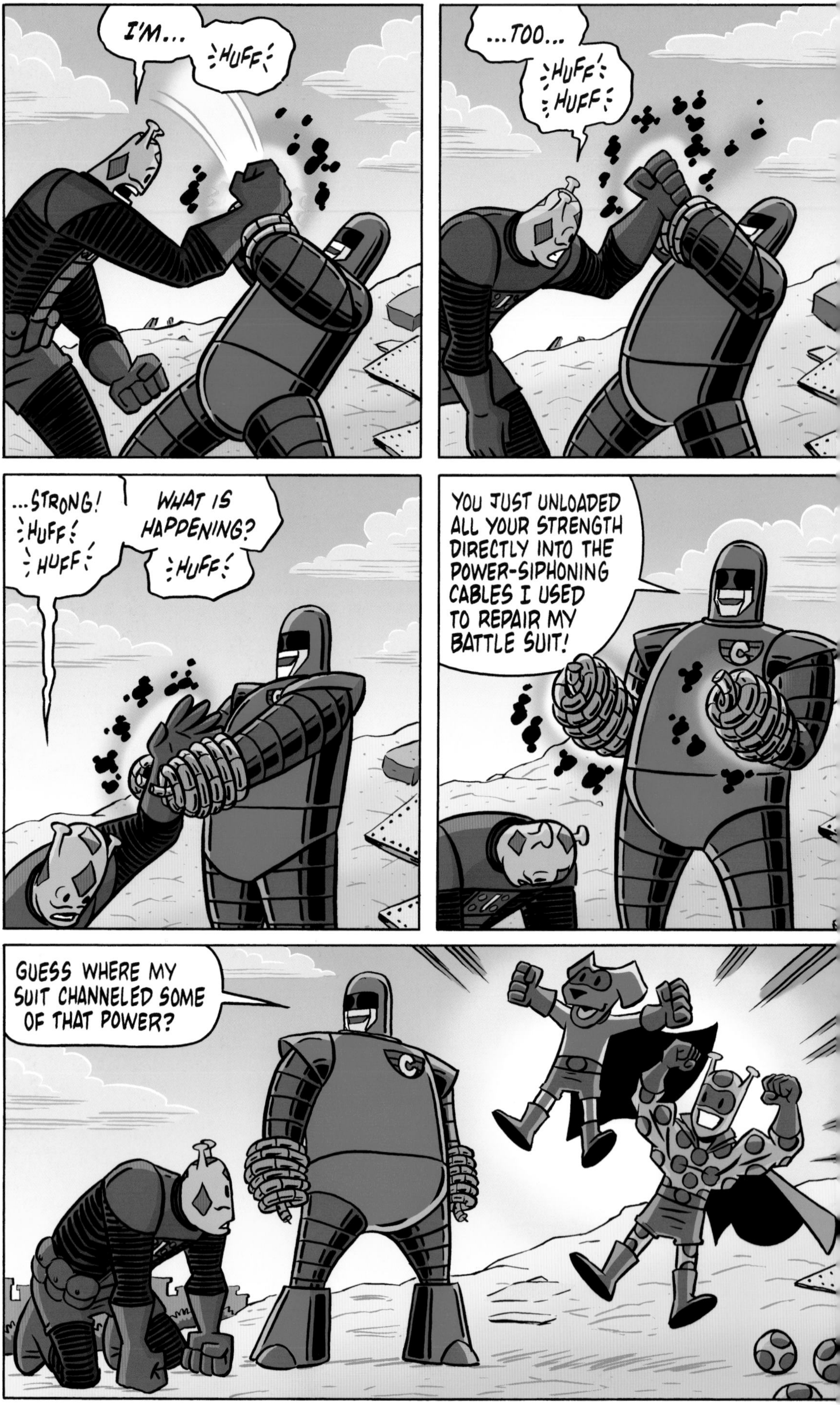
I'M...
HUFF
...TOO...
HUFF
HUFF
...STRONG!
HUFF
HUFF
WHAT IS HAPPENING?
HUFF
YOU JUST UNLOADED ALL YOUR STRENGTH DIRECTLY INTO THE POWER-SIPHONING CABLES I USED TO REPAIR MY BATTLE SUIT!
GUESS WHERE MY SUIT CHANNELED SOME OF THAT POWER?

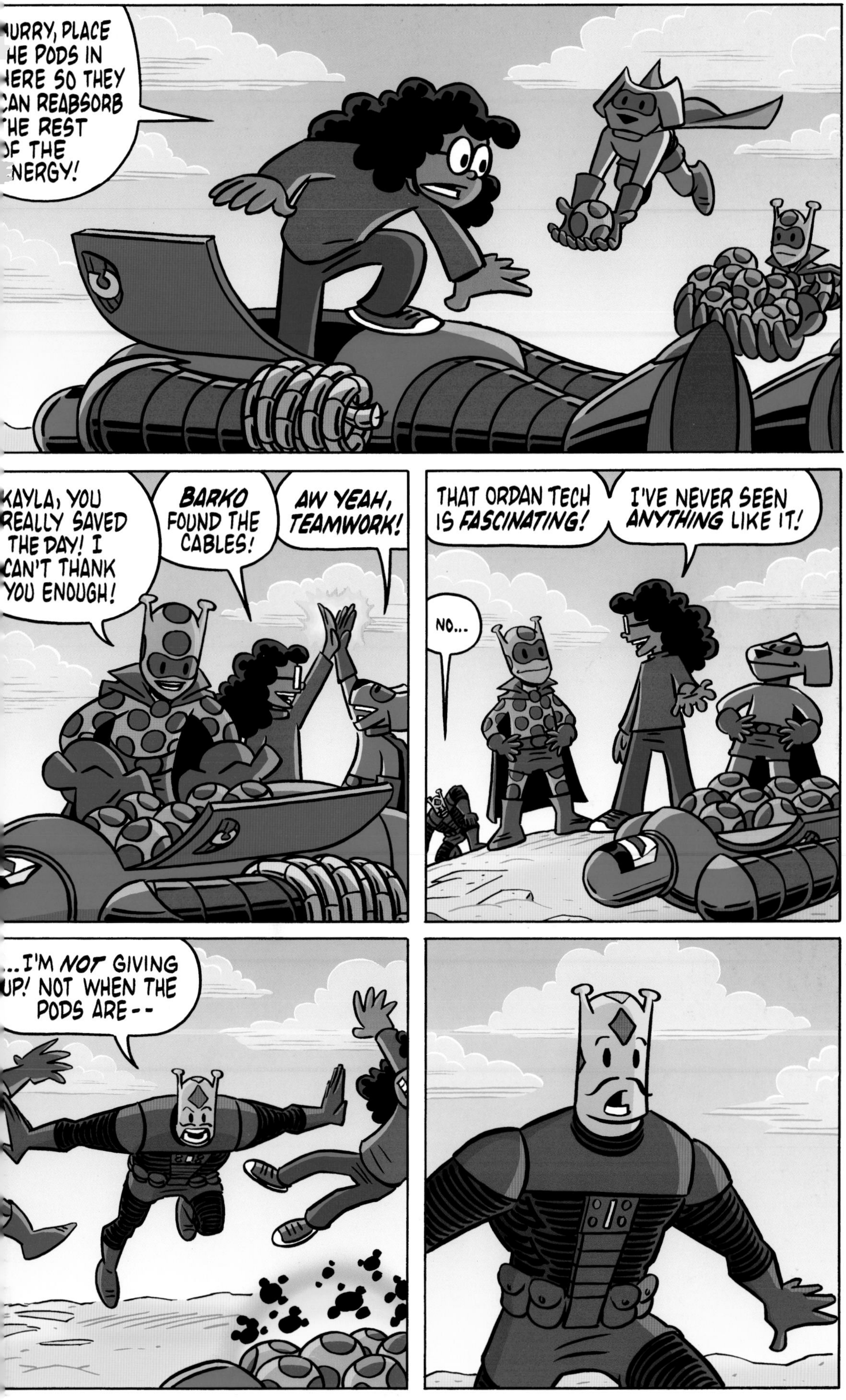

HURRY, PLACE THE PODS IN HERE SO THEY CAN REABSORB THE REST OF THE ENERGY!
KAYLA, YOU REALLY SAVED THE DAY! I CAN'T THANK YOU ENOUGH!
BARKO FOUND THE CABLES!
AW YEAH, TEAMWORK!
THAT ORDAN TECH IS FASCINATING!
I'VE NEVER SEEN ANYTHING LIKE IT!
NO...
...I'M NOT GIVING UP! NOT WHEN THE PODS ARE--

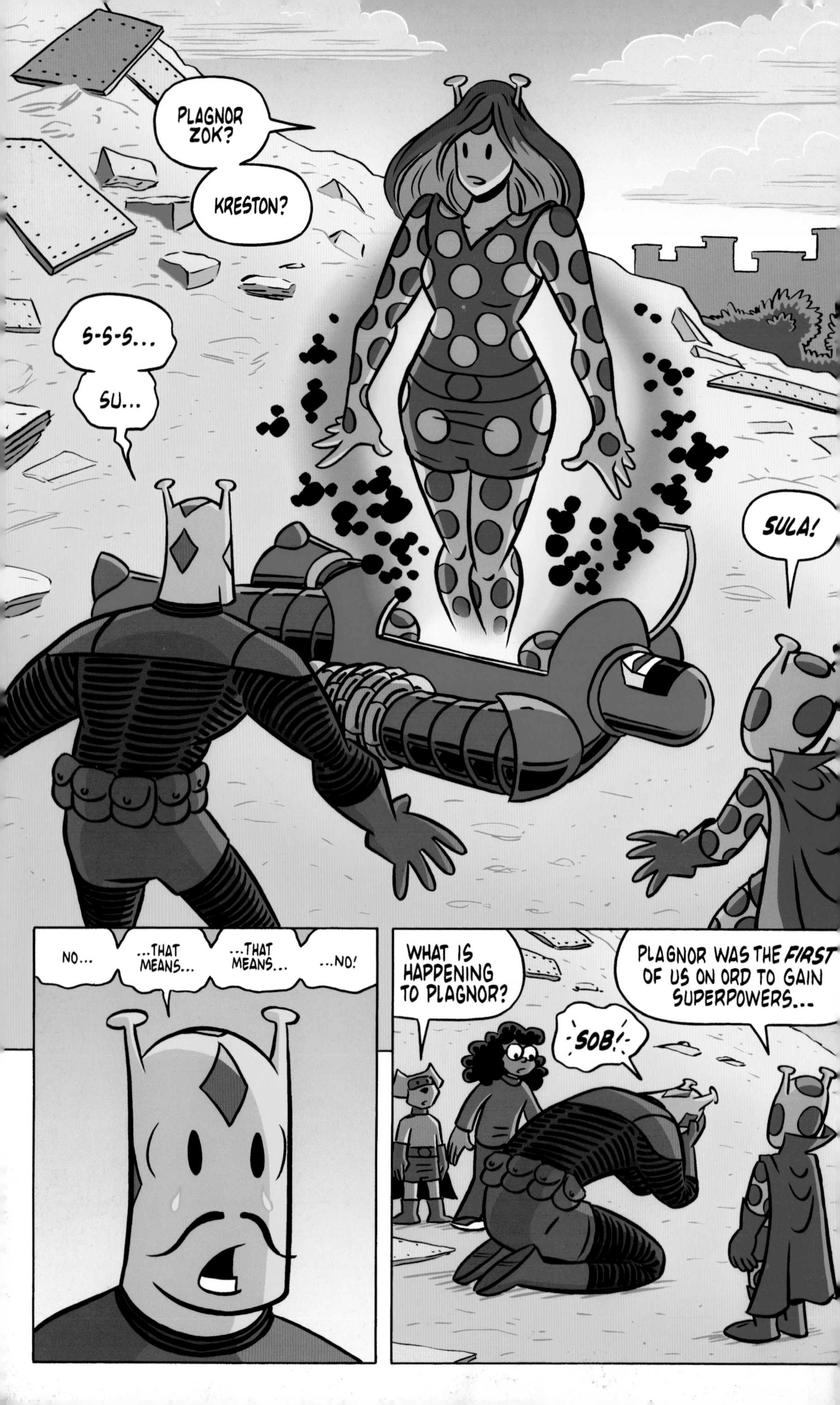
PLAGNOR ZOK?
KRESTON?
S-S-S...
SU...
SULA!
NO...
...THAT MEANS...
...THAT MEANS...
...NO!
WHAT IS HAPPENING TO PLAGNOR?
PLAGNOR WAS THE *FIRST* OF US ON ORD TO GAIN SUPERPOWERS...
SOB!

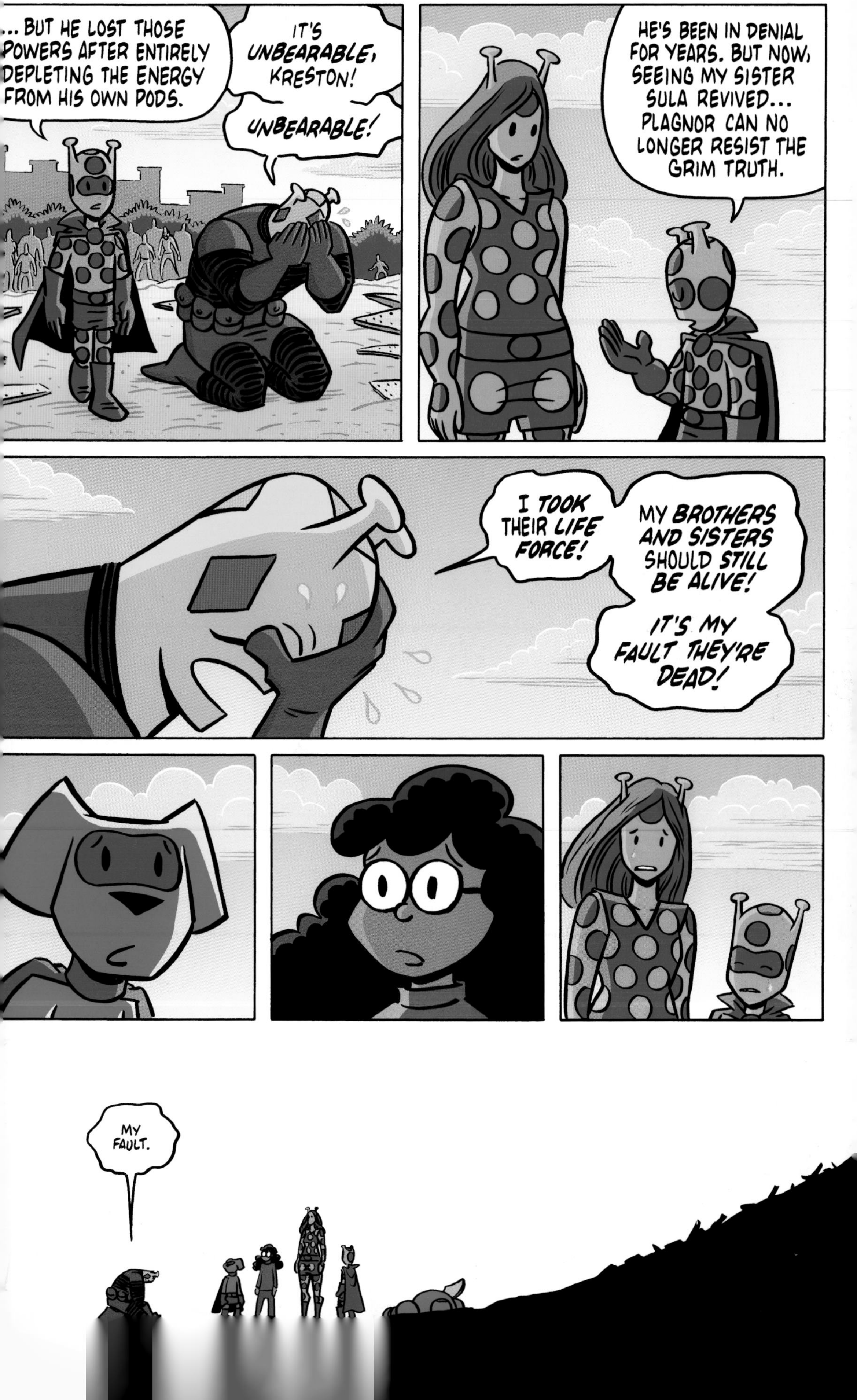

...BUT HE LOST THOSE POWERS AFTER ENTIRELY DEPLETING THE ENERGY FROM HIS OWN PODS.
IT'S UNBEARABLE, KRESTON!
UNBEARABLE!
HE'S BEEN IN DENIAL FOR YEARS. BUT NOW, SEEING MY SISTER SULA REVIVED... PLAGNOR CAN NO LONGER RESIST THE GRIM TRUTH.
I TOOK THEIR LIFE FORCE!
MY BROTHERS AND SISTERS SHOULD STILL BE ALIVE!
IT'S MY FAULT THEY'RE DEAD!
MY FAULT.

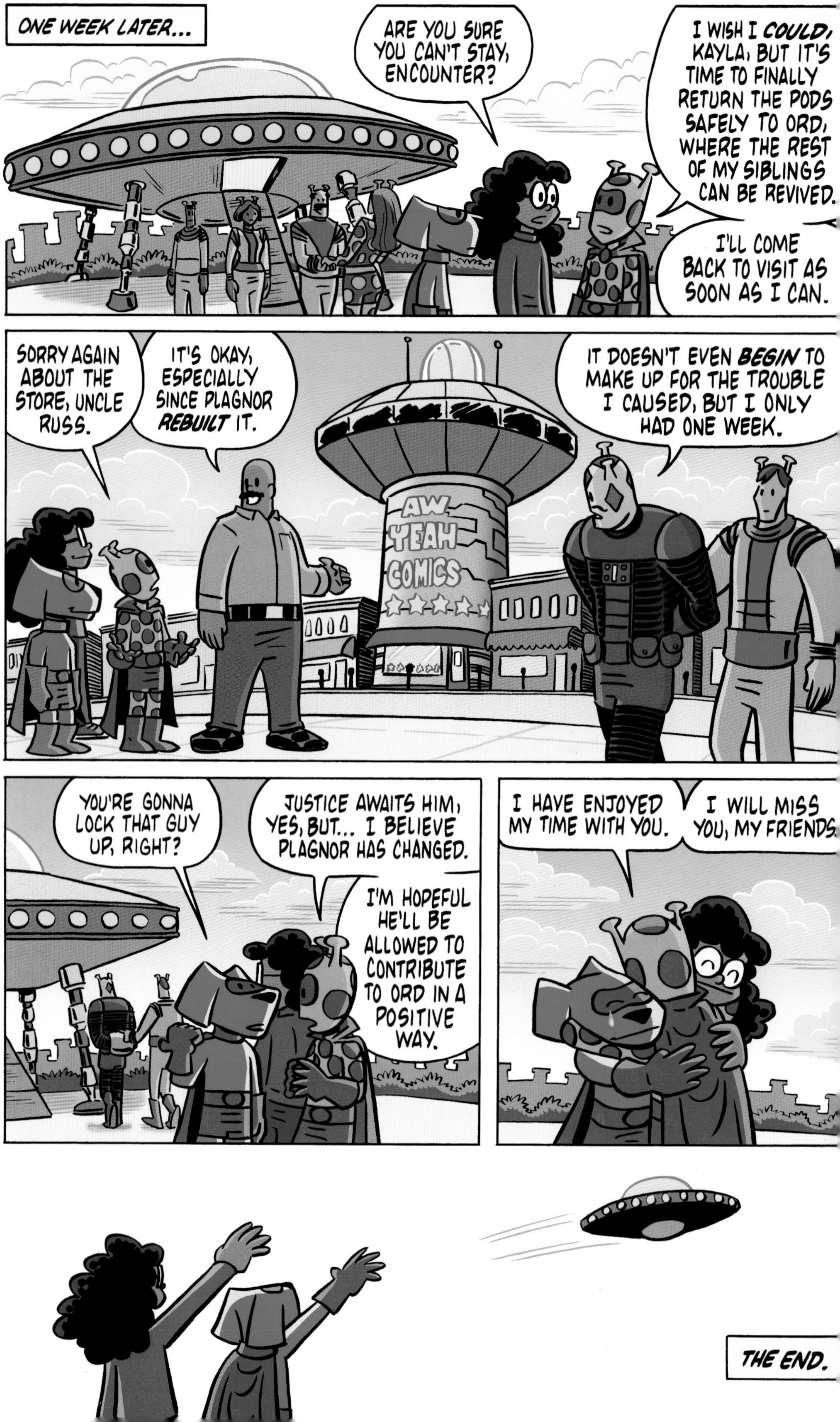

ONE WEEK LATER...
ARE YOU SURE YOU CAN'T STAY, ENCOUNTER?
I WISH I COULD, KAYLA, BUT IT'S TIME TO FINALLY RETURN THE PODS SAFELY TO ORD, WHERE THE REST OF MY SIBLINGS CAN BE REVIVED.
I'LL COME BACK TO VISIT AS SOON AS I CAN.
SORRY AGAIN ABOUT THE STORE, UNCLE RUSS.
IT'S OKAY, ESPECIALLY SINCE PLAGNOR REBUILT IT.
AW YEAH COMICS
IT DOESN'T EVEN BEGIN TO MAKE UP FOR THE TROUBLE I CAUSED, BUT I ONLY HAD ONE WEEK.
YOU'RE GONNA LOCK THAT GUY UP, RIGHT?
JUSTICE AWAITS HIM, YES, BUT... I BELIEVE PLAGNOR HAS CHANGED.
I'M HOPEFUL HE'LL BE ALLOWED TO CONTRIBUTE TO ORD IN A POSITIVE WAY.
I HAVE ENJOYED MY TIME WITH YOU.
I WILL MISS YOU, MY FRIENDS.
THE END.

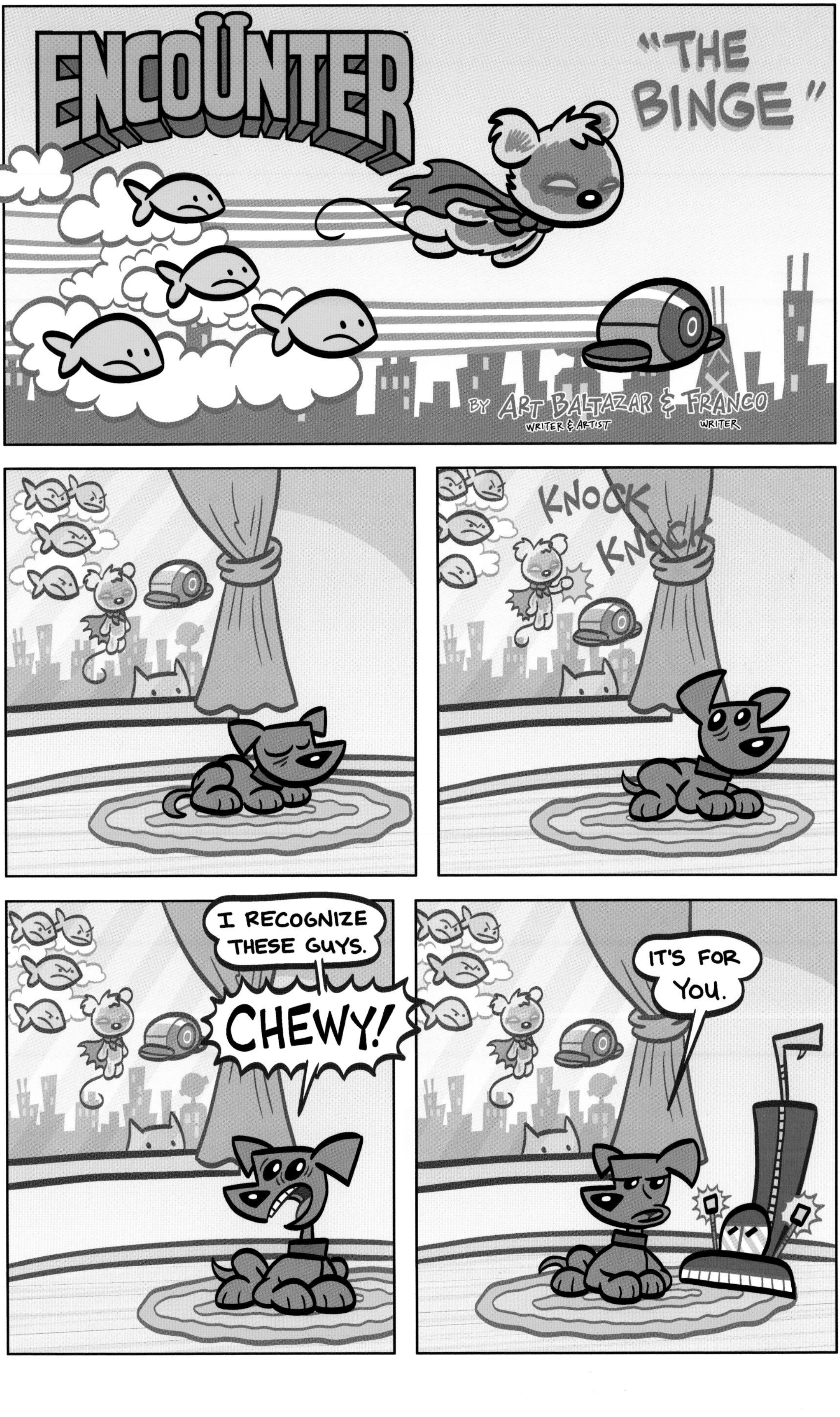
ENCOUNTER
"THE BINGE"
BY ART BALTAZAR & FRANCO
WRITER & ARTIST
WRITER
KNOCK
KNOCK
I RECOGNIZE THESE GUYS.
CHEWY!
IT'S FOR YOU.

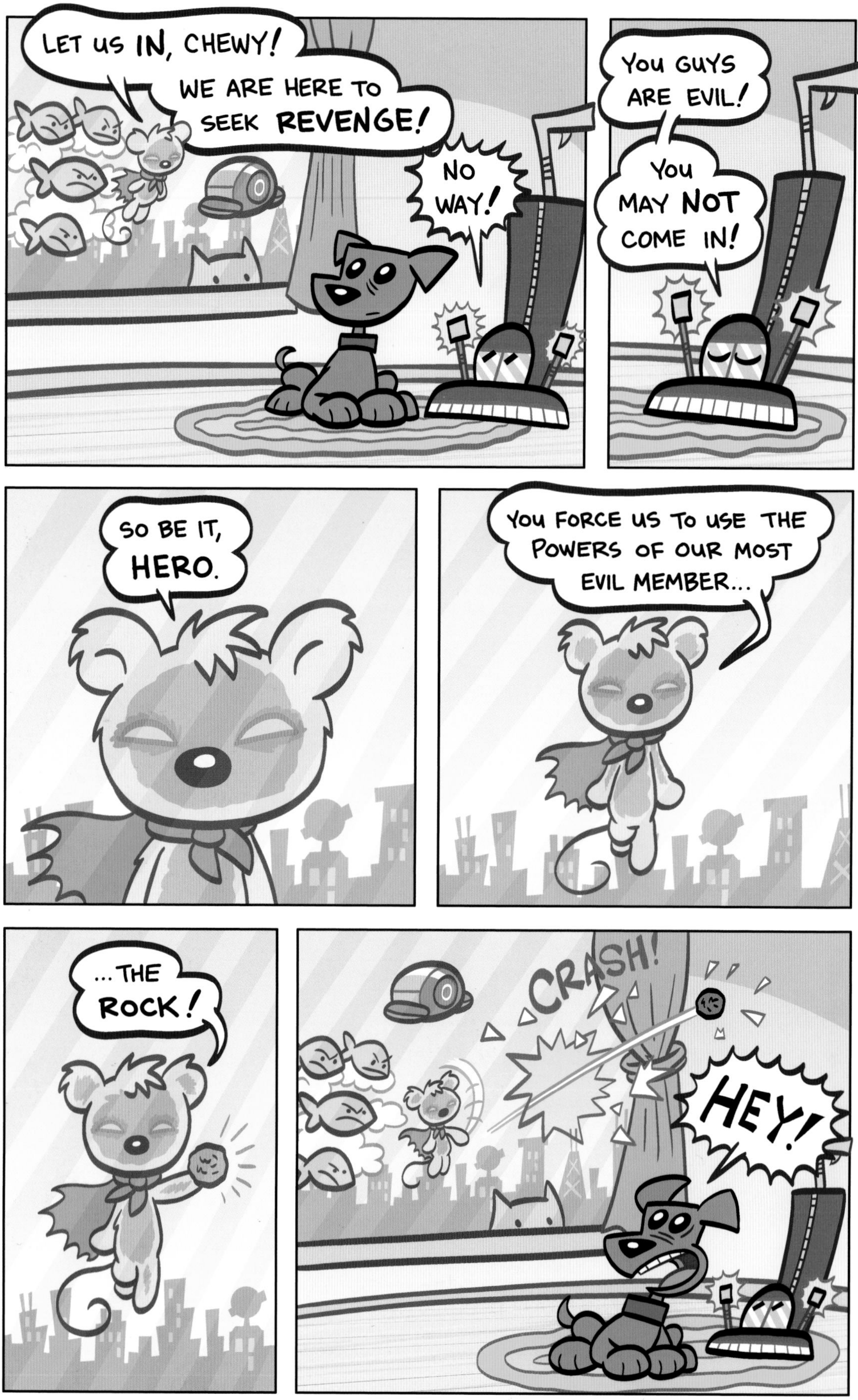

LET US IN, CHEWY!
WE ARE HERE TO SEEK REVENGE!
NO WAY!
YOU GUYS ARE EVIL!
YOU MAY NOT COME IN!
SO BE IT, HERO.
YOU FORCE US TO USE THE POWERS OF OUR MOST EVIL MEMBER...
...THE ROCK!
CRASH!
HEY!

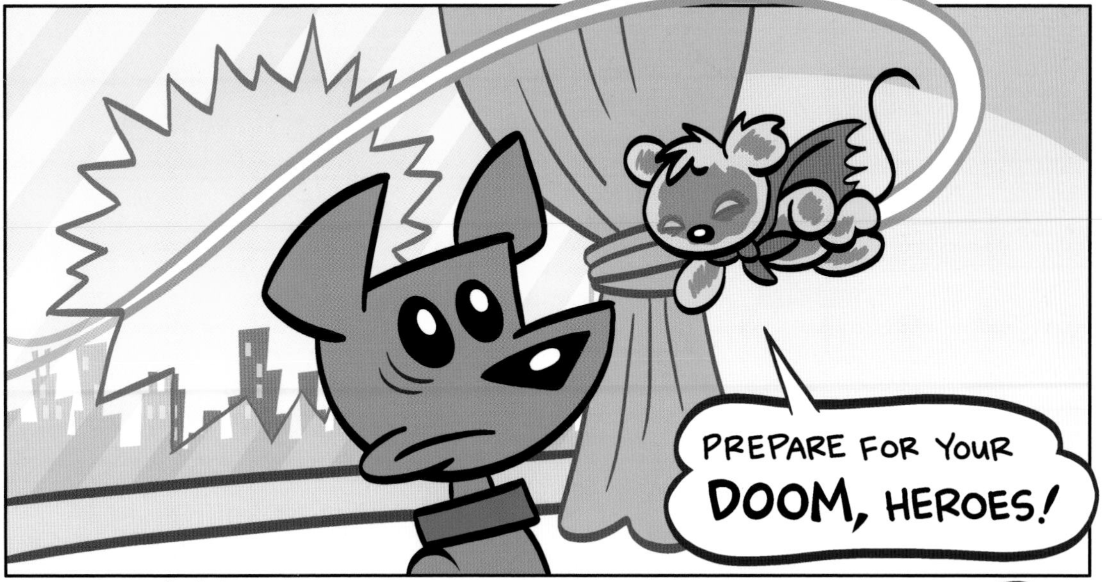
PREPARE FOR YOUR DOOM, HEROES!

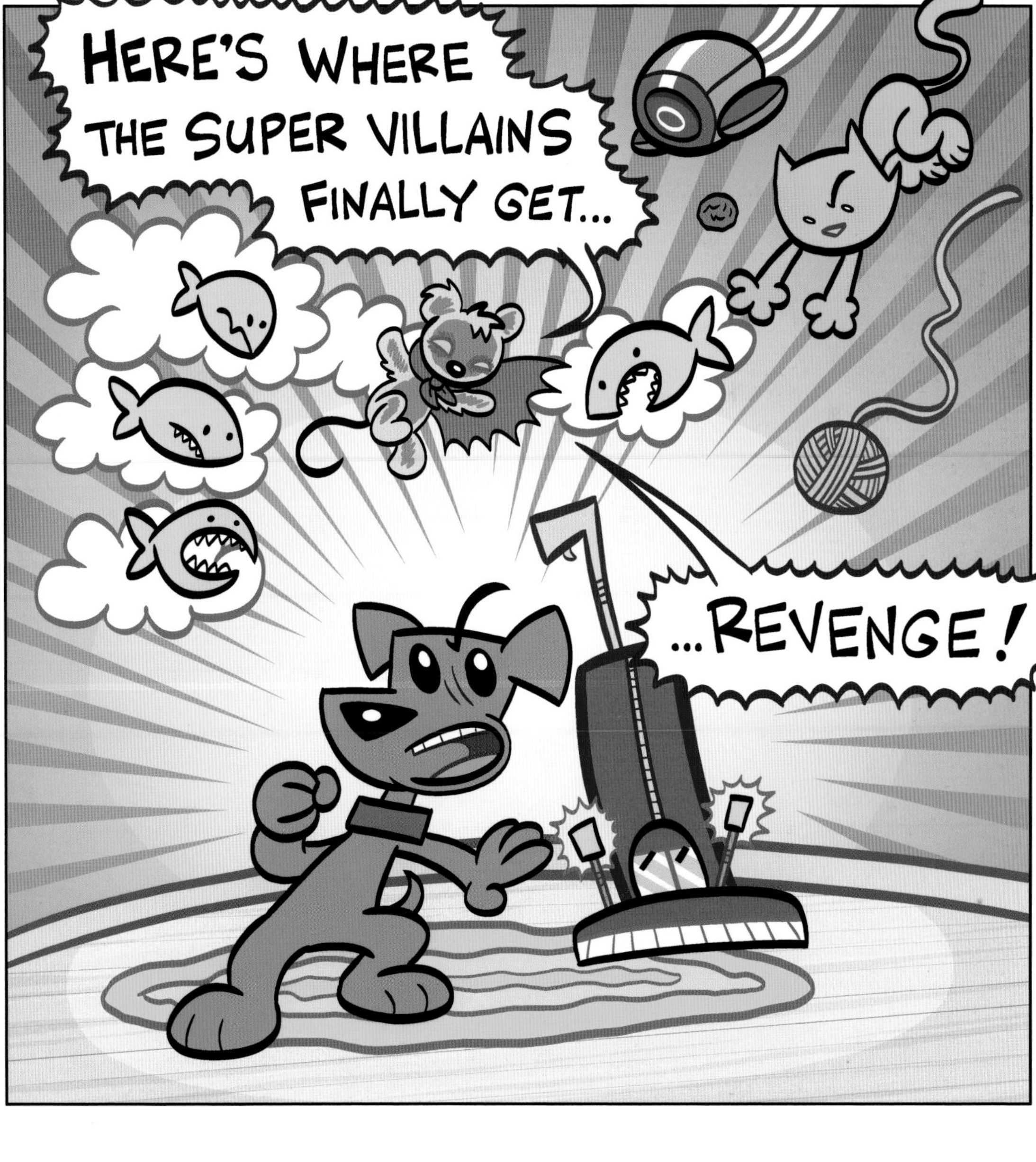
HERE'S WHERE THE SUPER VILLAINS FINALLY GET...
...REVENGE!

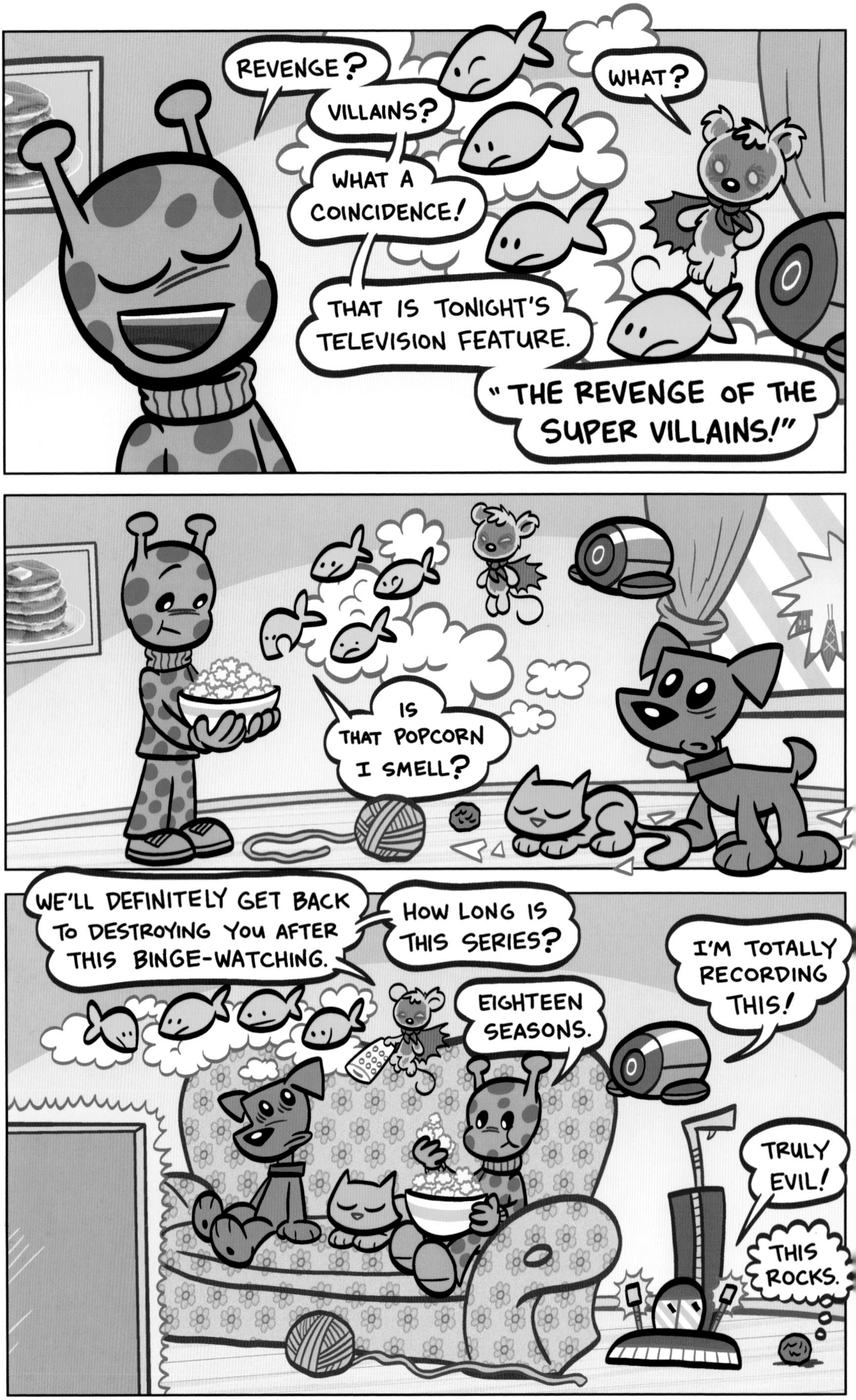
REVENGE?
VILLAINS?
WHAT A COINCIDENCE!
THAT IS TONIGHT'S TELEVISION FEATURE.
WHAT?
"THE REVENGE OF THE SUPER VILLAINS!"
IS THAT POPCORN I SMELL?
WE'LL DEFINITELY GET BACK TO DESTROYING YOU AFTER THIS BINGE-WATCHING.
HOW LONG IS THIS SERIES?
I'M TOTALLY RECORDING THIS!
EIGHTEEN SEASONS.
TRULY EVIL!
THIS ROCKS.

-END!

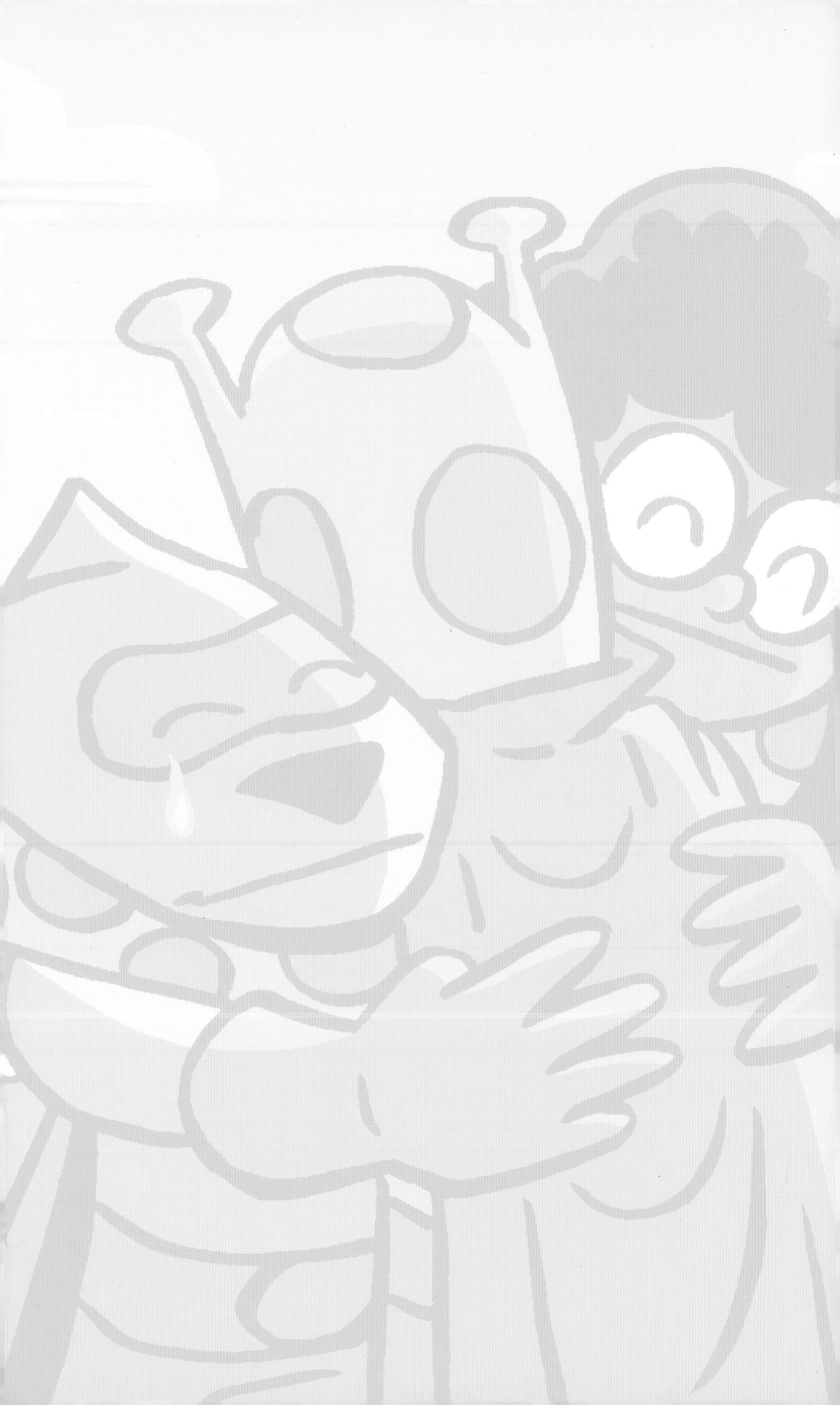

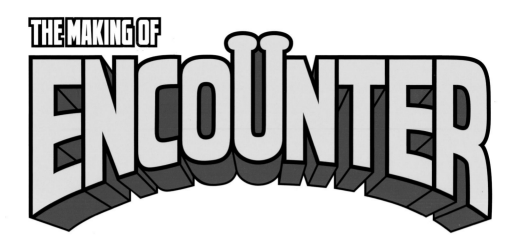

THE MAKING OF ENCOUNTER

BEHIND THE SCENES OF CREATING A COMIC

It's time for a sneak peek into the team behind the superhero team of Encounter, Barko, and Champion!

SCRIPT!

Where else would we start? It's the script! For Encounter, Art and Franco write the script together, using "thumbnails." Thumbnails are small, quick images that help an artist see what the authors had in mind for each scene.

CHAMPION
SO I'M GOING TO CATCH UP TO CHAMPION AND ASK SOME QUESTIONS
OKAY BARKO I DON'T THINK THIS IS A GOOD IDEA BUT YOUR MY FRIEND SO I'LL BACK YOU UP.
BARKO
IS... IS HE LANDING AT OUR HOUSE?
ENCOUNTER

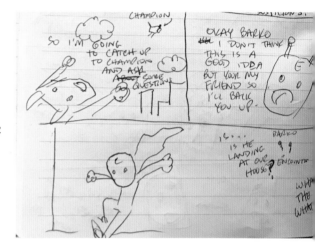

PENCILS!

After some editing, it's on to the pencils! Chris G. works his magic and brings to life the world Art and Franco created. As he's putting the story into panels, some dialogue and scenes change a little to make that storytelling really pop!

WELL I STILL THINK YOU'RE WRONG ABOUT CHAMPION.
I HOPE I AM WRONG, BUT WE NEED TO FIND OUT FOR SURE.
WHOA.
HOLD ON!
WHY IS CHAMPION GOING INTO OUR APARTMENT?

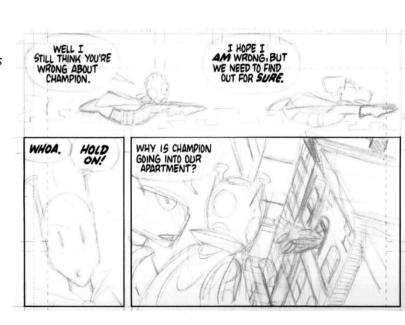

IKS!

ext up is inking those wesome pencils. Look all that detail! is is where Chris G. akes sure all the aracter designs and ckgrounds are all eaned up. The black es really grab your tention, right?

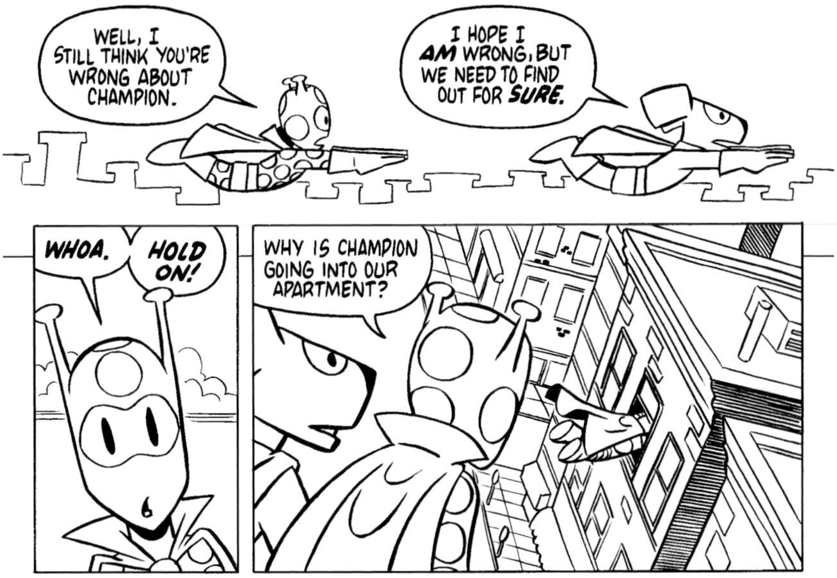

WELL, I STILL THINK YOU'RE WRONG ABOUT CHAMPION.
I HOPE I **AM** WRONG, BUT WE NEED TO FIND OUT FOR ***SURE.***
WHOA.
HOLD ON!
WHY IS CHAMPION GOING INTO OUR APARTMENT?

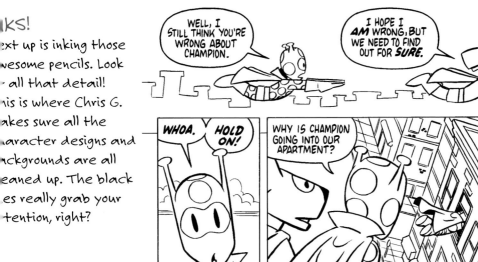

OLORS!

s off to Stephen Mayer for colors! First everything gets colored in, and then he adds me shadows and highlights. There's no mixing up any of the characters as they start oking ready to fight the bad guys and protect the pods.

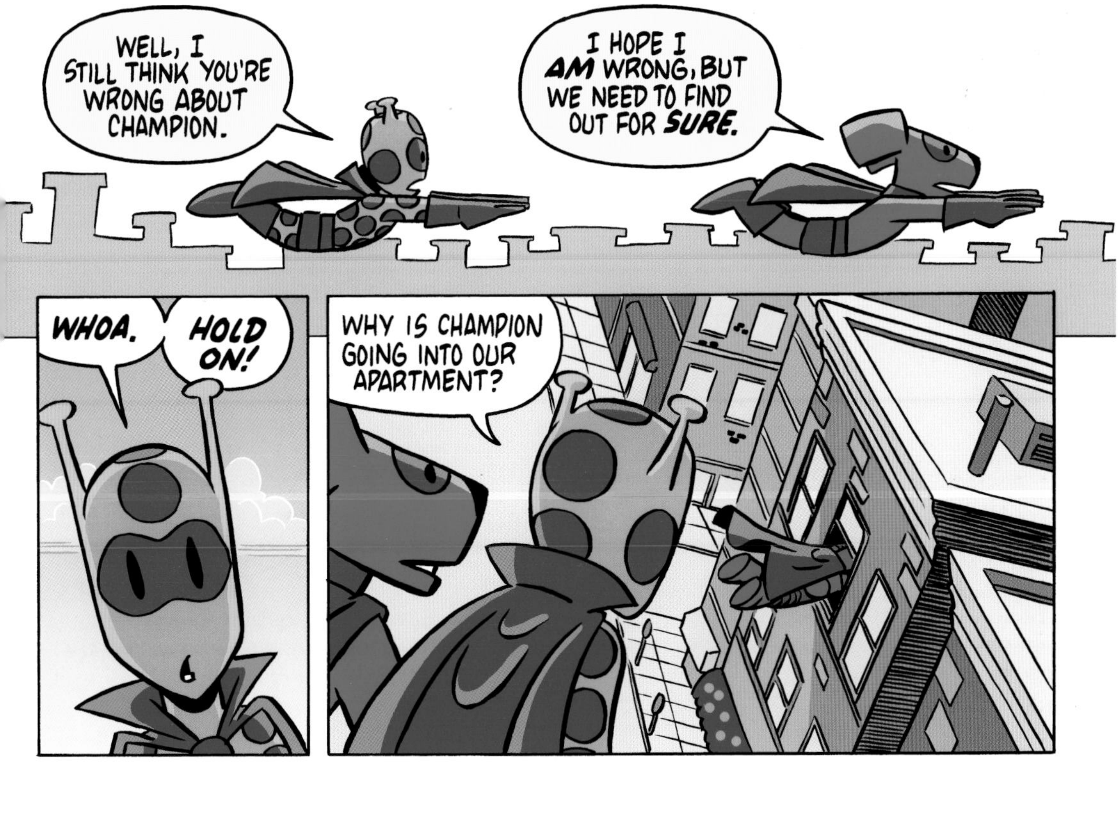

WELL, I STILL THINK YOU'RE WRONG ABOUT CHAMPION.
I HOPE I **AM** WRONG, BUT WE NEED TO FIND OUT FOR ***SURE.***
WHOA.
HOLD ON!
WHY IS CHAMPION GOING INTO OUR APARTMENT?

TEAM ENCOUNTER IS READY TO SAVE THE DAY, thanks to the creative team behind it all!

Famous cartoonist **ART BALTAZAR** is the creative force behind the *New York Times* bestselling, Eisner Award–winning DC Comics's *Tiny Titans*, co-writer for *Billy Batson and the Magic of Shazam!, Young Justice, Green Lantern: The Animated Series,* and artist/co-writer for the awesome *Tiny Titans/Little Archie* crossover, *Superman Family Adventures,* and *Itty Bitty Hellboy!* Art is one of the founders of AW YEAH COMICS comic shop and the ongoing comic series!

FRANCO is from the great state of New York. He and his forehead have traveled the world and in between he writes and draws stuff and sometimes throws paint around on canvas. He is the creator, artist, and writer of *Patrick the Wolf Boy* and *AW YEAH COMICS!* He has also worked on titles for various comic companies, including the critically acclaimed *Superman Family Adventures, Young Justice, Billy Batson and the Magic of Shazam!, Green Lantern: The Animated Series, Itty Bitty Hellboy, Battlestar Galactica,* and the *New York Times* bestselling, multi-Eisner Award–winning series *Tiny Titans.*

CHRIS GIARRUSSO is the Harvey Award–nominated artist and writer best known for creating, writing, and drawing *G-Man,* a series of books about a young superhero who gains fantastic powers when he wears a magic cape, and *Mini Marvels,* the comic series featuring pint-sized versions of Marvel's most famous heroes! Chris's work has been published by Andrews McMeel, Scholastic, Marvel, Image, IDW, and several independent publishers.